P9-AET-602

▶▶▶ACCEL·WORLD 09
THE SEVEN-THOUSAND-YEAR PRAYER

REKI KAWAHARA
ILLUSTRATION BY **HIMA**
DESIGN BY **bee-pee**

GREEN GRANDÉ

Green King, one of the Seven Kings of Pure Color. Nicknamed Invincible. Bearer of the large shield named Strife.

"————"

"Graaaaaaaar!!"

SILVER CROW
Duel avatar controlled by Haruyuki,
a boy in the lowest school caste.
Polluted by the Armor of Catastrophe.

"...I like you."

KUROYUKIHIME

Vice president of the Umesato Junior High student council. Controls the "Black King," Black Lotus.

"Haruyuki. You belong to me. I will not give up. I cannot tolerate losing you. Absolutely not."

"...Kuroyukihime."

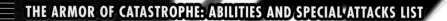

ENHANCED ARMAMENT

Drain
Absorbs the HP of the enemy avatar and charges its own HP. Default Armor ability.

Divination
Searches and scans enemy attacks in advance and displays information in one's field of view such as attributes, range, threat level, and attack trajectory. Default Armor ability.

Star Caster
Sinister longsword. Default Armor Enhanced Armament.

Flash Blink
A pseudo-teleportation that transforms the wearer into minuscule particles in order to move instantly to a distant location. Special attack of the first Chrome Disaster, Chrome Falcon.

Flame Breath
Flames released from the mouth to attack the target. The blaze continues to cause damage until it is extinguished. Second Chrome Disaster's special attack.

Wire Hook
An ultrafine steel wire released from the palm of the hand. When it hits its target, it becomes a hook and can reel in the target. Has a large range. The user can also move at high speeds by "hooking" immobile structures (obstacles). Ability of the fifth Chrome Disaster, Cherry Rook.

High-speed Flight
Wings on the back allow for the lone flight ability in the Accelerated World. Ability of the sixth Chrome Disaster, Silver Crow.

Laser Sword
Hardens the user's hand into a sharp sword to cut down enemies. Damage reaches even distant enemies due to power expansion. Special attack of the sixth Chrome Disaster, Silver Crow.

Laser Lance
Hardens the wearer's hand into a lance to skewer enemies, with an even greater range than that of Laser Sword. Special attack of the sixth Chrome Disaster, Silver Crow.

ACCEL·WORLD 09

THE SEVEN-THOUSAND-YEAR PRAYER

Reki Kawahara
Illustrations: HIMA
Design: bee-pee

YEN ON

NEW YORK

■ **Kuroyukihime** = Umesato Junior High School student council vice president. Trim and clever girl who has it all. Her background is shrouded in mystery. Her in-school avatar is a spangle butterfly she programmed herself. Her duel avatar is the Black King, Black Lotus (level nine).

■ **Haruyuki** = Haruyuki Arita. Eighth grader at Umesato Junior High School. Bullied, on the pudgy side. He's good at games, but shy. His in-school avatar is a pink pig. His duel avatar is Silver Crow (level five).

■ **Chiyuri** = Chiyuri Kurashima. Haruyuki's childhood friend. Meddling energetic girl. Her in-school avatar is a silver cat. Her duel avatar is Lime Bell (level four).

■ **Takumu** = Takumu Mayuzumi. A boy Haruyuki and Chiyuri have known since childhood. Good at kendo. His duel avatar is Cyan Pile (level five).

■ **Fuko** = Fuko Kurasaki. Burst Linker belonging to the old Nega Nebulus. One of the Four Elements. Lived as a recluse due to certain circumstances but is persuaded by Kuroyukihime and Haruyuki to come back to the battlefront. Taught Haruyuki about the Incarnate System. Her duel avatar is Sky Raker (level eight).

■ **Uiui** = Utai Shinomiya. Burst Linker belonging to the old Nega Nebulus. One of the Four Elements. Fourth grader in the elementary division of Matsunogi Academy. Not only can she use the advanced curse removal command "Purify," she is also skilled at long-range attacks. Her duel avatar is Ardor Maiden (level seven).

■ **Neurolinker** = A portable Internet terminal that connects with the brain via a wireless quantum connection and enhances all five senses with images, sounds, and other stimuli.

■ **Brain Burst** = Neurolinker application sent to Haruyuki by Kuroyukihime.

■ **Duel avatar** = Player's virtual self, operated when fighting in Brain Burst.

■ **Legion** = Groups composed of many duel avatars with the objective of expanding occupied areas and securing rights. There are seven main Legions, each led by one of the Seven Kings of Pure Color.

■ **Normal Duel Field** = The field where normal Brain Burst battles (one-on-one) are carried out. Although the specs do possess elements of reality, the system is essentially on the level of an old-school fighting game.

■ **Unlimited Neutral Field** = Field for high-level players where only duel avatars at levels four and up are allowed. The game system is of a wholly different order than that of the Normal Duel Field, and the level of freedom in this field beats out even the next-generation VRMMO.

■ Movement Control System = System in charge of avatar control. Normally, this system handles all avatar movement.
■ Image Control System = System in which the player creates a strong image in their mind to operate the avatar. The mechanism is very different from the normal Movement Control System, and very few players can use it. Key component of the Incarnate System.
■ Incarnate System = Technique allowing players to interfere with the Brain Burst program's Image Control System to bring about a reality outside of the game's framework. Also referred to as "overwriting" game phenomena.

■ Acceleration Research Society = Mysterious Burst Linker group. They do not think of Brain Burst as a simple fighting game and are planning something. Black Vise and Rust Jigsaw are members.
■ Armor of Catastrophe = An Enhanced Armament also called "Chrome Disaster." Equipped with this, an avatar can use powerful abilities such as Drain, which absorbs the HP of the enemy avatar, and Divination, which calculates enemy attacks in advance to evade them. However, the spirit of the wearer is polluted by Chrome Disaster, which comes to rule the wearer completely.
■ ISS kit = Abbreviation for "IS mode study kit." ("IS mode" is "Incarnate System mode.") The kit allows any duel avatar who uses it to make use of the Incarnate System. While using it, a red "eye" is attached to some part of the avatar, and a black aura overlay—the staple of Incarnate attacks—is emitted from the eye.
■ Seven Arcs = The seven strongest Enhanced Armaments in the Accelerated World. They are the greatsword Impulse, the staff Tempest, the large shield Strife, the Luminary (form unknown), the straight sword Infinity, the full-body armor Destiny, and the Fluctuating Light (form unknown).

1

Kill.
Kill them all.

All that existed was the urge. Already, it was beyond what could be called thought. The craving, the desire to hack and slash, to tear off his enemies' arms, legs, heads—the desire to rip them to pieces became a cold flame racing throughout Haruyuki Arita's entire body.

"*Grar...*" The low howl of an animal slipped out of his throat as he raised the longsword high.

The pure silver of the duel avatar Silver Crow had disappeared. In its place was a darker, more brutal chrome silver. His armor had also lost its original form: Previously slender, smooth limbs were covered seamlessly with sharp-edged metallic rings. Similar rings encircled his torso. But most sinister of all was his helmet, the maw of a carnivorous beast wrapped around the once-round head. Fang-like protrusions jutted out from the visor and hid his face completely; there was no sign left of the original, mirrored shield.

This armor was no mere equipped item, nor even a simple Enhanced Armament, within the fighting game of Brain Burst.

The strongest arms in the world were known as the Seven Arcs, aka the Seven Stars. The Destiny, the armor that was the sixth of these stars—the zeta—had fused with Star Caster, a high-level longsword. This combined form was then twisted by the raging grief of a particular Burst Linker of the past, at which point the Armor of Catastrophe, aka the Disaster, was born. Since the dawn of the Accelerated World, the legendary armor had brought about much destruction, always regenerating even when subjugated, never entirely disappearing. Its power surpassing even the Arcs, the Disaster now covered Silver Crow's lithe body completely.

In truth, the phenomenon did not stop at the level of "summoning" or "equipping." Haruyuki was now the Armor; the Armor was Haruyuki. The will to destroy housed in the Disaster had become one with Haruyuki's own mind, and he could no longer hear that gentle voice that had been whispering things in his ear all this time.

"You…," Haruyuki whispered in his own voice now. "I will kill you all."

Transformed into a demonic silhouette, as Haruyuki hovered with both wings spread out, he saw below him six Burst Linkers standing in a circle on the road of the Demon City stage—north of Miyashita Park on Meiji Street, in the Shibuya area of the real world—and staring up at him, the intruder. There were also two lights, shining weakly, in the center of this circle.

One was a grassy color. The other was gray. Death markers, appearing in the position where a Burst Linker died in the Unlimited Neutral Field. The grass-colored one belonged to Bush Utan, a member of the Green Legion, Great Wall. And the gray was the biker Ash Roller, Bush Utan's self-professed older brother and Haruyuki's longtime rival.

Five of the six Burst Linkers who had surrounded and repeatedly slaughtered the two dead Burst Linkers were faces he was seeing for the first time. But one of them, the avatar who had only minutes before dealt the death blow to Ash, was familiar.

He was slender and of average height, but there was a sense

of volume to his arms. His armor was a brownish dark green. Olive Grab, a main member of the Green Legion who had been teamed up with Bush Utan until mere days earlier. He obviously would have known Ash—he might have even called him a friend, in fact. And yet without the slightest hesitation, without showing anything even resembling emotion, Grab had stabbed him through the heart. He had tried to take all of Ash Roller's burst points and eliminate him from the Accelerated World forever.

Olive Grab—who was looking up at Haruyuki with a hint of doubt creeping onto his face mask—had an object embedded within his chest, as did the other five Burst Linkers around him. It was the same organic object in each case: a monstrous eye.

ISS kits were dark parasites that gave the wearer the power to control the Incarnate System, which itself was a super attack power outside the normal battle system. In the process, the kits multiplied the scope and intensity of negative emotions, going so far as to warp the personality of the real-world person. All six Burst Linkers were currently under the control of the kits, which was why they hadn't hesitated to attack Olive's senior in the Legion, Ash Roller, or Bush Utan, who had an ISS kit of his own.

However, all this no longer mattered to Haruyuki.

At the end of the day, Ash Roller was technically his enemy, a member of another Legion. And although his parent was Sky Raker, Nega Nebulus's second-in-command, Haruyuki had never actually met Ash in the real world.

But...

Ash was the first person Haruyuki fought as a Burst Linker. He was the first person he'd lost against, and the first he'd won against, as well. The biker seemed to enjoy every second of this landscape known as Brain Burst and, at some point, he had become a kind of foundation for Haruyuki. When he was struggling, when he was lost, Ash's extremely upbeat fighting style and the hearty roar of his American motorcycle got Haruyuki back on the right path as a Burst Linker. His duels with Ash were always intense, passionate, fun.

And so Haruyuki fiercely despised these six Linkers, who had tormented that same Ash with the overwhelming superiority granted to them by their number and power. Such emotion created an unusual contradiction, however, given that this very hatred and rage in Haruyuki's heart had brought back to life the Armor of Catastrophe after it had finally been returned to a seed state, sending Haruyuki charging down a path that was the total opposite of the true path of a dueler. Unfortunately, however, he was no longer capable of recognizing this.

Sending inky black sparks shooting off into the air, Haruyuki brandished the sharply tapered sword high above his head.

Likely judging this to be a hostile action, Olive Grab and the other five Burst Linkers on the ground raised their right hands in perfect unison and trained them on Haruyuki.

Palms of varying sizes became wrapped in dark overlays of, essentially, the same color. The viscous, dripping darkness instantly grew more concentrated and twisted the surrounding air, indicating a terrifying power.

At the same time, small English letters began to race across the additional gray layer blanketing Haruyuki's vision: PREDICTED ATTACK: INCARNATE ATTACK; RANGE/POWER ENHANCEMENT: NIHILISTIC ENERGY TYPE; THREAT LEVEL: 10.

From the six palms, faint, transparent scarlet lines stretched out soundlessly. These were not the actual attack. The Armor, from its vast wealth of accumulated battle experience, simulated the trajectories of incoming attacks and displayed them in Haruyuki's field of view.

It would have been an easy feat to evade this direct, long-distance group attack: It targeted his own chest and lacked any particular zigs or zags.

But rather than moving a single millimeter from the spot, Haruyuki tightened his grip on the longsword in his right hand, bringing the jet-black aura enveloping the blade to shudder violently. Although the coloring resembled the auras blanketing the six on the ground, if theirs were viscous, then Haruyuki's was a conflagration. A flame at absolute zero, layers of his wild rage and whetted bloodlust.

The Burst Linkers on the ground momentarily bent the fingers of their raised right hands before stretching them out once more. In one voice, they called out the name of the technique.

"Dark Shot!"

It was the first of two basic special attacks granted to ISS kit wearers. Three days earlier, the same dark beam shot out of Bush Utan's hand and ripped off one of Silver Crow's wings like it was paper. And now, six hands sent six dark beams charging toward him, leaving a sound of resonance in their wake. It was like the shriek of monsters.

Each one of the beams contained enough power to instantly eliminate any duel avatar, but Haruyuki let them close in on him until the very last moment—until the instant their trajectories crossed, and he casually sliced through them with the longsword Star Caster.

The brightly burning obsidian flames did not permit the dark beams to so much as touch the blade. The roar of impact threatened to shatter the air itself as the Incarnate attacks collided, and the six beams were knocked down to Haruyuki's right. Deep holes were instantly gouged out of the exceptionally hard terrain of the Demon City stage, and black flames shot out of them an instant later.

"Lukewarm," Haruyuki murmured in a cracked voice, without even glancing at the destruction.

It was, in the end, just a uniform Incarnate attack. They might have been able to mechanically cause an overwrite, but the core was empty, so weak it didn't begin to compare with the Dark Lightning Spike Takumu had unleashed while under the control of the same ISS kit the previous evening. There was simply no heart in their technique.

There existed inside Olive Grab nothing other than "hunger." A futile, single-minded urge to collect burst points. An ugly appetite to indulge in risk-free victories with instant power handed to him on a platter.

It was guys like this, with power like this, who had tormented Ash Roller to his death. These six had surrounded Ash, a man whose pride made him keep his distance from the Incarnate, a Burst Linker who had always worked to be a one-on-one fighter. And then they had killed him, over and over and over.

And that wasn't all. They had also hunted Ash's little brother, Bush Utan, who should have been one of them. The two death markers snuggled up against each other near the six Burst Linkers were proof of that. If they hadn't interfered, Ash and Utan would have joined up with Haruyuki and his friends in the Chiyoda area far to the northeast.

Earlier today—June 20, 2047—at seven PM, the six members of the Legion Nega Nebulus had carried out a mission to rescue Haruyuki/Silver Crow and Utai Shinomiya/Ardor Maiden from where they were held captive, deep inside the Castle towering at the center of the Unlimited Neutral Field.

In theory, the plan had been for Haruyuki and Utai to enlist the aid of Trilead Tetroxide, a mysterious Burst Linker they had met in the Castle, and escape through the south gate. At the same time, Kuroyukihime, Fuko, Takumu, and Chiyuri would divert the God Suzaku, the Super-level Enemy guarding said gate, and help the two get away.

In reality, Haruyuki and Utai were unable to simply fly straight out because Suzaku had materialized sooner than anyone expected. Just as the two fleeing avatars were about to be burned to a crisp by the God's flame breath, Kuroyukihime and Fuko, prepared to die to save Haruyuki and Utai, swooped in and made themselves Suzaku's target. But their death in that place would have been the worst possible outcome, both Legion Master and submaster deep in the territory of one of the Four Gods, trapped in a state of unlimited EK. So after entrusting an unconscious Utai to Takumu and Chiyuri, Haruyuki did a one-eighty and returned to help his beloved friends.

Grabbing them in his arms, he flew straight upward in the only route of escape left to them, but Suzaku relentlessly chased after them. Once the special-attack gauge that was the source of energy for his flying ability was drained, Haruyuki manifested a new Incarnate technique, Light Speed, and shot up through the stratosphere to reach the world of the stars.

Unable to fly with no air, both Haruyuki and Suzaku languished there, but Fuko, with her booster-type Enhanced Armament Gale Thruster, charged down with Kuroyukihime on her back, finally crushing the God with the Black King's lurid Incarnate attack, Starburst Stream. Although they didn't manage to strike the killing blow because of the Four Gods' ability to mutually heal each other at a distance, Haruyuki, Kuroyukihime, and Fuko did make it out of Suzaku's territory alive.

The six Legion members hugged one another fiercely and rejoiced in the success of the mission. But Ash Roller, who should have been there according to the plan, was not. When Haruyuki heard his rival never showed up at the meeting point, a terrible feeling that was hard to put into words came over him, and he flew off by himself to look for the man. And then he found—no, witnessed—*it*.

The very instant Ash was slaughtered by Olive Grab.

And the reason why Ash, a member of the Green Legion, Great Wall and thus ostensibly an enemy, would join up with the people of Nega Nebulus—and in the dangerous Unlimited Neutral Field at that—was because he intended to depart from his own beliefs and seek instruction in the Incarnate.

After the duel that morning before they went to school, Ash had told Haruyuki he didn't want to learn the Incarnate so he could fight no-holds-barred in the Unlimited Neutral Field. All he needed to do was strike one blow to wake up his little brother, Bush Utan.

There was no doubt that the reason he didn't show up at the meeting point was that he had run into Utan in the Normal Duel Field while on standby. Not letting that chance slip away, Ash had persuaded or begged Utan to come with him to the Unlimited Neutral Field.

And Utan had probably listened to Ash's persuasive/desperate words. He had resolved to get rid of the ISS kit possessing him and return to the true path of the Burst Linker once more. There was no doubt that the two of them had planned to meet here in the Unlimited Neutral Field and join up with Haruyuki and Nega Nebulus after they finished the Castle escape mission.

But Olive Grab and the other five Burst Linkers had figured out where Ash and Utan would be and ambushed them.

Haruyuki didn't know which of them had died first. But when he arrived on the scene, Ash had been almost clutching Utan's death marker to his own body to protect it. Since the marker was, as the name suggested, nothing more than a mark, there was no practical meaning in this, but he probably couldn't stop himself from doing it.

If there was a difference in the times of their deaths, then there would naturally be a time lag in their regenerations sixty minutes later. Even after one came back to life, the other would still be dead. In a helpless ghost state, they both had been forced to watch an adored brother be brutally killed over and over.

"...won't forgive." A hoarse voice spilled from Haruyuki's mouth once more. "I won't forgive you. I'll kill you. I'll kill all of you. I'll keep killing you until all your burst points are gone and you disappear from the Accelerated World."

The world-destroying conflagration raced through his body at a temperature of absolute zero, waiting impatiently for the moment of its release, internal pressure building endlessly. Rage and hatred melted into its flames, converging into a single purpose that burned white-hot.

"That's what you want, right? To fight, to kill. For you your-selves and even this world to disappear. So then I'll make your dreams come true. I'll make you all disappear."

The voice that slipped out from the brutal visor was also more monster than Haruyuki already. The voice of someone with the ferocity of a wild animal and the cool of steel.

No, that wasn't all. Somewhere far away, deep, deep down, another voice echoed faintly. The voice of someone trying intently to talk, lamenting and grieving...

But before their words could penetrate Haruyuki's conscious-ness, the six people below him lifted their right hands once more. They didn't seem the least bit shaken at the fact that six simulta-neous Incarnate attacks were repelled with a single sword stroke. They looked like they had power to spare, or more precisely, like emotion itself was being worn away.

In its place, the ISS kits parasitizing their chests glared at Haruyuki, crimson "eyes" filled with hatred. Viscous auras coiled thickly about the six arms, quickly concentrating in the palms, thin black sparks crawling through the air as if to hint at a power exceeding that of the previous attack.

In Haruyuki's field of view, the attack attribute information and anticipated trajectory were once again displayed. It was the same long-distance Incarnate attack, but the trajectory was dif-ferent. The clear red line spread out halfway, color fading as it did, and wrapped up a sphere in the air around Haruyuki. In other words, this was—

"Dark Shot!!"

The calls of the technique name were in perfect unison, as though one person were moving six mouths at the same time. The inky black beams emitted from the open palms surged ahead, scattering a fine spray. But unlike the earlier attack, they did not rush forward in a straight line. Twisting irregu-larly through the air, the attack charged toward him, still clearly aimed at Haruyuki.

Wordlessly, Haruyuki spread the metal wings on his back and

flew hard to his right. Instantly, the beams also bent sharply to follow. So it was a homing attack. Since the beams wouldn't overlap until the last moment, a defense using a single sword stroke was impossible. Even if he took one of them out with his sword, the remaining five would shower down on him. Because his health gauge, cut down in the battle with the God Suzaku, had been fully recharged when he summoned the Armor, they couldn't actually kill him with this one attack, but he would take a certain amount of damage.

As he twisted and turned hard to his left, the black beams came after him, radiating a ravenous hunger. No matter how fast he maneuvered, not one of the homing beams faltered in its unerring pursuit. He might have been able to shake them if he flew straight ahead at full speed forever, but that was no different from running anyway.

And he didn't have the slightest intention of fleeing. Instead, Haruyuki spread his wings and put on the emergency brakes; hovering in midair, he turned to face them.

The six beams pressed in on him, tangling up with one another in a complex way. Faint smiles bled onto the faces of the six Burst Linkers on the ground, perhaps taking Haruyuki's stopping as a sign of surrender. As if acting in concert, Haruyuki also smiled coldly under his thick visor.

Right hand gripping his sword, he crossed his arms in front of his chest. He arrogantly threw his head back and stared at the jet-black Incarnate bullets closing in on him. Stopped at an altitude of thirty meters, he drew the beams in and drew them still closer.

When they were on the verge of showering down on his entire body in a direct hit, he muttered quietly:

"Flash Blink."

Bwaan! Leaving behind only a momentary vibration, Silver Crow—or rather, the sixth Chrome Disaster, disappeared. Having lost their locked-on target, the dark beams raced around for a few seconds before erupting in black flames, some in the sky, some plunging through buildings on the ground.

Haruyuki, meanwhile, was already scattering a blackish-silver light as he materialized essentially right beside the six ISS kit wearers standing on the ground.

Flash Blink: The special attack of the ancient Burst Linker who gave birth to the Armor of Catastrophe in the Accelerated World—or more precisely, who twisted with his rage and despair the Destiny, the sixth star of the Seven Arcs, into the cursed Enhanced Armament the Disaster. The technique transformed his body into minuscule particles and pseudo-teleported them instantly to a distant location.

Haruyuki didn't even know that long-ago Burst Linker's name. His strange dream inside the Castle was all he had, a piece of a fragmented memory of something that had happened in the distant past. There shouldn't have been any way for Haruyuki to remember what he looked like or what techniques he had used. And yet he had understood—no, he had *known*. That the Haruyuki of that moment could use this power now.

One of the kit wearers—a duel avatar with dull, dark brown armor and a left hand with gun barrels for fingers—did indeed stare with surprise at Haruyuki's sudden appearance.

"Da…" He moved to thrust out his right hand as he called the name of the technique. But that hand was still facing straight up, not aimed at Haruyuki, and he tried to rotate it further back, ignoring his actual range of possible movement. And then a dark silver line ran across the base of his shoulder. The arm was quickly removed from the torso and fell to the ground of the Demon City stage with a noisy *clack*.

With lightning speed, Haruyuki had drawn the longsword in his right hand and severed his enemy's arm in the same stroke.

Similar to Flash Blink, this was not a technique he had originally been able to use. Unlike Takumu—Cyan Pile—Haruyuki had never studied kendo in the real world, and in all his time in the Accelerated World, he had focused on bare-handed fighting.

He didn't even know how to hold a sword-type Enhanced Armament, much less swing one. But he no longer cared what was happening to him. The intense urge to slice up the enemies before him and banish them from this world filled his head and heart.

The dark brown avatar stared down at his own arm rolling along the ground for a minute before finally twisting his face mask up in the slightest bit of fear. "What are you...What is this power..."

The voice leaked out from a mask fitted with round goggle-type lenses. The pain of the injury apparently caught up with him at last, and he pressed his left hand tightly over the opening at his right shoulder. Perhaps reflecting the wearer's agitation and suffering, the light from the eye on his chest—the ISS kit—also flickered irregularly.

But the kits of the five Burst Linkers standing to the rear all shone redly after a tiny hint of a delay. As if they were sending out energy, the kit in the brown avatar's chest also regained its fierce light. Apparently, these six belonged to the same "cluster," to use Takumu's words. The fact that their ISS kits were linked meant that they were as genetically close as clones—in other words, parent and child, or siblings. That said, linking them was only a temporarily advantageous agreement; it wasn't anything that could be called a "bond." The fact that they had mercilessly hunted even Bush Utan, ostensibly a member of the same group, was proof of that.

Bond...

The instant the word popped up in his mind, something ached deep inside Haruyuki. A sensation like a single ray of hazy sunlight shining in the frozen darkness. Someone's voice echoed from far, far, far away.

...emember...you, too...ave them...cious bonds...!

However, the overwhelming rage that immediately surged up in him again pushed the light and the voice away. "There's no point in telling you my name," Haruyuki muttered at the brown avatar before him, a pale burning blizzard of fury sinking into him. "Not when you're going to disappear right here and now."

"...Don't get...carried away..." The eyes in the lenses glowed red. The ISS kit pulsed in sync with the other five kits, like a heart. Apparently, this avatar was also no longer feeling any pain, although here in the Unlimited Neutral Field, it should have been double that of the Normal Duel Field.

The brown avatar made a small signal with his left hand as he pulled it away from his wound. Instantly, the other five moved quickly to surround Haruyuki. The brown one was apparently their leader, but now, having lost an arm, the spearhead of the opposition would have switched to someone else. Deciding to crush that one with his next blow, Haruyuki started to turn around.

But his feet abruptly, heavily stopped. When he looked down, he saw that at some point a gleaming green liquid had crept up to his feet, and two hands were reaching out from it to hold his ankles fast. It was almost, but not quite like the terrain effect Ensnare in the Cemetery stage. The liquid and the hands rising up from it were the melted arms of the duel avatar standing to the left. When the slender avatar met Haruyuki's eyes, a sneer crossed the simple elliptical mask. Olive Grab.

Haruyuki casually stabbed the hands grabbing his feet with the tip of the longsword dangling from his right hand. But the sharp metal met no resistance and simply sank in; it didn't appear to do any damage. Apparently, in this state, Olive was impervious to physical attacks as he held his target with incredible force. The Armor likely hadn't shown him this in the list of anticipated attacks because he had focused his gaze solely on the brown avatar.

The remaining five avatars spread out equidistant around the captured Haruyuki and raised their left hands in a perfectly coordinated motion. A viscous inky aura blanketed tightly clenched fists.

"Heh-heh, we'll squeeze all your points out of you, too, every last one," Brown said, in a creaking voice.

Now, again, text cut across his field of view: PREDICTED ATTACK/INCARNATE ATTACK; RANGE/POWER ENHANCEMENT/ NIHILISTIC ENERGY TYPE; THREAT LEVEL/30. The red predicted trajectory lines pierced Haruyuki directly from five different directions.

The five avatars brandishing their fists above their heads dashed forward together, shouting as one voice, "Dark Blow!!"

The straight punches cloaked in darkness shot forward, burning the virtual atmosphere. However great the Armor's defensive strength, if he was hit dead-on with five power-enhanced Incarnate attacks at the same time, he would take a fair bit of damage. But Haruyuki stared coolly at the approaching fists. Only their attack power was enhanced with Incarnate; the speed was not much greater than a beginner's. Given Haruyuki's rich history of special training to dodge the rifle bullets of red-type snipers, they were so slow, he was practically yawning. Once more, he drew the attacks well in, and then, when their auras were on the verge of making contact, he muttered the technique name beneath his visor.

Flash Blink.

Only a low vibration noise remained as the blackish-silver avatar disappeared from the spot. Olive Grab's liquid fists clutched emptily at the air. Haruyuki teleported three meters or so to the rear and rematerialized, still in his standing position. Before him, the five fists, having lost their target and with no hope of pulling back now, crashed into one another.

The sound of the collision was almost enough to rip the heavens open. Jet-black flames shot up and momentarily blanketed his field of view. He merely turned his face away slightly and allowed the flow of concentrated energy pushing at him to pass.

When the blanket of flames had dissipated, five duel avatars came into view, rolling around on the ground and moaning. All had lost their left arms, right from the shoulder. The wounds looked as though the arms had been ripped off; the pain was, no doubt, far beyond that of having an arm cleanly sliced off with a sharp blade.

"That...you..."

Olive Grab sounded stunned, but without so much as glancing at him, Haruyuki took a few steps to place his right foot on the chest of a particular fallen avatar. Owner of reddish-brown armor, leader of the six. Now that he was missing both arms, however, he could no longer use Dark Shot or Dark Blow. Unable to even speak, the other avatar simply blinked the lenses of both eyes.

"Don't fall for the same trick twice," Haruyuki said, in a low voice.

Getting caught by the same technique—in this case, narrow evasion with Flash Blink—in another battle on a different day was one thing, but in the same battle, it was the height of stupidity. The rivals Haruyuki had previously fought ruthlessly would have grasped the nature and power of the technique just by seeing him dodge the first beam and would have responded immediately. Naturally, those rivals included Ash Roller.

Ash must have hated it, being hunted by players like this, swaggering with easy power, forgetting the basics of the duel, relying on numbers. The instant this thought crossed Haruyuki's mind, his chest began to throb and ache again, but even that feeling was soon replaced by a blind rage.

Without considering how he must have looked to the eyes of Ash Roller in a ghost state awaiting regeneration very nearby, Haruyuki poured his strength into his right foot and the sharp talons readied there. Beneath his foot, he felt the ISS kit parasitizing the chest of the brown avatar pounding.

"Ngah...! Hnngh...Hah!" A clear cry of anguish gushed out from the avatar's mouth. Having lost both arms, he struggled and flailed as if trying to scratch at the earth, but the knifelike talons of the Armor dug deep into his chest to hold him fast. Finally, cracks radiated across the angular armor, and a florid light effect splashed out into the air.

Spurred on by his fury, Haruyuki brutally cut down the health gauge of his enemy, while one part of his mind raced with digital thoughts, an independent processor.

Was it possible to selectively destroy the ISS kits? If he could, he assumed something would probably happen when he did. He had noted earlier that the ISS kits were linked to one another through an invisible circuit. But rather than being a "peer-to-peer" type where kits with terminals were directly connected to each other, that connection was a central authority "client server" type. Perhaps it was possible that the instant a kit was destroyed, some sort of signal was sent to the main body of the kits that had to exist somewhere in the Accelerated World.

Still feeling the pulsation of the ISS kit under his foot, Haruyuki pushed his foot down mercilessly.

"Ngaaah! S-sto...Gah...Aaaaaah!!" The earsplitting scream rang out at the same time as the strange sound of the duel avatar's torso cracking into pieces. The avatar split into upper and lower halves to the left and right of Haruyuki's foot, and before he could let out one final scream, his health gauge dropped to zero in an instant, and a red light jetted from his body as he exploded into tiny fragments.

Haruyuki coolly observed the death of the opponent he had so cruelly slaughtered. Silver Crow's foot had indeed pushed through the ISS kit of the brown avatar. But judging from the death effect and the amount added to his special-attack gauge, he assumed that no Enhanced Armament destruction had taken place. Which meant that even if the ISS kit was pinpointed and attacked directly with a normal physical attack, only his opponent's health gauge would decrease. The kit itself could not be destroyed like that.

As robotic thoughts ran through Haruyuki's mind, one of the enemies he had knocked aside finally stood up to his right. "Fall back! Forget Cocoa Cracker!" he shouted briefly.

Cocoa Cracker was probably the name of the brown avatar Haruyuki had crushed and killed with his foot. Just like a hastily assembled gang to abandon their ostensible leader so easily. Olive Grab continued to stand motionless in front of Haruyuki, but the four avatars had no sooner nodded at one another than started to run south.

So they were planning to escape through the leave point at Shibuya Station, farther along down Meiji Street. Judging from the direction of his gaze, the unmoving Olive was waiting to build up his gauge to use his abilities again.

Haruyuki stood and stared at the four avatars racing off at top speed. He had not the slightest intention of letting them get away, however. He plunged the sword he clutched into the ground and raised his now-empty hands. He spread five sharp fingers wide and targeted the two on the ends of the fleeing foursome. He snapped his wrists back.

Ksshk! A small silver light launched from the lower part of his palms. He dragged out glittering platinum tails in the air, the lights chasing like gunshots after the two avatars running hard a few dozen meters away. They caught up to them immediately, and hit perfectly on target in the middle of the Armor on their backs. A dry, metallic sound echoed through the stage, but the pair continued to run, not even staggering. They appeared to have taken essentially no damage.

But…

When Haruyuki pulled his arms back a bit, he felt a heavy resistance, and the two Burst Linkers in the distance lost their footing. They stumbled and tried intently to kick at the ground, but their bodies did not move forward. Finally, they angled backward, their feet peeling away from the road, and they let out high-pitched cries as they flew back in a straight line. More accurate, they were pulled back, whether they liked it or not, by the extremely fine wires launched from Haruyuki's palms. The power of Wire Hook, an ability secreted away in the Armor of Catastrophe.

In the blink of an eye, Haruyuki had yanked them back to where they started. He plunged the talons of his hands into their backs down to the knuckles to hold them fast and lift them up.

"P-put me down!"

"No way! He's not using IS mode. How come he has this kind of power?!"

Their voices as they struggled and fought, insects stabbed with pins, were nothing more than cacophonous noise to Haruyuki. Concentrating an image in both hands, he uttered, in a nearly inflectionless voice, "Laser Sword."

Zzvsssh! A heavy vibration shook the earth. Long, endless Incarnate swords stretched out from the hands of Silver Crow clad in the Armor of Catastrophe, piercing the prey he had captured. But the swords were not their original silver; they were dyed with an inky black overlay reminiscent of the abyss of space.

Large holes ripped open their chests, much less the critical point of their hearts, and the two duel avatars rose up over a meter into the air from the aftereffects of the incredible attack power and shattered.

Haruyuki lowered his hands, the two death effect colors reflecting off his dull silver armor. Through his visor, he could see the remaining two enemies pushing themselves to flee at even greater speed. Already, they were almost a hundred meters away. Naturally, he could have caught them easily if he used the wings on his back. But Haruyuki instead grabbed his longsword from the ground, dropped his hips, and yanked the blade back hard above his right shoulder.

With the sharp tip of the sword, he set his sights precisely on the two avatars. Their silhouettes were already not even specks, but perhaps as an effect of the additional layer added to his field of view by the Armor, he experienced no loss of resolution. Coolly measuring his timing, the instant the bodies of the pair running started to overlap into one—

"Laser Lance."

The sword in his right hand charged forward at the same time as he called the technique name. The dark aura encircling the blade transformed into a lance and shot off into space. The movement to launch the attack was basically the same as the

Black King, Black Lotus's Vorpal Strike Incarnate attack, which it was modeled after, but Haruyuki was unconscious of this as he watched for results with narrowed eyes.

Off in the distance of Meiji Street, just as the two avatars were disappearing down the slope of Miyamasu-zaka, the Incarnate lance mercilessly skewered their backs. The avatars ran another few steps with massive craters in the middle of their bodies, as if they didn't notice what had happened to them, before finally staggering and exploding, accompanied by the faint noise of destruction and a burst of extinction light.

Shouldering the sword that he pulled back slowly, Haruyuki turned to his final enemy—Olive Grab, the avatar with the ability to turn to liquid.

This was not the first time they had squared off. After school on Monday, three days earlier, when he had tag-teamed in the Suginami area with the "shrine maiden of the conflagration," Ardor Maiden, she happened to select as their opponent the combo of Bush Utan and Olive Grab from the matching list. At that time, Haruyuki had been no match for Utan when he activated his ISS kit, but Maiden had gotten away from Olive without a scratch, even though he had to have been using the same dark Incarnate. Of course, she did have all the power one would expect from an Element of the former Nega Nebulus, but that probably wasn't the whole story. There had to have been some kind of overwhelming difference in affinities.

As Haruyuki coolly followed this thread, not a shred of emotion entering into his calculations, Olive continued to stand before him rather than fleeing. It wasn't as though he had a choice. Haruyuki wasn't sure if Olive was aware that he was the legendary destroyer Chrome Disaster, but either way, Olive was cowering with fear at the overwhelming battle prowess that had slaughtered his five companions before his eyes. As proof, his entire body, slickly shining as if it were wet, was trembling.

"Hurry...Hurry..." The hoarse voice that slipped out of his

mouth was directed at his own special-attack gauge. His eyes traveled back and forth and back and forth between Haruyuki, leisurely beginning to move, and his recharging gauge.

Right around the time the longsword came down from Silver Crow's shoulder to scrape dryly against the ground, Olive shouted, "Lipid Liquid!"

The call of the technique name was practically a falsetto. *Splsh!* His slender body immediately melted away. His avatar completely lost shape, transforming into a large olive-green puddle spreading out on the ground. In this state, he was likely invulnerable to all pure physical attacks.

And apparently, he still had the ability to move, since the puddle was charging toward one of the buildings lining both sides of the road, in a movement like the Slime that often showed up in fantasy-type games. If he fled into the elaborate terrain of the Demon City stage, it would be a pain to find him again.

But again, Haruyuki had not allowed Olive to use his special attack because he hadn't been paying attention. The greenish-brown puddle bulged in the center. Looking closely, he could see a black sphere wrapped up there. The ISS kit. Olive might have had the ability to become a liquid, but he couldn't change the kit, which was treated as Enhanced Armament, into one.

Haruyuki had deliberately brought about this situation. Staring at the slippery puddle as it receded, he took a deep breath. Soon, the sensation of something prickly bouncing about filled his chest. He let it build up and then blew it out as hard as he could.

Released from the maw of the brutal helmet was not simple air, but rather flames burning hot and red. The ability: Flame Breath.

Perhaps sensing something, the puddle moved intensely toward the building. But there was no way for it to escape the flames that radiated outward, scorching the air as they did. The instant the blazing breath touched it, the puddle burst into flames with a roar.

The breath soon scattered and disappeared, but the flames

blanketing the puddle did not. Almost as if the puddle itself was a flammable material—or rather, that was exactly what it was. The liquid that Olive Grab changed himself into was not water, but oil. The reason Ardor Maiden defeated him so thoroughly was because he was deeply incompatible with fire.

Even as a liquid, Olive wouldn't have lost his physical sensations. The lump of flaming oil bounced wildly from side to side. Haruyuki himself had been bathed in the fiery breath of the God Suzaku several times in the Unlimited Neutral Field, and the sensation of heat had been all too real. If Olive Grab was continuously experiencing anything on that level, the pain must have been unbearable.

But the Haruyuki of that moment did not care about the suffering of his enemies. He walked over to the puddle of oil, motionless now perhaps having exhausted even the will to writhe, and casually stretched out a hand. He dug his sharp fingers into the burning lump. Soon, they encountered a sphere about five centimeters in diameter, and he grabbed on to it tightly. He could feel the unpleasant sensation of countless fibers tearing away as he pulled out a red eyeball hidden almost entirely behind its lids—the ISS kit.

The handling of Enhanced Armament was a little different in the Unlimited Neutral Field than it was in the Normal Duel Field. First, once they were destroyed, external items did not regenerate even if the owner died and came back to life. In order to use Enhanced Armament items again, the owner had to exit the field through a leave-point and then return.

Also—and this depended on the type of item—it was possible to temporarily steal an item as long as the original owner was alive. To steal it, another Burst Linker needed to pick it up from the place where it was dropped or sever it from where it was equipped. Haruyuki was currently attempting the latter. Having rendered the liquefied Olive Grab helpless with his Flame Breath, he was ripping the kit out before Olive's HP gauge was emptied.

This way, the ownership would remain with Olive Grab in the system, but usage rights would transfer to Haruyuki.

Naturally, he had not the slightest intention of equipping it himself. His aim was just the opposite.

He had earlier confirmed that the kit itself could not be destroyed when the health gauge of the wearer dropped to zero in an attack. In which case, he would first separate avatar and kit, and then attack the kit itself.

A ferocious grin spreading across his face beneath his visor, Haruyuki concentrated his strength in his right hand. His razor-sharp talons dug into the rubbery surface of the eye. Instantly, the eyelids snapped open, and the bloodred pupil shuddered.

The blood vessel–type structure dangling helplessly from the rear of the eyeball writhed and came together in the tapered form of a drill. This drill bit then attempted to pierce the armor of Haruyuki's right arm—it was giving up on its original owner and trying to parasitize Haruyuki. Something similar had happened in the duel with Takumu the previous evening. The blood vessels of the kit had easily pieced Silver Crow's chest then, but the thick armor of the Armor of Catastrophe easily repelled the drill.

"Useless," Haruyuki said, and put every ounce of strength he had into his right hand.

Spplrrk! The sound of the rupture was disgusting, and was followed by an unusual metallic death rattle echoing through the air as the ISS kit crumbled into pieces and scattered.

Now that he had destroyed an ISS kit in the Unlimited Neutral Field, he was sure something would happen.

His expectation was not betrayed. From his right hand, a single thread of red light danced into the sky, turned sharply at a ninety-degree angle high up, and began to fly. The light was impossibly faint; if he didn't have the enhanced vision of the Disaster, he probably wouldn't have even noticed it.

Beside him, Olive Grab finally exhausted his health gauge and scattered as he returned to his original human shape. But Haruyuki did not so much as glance at him as he spread the wings on his back.

On the verge of taking off to chase after the light that had slipped out of the kit, Haruyuki caught sight of the two death markers nestled together a little ways off. One grassy green, the other gray. Bush Utan and Ash Roller, killed by the six kit wearers.

He had ostensibly raced over here to help them. But the priority he placed on them now had dropped to a relatively low level. What filled his heart instead was the urge to destroy and massacre, not placated in the least by routing the six Burst Linkers. If he stayed in that place any longer, he might attack even the regenerated Ash and Utan.

Thus, Haruyuki turned the focus of the rage that spurred him to destroy onto the ISS kits themselves. But, unaware of even these changes in his own heart, he turned aside and called back over his shoulder to the two avatars likely watching in a ghost state.

"When you regenerate, get out through a portal before those guys come back to life," he announced curtly, in a creaking voice, and then he took to the air from the scene of slaughter that the intersection had become.

2

Against the backdrop of the shades of black and blue of the Demon City stage, it was easy to pick out the red light that had escaped from the ISS kit. Ascending vertically until he was nearly at the swirling black clouds, Haruyuki caught sight of the luminous body flying quickly dead east.

"I won't let you get away," he started to say, but what spilled out from beneath his helmet was:

"*Graaar!*"

Nothing but the howl of a Beast.

He vibrated the now-sinister-looking metal wings with all his might. Looking very much like a bird of prey chasing its dinner, Silver Crow—the sixth Chrome Disaster sliced through the black clouds.

The rage that had boiled over in him immediately after summoning the Armor had vanished at some point and been replaced with something cold and honed that could have been called the will to destroy. Or perhaps this was something Haruyuki had unconsciously brought about himself to avoid attacking Ash Roller and Bush Utan, but his mind was in no position to recognize that at that moment.

In that instant, a single determination and two facts were pushing Haruyuki onward.

Determination: He could not forgive the ISS kit wearers or the makers of those kits.

Fact number one: Those Acceleration Research Society guys created and distributed the ISS kits.

Fact number two: The black layered avatar planned the incident that would serve as the trigger for the birth of the Armor of Catastrophe.

The layered avatar—Black Vise, the vice president of the Acceleration Research Society—had barged into the final stages of the battle against Dusk Taker and toyed with Haruyuki and his friends. A fearsome enemy equipped with a terrifyingly powerful Incarnate attack whose tone and attitude were very much not those of a junior high or high school student. And due to the brain implant chip he had in his head, he possessed the ability to "decelerate" and slow his thought clock, making lying in wait for a long time in the Unlimited Neutral Field, where time flowed a thousand times faster than it normally did in reality, an easy feat.

A very, very long time ago, this Black Vise set up a heartless trap and drove one Burst Linker to total point loss with the first Unlimited Enemy Kill in the Accelerated World. Due to the rage and grief brought about by that incident, the sixth star of the Seven Arcs, the Destiny, became warped, turning into the Armor of Catastrophe, the Disaster.

These were facts Haruyuki should not have actually known. The birth of the Catastrophe was at the dawn of the Accelerated World—seven years earlier. In contrast, only eight months had passed since he'd become a Burst Linker.

And yet he did not think it strange that the fathomless hatred and resentment toward the layered avatar Black Vise raced through his whole body as his own memories.

I will not forgive you. I'll never forgive you. All of you who created and distributed the ISS kits, led Takumu astray, hurt Ash.

I will find and kill the ones who murdered...with the fangs of the mythical beast Jormungand over and over and over. Just like that day, I will inflict the maximum amount of pain and suffering. I will keep killing them endlessly until their points are used up.

His determination hidden within him at absolute zero, Haruyuki flew intently after the red body of light. East from the northern part of the Shibuya area. He swept past Aoyama Street and the large school grounds beyond it in a single breath. The place coming into view up ahead packed with the small square stones was probably Aoyama Cemetery. The light flew along above the countless gravestones as if pulled in by something.

If this ball of light was the "core" of the ISS kit Haruyuki destroyed, then what lay ahead had to be the main body. In the middle of the previous night, Haruyuki had been sleeping while directing with Takumu and was led to the mysterious interior of the Brain Burst central server through the imagination circuit. What he saw there was a galaxy of light, interweaving all the data saved and processed in the Accelerated World, along with a lump of black meat, eating into a corner of the space and writhing—the main body of the ISS kits.

In this world, Haruyuki succeeded in destroying the kit housed in Takumu, but that made it seemingly impossible for them to return to the central server once more and attack the main body. When he thought about it, however, the fact that it was inscribed within the server as data meant that the main body existed as an object somewhere in the field that was the game world. Just like how the Seven Arcs, which glittered within the server like a constellation, existed in the field in the form of swords and armor.

And if the ISS main body *was* hiding, then it wouldn't be in the normal field, where creation and annihilation happened over and over; it would be somewhere in the eternal Unlimited Neutral Field. If he tailed the red body of light, he was bound to arrive at it. And wherever it was, one of *them* was bound to show up. Either the despised Black Vise or one of his friends.

"Grrr..." A groan he couldn't suppress spilled out of his throat. Now.

Now, finally, the time was at hand. The time for the revenge he as the Catastrophe had been waiting these many months and years for, as he moved through the minds of Burst Linkers. He would decapitate them all, tear their limbs off, smash them to pieces. No matter what came as a result. Even if he lost his last shred of reason and became a demon god, indiscriminately attacking every Burst Linker and destroying the Accelerated World itself. Actually, that was a fitting end to this savage world of battle.

Tearing the thick blanket of clouds immediately above his head with the shock wave emitted by the wings on his back, Haruyuki flew with single-minded determination. The red light fled intently a mere hundred meters ahead, almost as though it had a will of its own.

Beyond it, a remarkably tall building appeared. Judging from its position in relation to the road, the building, surrounded by decorative pillars with the sharp edges characteristic of the Demon City stage, was Tokyo Midtown Tower, the mixed-use commercial structure in Minato Ward's Akasaka in the real world. The body of light appeared to be descending, aiming for somewhere near the top floor of the building. This was it. The physical main body of the ISS kits in the Unlimited Neutral Field.

I will crush it!!

Brimming with the desire to destroy, Haruyuki pushed his flying speed to the limit.

Or he was going to. Immediately before he could, somewhere below him to the right, he felt like he could hear a voice. And no mere words. The call of a technique name.

"Parsec Wall."

It was unfamiliar, the low, solemn voice of a boy, reminiscent of stark, craggy mountains. At the same time, Haruyuki's field of view was painted over by a dark-green light.

A wall. One after another, countless large green crosses—bigger than a person—appeared and joined seamlessly together to create a very wide and very tall wall. He couldn't tell how far it continued in any direction, and if he detoured around it, he might lose sight of the body of light flying on the other side. Rather than finding the Burst Linker who produced this wall, his top priority was on discovering where that red light was going. He could deal with any intruders some other time.

"Raaah!" With a low roar, Haruyuki brought up a black Incarnate overlay in his left hand. Without the slowing down, he brandished his fist and smashed it into the green wall.

The instant the dull silver aviator and the rich green defensive wall collided, the incredible impact set heaven and earth shaking in the Accelerated World. But the wall did not break. The herd of crosses slid back and forth incrementally, absorbing the collision and sending it radiating outward to stop Haruyuki's charge.

The current Haruyuki was no longer Silver Crow, whose only strength was speed. He was now the ultimate fighting machine, layering power and defense onto that speed, the sixth Chrome Disaster. And he also had the thick Incarnate aura on his fist. The fact that the wall had repelled this blow most certainly meant that it was the product of someone's Incarnate technique.

"Grar…" A groan of annoyance slipping out, Haruyuki pulled back the left fist he had thrust forward. There was no damage to his armor or his health gauge, but there was also no sign of a crack in the green wall. Spreading his wings to hover, he slowly turned his head and peered in the direction of the earlier technique call.

To the right—basically, due south. At a point about five hundred meters away, the space separated by the elevated Shuto Expressway No. 3, a building roughly as tall as Midtown Tower rose up into the sky. The main tower of the similarly large-scale mixed-use Roppongi Hills.

On the roof was a large heliport, and in the center, two human figures stood. One had his left hand held high, a dazzling green overlay gushing from it. No mistake, this was the source of the Incarnate wall repelling Haruyuki.

"Then I'll take care of you first," he muttered, and leisurely changed his orientation. The body of light he had been chasing, the core of the ISS kit, had probably slipped into Midtown Tower by now. It wouldn't be easy to hunt down the kit's main body in the enormous building, but if he had to, he could just destroy the building itself. He would think of this battle with the two intruders as a way to recharge the special-attack gauge he had used up flying at full speed.

Resting the sword dangling from his right hand on his shoulder, Haruyuki started flying again.

The roof of Roppongi Hills Mori Tower was about a hundred meters lower than the altitude he had been hovering at, so he basically only had to glide in. Clawing at the hard tiles with the talons of both feet, Haruyuki landed on the northern side of the heliport.

He turned his gaze to first stare at the Burst Linker using the large-scale defensive Incarnate technique, but the second Burst Linker quickly pushed in front. It was a duel avatar he'd never seen before. Medium build. Basically the same size as Haruyuki in his current incarnation. The silhouette was orthodox, but two things drew his eye.

One was the fact that both hands were ridiculously large. And they didn't look like they had been enlarged like Olive Grab's, but rather as if they were wrapped in round, thick gloves. And the second characteristic was the color of the Armor. The dull gleam reflecting the hazy sunlight was clearly metallic. There was no doubt he was looking at one of the few metal colors in the Accelerated World.

Haruyuki then shifted his gaze to the one behind the metal avatar, the large duel avatar who continued to hold his left arm up into the sky.

He had seen this one before. And not just that. The color, the form. He had come face-to-face with him only once before, but even if he tried to forget, the other avatar was filled with such an absolute sense of presence, forgetting him was almost impossible.

The Armor plates, radiating a weightiness, were a green so pure, it could almost be compared with nothing else. The limb and chest plates were fat and thick, but the key points were tensed, so there was nothing lumbering in the impression he made. To sum it up in one phrase, a great tree—ruler of the earth, towering forever above the land without the slightest tremor in the face of any storm.

It wasn't possible to mistake a Burst Linker with this kind of pressure for anyone else, but Haruyuki, his mind fused with the Armor of Catastrophe, still found it hard to believe. Given that they had interfered with his pursuit of the body of light, he had to conclude that the pair were ISS kit makers—in other words, members of the Acceleration Research Society. But Haruyuki had seen the green avatar seated at the meeting of the Seven Kings the other day. And not as an attendant, but as one of the key players at the meeting.

When Haruyuki soundlessly focused his gaze on him, unable to completely push aside his misgivings, the green avatar abruptly lowered the hand he had held aloft all this time. At the same time as the intense overlay housed in his arm weakened, the wall embedded in the sky vanished from the corner of Haruyuki's eye.

But the light didn't completely disappear. Still lodged in the avatar's left arm, it spread out into a square and gained substance. What appeared was a shield, glittering a remarkably pure green as though an enormous emerald had been carved into a panel.

The priority, which was enough to faintly distort the surrounding air, was not something regular Enhanced Armaments had. Which meant it was an Arc. The large shield was the gamma of the Seven Stars, the Strife.

There was definitely no doubt now. The green avatar who had generated a wall large enough to connect earth and sky with an Incarnate technique and repel Haruyuki's forward motion was one of the Seven Kings of Pure Color, ruler of the major Legion

Great Wall, the strongest person reigning in the Accelerated World.

"Green King...Green Grandé." Haruyuki said the name in a hoarse, creaking voice.

There was, of course, pressure in being face-to-face with a king, but the emotions beyond that made him forget his fear. An aura of black flames dancing around his body, he turned toward the avatar, who was a head taller than himself. "Are you...the mastermind?" he asked. "Was it you who made the ISS kits and distributed them?"

If his opponent moved his head in the slightest gesture of assent, Haruyuki was ready to use the sword in his right hand to cut him down without a moment's delay. But the Green King only looked quietly at Haruyuki with strangely amber-colored eye lenses, evincing no reaction at all.

"What the—?!" the metal color standing in front of the king shouted back instead. His head was a simple cylindrical shape, but that gave it a sense of toughness as the avatar shook it and turned a glove-shaped fist toward Haruyuki.

"Silver Crow—no, Chrome Disaster! You're the ally of the Society here!" he spat. "That filthy overlay is proof of that! The Six Kings were kind enough to give you a whole week to purify yourself, and here you are sneaking around behind the scenes, the height of cowardliness! You really are the child of the biggest traitor in the Accelerated World!"

The instant this line echoed through his brain, something pinched unexpectedly within Haruyuki. He wouldn't simply kill this one. As he resolved himself, a part of his brain was analyzing the information like an automated digital circuit.

These two were already aware that the duel avatar standing before them was Silver Crow after summoning the Armor of Catastrophe. Still, that wasn't especially strange. Although the Accelerated World was large, even newbies knew that the only one who could continuously fly was the crow from Nega Nebulus, and the kings and their closer associates would naturally

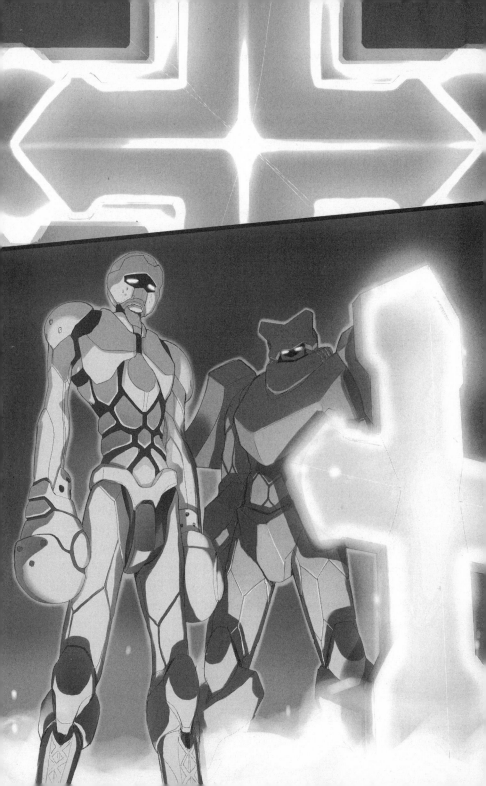

have the information that Silver Crow had been parasitized by the Armor of Catastrophe. And Haruyuki's current form had been revealed before the eyes of several hundred spectators in the final stages of the Hermes' Cord race the other day.

Setting aside the question of the Green King, Haruyuki should have actually commended the courage of the metal color, perhaps, who not only did not tremble in the face of the legendary destroyer, but even spit such challenging words at him. Naturally, he gave voice to none of this and simply let his thoughts run further along.

If he was sincerely cursing Haruyuki out for being a friend to the Acceleration Research Society, that meant the two Green Legion avatars were not members of the Society. But if that was the case, then why would they interfere with Haruyuki chasing that body of light? And there was one more thing he definitely could not shut his eyes to. Before they fought, he had to ask this at least.

"If you say you're not allies of the Society," Haruyuki began, staring at the headgear-shaped face mask of the metal color, "then how can you just be standing around here?"

"What's that supposed to mean?"

"A mere three kilometers away, only a few minutes ago, two members of Great Wall were murdered several times by ISS kit wearers. If you were this close, why didn't you go help them?"

As he gave voice to this question, the image of Ash Roller being pierced through the chest and scattering in all directions flashed across the back of his mind, and Haruyuki once again felt the absolute-zero rage race through his veins. A howl he couldn't suppress slid out from under his visor, a growl.

"Ngh!" The metal color swallowed his breath.

Haruyuki took a step toward him and glared at his opponent from beneath his visor. "Or is it that you don't give a crap how much the subordinate members of your Legion suffer, or if they end up in total point loss?" he said, in a voice that was almost not a voice. "And you think someone like you has the right to call anyone a coward or a traitor?"

Spitting words like pale flames, Haruyuki was still not aware of another enormous contradiction that existed within his own self. What he desired as the sixth Chrome Disaster was revenge on the layered avatar Black Vise, who had killed his beloved in the distant past, and the end of the Accelerated World itself, which was nothing more than a cradle for this kind of tragedy. And naturally, that included the annihilation of the people Haruyuki now loved.

However, the Haruyuki left inside the Armor as Silver Crow still believed in and desired the many bonds he had built in this world. Which was exactly why he got angry when his parent Kuroyukihime was insulted and felt that he couldn't forgive the Green Legion senior members for not protecting Ash Roller. Perhaps this double standard was proof that Haruyuki was still not completely fused with the Armor of Catastrophe, or perhaps it was because the Enhanced Armament Destiny itself had originally possessed these two faces. That said, this internal struggle did not show on the outside. Haruyuki took another step, an ever-more-intense aura gushing out of him.

"Th-that was..." The dull gray metal color, holding his ground, hung his head slightly and groaned. "We have something important—"

"There's nothing more important than the lives of your Legion members! Guys who don't even try to protect their friends are worse garbage than the Acceleration Research Society. Right now...I am going to make you both disappear from the Accelerated World!!" Crying out sharply, he sliced sideways with the longsword on his shoulder.

The eyes of the downcast metal color shone, accompanied by the heavy sound of vibration. Slowly raising his face, he stared at Haruyuki. "What do you...know? We, our king...Do you know how much time we've sacrificed for the Accelerated World...Who exactly has been protecting and maintaining this world you all happily come to have fun fighting in…"

At that moment.

The Green King, who had kept silent until that point, made a move. That said, he simply took a step back and crossed his arms behind the great shield. However, the metal color seemed to take some kind of intent from this movement and stopped speaking, dropping his head as his entire body stiffened with a snap once more. Finally, he lifted his face and spoke as if he had decided something.

"Right from the get-go, I didn't think we could do this without fighting you, aka the Catastrophe. *Action* before words. All that's left is to talk with our fists." He drew back his right foot, bending at the knee, and in a sudden change, danced about with light, nimble footwork. He raised his massive fists and readied them in front of his body side by side. "Third seat of Great Wall's Six Armors, level seven, Iron Pound. We're not waiting for the meeting of the Seven Kings in three days; we're getting rid of you right here and now!"

Taking in the proudly shouted name, Haruyuki opened his mouth under his helmet. But he couldn't name himself, couldn't shout back, *member of Nega Nebulus, Silver Crow*. Even if his mental state was abnormal, he was all too painfully aware that the way he was now, he had no right to that title. Thus, he murmured the name of the cursed armor, "Sixth Chrome Disaster."

Perhaps in response to this name, the dark aura rising up from all over the Armor abruptly increased in strength. As his upper body continued to sway rhythmically, the enemy metal color Iron Pound responded with a pale-blue aura lodged in his glove-shaped fists.

If the Six Armors was the name of a leader group equivalent to the former Nega Nebulus's Four Elements, then the avatar before him was a powerful fighter who was ranked fourth in the enormous Legion Great Wall. And he was two levels ahead of the currently level-five Haruyuki. This opponent had power on such a different level that, normally, Haruyuki's chances of victory would be slim, even if he took on the challenge prepared to die.

But now, he thought of Iron Pound up against him as nothing more than an annoying object. His true objective was the Green King. The distrust and rage he felt toward Green Grandé—not only had he not gone to rescue Ash Roller, supposedly a subordinate in his Legion, but he had interfered with Haruyuki's pursuit of the ISS kit—would not subside until he had taken the king's head.

First, he would take care of this interloper with a single blow. Making this resolution to himself, Haruyuki placed his left hand on the hilt of the longsword and brandished it high in the air. The tip stopped at the peak, and just as he was about to start moving it, a vivid red line pierced his washed-out field of view—the attack prediction line. At the same time, the attack attribute information display began. PREDICTED ATTACK: INCARNATE ATTACK; RANGE/POWER ENHANCEMENT: STRIKING TYPE...

But that was as much of the small text message as he got to read. Because with almost no delay after the moment the prediction line appeared, the enemy launched his Incarnate technique.

There was just the blink of a blue light, which even Haruyuki could not make out, despite the fact that his eyes could pick out a bullet fired from a rifle in the Accelerated World. Iron Pound launched a series of frighteningly fast left punches, blow after blow shooting out beyond his actual reach—which Haruyuki understood only after they slammed hard into his face and sent him reeling.

"*Grr...raaaah!!*"

A howl of rage slipping out, he braced his feet and forcefully brought down the longsword. The blade, tinged with the dark aura, came down on the head of the enemy just as he finished his attack.

Or not. What the sword actually caught was the afterimage of

Iron Pound left in Haruyuki's vision. The point of his sword dug deep into the heliport on the roof of Mori Tower, and the aftershocks from the power it contained produced sharp cracks several meters away. By that point, however, his enemy had already cut around two meters to the left, and his fist glittered once more.

Bam! Babam! The blows popped the sides of his helmet rhythmically. This time, there was no chance for the attack prediction lines to be displayed.

So fast!!

An incredible speed, exceeding even the calculation abilities of the Armor of Catastrophe. The force of a single blow wasn't that great, but because there were so many of them, Haruyuki's health gauge was shaved down nearly 5 percent. Given that this small technique was breaking past the incredible defensive power of the Armor, it was clearly an Incarnate attack, but the ease of use was somehow different from the techniques he had been hit with before.

As he pulled his sword from the floor and readied it in front of his chest to check the enemy's movements, Haruyuki searched for the reason for this dissonance, and then realized what it was. Pound wasn't calling the technique name that always accompanied an Incarnate attack. So the launch of the technique was abnormally fast, and it was also hard to get a grip on the timing. In the depths of his mind, fragments of the lecture from the Red King Scarlet Rain came back to life from what already felt like the long-distant past.

"The heart of an Incarnate technique is whether or not the image is firmly fixed in your mind. Ideally, you wanna be able to call it up as naturally as you do the abilities and special attacks you had from the start. You were concentrating for nearly three seconds from the time you crouched down to the time you moved. That's way too slow! So first, you give your technique a name, so then you superimpose over the image with you shouting the name as the trigger..."

Something deep in his heart throbbed, but Haruyuki forcefully erased that emotion and sorted through the information in those words.

Just as Niko had said, unlike a normal special attack, calling out the technique name was not an action required by the system for an Incarnate attack. The purpose of shouting the name of the technique was to semi-automate the focusing of the imagination as a conditioned reflex, so to speak, and speed up activation. Currently, it took Haruyuki approximately 1.5 seconds to go from a natural, relaxed posture to finishing the release of his Incarnate attack Laser Sword. However, without calling the technique name, it took more than four seconds.

But the reason calling out the technique name was required to begin with for normal Brain Burst special attacks was because it was one restriction on releasing a powerful attack. Obviously, it made surprise attacks from behind impossible, but more than that, it informed the enemy of the attack timing and gave them precious moments to respond. Which was why the strongest attack was actually a silent special attack. And the attack Iron Pound was pummeling him with at that moment was precisely that. A special attack without the call of the technique name. He barely took even a tenth of a second from readying his fists to launching the punch. It was only natural that the Armor's attack prediction line display couldn't keep up.

However, no matter how fast, the attack was, in the end, nothing more than a bare-handed punch. Pound's reach also appeared to be extended with Incarnate, but it still wasn't greater than the reach of Haruyuki's sword. If he met his enemy's initial onslaught with a slashing attack, the sword would land first.

Leisurely raising the sword to chest level, Haruyuki concentrated on his enemy's movements. The way Iron Pound danced about in small steps, his heels almost floating, made it hard to predict what he would do next. But although he could neglect the technique call as much as he wanted, he couldn't hide the increase in overlay accompanying the activation of an Incarnate attack.

"Sh!" A sharp breath.

At the same time, Haruyuki saw the aura enveloping his enemy's left fist flash brightly.

The timing of his counterattack was perfect. Immediately before Iron Pound launched his punch, Haruyuki sliced downward with his longsword. The distance between them was just enough that his opponent's fist could not reach him, but the tip of his sword could just barely reach his opponent. The power in the blade could easily slice through even the structures of the Demon City stage, so it should have bisected his enemy's headgear mask. And yet...

In a move Haruyuki's experience had led him to believe was impossible, Iron Pound threw only his upper body back, leaving his feet planted where they were. The deadly blade flowed straight down into nothingness, leaving a few sparks in its wake.

A feint.

The enemy pretended to throw a left jab, inviting Haruyuki's attack. Successfully luring the sword in, he dodged it by simply leaning back, and then, no sooner had Haruyuki been drawn in deep than his enemy immediately shot his *right* fist out in a straight line, a large rifle bullet.

Again, there was no technique call. But the powerful, focused right hook of his enemy, wrapped in a thick aura, delivered a scathing shot to Haruyuki's face the instant he finished swinging his sword. The impact was so great that he was surprised his helmet wasn't shattered; in fact, the only reason Haruyuki managed to avoid that level of damage was because he had reflexively flapped his wings with all his might to push himself backward. Even still, the instant the bomb hit him, his head snapped back and his field of view went white. The power of the punch and the force of his own retreat sent him flying more than ten meters backward, reeling.

"*Graar!*" A howl of rage slipping out, he pulled his face back down. Tiny fragments of metal fluttered off from the cracks in his visor. Somehow, he managed to get the fitful magma of rage erupting in him under control enough to speak. "That technique," he muttered. "Boxing?"

"Yeah." Iron Pound nodded before him, smoothly pulling his extended fist back to bring both hands neatly in front of his mouth again. "There are basically no boxing-type Burst Linkers, so I guess I'm pretty hard to deal with at first glance."

He spoke the truth. Haruyuki had never once before dueled a Burst Linker who used boxing techniques. There were a lot of blue-type "strikers," who had hands specialized for punching attacks, and he had fought them any number of times. But this was the first opponent he had faced who had mastered techniques from the sport of boxing to this extent and whose duel avatar was a perfect boxer form as well.

Most likely, the flesh-and-blood player in the real world also trained as a boxer. It would be hard to otherwise explain the perfect succession of those terrifyingly fast left punches (jabs), or the defensive maneuver of throwing his body back like water flowing (swaying), and the single-blow special attack of the right punch (a straight).

The heavy weighting of "player skills"—abilities the flesh-and-blood player possessed in the real world—in full-dive VR games was said to have come about a few decades earlier. The tendency for players who did kendo or who excelled in memorization to do well in sword-and-sorcery VRMMO worlds was also carried over to the VR fighting game Brain Burst.

But this so-called initial ability bonus was not large enough to upset the balance of the Accelerated World. One reason was that there were very few sporty Burst Linkers to begin with. Given the fact that Brain Burst was in the end a net fighting game, most of its players were children who liked games, i.e., the indoor type.

Naturally, there were exceptions like kendo-team Takumu and track-and-field Chiyuri. But it wasn't the case that the skills the flesh-and-blood player had learned were always reflected as is in the duel avatar. In fact, there were almost no such examples. Takumu's Cyan Pile had been created with a pile rather than a sword, although he was a blue type, and Chiyuri's Lime Bell was not a particularly high-speed-motion type. And Haruyuki himself, his obsession with first-person shooters would have been put to better use if he had been born a red type equipped with at least one gun rather than the empty-handed Silver Crow. This discrepancy itself was the second reason the initial bonus didn't really affect the duel balance.

Still, that said, very rarely, a duel avatar was generated reflecting the knowledge, experience, and abilities of the flesh-and-blood player as-is. Avatars like that were called...

"Perfect Match," Haruyuki murmured.

Iron Pound nodded. "But," he said, "that's not the only reason you can't beat me. At Great Wall, yeah? We've spent the last few years exhaustively researching the Armor of Catastrophe, so that the next time for sure, you wouldn't be allowed to wreak whatever havoc you wanted and we could completely eliminate you from the Accelerated World."

"...Researching?"

"Exactly. Unfortunately, because of the mutual nonaggression pact between the six major Legions, we couldn't touch the fifth when he showed up north of Shinjuku six months ago. But the sixth...We're not letting you get away. We were planning to wait until the bounty was officially announced, but running into you here like this, we have no reason to hold back on subjugating you."

As Iron Pound spoke his very composed words, Haruyuki stared at him coolly through his cracked visor. No matter how much of a Perfect Match boxing type he was, now that Haruyuki knew that, he had any number of ways to attack him. Or rather, the moment Pound acknowledged that he was a boxer, he essentially revealed he was only adept at close-range fighting, at best six meters—the length of one side of a boxing ring. No matter how fast he was within that distance, once Haruyuki maneuvered deep inside or outside that range, it would be a simple enough matter to negate those abilities.

First, he would catch him. And then he would skewer him with his Incarnate sword and throw him off the edge of the building, and that would be the end of it.

"Then I'll show you that your research or whatever was absolutely useless." Haruyuki quickly thrust his left hand forward. The palm, flanked by five open fingers, snapped backward. From the base of his wrist, a silver light shot out with a faint rasp. Wire Hook. Once the hook grabbed on, no avatar could get away from him.

Originally, this had been the particular ability of Cherry Rook, the fifth Disaster. Like the first's Flash Blink and the second's Flame Breath, the Armor had copied it. Using it required him to be exceedingly synchronized with the Armor, but Haruyuki had reached that depth. Being able to use the powers of past Disasters could actually have been the greatest power of the sixth.

Only moments earlier, Iron Pound had said they hadn't touched the fifth, so they shouldn't have even been aware of the existence of Wire Hook. There was no way he would be able to dodge at first sight a hook that was so small it was practically invisible, flying at a speed equivalent to that of a bullet—

Claaang! The dry metallic noise echoed across the roof of Mori Tower.

And then Haruyuki saw it. The ultimate capture technique, Wire Hook, wielded so powerfully against countless avatars including Silver Crow himself, had made a direct hit with Iron Pound's rounded left shoulder and bounced off emptily.

"—!!"

By the time Haruyuki had swallowed his breath, the veteran boxer was already closing the distance between them in a terrifyingly fast charge. The two gloves readied in front of his chest began to shine a fresh blue.

"Hammer Rave!!" This time, the technique name was shouted sharply.

Countless fists covered his entire field of view. A storm of machine gun–like jabs launched from the left. In between, surging in from the right came straights, like rifle bullets and hatchet-like hooks. The total number was probably more than ten blows a second.

Haruyuki didn't even have the luxury of tightening his guard. Fierce blows slammed into every spot on his upper body, pushing him up several dozen centimeters into the air, chin and arms thrown clumsily upward. Unable to counter or even move, he was in a state of shock delay.

Iron Pound slid in close to the reeling Haruyuki, drawing a blue afterimage in the air. He dropped down, and an even more concentrated overlay came to life in his right fist. Intuitively understanding that the finishing blow was on its way, Haruyuki frantically tried to command his metal wings. But they were much larger now, and the reaction time was the slightest bit duller. Just as he was finally able to generate some lift—

A right uppercut like the main artillery of a battleship caught Haruyuki squarely on his totally exposed and defenseless jaw, carving out a blue arc as it plowed into him.

The impact nearly knocked the brain right out of his head, and he rose up into the air, all four limbs splayed. Finally, he reached the pinnacle of the parabola and fell for a few seconds. *Kawhud!* His back hit the floor, and after bouncing once, he came to rest, arms and legs still shooting out at all angles.

In the upper left of his field of view, his health gauge was dyed yellow, half of it whisked away all at once. Although he knew he had to stand up, the impact was too deep—his thoughts were filled with failure, and a desire to not admit the truth of the situation had pushed Haruyuki to the precipice of a zero fill state.

Through the floor beneath his back, he heard sharp footsteps. And then a voice: "That's the weak point for *all* of you. Doesn't matter which one you are, something all you Chrome Disasters have in common."

"Weak point," Haruyuki groaned, lifting his head to glare intently at Iron Pound, who stood two or so meters away, showering him with a cool gaze.

"The performance of the Armor is definitely incredible," the Perfect Match boxer started, sounding detached, a somehow pitying look popping up in the simple shape of his eye lenses. "And it looks like it's eaten so far into you that you can even use the abilities of its former owners. But in the end, it's still the power of something *borrowed*. It's like a little kid without a license driving a super car with a thousand horsepower. You might be able to recklessly slam your foot down on the accelerator on a straight course and go as fast as possible, but you can't take the corners properly. You're wielding a power that's not your own, so the most basic of all fighting basics...You don't even see your opponent's attributes anymore."

He raised his glove-shaped right hand, and with his thumb (his only free finger), he tapped his left shoulder—the very spot Haruyuki's Wire Hook had bounced off.

"I'm iron, which has the greatest piercing defense of even the metal colors. Even when I'm not enhanced with Incarnate, *as if* your little hook could stab me."

So that's it. Haruyuki finally became aware of his own mistake, his clenched fists creaking.

Metal-color duel avatars, not belonging to the normal color wheel, were as rare as or rarer than Perfect Match avatars. The only ones Haruyuki knew of—in addition to his own Silver Crow—were Cobalt Blade and Manganese Blade, close associates of the Blue King, and whoever it was that had given birth to the Armor of Catastrophe in ancient times, crowned with the name Chrome. Which was basically equivalent to his having no experience fighting them.

Thus, having enjoyed for such a long time the advantages of

being a metal color, excellent at all kinds of defense, he hadn't even imagined the disadvantages when that metal color was an enemy. If that wasn't careless, then what was?

But it wasn't just that. When the Wire Hook bounced off Iron Pound, if it had been a technique he had generated himself and used for many years, he would have instinctively understood which opponents it wouldn't work as well on. And during the fight with the fifth Disaster, aka Cherry Rook, six months earlier, Rook indeed hadn't tried to use the Wire Hook on Haruyuki. That was probably because he knew it was likely to bounce off his metal-hued armor.

The power of something...borrowed. Still flat on his back, Haruyuki had barely digested those words when Iron Pound spoke again, even more quietly.

"After analyzing the Armor of Catastrophe and searching for a way to fight it, we came to a single conclusion. It's not the power of numbers or a superstrong Incarnate technique that can defeat the Disaster, it's just thoroughly polished basic techniques. Ever since, the Six Armors of Great Wall have spent an enormous amount of time refining our techniques, in order to bring our strongest basics into the domain where they exceed even the most powerful Incarnate. So that the next time, for sure, we would eliminate the curse gnawing at the heart of this world, without having to rely on the power of the kings."

Fshk! The air snapped. Pound had probably sent off a left jab into the air, but Haruyuki's eyes couldn't catch even the afterglow of the aura piercing the space.

"All five Disasters who've shown up so far were dealt with by the kings themselves. Heading into the field, courting the risk of the sudden-death rule that comes with level nine, right? But there's no greater disgrace for those of us who guard the king. This time for sure, we—no, *my hand*—will stop the Catastrophe. Sorry, but you're outta here, Silver Crow. While you're the newborn...and *weakest* Disaster."

Weakest.

The instant the word resounded inside his helmet, a boiling storm of emotion whipped through Haruyuki's entire body—before concentrating in a single point on his back.

Kill. Kill, kill, absolutely kill!!

The rage was dizzying. Rather than settling into the depths of the Armor, this energy took form, jetting out through a gap in his back; it felt like something being yanked out of him. And then stretching out behind him were countless long, sharp metal segments joined together—a tail. The emblematic organ of the sixth Disaster Haruyuki had himself severed with his own Incarnate at the end of the Hermes' Cord race.

The tapered knifelike tip of the tail stabbed into the floor, and using the reactive force from that alone, Haruyuki gradually pushed his body up, arms and legs still splayed. When he was finally standing again, he leaned forward, armor clanking. Gripping the longsword in his right hand, shaking the talons of his left, he howled like a beast.

"*Grar! Raaaar*...Kill...Kiiiiilllll..." The bloodlust and rage racing through him became an inky black aura and shot outward, sending cracks radiating through the Demon City stage. His earlier reflections on his error also were sent flying off somewhere, and he tensed himself to slice out blindly.

Iron Pound didn't seem to even flinch when faced with this Haruyuki. He simply readied his fists peekaboo style. In the eye lenses that could be seen on the other side of those iron gloves was an unwavering resolution and confidence, and a hint of pity.

I've seen those eyes somewhere before, Haruyuki thought, with what shred of rationality remained to him.

It was...Right, when he had taken part in the battle to subjugate the fifth Chrome Disaster six months earlier. At the very end of the intense fighting, when the Red King Scarlet Rain was on the verge of eliminating her own parent, the fifth Chrome Disaster, with her Judgment Blow—she had had the same look in her eyes then. Cherry Rook, drowning in the Armor's power and swallowed up by rage, existing only to attack and devour others…Niko had gone to free Haru from the curse that was this armor.

The instant he became aware of this, Haruyuki raised the sword in his right hand up high and thrust it down at his feet as hard as he could. He peeled away one stiff finger at a time and let go of the hilt, and then let his arm fall away, an attempt to control the spasming violence sweeping through him.

Abruptly, in the back of his mind, he heard a howl of annoyance.

WHAT ARE YOU DOING?! TAKE UP YOUR SWORD. CUT DOWN YOUR ENEMY, RIP HIM APART, DEVOUR HIM SO THERE IS NOT A SHRED LEFT.

The one speaking to him was the Beast living in the Armor of Catastrophe, a pseudo-intelligence that had spent an eternity inside the Armor, made up of the concentration of negative wills carved into the Disaster by its previous owners.

All data in the Brain Burst central server—also known as the Main Visualizer—were supposedly stored and calculated in a form based on human memory. Thus, an object stained with a very strong emotion had something that could have been called an independent mind—this is what Haruyuki had been told before. But the Beast was much too dominant to be called a simple pseudo-intelligence. The instant the warped voice echoed in the back of his mind, Haruyuki's own thoughts almost scattered once more, but he endured it intently.

Shut up!! he shouted back with his heart. *I can't beat him if I just run around in a blind frenzy!! I— No matter what, I want to beat him, I have to beat him! I can't lose to anyone who'd say there was anything more important than their friends' lives!!*

A groan coated with irritation came back soon enough.

GRAAR! IN THAT CASE, YOU NEED MY POWER MORE THAN EVER. YOU ARE NOTHING MORE THAN A TINY, HELPLESS CROW.

Yeah, I am. I admit it. But, like…I can't master all the Armor's powers right now. With his speed, unless I'm using techniques I've practiced and practiced, I can't fight back. So just shut up and give me strength!! You don't want to disappear here, either, do you?!

This exchange was actually carried out in a relay of wordless thought in less than one-tenth of a second. And although the Beast howled unhappily once more, it apparently agreed with Haruyuki's assertion, and surrendered part of its control over the avatar.

Naturally, this didn't mean Haruyuki's own rage had vanished. But it was a little different from the earlier crimson inferno that threatened to indiscriminately burn anything and everything. It was more sharply honed, fluid like a pale plasma, seemingly filling his avatar to its extremities.

With sharp talons stretched straight out, Haruyuki brought his hand neatly up in front of him and lowered his stance.

Iron Pound, who had started to close the distance between them, narrowed his eye lenses slightly. Apparently trying to gauge Haruyuki's intentions in throwing down his sword, the pugilist stopped his advance just barely in range for a left jab, and considered his enemy.

Haruyuki didn't move. He held his left hand in front, right behind, one leg bent at the knee, the other stretched out behind him. He simply focused his entire being on the fists of his opponent.

Now that he had somehow managed to succeed in cooling his head, it seemed like dodging or a surprise attack using the pseudo-teleportation ability Flash Blink might work. But given that it was a special attack, he would absolutely have to utter the name of the technique. And after seeing his enemy's super-high-speed punch, he knew he wouldn't be able to make it in time if he did. Even if he got the initiative, once he revealed the technique, it wouldn't work again.

Though, since his special-attack gauge was essentially fully charged, he could also use the wings on his back to hover just beyond his opponent's reach and attack with the long-distance attacks Flame Breath or Laser Lance. However, his opponent already knew that the sixth Chrome Disaster was Silver Crow, so Haru had to assume Pound had naturally prepared some strategy against his flying ability. And he couldn't forget about Green Grandé, standing off to the side, arms crossed, silent like a statue. If Haruyuki tried a unilateral attack from up in the sky, the Green King could activate that Incarnate technique Parsec Wall again.

He needed to kill Iron Pound instantly while the king was silently watching. Even with the Disaster's power, this was a very tall order, but he had no choice but to do it—he had to neutralize these two interfering with him, break into Midtown Tower, destroy the ISS kit main body, and if there were any members of the Acceleration Research Society nearby, he had to rip them to shreds; this was Haruyuki's sole remaining reason for existing.

"Come," he said quietly, a thin, dark aura enveloping his body.

In response, Iron Pound's upper half swayed, and he began gracefully dancing about. With his nimble, rhythmic footwork, he steadily closed the distance between them.

Just like he'd said before, the Incarnate jab released from the left fist with no movement and no command was Pound's greatest weapon. The damage from one blow wasn't all that bad, but because the blows came in rapid succession and left you essentially stunned, you couldn't dodge the heavy-hitting right straight that followed.

If this were a boxing match against a nimble out-boxer, Haruyuki would be advised to tighten his guard and close the distance while repelling the jabs. But this was not a six-meter ring; it was the large heliport on the roof of Mori Tower. There was too much space to retreat and come around from the side. Even if he did solidify his defenses, he wouldn't find a chance to counter. His health gauge would only be carved away instead.

So his only chance at victory was to break through that Incarnate jab.

Hey, Beast. Right hand still raised, guard up, Haruyuki again started talking to the intelligence that lived at the back of his mind within the Armor. *Your attack estimate precision's better than mine. Pick out just when he launches that jab. I'll handle it after that.*

He received no reply in words, but he did hear a definite, faint howl of agreement—although it was almost indistinguishable from the anger.

In the next instant, the overlay wrapped around Iron Pound's left fist grew faintly thicker. At the same time, a vivid red line—the attack prediction line—cut through Haruyuki's view.

Reflexively, Haruyuki straightened his right hand and it glittered in a spiral motion. Pound's Incarnate jab came flying at him almost immediately after the prediction line appeared; meeting the attack after visually confirming it would be impossible. Haruyuki could only rely on his instincts.

As the palm of his hand moved from outside to inside in a circular motion, Haruyuki felt a prickly, burning sensation. It had touched the glove in the trajectory of its straight-line attack. But if he simply repelled it here, the fist would quickly be pulled back, only to have the next punch launched, and then the next.

So Haruyuki didn't repel it; he pulled it into his own movement.

Focusing on the image of sucking Iron Pound's jab into his palm, he bent its trajectory down and to the left. The high-level technique of interfering with and defending against the vector of the enemy attack rather than the energy it contained was known as the "way of the flexible"—guard reversal.

Even an old hand like Pound probably wasn't anticipating that his jab would actually be sucked in instead of blocked. His upper body shook, and his footwork became disordered.

Instantly, Haruyuki shouted inside his helmet, "Flash Blink!"

The avatar clad in the dull silver armor became substanceless particles and moved a mere meter. He slipped by Pound's body on the side—all to reappear behind him.

·Whirling around as he rematerialized, Haruyuki pressed the tips of his fingers against his enemy's defenseless back and cried out, "Laser Sword!!"

Compared with Pound's Incarnate jab, Haruyuki's Incarnate attack took far longer to activate. If Pound had immediately taken evasive action, he might have avoided a direct hit.

But the Perfect Match boxer's reaction was slow precisely because he was so perfectly matched. In boxing, hitting the back was a violation of the rules. Your opponent would never actually go around and attack you from behind.

Naturally, Pound also knew all too well that there was no such rule in the Accelerated World. But it wasn't such an easy thing to erase the reaction drilled into his real-world body. It was the same with Takumu, who been traumatized by the jabbing technique in kendo and so had stiffened up in the face of Dusk Taker's piercing attack to his throat. And that was to say nothing of the irregularity of an attack on the back after a very short teleportation.

The momentary stiffening that came over Pound was Haruyuki's greatest and last chance in this duel. The jet-black blade that surged out of his right hand made contact with a *crash*.

Even the iron armor and its superior physical defenses could not defend against an Incarnate attack launched from a distance of zero meters. The sword pierced the critical point of his heart, and Iron Pound threw his head back, a cry of anguish slipping out.

"*Ngah!*"

But Pound was level seven. He did not die in that one blow, but instead tried to get distance with a desperate forward dash.

Normally, Haruyuki wouldn't have been able to follow with a pursuing attack, given that his right arm was fully extended and his big technique was newly spent. But in another reaction of instinct, he fluttered his right wing with all his might. The kinetic energy generated gave his avatar just enough torsion power to attack. Generating instantaneous thrust with his flying ability in the middle of battle to maneuver in three dimensions was Haruyuki's own original technique, Aerial Combo.

Haruyuki roared, transmitting the sharp spiral force from his back into his shoulder and then down into his right arm. "Unh... Aaaaaah!!"

Skreeeenk!! The earsplitting sound of metal ripping apart metal reverberated and then disappeared.

Silence fell over the roof of the evening-clad Mori Tower. The silhouettes of the two fighting melted into each other completely and cast a long shadow on the broad floor.

Both arms dangled loosely from Iron Pound's sides, and the strength slid out of his legs as well. Supporting this tough body was the right arm of Chrome Disaster, penetrating deep into his chest from behind. The sharp talons had dug into the opening gouged out of the Armor by the Laser Sword.

Arm buried in Pound's body from the flat of his hand up to his shoulder, Haruyuki abruptly heard a low voice in his ears.

"If you've...mastered...this kind of technique...then why... the power of darkness..." Having gotten this much out, the Perfect Match boxer turned into countless polygon fragments and scattered.

Once the massive light effect was over, all that was left was a small flame—the dull gray of Iron Pound's death marker flickering at Haruyuki's feet. Looking down at the flame, Haruyuki shot off in a cracked voice, "What cultivated the Catastrophe to this point...was probably your rejection and lack of understanding."

Naturally, the shimmering marker no longer responded. But Haruyuki continued quietly. "This darkness...is definitely in anyone's..."

The rest was swallowed up in his chest, because in the back of his mind, the Beast raised its sinister voice.

I know, Haruyuki responded to that voice. *The real show starts now, huh...*

He turned around, armor clanking.

His gaze landed on an enormous figure carrying a massive

cross-shaped shield, arms casually folded. The Green King, Green Grandé, nicknamed Invincible. Although his right-hand man had just been taken down before his eyes, those amber lenses were filled only with a tranquil and mysterious light.

According to the fragmentary memory Haruyuki shared with the Beast, the Green King was the lone Burst Linker who had been present at the destruction of all of the first four Chrome Disasters.

He hadn't attacked them directly, but he had held fast against the attacks of the rampaging Disaster with his great shield Strife and created the moment for those fighting with him to attack. In other words, if the Green King hadn't been there, the destruction brought about by the Armor of Catastrophe would likely have been two or three times as great.

The Green King himself was, for the Armor and the Beast that lived in it, a most bitter enemy. The howl that echoed and bounced through Haruyuki's mind was filled with such murderous lust that he was unable to control it. It threatened to explode even now.

Control yourself. This guy for sure, we can't beat him by just attacking at random, Haruyuki said to the Beast, and slowly approached the enormous green avatar one step, then two.

"If you guys aren't in league with the Acceleration Research Society like Iron Pound said," he began in a low voice, staring at the king, who didn't so much as twitch, "then why did you get in my way before?"

He waited three seconds, but of course, no answer came back to him. At the meeting of the Seven Kings a few days earlier, Green Grandé had said not a single word from start to finish.

"I guess it's pointless to ask. Which means I'll just have to have you tell me with your fists." He muttered it half to himself, before dropping his stance to take on a battle posture.

But just before he could—

"If you wait a little longer, you'll understand the reason."

*　　*　　*

Although it was colored with a strong effect, the voice was clear and bright. There was no mistake. It was the same male voice as the one that had called out the name of the large-scale Incarnate technique Parsec Wall earlier. However, because it sounded like it was gradually rising up from the field at his feet rather than coming through the air, Haruyuki couldn't be sure that it had come from the avatar before his eyes.

He stared hard, but the Green King still did not twitch, as usual. His bulk, arms crossed, was turned toward the northeast, at an angle of thirty or so degrees away from Haruyuki. Unconsciously following the man's gaze, Haruyuki understood that he was staring at another mixed-use commercial building soaring up and sandwiching Shuto Expressway No. 3, the main tower of Tokyo Midtown.

The enormous spire, decorated with the sharp ornaments characteristic of the Demon City stage, caught the light of the sun as it was on the verge of setting and glittered redly. The roof, unlike that of the Roppongi Hills Mori Tower, tapered into a narrow needlepoint, and other than the small flying Enemies circling it, there was absolutely no movement in the building.

But somewhere inside that tower was the main body of the ISS kits, as it blackly devoured the Accelerated World. If it was completely destroyed, the terminal kits currently infecting a minimum of fifty Burst Linkers would have also stopped functioning.

The Haruyuki of that moment was not particularly interested in trying to save the Accelerated World or anything of the like. Just the opposite, in fact—more than half his brain was ruled by a destructive urge to systematically slaughter any and all Burst Linkers who stood in his way as enemies, and he didn't care anymore if Brain Burst itself declined or disappeared as a result. But he first had to slaughter the Acceleration Research Society, which had made and distributed the ISS kits. It wasn't just about the kits. They had set a cowardly trap for…and as they inflicted incredible pain and suffering on her, over and over and over…

"Ngh!!"

Suddenly, a fierce pain, a high-voltage current, pierced him from the depths of his back to the center of his head, and Haruyuki's entire body stiffened.

The Beast, which he had kept under control to a certain extent up to that point, let forth a ferocious roar. Because the pitch of the cry, filled with overwhelming rage and bloodlust, was much higher than any that had come before, it sounded even more like a sobbed shriek.

The dark aura constantly blanketing the Armor of Catastrophe became ebony flames and spurted outward. The edges of the Armor covering his body seamlessly stood up like sharp blades, and the talons of his hands and feet took on an even more sinister form. The tail on his back flew whiplike out on its own, wound around the hilt of the longsword, and plunged into the ground a little ways off.

It yanked the blade out with a rasp of metal and stabbed it down once more, immediately in front of Haruyuki. The blade, dark yet mirror smooth, reflected the figure of Chrome Disaster, stooped body spasming irregularly. In the darkness beneath his cracked visor, eye lenses foreign to Silver Crow blinked strongly, tinged with an ominous crimson light.

"Grar...raaaaaaaar!" the Beast—and Haruyuki himself— roared, low and heavy. Thought and reason were blown away, and his head was filled with only a boiling bloodlust. It was clear that this was the "overflow" phenomenon, a fitful rampage of the negative will, but Haruyuki was no longer capable of being aware of this fact.

Forgetting even the presence of the Green King standing nearby, Haruyuki spread the metal wings on his back. He pulled the longsword in front of him out with his right hand and swung it to the side, readying himself to fly off the Mori Tower to raid Midtown Tower. But before he could—

"Wait. It's not time for that yet."

"...*Grar...*" Haruyuki turned to his right, a howl thick with bloodlust slipping out.

The Green King turned his heavy face mask toward Haruyuki. The mysterious amber eyes were quiet in contrast with the Disaster's. There was no rage, no impatience, not even concern there. He was simply standing calmly, an ancient tree in the forest that knew everything and watched over all.

But for Haruyuki at that moment, the Green King's attitude appeared to be a challenge he could not shut his eyes to. If he was going to interfere, then just cut him down. Spurred on by a senseless impulse, Haruyuki slowly brandished the sword in his right hand. He also placed his left hand on the hilt and creakingly bent his body, so that with a single blow containing all his power, all his speed, all his Incarnate, he could slice his enemy in two.

Of course, Haruyuki had no experience training with a sword in either the real world or the Accelerated World. So this technique was a borrowed power, as Iron Pound had perceptively pointed out earlier. It wouldn't work in a battle competing at the ultimate speed.

However, right now at least, Haruyuki was already more than 90 percent not himself. His rampaging Incarnate had brought "Silver Crow wearing the Enhanced Armament Disaster" closer to the "true Chrome Disaster" than ever before.

Haruyuki didn't know their name, but the third Disaster had been a blue-type double-handed sword user. Renowned for their skills, they could stand alongside even the Blue King, Blue Knight—aka Vanquisher—and in the end, they were banished from the Accelerated World by the sword of that very king.

The technique the third had left in the Armor moved Haruyuki's body now. It was the same as with the Flash Blink of the first, the second's ability Flame Breath, and the fifth's Wire Hook. By syncing tightly with the Armor, or rather the Beast living inside the Armor, he could make the powers of the previous

Chrome Disasters his own. This itself was the true power of the Armor of Catastrophe—no, of *Haruyuki*, who was now the sixth generation.

The Green King also seemed to recognize the rampaging depths Haruyuki had fallen to. He set his right foot out a step and now turned his entire body to face Haruyuki. The avatar was more than half-hidden behind the massive cross shield, but regardless, Haruyuki drew his own body back like a bow. The tip of the brandished longsword went over his back and touched the floor, lightly stabbing into it. Bent as far back as he could go, the avatar strained and creaked dully. The instant this tension had reached its limit—

"*Gr...aaaaaaaar!!*" Roaring out of him like an explosion, Haruyuki released every ounce of strength he had.

He charged forward with utmost determination, riding the propulsive force of his wings. The virtual air was compressed and rebounded, turning into a shock wave to rip a V into the hard floor of the roof.

The distance between them, more than ten meters, was a bit too much for a close-range-type attack. But Haruyuki closed the gap in nearly zero time, and Green Grandé appeared to never have had any intention of trying to get out of the way, at any rate. Even as he watched the blade cutting out a jet-black crescent as it poured down, his feet did not even twitch; he merely raised the great shield on his left arm a little higher.

Enhanced Armaments often changed color to match the avatar who owned and equipped them, and the Green King's great shield and the Blue King's double-handed sword were thought to be of this type. But the shield blocking Haruyuki's way now looked like it shone a slightly clearer, deeper emerald green than the king's armor.

Against this green wall rising up, with a sense of presence like a deep, ancient forest, Haruyuki brought down the longsword with the absolute maximum attack power he could currently produce.

A pure and vast energy, impossible to depict with sound and

light effects, sprang up where shield and sword touched. Distorting space itself, abnormal vibrations threatened to shatter the world as they radiated outward, and the top half of the enormous Roppongi Hills tower shuddered in rippling waves.

And then the building, which should have been stronger than any other due to the characteristics of the Demon City stage, broke from its midsection into a myriad of minute fragments.

Having lost their foothold, Haruyuki and Green Grandé began to slowly fall among the object fragments raining down. However, they fell with sword and shield still locked; neither moved a muscle. The Incarnates of the two avatars facing off overwrote the reactions that normally would have occurred, allowing them to remain fixed in place as they fell.

In a movement reminiscent of sprouting vines, the green aura radiating from the great shield Strife went to wrap around the longsword that had once been called Star Caster. The inky black overlay that surrounded the blade burned the green back time and again, but the verdant aura sprouted endlessly and showed no sign of withering. So much like an enormous tree—the World Tree supporting the nine worlds in Northern European mythology.

I support the world.

The instant these words cut through Haruyuki's mind, an image—or maybe a memory—infused within his consciousness. A vast, incredibly vast, time, and a battle repeated ad infinitum within it. But his opponent was not a Burst Linker. It was an enormous monster with a form that was not human—an Enemy.

Finally, the pair landed with a heavy *thud* on the mountain of fine rubble that was once the top half of the Hills Tower. At the same time, their auras waned, and, following suit, sword and shield also pulled back. Compared with the scale of destruction, it was an almost impossibly quiet curtain falling. When Haruyuki came to, the storm of anger raging within him had died down as if it had never been; even the Beast was silent.

"Taking a blow like that so coolly," he murmured. The dark

effect had faded from his voice, and even the phrasing brought his own sensibilities to the front. But unaware of this, Haruyuki lightly jumped back to gain some distance. The sand crunched softly when he landed, and he lowered his blade.

Also lowering his shield, the Green King shook his head solemnly, eyes still on Haruyuki. He indicated a spot on the shield with his right hand, as if to say he was not cool.

When Haruyuki looked very closely, the upper edge appeared to be chipped a mere three millimeters or so in one place. Having made nothing more than a scratch that could hardly even be called a scratch, Haruyuki felt he had just been told *you win*, and he grinned wryly, unconsciously.

"I was trying to cut you down along with that shield, you know," he remarked as he glanced around.

Due to the surplus energy of their clash, Mori Tower had been reduced by 50 percent, half as tall as it had originally been. The surrounding buildings also leaned and crumbled on one side.

The small flame shimmering a dull gray on the sand a little ways off was no doubt Iron Pound's death marker. It had fallen along with them in the building's destruction. Right now, Pound was no doubt anxiously observing Haruyuki and Green Grandé facing off in his ghost state, where all he could do was watch over the situation around him.

Through the direct clash of his Incarnate alongside the Green King's, and the glimpse of his opponent's memories, Haruyuki felt like he could understand to a certain degree what Iron Pound had said before the fight, about how much time their king had sacrificed to the Accelerated World. He turned his gaze back on the king.

"The majority of the points supplied through Enemy hunting in the Accelerated World...You actually earned them by yourself, huh?"

No answer. But the silence was colored with an air of affirmation.

For the thousand or more Burst Linkers who existed, burst

points were in-game currency, experience points, and life itself. Their number increased if you won duels and decreased if you lost, but a large quantity were also exhausted in using the acceleration commands, buying items in the shop, and processing level increases. Considered rationally, the supply of points didn't seem to match up against that pace of consumption. The fact was that each month, Burst Linkers used up an amount of points largely in excess of the monthly increase brought to the world by new Burst Linkers' initial hundred points.

The shortfall was supposedly made up for by high-level Linkers hunting Enemies in the Unlimited Neutral Field, but still, Haruyuki had always thought it strange that those points were so widely redistributed in the Accelerated World.

The Green King had hunted the high-ranking Enemies that lived in dangerous dungeons, transferred the vast sum of points he'd earned onto various blank cards from the item shop, and then fed those cards to the lower-ranking Enemies living in the field, which would then drop as loot. At some later point, other Legion hunting parties would then defeat those Enemies that had eaten the cards, in turn receiving an enormous amount of points as a bonus to the initial kill. As a result, his farmed points spread out among the low-level Linkers of the midsize and small Legions.

Not unlike a great tree supporting countless smaller lives with the sunlight and water stored in its massive body.

But no matter how he thought about it, Haruyuki didn't understand the reason the Green King had provided this service for free for so many years. The hunters of the Enemies who had eaten the point cards wouldn't necessarily be members of the Green Legion. In fact, the opposite case would naturally have been the overwhelming majority. In other words, the king's actions substantially benefitted other kingdoms. Looking back on it, Haruyuki himself remembered being overjoyed when the prey he had brought down with an Enemy hunting party he had been a part of spit out an essentially impossible number of points.

"Why?" Haruyuki asked in a whisper, unable to understand the foundation for the king's actions. He had shared points with all, even enemy Burst Linkers. But on the other hand, the lives of his Legion subordinates Ash Roller and Bush Utan had not been priorities.

There likely would be no response to this question, which could not be answered with a yes or a no. That was what he expected.

"It was all to stop Brain Burst 2039—also known as Trial Number Two—from ending in vain." The silent king uttered his longest string of words so far, but the blow to Haruyuki's soul came more from the details contained in those words, even if he didn't really understand what they meant.

"Trial...Number...Two?"

"Aye. A long time has already passed since Accel Assault 2038 and the following Cosmos Corrupt 2040 were abandoned. It's likely that this Number Two is equipped with whatever elements were missing from Number One and Number Three. Until those elements are embodied, we can't let this world be closed."

The information the Green King put into words in his stubbornly tranquil voice far surpassed Haruyuki's processing abilities. Even so, he managed to summarize it into three key points and list them in his heart.

One: Brain Burst—in other words, the Accelerated World—was not the one and only.

Two: The Green King, Green Grandé, was working to maintain or prolong the life of the Accelerated World.

Three: Green Grandé *knew the reason this world existed.*

"You the GM?" Haruyuki questioned the giant in a tense, creaking voice. "Are you— Is it actually you who's the admin for Brain Burst? Is it you manipulating thousands of Burst Linkers, making them dance? Making them fight?" He waited for a response with bated breath, not considering what he would do if the Green King assented.

Two seconds later, the king shook his thick face mask once. "Negative." He paused for another second and then continued, "The authority we have been given is no different from yours. If this head is cut off, I will die, and if I die, I will lose points. Once my points are exhausted, I will disappear from the Accelerated World."

"Then…why do you know things like that, that no one else knows?!"

"That is also negative. I am not alone in knowing the name Trial Number Two. Of the Originators, there likely exist some who possess more information than I."

"…Origi…nators." This wasn't the first time he'd heard the word he parroted back. After the meeting of the Seven Kings four days earlier, the Red King Niko had uttered it in a trembling voice after appearing suddenly at his house. She hadn't told him the specific meaning, but now he could hazard a guess. Most likely, the word indicated the first Burst Linkers, the ones without parents.

Hey, Beast. In the back of his mind, Haruyuki unconsciously called to the destroyer lodged in the Armor. *Whoever it was who first gave birth to you was an Originator, too, right? You know anything?*

In return, he heard an annoyed groan from the Beast, which had maintained its silence for several minutes even in the middle of the heated battle.

GRAAAR…I DO NOT. I ALSO HAVE NO INTEREST. MY OBJECTIVE IS DESTRUCTION AND SLAUGHTER ALONE. YOU, TOO, WOULD DO BEST TO THINK OF NOTHING BUT THE SLAUGHTER OF THE ENEMY BEFORE YOU.

This answer very nearly made Haruyuki smile wryly, but he got himself under control again before the grin reached his lips. The Beast might have been tame at that moment, but it had to have been vigilantly awaiting its chance to overtake Haruyuki over again. And more than that, Haruyuki was not Silver Crow now, but the sixth Chrome Disaster, so this was no time for laughing. He didn't have the right to laugh, either.

I get it, he murmured. *But you have to know, even from that one blow, that I can't beat this guy so easily as all that. And...something's weird. Even if we do fight, I want to get as much information as I can before that.*

The response he got was the Beast simply returning a short howl, and then pulling back into the Armor.

Haruyuki took a deep breath and switched gears, staring once more into Green Grandé's eyes. The amber eye lenses, not allowing a single emotion to slip out, looked back at him quietly.

"I get that for some reason, you've been trying to prolong the life of the Accelerated World, and that you've been hunting Enemies all this time by yourself to that end," Haruyuki said, and then raised his voice. "But then why are you getting in my way now? It's obvious that the Acceleration Research Society and the ISS kits are trying to destroy this world. I'm sure that building—Midtown Tower—is their base. My goal is to *crush* that base!"

"I told you. Wait a while and you'll see," came the brief reply.

The Green King turned his eyes up toward the building in question, soaring in the northeast, and reflexively, Haruyuki traced his gaze. Because Mori Tower was now half what it had been, the other tower seemed twice as tall. The blue-black spire had fallen silent; not a hint of activity could be seen.

"I've waited plenty long. If you're trying to buy time...," Haruyuki started to say, until—

Suddenly, far, far off in the eastern sky, he heard a mysterious sound. Like the ringing of an infinity of bells, the fleeting echo of thin glass shattering.

Turning his gaze forty-five degrees to the right, Haruyuki saw a thin seven-colored veil rip through the thickly hanging clouds hanging low over the Demon City stage. The aurora—no, that wasn't it. It was a light signaling the start of the end of the world.

"...The Change," he murmured, and the Green King nodded heavily. So *this* was what the king and Iron Pound had been waiting for?

"The Change" referred to the phenomenon in the Unlimited Neutral Field of the switching of stage attributes—Demon City, Purgatory, Primal Forest. When the Change occurred, hunted Enemies repopped, and destroyed objects were completely recovered. Naturally, the appearance and terrain effects of the field were also completely transformed, and any duelers or Enemy hunters caught up in the Change were required to abruptly change strategies.

The timing of the Change was random, but it was said that it happened at its quickest in three days of internal time (just over four minutes, real-world time) and within ten days at the latest. Since it was impossible to predict the timing, Green Grandé and Iron Pound must have been simply waiting in this place for days.

But why?

Even while Haruyuki tried to guess at their intention, the aurora wall approached at an incredible speed. When he looked closely, he could see that at the base of the light pouring down from the sky, the buildings crowded together in central Tokyo were instantly being overwritten with new colors and shapes.

Without even a mere thirty seconds passing from the time he first heard the sound of it, the aurora had reached Roppongi Hills and painted everything in a glimmering rainbow, transmitting a faint pressure to Haruyuki as it did. Immediately, a sensation of ascent, like being in a high-speed elevator, enveloped his body—but he wasn't flying with his own wings. Because the half-destroyed Mori Tower had started to rapidly regenerate, Haruyuki and the Green King were being pushed up to the roof, where they had originally stood. At the same time as their ascent stopped and his feet stepped onto the hard floor once more, the seven colors of the rainbow faded and disappeared.

After watching the aurora wall charging off to the west, Haruyuki looked at his surroundings.

The gloomy dark blue of the Demon City stage was completely gone. In its place, the world was dyed a concentrated muddy red. The ground and buildings were all gray tiles, but from the obvious seams oozed a viscous red liquid—in other words, blood seeped out, flowed, and pooled everywhere. The sky was also a garish red different from the sunset. The very infrequently occurring Deadly Sin stage.

Unlike the Demon City, this stage had annoying attributes with a mountain of special effects, but of these, the one Burst Linkers had to be careful of was the fact that half of the damage done in direct physical attacks would bounce back at the attacker. In other words, it was very advantageous to long-range duel avatars. At least there weren't any red types there now.

Chiyu's super bad at this stage. She's probably freaking out and complaining right about now.

After this momentary thought, Haruyuki forcefully cut off the flow of his thinking. If he thought even a little more about his friends in Nega Nebulus who were waiting for him at that very moment near the southern gates of the Castle, far off to the North, he had the feeling he would simply fly apart.

Focusing on freezing his heart, he shifted his gaze and confirmed that the Green King was still in his daunting pose a little ways off before he opened his mouth.

"So? The Change happened and now what?"

Other than the slickly bloody exterior, nothing appeared to have changed with Midtown Tower rising up to the northeast. He still did not understand the Green King's reason for blocking his approach.

The reply to Haruyuki's question came not from the king but a quiet voice behind him.

"It means…we missed this time, too."

Turning around, Haruyuki saw the iron boxer sitting crosslegged in a pool of half-dried blood, dropping his shoulders lifelessly. It was Iron Pound, despite the fact that not even thirty minutes had passed since he was defeated by Haruyuki and died. Haruyuki thought, suspiciously, that it was too soon for Iron Pound to have regenerated—when he realized that the Change had one other effect: to ignore the sixty minutes of wait time for regeneration for Burst Linkers in the ghost state and bring them back to life.

Although he had managed to get away with only half of the dull, boring regeneration standby, Pound didn't seem the least bit pleased. The boxer rested his slack gloves on his legs, resigned.

"Missed?" Haruyuki asked, furrowing his brow. "The Change now? What exactly were you guys waiting for?"

"Did you know that to a certain extent, there's a pattern in the change?"

His question met with a question, Haruyuki's scowl grew deeper. But he restrained himself and obediently shook his head.

Pound nodded once and then continued, "Just like duel avatars, you can divide the various attributes of the duel stages into rough groups. You could say the Ice stage and the Drizzle stage are water types, Lava and Scorched Earth are fire types, Primeval Forest and Corroded Forest are wood types, and Demon City and Steel are metal types. On top of these so-called natural stages, you have dark types like Purgatory and Cemetery, and holy types like Aurora and Sacred Ground. You with me so far?"

At these teacherly words, the Beast let out a groan of dissatisfaction before Haruyuki could, but thanks to that, Haruyuki himself lost the chance to be annoyed. When he silently gestured for the other avatar to continue, Iron Pound opened his mouth once more, standing up leisurely.

"Normally, there aren't two stages in a row belonging to the same overall category. And the appearance rates for the eight categories of earth, water, fire, wind, wood, metal, light, and dark are basically equal. But, rarely, only the first six natural categories go on for a long time. In that case, the dark- or holy-type stage that appears after that has a very high level of purity in the attributes. Basically, it's incredibly evil or incredibly divine. There are some other, detailed rules, but this is the rough idea. Through our analysis of the long-term patterns, we predicted a super-evil stage would appear at this time today, and we were waiting for it."

"So then you've achieved your goal. There isn't a stage more evil than Deadly Sin. It's not a miss, it's a bull's-eye hit, isn't it?" Haruyuki remarked.

"That is true." Pound nodded lightly before shaking his head slowly from side to side. "But...this still isn't enough. What we need is the darkest of the dark, the ultimate evil...the Hell stage."

"..."

It had been eight months now since he became a Burst Linker, and having reached level five, Haruyuki couldn't be said to be a newbie anymore. But still, when it came to the Hell stage, he had heard the name only a few times. Since he had merely the haziest idea of its special effects and looks, he didn't react immediately. From the explanation up to that point, though, he had learned nothing more than the fact that Iron Pound and Green Grandé had been waiting for something, but Iron Pound hadn't said one word about why.

"So you're saying there's some connection between the Unlimited Neutral Field turning into hell and you guys getting in my way here?" Haruyuki asked as he took a step forward from the tile oozing blood at his feet. It was getting harder to control his irritation.

Standing a few meters ahead of him, Iron Pound slowly raised his right fist, mouth still closed. The iron glove, open until that moment, was clenched into a tight fist with a *squeak*.

Haruyuki narrowed his eyes under his visor, but it appeared that Pound wasn't trying for a rematch. He opened his left glove and held Haruyuki off, before turning his body toward Midtown Tower, soaring up five hundred meters to the northeast.

"If you look at that, you'll understand whether you like it or not," the iron boxer murmured, striking a curious, very unboxing-like pose. He spread both legs far apart, thrust his wide-open right hand straight ahead, and placed his left hand on the elbow joint of his right arm.

Immediately, an intense blue light effect enveloped the tightly clenched glove. A special attack. Reflexively, Haruyuki braced himself, but no line of predicted attack popped up from the Armor. Pound didn't even glance at Haruyuki, who was holding his breath. Instead, he glared at the enormous spire dripping with blood off in the distance, as he shouted the technique name.

"Rocket Straight!!"

The boxer's right arm exploded, just a little below the elbow.

No, that wasn't it—it *jettisoned*. The round glove and forearm cut away from the avatar and flew off, trailing bright-red flames. Even now that he had become the sixth Chrome Disaster, Haruyuki couldn't help but be slightly baffled by this. This technique most certainly did not exist in traditional boxing, or any fighting technique, for that matter.

So you're not a Perfect Match boxer avatar? Haruyuki suppressed the urge to shout it and chased after the flying fist—the rocket punch—with his eyes.

Whether it was orthodox or not, given that the technique took just five seconds from preparation to activation, it was wonderfully fast. It had an impact almost on par with the main artillery attack of the pure long-distance type, the Red King Scarlet Rain. Drawing out a long trail of smoke as it charged forward, the punch soared past the Shuto Expressway No. 3 and the buildings of Roppongi in the blink of an eye and closed in on Midtown Tower in the distance.

At that moment, Haruyuki saw *something* move near the very top of the massive, sharply tapered tower. It was unbelievably big—that was all he knew. The reason he couldn't pick out its precise size or shape was because it was almost completely transparent. Even with Disaster's super resolution power, all he could see was the strange distortion of the red ambient light around the pinnacle.

Straining his eyes intently, perhaps through some ability of the Armor or generosity of the Beast, the silhouette in the air where the light was distorted was emphasized and popped up clearly in his view. Colored a pale gray, the silhouette was strange: It was like a person, but also like a bird. It held tightly on to the tower with at least ten limbs, and an excessively round, enormous head turned toward the charging rocket punch.

"Ngh!" Haruyuki's entire body stiffened unconsciously.

From the back of the transparent something, a wide, thin film spread out to the sides. No doubt about it: wings. Their span exceeded the fifty-meter breadth of Midtown Tower. The entire creature might have even been larger than the Super-class Enemy guarding the southern gate of the Castle, the God Suzaku.

The large, transparent wings were tinged with a dim white light. And then in the next instant, a beam of light jetted out from the center of the massive head.

The intensity of the light was such that Haruyuki's enhanced vision burned pure white momentarily. The bright line, far beyond a mere laser, contained a terrifying amount of heat and swallowed up Iron Pound's right fist as it soared forward to smash into the wall of the building. The fist evaporated in short order.

The laser beam kept going, shooting several hundred meters into the streets of Roppongi. The beam concentrated on one spot for a brief moment, and then there was an incredible explosion, like the impact of a large meteor.

"Hngk!!" At the same time as the choked cry slipped out of Haruyuki, the Beast also moaned quietly somewhere deep inside the Armor. The shaking that assaulted them was so fierce, it threatened to destroy the Roppongi Hills tower, even though it should have been sufficiently far away. While Haruyuki and Pound braced their feet to ride it out, the Green King alone stood as calm as ever. But Haruyuki caught a glimpse of the tiniest stiffening in even that broad back.

The strength of the ray of light that the transparent *something* released to meet the rocket punch far exceeded the level of power any duel avatar could muster up. That was clear from the width and depth of the crater left at the center of the explosion. So it wasn't a Burst Linker, which meant that it had to be an Enemy. But if that was the case, the power of this Enemy was on par with that of the Four Gods—actually, taking into consideration the fact that its body was transparent, which made it hard to find the right moment to attack, this Enemy could perhaps even be said to rank equal with the Gods.

But why? Tokyo Midtown was supposedly nothing more than a simple landmark, far from the Castle. Why would such a powerful Enemy be guarding it?

"You see it?" Haruyuki heard the now-armless Iron Pound whisper nearby. Without waiting for Haruyuki's reply, he continued, "Its proper name is the Legend class Enemy, Archangel Metatron. The last boss of the massive dungeon beneath Shiba Park. Or least it was."

"Meta...tron." He felt like he had come across the name in games and manga besides Brain Burst, but a large contradiction caught his attention, and he opened his mouth again. "The dungeon's...last boss? But, I mean, not only is it not underground, it's up on the top of Midtown Tower...?"

"I said, it *was*. Someone moved it. Probably they tamed it."

"*Tamed*...the *last boss*...Can you even do that?"

"It's impossible. Everyone thought so. Until about a week ago, real-world time, when Metatron suddenly appeared on the tower," Iron Pound said, almost groaning, and then glared at the figure of the "angel," which had disappeared completely once more.

"Contrary Cathedral, the massive labyrinth under Shiba Park, is one of the four great dungeons. And just like the name says, it flips internal attributes one hundred eighty degrees when a duel avatar steps on particular panels. From the holiest of sacred stages, Heaven, to the darkest of dark stages, Hell. And then back again. That last boss there, Archangel Metatron, has the totally annoying status of being invisible with a sudden-death attack and impermeable to all attribute damage. Its power weakens only when the dungeon attributes are Hell, and then our attacks can actually hit it...So as long as it's where it belongs—in the depths of Contrary Cathedral—it's not such a terrible enemy. I mean, it's a bit tough, but as long as you step on the control panel for the boss room, you can force Hell attributes to appear whenever you want. At the very least, it's waaaay easier to fight than the Four Gods at the Castle. But..."

Having heard this much of Pound's explanation, Haruyuki finally felt like he was able to see the bigger picture. Without realizing it, he gave voice to a hazy supposition. "But once Metatron gets outside...the Hell stage almost never appears, so..."

The boxer nodded in a creaking motion. "Completely invincible," he spat. "You can't see it, and there's no way to defeat an Enemy if your attacks can't hit it. Right now, the area within two hundred meters of the top floor of Midtown Tower there is completely impenetrable; no one can get in. It's basically a tiny Castle..."

Naturally, Iron Pound had no way of knowing that Haruyuki and the other members of Nega Nebulus had not more than an hour ago succeeded in their Castle escape mission. But they had been helped by so many coincidences that their success was more miracle than anything else. One wrong step, and he could have easily ended up in a state of unlimited EK with his beloved swordmaster and teacher.

Once his brain had gotten to this point, he clenched his hands tightly again, and cut off that line of thought. He squelched the smiling faces of his loved ones springing to life in his mind and painted over them with a black brush.

"So if you get close, and die in an instant, do you stay there in unlimited EK?" he asked in a low voice.

"No," Pound replied, without looking at Haruyuki and seemingly oblivious to his momentary inner strife. "You die instantly, but the attack is just too intense. You can't get that far into the Enemy's reaction range, so you don't end up in unlimited EK. If you put everything you've got into a dash right after you regenerate, you can just barely make it without taking the next laser. I tested that out myself."

An ironic smile spread across the mouth covered by headgear, but soon disappeared.

"Our king has the greatest defensive power in the Accelerated World, and even he could only last five seconds against that light beam with full Incarnate defenses deployed, so there's no way someone like me could do much of anything. Anyway, now you know the situation. What we're waiting for here—and why we stopped you from charging into Midtown Tower."

Even after Pound closed his mouth, Haruyuki remained silent for a while. He did indeed finally understand the situation. Iron Pound and Green Grandé had found the pattern in the change, so they were waiting up here on the roof of Mori Tower for the Hell stage that might appear during the next one. Because only in hell did the Archangel Metatron guarding Midtown Tower lose its power and become susceptible to attack. And the reason the Green King had gone so far as to deploy his Incarnate technique Parsec Wall to repel Haruyuki's flight was...

"Are you trying to say...that was to save me from Metatron's instant death attack?" Haruyuki asked, in a dangerous voice.

Pound shrugged lightly. "If we had known from the start that you—that Silver Crow had gotten so 'Disasterfied,' we prob'ly would've let you keep going. Save ourselves the trouble, and the points to set a bounty."

Haruyuki gritted his teeth tightly, and the Beast roared briefly again. The dark aura rising up from his entire body shimmered and shook, but he suppressed the urge to attack. The hardness of Pound and the Green King had been beaten into him mere moments earlier. They were not opponents he could defeat by slashing wildly.

"Chances for the Hell stage to appear next increase three days from now in real-world time, on Sunday evening." Glancing at Haruyuki out of the corner of his eye, Pound waved the remainder of his right arm around in circles as he spoke. "After waiting up here on this roof for nearly three months, we're tired—no big surprise there. So the king and me are going to log out for a bit. You…at any rate, I'll just say thanks. Looks like you helped out our Legion members."

He stopped speaking for a moment before saying, as if to himself, "You're seriously a weird one. You're so deeply Disasterfied, and yet we're having a conversation like this."

"If you're going to thank me, then you yourself…," Haruyuki replied, quietly, ignoring the last bit of Pound's muttering. But he cut himself off midsentence.

Pound and the Green King had apparently been waiting here for over three months of inside time for the Change now. If that bout of asceticism was for the purpose of attacking Midtown Tower, it meant that they too were deeply alarmed at the spread of the ISS kits and were working hard in their own way. They already knew that there was no point in smashing the terminals of the lower-level members; they had to destroy the main body.

"Bush Utan of Great Wall lost once to the temptation of the ISS kit, but he tried to get rid of it of his own volition before. That's why he was attacked by the kit wearers. So…" Once Haruyuki had gotten this far in his strangled voice, Pound nodded lightly as he turned around.

"Yeah. The policy of the king and the Legion for this whole thing's not to just go and pass Judgment on anyone. Most likely, at the meeting of the Seven Kings three days from now, the six Major Legions will agree on a unified policy for dealing with the Incarnate study kits or whatever…Although, naturally, that'll be *after* they've decided on the number one item on the agenda, the Armor of Catastrophe."

The iron boxer finished this little businesslike speech and

walked over to the Green King a few meters away. They briefly exchanged words before starting to walk together. They were probably going to take the elevator at the southeast edge of the heliport down into the building, and then use a nearby portal to return to the real world.

Watching their backs as sure steps took them farther and farther away from him, Haruyuki thought with a mind that was somehow numb. *Guided by anger and hate, I summoned the Armor of Catastrophe, and now this time, I really am the sixth Chrome Disaster. I tore apart those six ISS kit users who attacked Ash and Utan. I slaughtered them with an overly strong power that really doesn't belong to me. I'm basically tracing out the same path as Takumu yesterday. With the darkness generated by the ISS kit, he completely and utterly crushed the PK group Supernova Remnant after they attacked him. What did I say to him then?*

The instant his thoughts made it this far, his own tearful voice was replayed from a great distance in the back of his mind. *I know you can fight this black power, too! You can fight it and break it and move forward again! You can, Taku!!*

And then Takumu had stood and faced the darkness hiding inside him, just as Haruyuki had insisted he could: He had brandished his sword and magnificently cut free of the ISS kit parasitizing him.

I can't do that, Taku. Looking down at the sinister talons of his own right hand, Haruyuki muttered to himself with a self-deprecating air, *There's not the tiniest bit of strength left in me, separate from this armor...but I've fused so deeply with it and the Disaster, maybe I didn't have any real strength to begin with. The fight with Great Wall's third-in-command was super hard, and I barely made a mark on the king. So the fourth I saw in the replay, and the fifth, who sent the Yellow King running with one blow, were way stronger. And if even they couldn't escape the control of the Armor, then there's no way someone like me's going to be able to fight back now...*

If Kuroyukihime had been there at that moment, she would perhaps have been exasperated—"Quite the trick there. You turn into Chrome Disaster and become so utterly negative!" But, naturally, he didn't hear that voice now. Instead, from somewhere near the base of the tail growing out of his back, he heard the Beast speak, words mixed with a howl.

GRAAAR. YOU ARE THE PERFECT VESSEL BB PLAYER, THE ONE I HAVE SOUGHT FOR MANY YEARS. YOU ARE THE FIRST ELEMENT TO HAVE FOUGHT TO SUCH AN EXTENT SO SOON AFTER FUSING WITH ME.

What? Haruyuki lifted his hanging head and replied with a thought colored with a wry smile. *Are you...comforting me?*

GRAR!! Instantly, a howl thundered explosively in his mind. IF YOU HAVE THE TIME TO OFFER WANTON JESTS, THEN GO AND FIND OUR NEXT PREY!!

Still, you know, we first had our eyes on Midtown Tower, but we're not going to be able to attack with any normal means, huh? You saw it, too, that serious laser before.

RRRRR. IF WE COULD OBTAIN THE THEORETICAL MIRROR ABILITY. OR...

At some point, he had started having a conversation with the Beast nesting inside of him. And then Haruyuki realized that Iron Pound, who he thought had left a while ago, was standing in front of the elevator tower, staring at him over his shoulder.

Wondering if he wanted a rematch maybe, Haruyuki shot a glare at him in return, and the boxer moved his truncated right arm as if to say Haruyuki had the wrong idea, before he opened his mouth.

"Nah, don't worry about it. My eyes were just playing tricks on me, I guess. For a second, the color of your armor..."

Reflexively, Haruyuki looked down at his own body, but naturally, all he saw there was the evil form of the Armor. The color was, of course, the shadow-tinged chrome silver.

"Just forget it," Iron Pound called to Haruyuki as he lifted his face again, and then shouted, "Listen, Silver Crow! You have three days left in the deferment they gave you! If you don't completely remove that Armor there from your avatar before Sunday at one PM, the highest bounty in the Accelerated World will be put on you!!"

"And when it is, make sure you're the first to come for my head. You want a rematch, don't you?"

Not responding to Haruyuki's retort, Iron Pound turned his back and quickly thrust his left glove up into the air—maybe a sign that he wouldn't lose the next time? He then followed the Green King into the bloodstained elevator. The box covered in dirty tiles disappeared to the lower floors with an unpleasant slithering sound.

Left alone on the rooftop of the Deadly Sin stage building, Haruyuki murmured out loud, unconsciously, "Three more days, huh…"

If he thought about it calmly, that was the rest of his life as a Burst Linker. No matter how strong the Armor—the Enhanced Armament Disaster—might have been, if duelers came after him single-mindedly one after another whenever he was connected globally, his own powers of concentration would soon be exhausted. And you could have the most expensive sports car in the world, but if you drove it half-asleep, you'd get in an accident soon enough—well, the control AI would forcibly take control before that happened. There was nothing so fragile as a Burst Linker who couldn't concentrate. In fact, basically all the Chrome Disasters, first to fifth, had lost in this way.

"Hey, what're we gonna do, Beast?"

Naturally, it wasn't as though his rage and urge to destroy had disappeared, but perhaps they had been burned up to a certain extent in the intense fighting with Iron Pound and Green Grandé; right now, resignation, emptiness, and self-loathing, seasoned with a dash of despair, were the stronger emotions in him. He was already annoyed with thinking about this and that, and when he started talking to the creature casually, it quickly responded with thoughts like a flare-up.

WE MUST GROW STRONGER, MUCH, MUCH STRONGER. STRONG
ENOUGH TO EASILY SLAUGHTER AND DEVOUR THE ENEMY,
WHETHER THAT BE AN ORIGINATOR OR A PURE COLOR...

"You sure are full of life, huh?" Haru laughed briefly beneath
his visor.

The Beast—more precisely, the many negative memories and
feelings incorporated into the Enhanced Armament Disaster—
functioned like a pseudo-intelligence through the special characteristics of the memory medium. And its objective was very
simple: Treat all Burst Linkers as enemies, fight them, beat them,
devour them. Due to this simplicity, its mental control was very
strong. The first, who had given birth to the Armor of Catastrophe itself, and the second and third, had, to greater and lesser
extents but without exception, had their minds eaten into by the
Armor and been transformed into terrifying berserkers. The
number of Burst Linkers their hands had forever banished from
the Accelerated World definitely didn't stop at a hundred.

In other words, if he thought about it mechanically, currently,
more than the ISS kits or the Acceleration Research Society, this
Armor of Catastrophe = Beast = sixth Chrome Disaster = Silver
Crow was a much more enormous threat, an enemy of the entire
world.

In the final stages of the Hermes' Cord race two weeks earlier, Haruyuki had summoned the Armor once, and he had not
stopped at instantly killing the enemy before his eyes; he had
tried to attack even the hundreds of people in the Gallery. He
had just barely been pulled back into his original state with Lime
Bell's special attack, but he had felt then that the next time he
called the Armor, he probably wouldn't be able to return to his
normal self again. That his own mind would be instantly erased,
and he would simply be a presence raging in the darkness.

And now Haruyuki had actually set foot into that boundary
region. He had summoned the Armor a second time, become
more deeply fused with it than before. He had indeed let the

anger take over and run wild for a time. But something had started to change in the middle of the fight with the difficult Iron Pound and through the great clash with the Green King. He was strangely quiet now, for some reason.

Was this proof that Haruyuki had already completely become one with the Disaster? Or was it not Haruyuki at all, but some factor within the Armor, on the Beast's side?

"Hey, you…So, like, you…," Haruyuki began saying to the Beast. And yet for so long, all this time, he had thought of it as the terrifying root of all evil, basically a time bomb lurking within his own self. "If you fight your enemy and win, and win and win and keep winning, until you beat the very last one, what're you going to do after that?"

For a while, there was no reply. He wondered if maybe the creature hadn't actually thought about what came after that, but finally, a low roar thundered deep in his head.

I DO NOT KNOW. IT DOES NOT MATTER. OUR PURPOSE IS SIMPLY TO DESTROY THE ENEMY BEFORE US AND NOTHING MORE.

"Heh, ha-ha. I guess so." Haruyuki laughed briefly and nodded.

Now that had he summoned the Catastrophe of his own will and completely awakened it, there was a strong possibility that even if he turned to Lime Bell's Citron Call and Ardor Maiden's Purification, he wouldn't be able to go back to normal. In other words, just like the Beast, Haruyuki no longer had anywhere to go home to. Because he had no guarantee that the instant he saw the faces of his friends in Nega Nebulus, he wouldn't lose all reason like he had before and slash at them wildly.

Of course, at some point, he would have to leave the Unlimited Neutral Field and face Chiyuri, Takumu, Fuko, Utai, and Kuroyukihime in the real world. But Haruyuki had no idea what he should do or what he should say to his loved ones when that happened, to the point that he even had the thought that his only choice was to simply continue to wander in the Unlimited Neutral Field, where time flowed accelerated by a factor of a thousand. Attack anything that came into sight without discrimination, Enemy or Burst Linker, and defeat it. Wear himself down during the long, long hours, until he was on the verge of disappearing.

Then he might be able to get through it without feeling too sad. Even if he had to say good-bye to those very important people only halfway through their journey.

"Looks like we're gonna be spending a lot of time together, huh, partner?"

All Haruyuki got in reply was a brief, displeased roar.

I can't believe I can chat like this with that terrifying Beast now. And animals don't usually really like me... As this thought wandered through his mind, he decided to head east for now, toward Ginza. He walked toward the edge of Mori Tower.

At that point, Haruyuki didn't bother to concern himself with two important facts.

One was that if he had truly become one with the Armor of Catastrophe, aka the Disaster, then he wouldn't be able to hear the Beast's voice to start with. In fact, for a while after he summoned the Armor an hour earlier in the northern part of the Shibuya area, Haruyuki had been basically unaware of the existence of it—because he himself had become "the Beast" and had been rampaging.

He had become able to hear the consciousness's voice in his head in the instant he tried to fight the control of the Armor with his own will—in the middle of the fierce battle with Iron Pound. Ever since, Haruyuki had fought while communicating at super-high speed with the Beast. In other words, battle power aside, this could actually be seen as proof that his level of fusion with the Armor was low on the mental side...but the Haruyuki of that moment wasn't able to recognize this.

And the second fact, which Haruyuki had completely forgotten:

An hour earlier, as he had been about to leave the members of Nega Nebulus in front of the southern gates of the Castle and fly off to look for Ash Roller, Chiyuri had said, *Haru, if you're not back in an hour, we'll pull the cable on the other side, okay?*

As he prepared to fly off aimlessly from the eastern edge of the roof as a wandering mercenary, a reddish-purple system message flashed fiercely in the center of his field of view. DISCONNECTION WARNING. He was being disconnected.

It took a few seconds for him to realize what was happening. His friends had returned to the real world ahead of him through a leave-point, and now they were physically pulling out the XSB cable connecting him to the Unlimited Neutral Field out of his Neurolinker. The bloodstained scene of the Deadly Sin stage began to disappear, stretching out vertically like toffee. On the verge of being cut loose from the Accelerated World, he heard the brief howl of the Beast.

In addition to the usual rage and annoyance, the voice seemed like it also held the slightest note of some other, unfamiliar emotion.

3

The first thing he felt was not the dull weight of his real world body, nor the elasticity of the sofa up against his back, nor even the cool air emitted by the air conditioner. It was the sensation of someone's hand squeezing his left shoulder tightly, the faint scent of something sweetly minty, and hair like silk tickling his cheek.

Before even opening his eyes, Haruyuki knew there was someone right in front of him. Even still, the instant he saw Kuroyukihime barely thirty centimeters away, eyes like the starry sky wide-open, he couldn't stop himself from trembling at the feelings that filled his heart.

Kuroyukihime was gripping his shoulder with her right hand, and in her left, she held the XSB plug she had just pulled out of his Neurolinker. Apparently, she had been the one to carry out the physical disconnection, rather than Chiyuri.

"Haruyuki." She parted her smooth, faintly cherry-colored lips, and a slightly strained voice came out. "We waited for an hour, but you didn't come back, so apologies, but we took the liberty of activating the emergency disconnect safety."

"...Right." He somehow managed to produce that much of an answer, but his voice was so raspingly hoarse it surprised even him. The inside of his mouth was completely dried out; his tongue wouldn't move properly.

A glass of iced oolong tea was swiftly proffered from his right. Holding it was Fuko Kurasaki, looking as worried as Kuroyuki-hime, if not more so. Bowing his head slightly, Haru accepted the glass and drank the chilled tea down in one gulp. The pain in his throat finally subsided, and he let out a small sigh.

As if she had been waiting for him to relax a little, Kuroyuki-hime opened her mouth once more. "Did something happen? Right before we moved to exit through the leave-point at the police station, the closest one to the Castle's southern gate, we saw a tremendous explosion in the south, probably in the direction of Akasaka. You couldn't have actually..."

Oh, right, he thought. All he had said to Kuroyukihime and the others when he left them at the Castle's southern gate was that he was going to look for Ash Roller, so naturally none of them knew anything. Nothing about the many—too many—events that had happened in the following hour.

Still holding the now-empty glass with both hands, Haruyuki quietly looked away. Kuroyukihime was directly in front of him, one knee on the sofa, almost bending forward. To her right, kneeling on the carpet, was Fuko. Farther to the right, sitting on her knees alongside Haruyuki on the sofa, was Utai Shinomiya.

When he turned his eyes to the opposite side, Takumu Mayuzumi and Chiyuri Kurashima were leaning forward, shoulders almost pressed together. All the members of the second Nega Nebulus had a shared look of sincere and deep concern for Haruyuki on their faces.

And yet.

And yet, their faith in me, I...

Forcing that momentary thought out of his mind, Haruyuki somehow succeeded in bringing an awkward smile to his face. He looked at Kuroyukihime again. "Oh, uh, I'm okay," he said, clumsily, still unable to meet her eyes. "I wasn't pulled into that explosion. And I didn't die. I was pretty close to a portal before I logged out, so it'll probably be easy to leave normally."

Once he had gotten this much out, a hint of relief rose up on the faces of everyone present. However, the moment he saw that, a feeling of guilt like a sharp needle plunged into Haruyuki's heart. He had to tell them. Everything. What he had done. That he had given himself over to anger, lost his senses, and destroyed something precious—something called *possibility*. Not just for Haruyuki, but the future of the Legion Nega Nebulus itself.

Suppressing the urge to sob and wail like a small child, Haruyuki focused on keeping a smile on his face as he gently pushed Kuroyukihime's hand away from his shoulder. His beloved swordmaster leaned back, brow furrowing slightly, and didn't quite stand while rearranging herself on the sofa.

He reached a hand out and placed the empty glass on the coffee table before lifting his face. "Um, I'll start at the beginning, okay?" He looked at Fuko first and gave her a nod. "Master, I found Ash Roller a little north of Shibuya Station. Apparently, before meeting with all of you, he planned to pick up Bush Utan in Shibuya and bring him along. But they were attacked by a group wearing ISS kits."

"What?!" Fuko gasped, her eyes flying open.

Haruyuki nodded briefly again. "It's all right. It looks like the attackers stole points from them a few times, but neither Ash nor Utan got to total loss. They should be leaving normally through the portal at Shibuya Station right about now."

"I see." Fuko let out the breath she'd been holding and furrowed her brow. "Even though I knew it would be far too late, I was this close to running down to the parking lot and pulling off Ash's Neurolinker. Honestly, no matter how many times I say not to, that child's habit of running off cannot be corrected...I must make sure I give Ash the superspecial course from the Incarnate training menu."

UI> DON'T BE TOO HARD ON ASH, Utai replied in the chat window, pulling her shoulders in for some reason, and Kuroyukihime, Chiyuri, and Takumu laughed together.

"Um." Haruyuki worked intently to relax his cheeks and somehow put something resembling a smile on his face as he recommenced his story. "So after I managed to beat back the kit users, I saw one of the ISS kits fly off to the east, so I went after it. It moved to the area around Roppongi Hills, but I ran into members of another Legion there, so I got into another little fight, but I managed somehow...And then right after they left through the Mori Tower portal, you pulled the cable out for me, Kuroyukihime, and I burst out, too. The explosion you guys saw was caused by this massive Enemy nearby, but it wasn't like it was targeting me, so..."

Haruyuki closed his mouth here, but given how many details his explanation omitted, it was no surprise when his friends exchanged looks that said something didn't quite click for them. Kuroyukihime gave voice to the questions.

"The most important thing is that you're safe, Haruyuki. Just now, you said you...beat back the group of ISS kit users, yes? Does that mean that you defeated several IS mode users by yourself? Oh, I don't mean to cast doubt on your actual abilities, but..."

"Uh, um..."

"Kuroyukihime, when Haru does something, he really does it, you know!" Chiyuri spoke up brightly, perhaps keenly sensing that Haruyuki was hard-pressed to answer. "Lately, if you let him use a sneaky trick or two when he's down, he'll come out better than the Yellow King!"

"...Chiyuri, was that a compliment?"

Takumu, Fuko, and Utai all smiled at this exchange between the two girls. Haruyuki tried hard to join them and push something like a laugh out of his throat. But at the same time, the feelings he had been desperately trying to dam up in the bottom of his heart were about to burst forth.

The cheery voices of his friends were just too warm, their faces too dazzling. Until the instant they dove into the Unlimited Neutral Field together—mere minutes before, according to the clock on the wall—Haruyuki had been a part of the small but strong circle of Nega Nebulus. He had believed that he would rescue Ardor Maiden from the mouth of the God Suzaku, be purified of the parasitic element of the Armor, and then fight alongside all of them forever. And yet...And yet...

"Haruyuki...?" At the sound of Kuroyukihime's bewildered murmur, Haruyuki finally realized that a tear was sliding down his own right cheek.

"I-I'm sorry." He hurriedly wiped at it with the back of his hand several times and put a smile on his face once more. "It's nothing. I'm just relieved now that the mission to rescue Shinomiya's over, and..." He managed to quickly push this out, but then his real-world body rejected his control, and large drops began to spill from both eyes, one after another. His face screwed up, and his chest heaved.

"Haruyuki." Kuroyukihime said his name in a clear voice, and reached out with a pale hand.

He gently, but still with some force, pushed back with both hands. Kuroyukihime's slender body had no sooner moved away from him than he was springing up from the sofa and running heavily toward the living room door. With his hand on the door-knob, Haruyuki looked back and said to his wide-eyed friends, "I'm sorry, guys. I'm really sorry."

"Wh-what's wrong, Haru?" Takumu shouted. "At least tell us first. We promised not to hide things from each other anymore, didn't we?!"

Haruyuki started to reflexively lower his eyes, but then stopped and endured their gazes at least. To these people he loved, sitting about in the center of his blurry, hazy vision, he said hoarsely, "I'm not Silver Crow anymore. I'm the sixth Chrome Disaster."

He felt them all gasp as one, but he couldn't make out the details of their faces through his veil of tears. Thanks to that, he was able to string a few more words together.

"The Armor's totally become one with my duel avatar. It's too late to go back or to purify it...I'm sorry, Kuroyukihime. I...I...you..."

I wanted to see the farthest reaches of the Accelerated World with you. Swallowing this, Haruyuki turned without waiting for Kuroyukihime's reaction. He pushed the door open and flew out into the hallway.

Behind him, he heard the footfalls of what was probably Takumu and Kuroyukihime. Running toward the front door, Haruyuki accessed his home server and opened a holowindow to press his finger down on the FORCE LOCK button in the security settings tab.

"Haru!!"

"You have to wait, Haruyuki!!"

As if fleeing from their voices, he shoved his feet into his sneakers at the same time as he pushed open the entryway door. He had no sooner stepped out through the gap into the shared hallway outside than he was pushing the door shut again with his body and hitting the LOCK button.

Chak! The sound of the lock rang out like something had been severed. Immediately after that came the sound of the handle of the door being pushed down several times, and then that of the dead bolt being turned, but the door did not open. No one but Haruyuki, with his administrator privileges on the Arita home server, could unlock that door.

Flicking around in the window, he set the maximum fifteen minutes for the time to maintain the lock and then started talking to Kuroyukihime, who was still calling his name on the other side of the five-centimeter-thick door.

"Kuroyukihime. I—I summoned the Armor of Catastrophe of my own will. Just when—just when all of you were working so hard to purify the seed parasitizing me...even though Mei made it out of the Castle alive...I made it all worthless..."

How could it be worthless?! Do you think I don't at least understand you would do that to save a friend you care about?! I will cut that Armor away from you in a single blow! So open the door, Haruyuki!!

Even separated from him by the layers of aluminum, Kuroyuki-

nto full view in pieces. Above the plaid skirt: an ivory school ca...
igan. At the neckline, a ribbon of the same pattern as the skirt
f it was a school uniform, it was a fairly stylish design. Over it, ...
mallish shoulder bag hung diagonally. The girl was probably in
unior high, but she was quite slender and small. Thin arms were
pread out at an angle of about thirty degrees; she was extremely
erious about blocking Haruyuki.

Even more dumbfounded, he finally looked at his opponent's
ce. Like the voice and the uniform, it was unfamiliar. Her fea-
res were sharply put together, with something boyish about
hem, and her hair was short and slightly unkempt. Haruyuki was
ad at remembering faces, but still, there was very little doubt that
his was the first time he'd ever seen this girl. However, he couldn't
efinitively declare this to be true, seeing as how he'd only looked
 her face for a moment before reflexively sliding his eyes away.
And that was because the mysterious girl had downturned eyes
et with tears, on the verge of spilling down her cheeks.

There was no reason for him to even try to figure out why a
nior high girl on the verge of tears was not letting him pass in
e middle of a mall full of shoppers; the whole thing made no
nse at all. Haruyuki somehow managed to turn off his "sur-
rised" switch before he went into full-on, frozen shock.

"Um," he whispered, "I—I think you have the wrong person.
xcuse me, I'm in a hurry, so…" And then he changed course for
e third time, trying to slip by on the left.

The half-crying girl reached out to grab his wrist with unex-
ected force. "I don't have. The wrong person," she told him in an
en thinner voice. "I can't. Let you go."

"Huh?! Wh-why…I haven't done anything!" Haruyuki said,
urriedly, feeling the eyes of passersby finally turning on them.
The girl's response to this was further denial.

"No. You did. You. Saved. Me," she announced haltingly, tears
uilding up in her single-lidded eyes.

"I'm. Ash. Roller."

hime's voice reached his ears very clearly. And the vibrations of
her pounding steadily on the door with all her might felt like
they came directly through his back and into his heart.

"If we go on like this, you and everyone in the Legion might
end up being investigated, too, at the meeting of the Seven Kings
on Sunday. And if everyone gets a bounty put on their heads…
Nega Nebulus will disappear. I have to make sure that doesn't
happen, at least." The vibrations stopped at this. In the brief
silence, Haruyuki focused on giving voice to his last words.
"I'll finish things with the Armor of Catastrophe myself. Please
wait…I know I'll come back. To you…to everyone."

That was the first big lie Haruyuki had told since he'd become
a Burst Linker as Kuroyukihime's child. The Armor could no
longer be cut free. Even now, while he was in the real world, he
felt that Beast breathing somewhere deep inside him. There was
only one thing he could do: disappear along with it. After fighting countless battles, wear his existence itself out.

I'm sorry. Good-bye, Kuroyukihime. Good-bye, Master. Sorry,
Taku, Chiyu. And…Shinomiya.

Whispering this in his heart, Haruyuki peeled his back off the
door. He clenched his hands into tight fists and started running
for the elevator. The time display in the lower right of his field of
view said 7:20 PM, still a time when a junior high school student
would be allowed to be walking alone outside. If he went back
into the Unlimited Neutral Field again right away from a dive
café somewhere, he should be able to finish everything before he
was chased out of the café at ten.

Even in the midst of his confusion and worrying, the thought
did indeed cross his mind that perhaps his own actions were a
little too rash. But he could not forget the fact that the Armor of
Catastrophe gradually ate into even the personality of the Burst
Linker wearing it in the real world. Haruyuki could not repeat
the tragedy of the fifth Disaster Cherry Rook trying to eat his
own child and Legion Master Niko. At least that, he could not
allow. Absolutely not.

In his last dive, Haruyuki had only lost himself and attacked Olive Grab and the other ISS kit wearers. In the fighting with Iron Pound and the Green King, he had started to rampage twice, but fortunately, it hadn't reached the level where he lost his reason or his memory. He would settle this while he could still be himself.

Carving this into his heart, when he went to get into the elevator, his VOICE CALL icon began to flash, accompanied by a light synthetic sound. The caller was…Chiyuri.

Haruyuki clenched his hands as tightly as he could and rode out the desire to push the icon. He apologized in his heart as he cut all network connects from his Neurolinker. And then, instead of using the now-disabled AR button, he specified the first floor with the control panel in the elevator, something he had no memory of ever using.

The basement up to the third floor of the multi-use high-rise condo in northern Koenji where Haruyuki, Takumu, and Chiyuri lived was taken up by a large shopping mall. Even though it was a weekday evening, the central walkway on the first floor was quite busy with families and couples. As he trotted ahead, ignoring all the smiling faces and the fun these people were having, Haruyuki felt a little sense of déjà vu.

Right. It had been in April…the day Haruyuki's lone power, his flying ability, had been stolen by the Burst Linker who suddenly appeared at Umesato Junior High, the Twilight Marauder, Dusk Taker. After he had been ordered to pay a tribute of burst points every day, Haruyuki had raced through the shoppers, holding back tears just like this.

In the end, he'd been saved by Ash Roller, when he had challenged him to a duel on Kannana Street. Ash had taken Haruyuki to meet his parent Sky Raker, and she had given him the two powers: that of the Incarnate system, as well as that of the Gale Thruster, all so that he could defeat Dusk Taker in the final battle.

This time, however, he couldn't rely on anyone else. Because, if

…e faced them in the Accelerated World, Haruyu… …riminately attack them. Given this risk, the act… …e Unlimited Neutral Field itself was full of dang… …y that he wouldn't run across someone there w… …n fight. Maybe it would be better to pull the Neu… …ck and smash it or throw it into the fountain. … …stalled BB program itself might be the only … …rmor of Catastrophe…

And then a pair of neatly lined-up shoes came … …ld of view ahead of him, as he headed for the e… …had hanging. They weren't new, but the black l… …well cared for. White socks, slender calves. A pl… …swinging slightly above small knees.

Someone, probably a girl, was standing in Har… other words, smack in the middle of the centra… shopping mall. She might have been manip… tual desktop, but it was still a serious violation… of course, he did not have the nerve to just cha… shove her aside, so he changed course to the left… up at the other girl's face.

But, shockingly, the black loafers also took a s… continued to block his path.

Finally, feeling mildly irritated, Haruyuki sh… right. But the owner of the shoes also moved i… tion. The distance between them was cut down… was forced to stop.

"Excuse me," Haruyuki whispered, stubborn… "I'm coming through here."

Ah! I'm sorry! was naturally the reaction … But…there was a bit of a pause, and then a fa… something beyond unexpected:

"I. Won't let you."

Huh?! Things having reached this point, the… even Haruyuki could help but straighten his r… As he lifted his eyes, the mysterious path-l…

4

Many abilities were required of those who would be Burst Linkers, but the most important was the ability to react to a situation.

Anything could happen in the middle of a duel, even if your opponent was a duel avatar you knew well. Your chances at victory in an unimaginable situation were slim if you didn't react quickly. The chance to collect information and act. You could leverage the performance of your avatar or you could be killed, depending on whether or not you could make this process happen in a short time.

The foundation for Silver Crow's speed, his greatest strength, was Haruyuki's own reaction speed. And it wasn't as though he had only recently developed the ability to race through a moment of paralysis during a duel.

However...

Now Haruyuki's thought clock dropped to below a single hertz, and he could do nothing other than gape, eyes and mouth wide open.

Ash Roller. So...Wait. Who?

It's...Ash. He answered his own lagging thoughts. *Rides the antique American motorcycle. With the skull helmet. All shrieking with laughter, thinks he's so hot.*

Huh? This is what's inside Ash? This quiet girl?

Haruyuki used up a full ten seconds before finally processing even a fragment of this new information, but there his thoughts stopped once more. For an instant at least, his own predicament flew completely out of his head, and in the blankness there, a tiny motorcycle zoomed past within his mind. And yet he still stood frozen in the middle of the crowded shopping mall.

The girl with the teary eyes gave his wrist another tug. "Um," she said quietly. "Let's. Go somewhere. Else."

Essentially brain-dead, Haruyuki allowed himself to be led to the large parking area on Basement 2 of the mall. They cut through the orderly rows of EVs, and a familiar compact car appeared. Fresh canary yellow, Italian five-door hatchback—the beloved car of Sky Raker, aka Fuko Kurasaki (or, more precisely, Ash's mother).

The girl apparently had a remote key because she made a quick gesture with her right hand, and the doors were unlocked, accompanied by the flashing of the car's turn signals. She pulled the rear right door open and pushed Haruyuki into the backseat before sliding in after him.

He could take the fact that the girl had been given the key to this car as proof that she knew Fuko. Still, he simply could not process the claim that the junior high school girl with the messy short hair plopped down beside him was *the* Ash Roller, and he sat there emptily. In comparison, it had all felt so much more real when he learned that the little girl who had slipped into his house under the pretense of being his relative Tomoko Saito was actually the second Red King, Scarlet Rain.

However, he couldn't stay frozen like this forever. Seven minutes had already passed since he flew out of his house in his sloppy T-shirt and long shorts. He had eight more minutes before the emergency lock function of the Arita house automatically unlocked and released Kuroyukihime and the other four, after which they would no doubt come running after him.

Finding him in the enormous condo complex when he had cut

his Neurolinker off from the network would probably be difficult, but they had Chiyuri and Takumu on their side. When the three of them were little, they had played countless games of tag and hide-and-seek with this building as their staging ground, and Haruyuki's win ratio was far and away the lowest of all three. With Chiyuri's weird animal instincts, once they got around to the ice cream of Enjiya, they would sniff out his location in minutes. Which meant if he really intended to settle the situation by himself, then he had at best ten minutes before he needed to be outside the condo.

Having succeed in rebooting his brain with this little detour, Haruyuki glanced over at the girl, still sniffling beside him, and managed to open his mouth.

"Ummmm, so…what you said before, Ash Roller? So you're, like, Ash's friend or messenger…or something?" he asked first, betting on the unlikely possibility that he had misheard her before.

But clutching the white handkerchief she had pulled out at some point in both hands, the girl made a clear gesture of denial, shaking her soft hair. She hung her face, which was for some reason a little redder now, and in a voice that threatened to disappear, oozing shyness, she said, "I'm Ash."

His thoughts threatened to shut down once more. But he still couldn't actually believe it.

In the expansive Accelerated World, there were people for whom the images of their duel avatars and their real selves were far apart. Haruyuki himself could be said to be one of them. If you only knew the slender-to-the-extreme body of Silver Crow, you wouldn't really be able to imagine that this rotund eighth-grade boy was the true identity of that duel avatar.

But that sort of thing happened mostly with external appearance. There wasn't much divergence in the tone of voice or the way a person held themselves—their "spirit," as it were. Burst Linkers Haruyuki knew in the real—Kuroyukihime and the other members of Nega Nebulus, Niko and Pard from Prominence, and even that crafty Dusk Taker—were no exception.

In contrast, the girl beside him and Ash Roller had not a single point in common—or at least, that's how it looked. The words they used, their gestures, their personalities were so different, they could only be called polar opposites. And no matter how he looked at it, that biker was a male-type avatar, wasn't it? And in Brain Burst, if the person was a girl, then they would definitely get a female type...

"Oh!" Haruyuki let out a small cry as he remembered a certain scene. He threw his body back to the right and stared straight on for the first time at the teary face of the girl.

She shrank back slightly even as she returned his gaze, her face housing a soft weakness and coolness at the same time. She was indeed a girl, but her appearance gave the faint impression of a nerdy boy. Her face did somehow resemble the "bare face" of Ash Roller hidden beneath the skull-patterned helmet shield.

"...You...really...but why..." Haruyuki asked an entirely too vague question.

The teary-eyed girl replied in action rather than words. She opened the small shoulder bag on the knees of her skirt and tucked away the handkerchief before pulling out something else in its place. Right and left arms folded up, dark metallic gray—a Neurolinker.

Huh? he thought, as he shifted his gaze to the girl's slender neck. Already equipped there was a cute pastel-green quantum communication terminal. Given that she had unlocked the car earlier with a wave of her right hand, it would naturally be strange if there wasn't.

But then, here came his second question.

Neurolinkers were mobile devices in a line descended from the old cell phones and smart phones, but that was not all they were. They were business cards, wallets, personal identification. The particular brain waves of the user and the particular ID burned into the core chip were linked; just by wearing it, you proved who you were. So that ID was, for all intents and purposes, a "citizen number."

Put another way, the Neurolinker was a "tagged necklace" the government gave citizens. Reinforcing that, ownership of multiple Neurolinkers was prohibited by law. Of course, there were several ways to get a hold of a second or third terminal, but there was no point in getting just the machine, given that only one key core chip was issued per person, and the chips could be transferred (i.e., to a new model) only at a ward office or government-approved shop. Even *the* Kuroyukihime had only one Neurolinker. If she had had two, she wouldn't have had to stay disconnected from the global net for over two years in order to hide from the assassins of the Six Kings.

For all these reasons, Haruyuki was honestly stunned at the second Neurolinker the girl pulled out. "I-is that…yours?" he asked hoarsely. "Y-you can use it?"

"I. Can," the girl replied, tilting her head at a very slight angle. "But. It's. Not mine. This was my. Older brother's. Neurolinker."

"I-it *was* your older brother's?" he parroted, dumbfounded, and the mysterious girl nodded sharply, turning her entire body toward him on the leather seat. However, they were inside a car, so this essentially amounted to her twisting her torso, inevitably yanking up the hem of her skirt to reveal a fair amount of her pale legs.

Even in this increasingly complex situation, Haruyuki, being Haruyuki, could only freeze his eyeballs unnaturally in panic. But the girl seemed unconcerned with his reaction and snapped her back up straight while taking several deep breaths. It was almost as though the girl was just as nervous in this situation as Haruyuki. Placing the gray Neurolinker on her lap, she squeezed both hands tightly as if telling herself, *You can do it.*

Finally, she took another breath before turning eternally teary eyes back toward Haruyuki. "I— My name is. Rin Kusakabe," she said, in a clear voice. At the same time, she made a small gesture with her right hand, and a pale-green rectangle appeared in his field of view. A name tag sent via an ad hoc connection. The kanji characters displayed there read RIN KUSAKABE. She was born in 2033, making her an eighth grader in junior high, just like Haruyuki.

"Uh, um, I'm Haruyuki Arita." Reflexively, he gave his name as he pushed the button to send his name tag in return. The girl, Rin, dropped her eyes to glance at the tag and smiled the tiniest bit, the first time since their chance meeting.

Pressed into an even more panicked state, he gave voice semi-automatically to a question not high up on his list of priorities. "Th-th-that reminds me. In the mall before, how did you know I was Silver Crow?"

"That…A few minutes after. I burst out in the car. I got a voice call from Master. Your picture was attached. And she ordered me to. Do whatever it took to catch you. Before you left the condo."

"Master? You mean Sky Raker, right?" he confirmed, and then his brain took a shortcut, moving sideways.

The combination didn't entirely make sense. On the surface at least, Fuko Kurasaki was basically a graceful, upper middle-class high school student, and yet she was parent to the arrogant and insolent fin de siècle rider. From that point of view, the girl before him now no doubt had much more in common with Fuko, but this didn't answer the fundamental question.

As Haruyuki fought the urge to hold his head in his hands, Rin Kusakabe took the metallic-gray Neurolinker in her hands once more. Each time she moved, a faint floral scent wafted through the car, decelerating his thoughts. When she started speaking again, Haruyuki hurriedly sat up straighter.

"Um. I'll start. From the beginning. Why. I became. A Burst Linker."

"My brother's name was Rinta, and he was an ICGP racer."
This was Rin's beginning.
ICGP was a category of two-wheeled—in other words, motorcycle—racing. IC stood for "internal combustion." In

an age where electric vehicles had conquered even the world of motorsports, this was, to be blunt, an old-fashioned race, a lingering obsession with gasoline-engine vehicles that had no AI controls.

Nevertheless, compared with the strong, silent, and smart impression of electric racing machines, gasoline vehicles had an appeal that was hard to deny, with their roaring exhausts and wild spins. It wouldn't be a surprise if this category of racing, under attack for years as a symbol of environmental destruction, disappeared at any time, but Haruyuki himself had pushed back his sleepiness to watch the midnight broadcasts any number of times.

"My brother was. Six years older than me. And I know I'm the one saying it, but he. Was a talented rider. Two years ago, if he did well domestically. He'd get to go to Europe. It was a chance he embraced." As she falteringly told the story, Rin's eyes welled up with transparent droplets once more. "But in the last race. From the inside. He was hit by another car. I was there cheering for him. He was. Crushed right in front of me. Fortunately, they saved his life. But he's been unconscious ever since. This whole time. Even when they. Force him into a full dive with a medical Neurolinker. There's only. The faintest reaction…"

Unsure of how to respond, Haruyuki simply continued to stare into Rin's wet eyes.

In EV races, where AI controls were the rule, there were essentially no accidents caused by one car touching another. This meant viewers did not get to see thrilling passes or the neck-and-neck fights, sparks shooting out from the wheels of both cars, so this was a selling point for ICGP and IC Formula, which had exactly these elements. But it was inevitable that the number of serious accidents was an order of magnitude higher.

Rin blinked several times and calmed her breathing before continuing, "For the last two years. My brother's been in a large hospital. In Shibuya. I live in Egota, in Nakano Ward. But I chose a private. Junior high in Shibuya."

"So you could go visit him?" Haruyuki asked in a small voice, and Rin nodded sharply.

"The doctor said. His chances of recovery are higher when. He can hear the voices of his family. And have us hold his hand in the real world. I stop at the hospital every day. On my way home from school. I wanted to go every day during summer vacation, too. But I felt shy about asking. For a bus pass just for that. And then, last summer, in the hospital cafeteria, his primary doctor. Suggested I work there part-time just for summer vacation."

"I—I get it."

With the easing of restrictions on hiring minors in the revision of the labor standards, junior high school students were also now able to work the part-time jobs they had previously been forbidden, although the hours they could work were limited. Still, Haruyuki had never once thought about working to earn money himself, and he unconsciously let out a sigh of admiration.

"Wow. I mean, working the whole summer vacation for your brother's sake..."

"No." Eyes still damp with the ever-present tears, Rin smiled very faintly as she shook her head. "I'm just clumsy at work. Last summer alone, I broke ten plates. And glasses."

"Y-you did?"

"And not just. That. Once, I dumped ice water. On a patient's lap."

"Y-you...did?"

"Fortunately, the patient was very nice. A little older, but a junior high student like me. And our schools are close to each other, too. We got closer after that. We talk about where we'll go to high school. About my brother, all kinds of things."

"Mm-hmm." Unable to see where this was going, Haruyuki forgot his own predicament a little and leaned forward. The time display in the right of his view was second by second approaching the fifteen-minute limit from the time he'd flown out of the house, but he wasn't paying attention to that.

Last summer. So about ten months earlier. Right before Haruyuki became a Burst Linker at Kuroyukihime's invitation.

Rin stared back at him with damp eyes and continued, "After meeting several times, she. Saw through. To my 'mental scars.' And then said there was another form. Of the city of Tokyo. And that there. Maybe I could find the answers I was looking for."

"Your mental scars. Another Tokyo," Haruyuki murmured, before belatedly understanding what those words meant.

The urban center of virtual Tokyo where boys and girls with pain in their hearts came together and fought. The Accelerated World, the hidden battlefield produced by the Brain Burst program.

"So then this person is your parent Burst Linker?"

"That's. Right. My kind. Harsh Master," Rin said, nodding, and Haruyuki gasped.

He had actually almost forgotten, but the girl before him was asserting that she was *the* Ash Roller. If that was true, then that meant the junior high student Rin had met in the hospital cafeteria was Haruyuki's own teacher, the level-eight Burst Linker "Strong Arm" Sky Raker, aka Fuko Kurasaki.

He hesitated to actually say Raker's real name out loud in case Rin was a hostile Burst Linker approaching him with some sort of hidden agenda, although that was hard to imagine at this point. Perhaps understanding what was in Haruyuki's heart as he fell silent in a momentary indecisiveness, perhaps not, Rin slowly lowered her eyes.

"When I heard the explanation of the conditions for installing the program Brain Burst 2039…I—I thought it would be. Impossible. I only got my first Neurolinker right before I went to elementary. School."

"So then you couldn't meet the first condition…right?"

Rin bowed her head slightly in agreement.

The very first requirement to be able to install the Brain Burst program—to become a Burst Linker—was to have been wearing a Neurolinker since immediately after birth. Most parents wouldn't go to that extreme unless they were very enthusiastic about child-rearing, or the exact opposite of that.

"I. Explained that. But Master smiled. And said. 'I feel. The light of. A strong will in you. My. Instincts about this. Are never wrong.'"

This sort of gentle and kindly controlling statement did indeed sound like something Fuko would say. But although she might have been the "actually really scary Master Raker," even Fuko couldn't fake meeting the first requirement of Brain Burst. Haruyuki cocked his head to one side, and Rin once again lifted up the item she held in both hands.

"Then," she said. "I. Remembered…when my brother—Rinta. Was little, he was a troublemaker. He wasn't just going to be an ICGP rider. He was going to make me one, too. So when I was a baby. He used to sneak his Neurolinker onto me. My parents. Said he showed me race videos."

"Y-your brother's kind of amazing, huh?"

A stiff smile spread across her face, and she blinked in surprise. They might have been brother and sister, but a different person was still a different person. Even if her brother had put the Neurolinker on her, wouldn't it have been impossible for her to activate it?

As if guessing the question in Haruyuki's mind, Rin nodded. "A newborn's brain's not. Fully developed until they're a toddler. So apparently, the particular brain wave pattern can't always be read. Well. Of course, these are rare cases. But Rinta's Neurolinker apparently recognized. Baby me as a user, too. And ever since I can remember. Until my parents bought me my own, I borrowed my brother's sometimes. To read picture books. Do full dives. That was. This Neurolinker."

What Rin held so carefully in both hands was a worn-out, metallic-gray wearable device.

As he stared at it incredulously, Haruyuki realized something. He hadn't noticed it until now because of the gloom in the car, but in addition to the peeling paint and wear from normal use, the external plastic shell had a crack like a bolt of lightning racing across it, likely made in some kind of intense impact.

"My brother. Kept using the first Neurolinker he got as a kid all that time. He just changed the shell. To an adult size. He said he could race faster with it. After junior high, he didn't go to high school. He went straight. Into the world of motorcycle racing. And. All this time…"

Although the ICGP races that Rin's older brother, Rinta, was part of were old style with no AI control, the riders wore Neurolinkers for the bare-minimum AR display and communication with the pit.

In which case. The machine Rin held in her hands—

"That Neurolinker…In the crash two years ago, your brother was…?"

The girl moved her head slowly up and down at Haruyuki's hushed question.

"My brother's team's. Coach gave it to me at the circuit. Where the accident was. He probably meant for it to be. A memorial. I think. Rinta's life was saved, but ever since, he's. Been in a coma. But it's strange." She cut herself off and smiled gently. "When Master was explaining. The installation of the BB program. I took off my own Neurolinker and tried putting this one on. The last time I'd borrowed it from my brother was. Right before I went to elementary school. A long time ago. Over eight years. I thought I wouldn't be able to activate it anymore. But the machine. Worked."

Haruyuki took a sharp breath. That meant that the girl before him, Rin Kusakabe, used two Neurolinkers, something that should not have been physically—or legally—possible.

Of course, as long as you weren't a criminal or something misrepresenting yourself and up to no good, there wasn't really any point in using multiple Neurolinkers. But using the Neurolinker she had used as a baby was probably an effective way to meet the conditions for installation of Brain Burst.

Because both the first condition of having worn a Neurolinker since infancy and the second condition of having long-term experience with full dives were, in the end, interrogating the affinity and responsiveness between brain and machine. Since there were individual differences in the Neurolinker quantum connection devices, it was possible that the machine you first used after you were born was the one your body—no, brain—was most familiar with.

"So then...the Brain Burst program isn't in this green one now, but in your brother's Neurolinker?" Haruyuki asked.

"Yes." Rin bobbed her head up and down. "Since Master said we could only try to install it once. I was a little hesitant. Before. When I said it was strange. After I put on this Neurolinker. In the middle of the virtual flames from the BB program. When I was waiting for the indicator to advance. I heard. My brother's voice."

"Huh?"

"'You race. Down your road....I'm right behind you, pushing you forward.'" Eyes full of transparent tears, Rin smiled the clearest smile she had since this strange conversation began. She gently opened the lock arms of the battered Neurolinker as she continued. "The installation. Succeeded. But. When I first went with Master to the duel stage. And I saw my own avatar. Without thinking. I laughed."

She stopped, and the slightest of giggles actually slipped out of her.

"Leather jacket, flashy helmet. The big, shiny American motorcycle. The machine my brother said he was going to. Ride for himself when he. Was a champion in Europe. It was that very. Machine. Telling me to. Go down my own path, and then. My avatar's exactly like. His own dream. He really. Has always..."

Large droplets on the verge of spilling out were caught by her eyelashes, while Rin held the metallic-gray Neurolinker lovingly to her chest.

Haruyuki smiled at this gesture. "Right. So then, you in the Accelerated World—Ash Roller is like, um...maybe like role-playing? That tone, the style of fighting...you're acting like you think your brother would?"

Even still, the teary-eyed girl before him and the century-end rider in the Accelerated World were simply too far apart, but given the depths of her feelings toward her sleeping brother, he got the feeling that he might just barely get it.

While he forced himself to digest the situation, Rin looked up abruptly.

"It's. Not. Weird, is it?" she said unexpectedly. "It's. Cool, right?"

"Huh?! Cool? You mean, Ash?"

Her bobbing head sent her short hair swinging and then kept charging forward. Closing the distance between them, Rin spoke in a quiet but passionate voice. "The skull helmet. The spiky leather jacket. And the missiles on the bike are cute, too."

The words were too startling coming from a girl raised quite properly, clad in the uniform of a rich girls' school, and although Haruyuki bobbed his head up and down, his mouth stiffened up slightly. And then Rin took a sharp breath, as if coming back to herself, and dropped her head in embarrassed mode.

"I-I'm sorry. I. When it comes to the Accelerated World. I just get carried away. In duels, too, actually, it's. Like that. Maybe because I get too. Lost in it. Thirty minutes goes by in the blink of an eye. Even when I come back to the real world, I don't. Really remember. The duels."

"I—I get it." Haruyuki kept nodding and quickly considered the situation.

The sense he got from what Rin was saying now was that Ash Roller was not a simple performance, but rather to make it through the extreme and intense duels, a second self. So maybe she half-unconsciously borrowed her brother's personality or something? When he got wound up in the Accelerated World, Haruyuki himself sometimes switched from his normal way of talking to something a little tougher, and his tone also got about one and a half times wilder, so it made sense.

As he became lost in thought, Haruyuki felt a slight change in the air, and lifted his eyes.

…To meet those of Rin fairly close up, after her earlier unprecedented push forward on the leather seat. The irises, still plenty damp, were tinged with gray and made him feel a depth like he was peeking into an ocean.

"But there is. Just one thing I remember. More clearly than memories of the real world." Rin's voice was thin and halting, as always, but it echoed as clearly as neurospeak through a direct cable in the sealed car.

To get his once again rapidly rising pulse under control, Haruyuki chanted to himself, *She's Ash Roller, she's Ash Roller.*

But…

The girl who was supposedly the insides of that century-end rider brought her face another centimeter closer and whispered in a weak and yet heated tone, "That's. You. The first time we fought. We both won once, lost once. Ever since that day. The way you look, your voice. They've never. Disappeared from inside me."

"…K-Kusakabe…" His thoughts, which had started to cool down, shot up again into the red zone, and Haruyuki opened and closed his eyes intently at top speed. Each time his eyelids cut across his field of view like a shutter, he felt like Rin's damp eyes had gotten still closer.

"No other. Burst Linker even noticed it, but you. Figured out the structural features. Of an internal combustion engine motorcycle and defeated. Me. My brother always. Used to say, 'Front wheel spinning? That's no motorcycle.' He was probably annoyed. At losing to you. Lower level and still a newbie on top of that. But I think. In his. Heart, he was also glad."

The distance between their faces was already down to twenty centimeters, and Haruyuki's brain, running at only 10 percent of capacity, couldn't see the strangeness of what Rin was saying. And almost as if she was also not really aware of what she was saying—or doing, she continued to sidle up to him.

"But. The thing that's most. Clearly carved into my mind is… you with your wings spread, flying in the sky. Faster than. Anyone. Piercing the wall of air. Almost like. Almost like my brother then. When he would race through full throttle on the circuit's. Homestretch..."

And here, the large droplets that had been held back by her eyelashes through some curious equilibrium until that point spilled out onto her cheeks. The tears dripped down from her sharp, boyish jaw, and fell onto Haruyuki's T-shirt.

"I. Liked watching you flying in the sky of the Accelerated World. I liked. Dueling with you, racing along at full speed on the ground. To chase you up in the air. The way you look. Like the materialization of the word *speed* itself." Her voice shook, trembled, and stopped.

She lowered her eyes, and several tears that had formed anew spilled out. She took a deep breath and held it for a few seconds before suddenly continuing in a voice colored with grief. "But. But I. The foolish thing. I did. Without thinking of the consequences. I pushed you into. A dangerous situation."

Huh? What's she talking about? After a moment of confusion, Haruyuki finally remembered the predicament he was in.

Spurred on by anger, he had summoned the Armor of Catastrophe, and completely fused with it to become the sixth Chrome Disaster. And on top of that, to protect his Legion, he would have to draw the curtain on his life as a Burst Linker himself. The reason he had ended up in this situation was indeed as Rin said—the fact that he had seen the scene of Ash Roller's death in the Unlimited Neutral Field.

And he had to say that the reason Ash had ended up back against the wall, repeatedly hunted by Olive Grab and the other five ISS kit wearers, was because he (or she) had ignored the instructions of his Master, Sky Raker, dove into the Unlimited Neutral Field earlier than the meeting time, and then traveled a dangerously long distance inside by himself. But he had done so because he was trying to save Bush Utan, who was like his younger brother. To help Utan—who, like Olive and the others, was parasitized by an ISS kit, but unlike them, was trying to break free of its control of his own will—Ash had moved under his own judgement. He'd had no choice. Who exactly could fault him for acting…

"Oh. Th-that reminds me." Having gotten this far, Haruyuki finally reached the question he should have asked much earlier. "D-did you and Bush Utan make it out through a portal okay…?"

"Yes." Rin leaned forward, perilously close to him. "Just as you instructed. As soon as we regenerated. We ran together, to Shibuya Station."

"Y-you did?" Haruyuki let out a sigh of relief. "Good. That's great."

At that moment, Rin's hanging head shook and tilted and bumped into the chest of his T-shirt.

Helplessly, Haruyuki froze completely, and a small hand pressed gently, but with sure power against his back. On the surface, it appeared that the two of them were alone in a car hugging, and in this situation, the chant "this girl is Ash" lost its efficacy. His internal brain clock dropped to the bare minimum, and yet his heart pounded out a beat at top speed…It was a contradiction with the mental clock acceleration of Brain Burst, wasn't it?—

With the vestiges of mental ability left to him, Haruyuki considered ideas that bore no relevance to the current situation. Then, through the body pressed up against him, he heard an almost vanishing voice.

"I. Saw it. To save me and Utan, you. Summoned that terrifying Enhanced Armament. That's the Armor of Catastrophe, right? If only I hadn't. Gotten in the way, it was supposed to be. Purified today."

Unable to answer yes or no, he simply opened and closed his mouth. Rin's hair so close to his respiratory organs was shining finely, the faint smell of flowers drifting up from it. As he took in the sweet scent, Haruyuki was aware of a strange sensation rapidly surging up from the depths of his heart. It resembled panic or anxiety, but it was a little different. A sad throbbing, like being stabbed with a soft needle.

"Me being saved. Just me. And you not. Being able to fly in the Accelerated World. It's wrong."

Without being aware of it, Haruyuki had been on the verge of trying to take some kind of action when Rin started speaking again, and his hands froze in midair, dangerously close.

"I mean. The reason I've been. Able to keep fighting in the beautiful and cruel world. Is because you were there. Because I wanted to. See you flying in the sunset of the Twilight stage. In the Century End stage, reflecting the bonfires. In the bus on my way to school. Back home. I would think about whether I'd challenge you. Or you'd maybe challenge me. I. Looked forward to it."

Here, the thin, passionate voice cut off, and Rin lifted her face. She looked straight at Haruyuki, tears dripping from her eyes, and the girl who was *the* Ash Roller—the roaring, racing century-end rider, Haruyuki's *hya-ha-ha-ha*, *mega-lucky* eternal rival—released a single sentence from her cherry-colored lips.

"I like you."

Instantly, all activity in his body shut down—at least subjectively— and the abdominal and spinal muscles that had supported Rin's meager weight until that point went limp.

Thud! They fell onto the seat with Haruyuki on the bottom. The five-door hatchback by the famed Italian manufacturer was plenty spacious in the rear, but of course, Haruyuki bumped his head on the inside of the door. But this impact might well never have happened. Because the sensation of contact along the front of his body and the destructive power of the words just uttered had begun to peel his soul from his physical body.

"B-but..." Although it was completely turned inside out and totally hoarse, the fact that he somehow managed to produce a voice in response was essentially a miracle. "But in the real, I'm like this."

Haruyuki at that moment didn't even have the extra brain-power to think he was pathetic, spitting something like that out at this stage of the game.

But not only did Rin not pull away from him, she pressed her body closer as she whispered in a teary voice, "I. Actually found out your. Real a little while ago."

"What…H-how?"

"It's just. After our duel on Kannana Street, you were standing forever. In the position where your avatar appeared. On the pedestrian bridge. I passed under you. On the bus."

To this, he had no immediate reply. If you were going to duel in open, public spaces, then the most basic of baby steps was to move once you were done. But for Haruyuki, when the duel was too superheated, a famed contest, he had the bad habit of spacing out and replaying the fight in his mind after he burst out. Apparently, he had somehow been perfectly picked out there by Rin, through the window of the bus.

"But—then, now— If you knew my real, why…someone like me?"

"I mean. You have. Wings. Not just your duel avatar. You in the real world, too. You do. I can see. Those wings so clearly." Rin's hand, still wrapped around Haruyuki, slowly stroked the center of his back.

A sensation that was hard to put into words shot through him from the tips of his toes to the crown of his head, causing him to hold his breath.

A bewitching smile rose up on Rin's face as tears continued to drip from her eyes onto his neck. "Ever since that day," she said, "I. Decided. If…if I ever got to meet you in the real, I would make sure. To tell you. That I like you. That I've always liked you. Ever since you were in level one. I'm glad. I got to tell you. I'm glad. In the end, we got to be. Like this, alone together."

"Huh? I-in the end?" Haruyuki asked, dumbfounded.

This girl, Rin Kusakabe, who he had basically never met before, sighed heavily before making both her face and voice resolute. "The Armor of Catastrophe you summoned. I'll get rid of it," she announced. "With my body. With my heart. I'll get rid of it."

"That…What does that mean?"

"I'll take. All of your anger and hatred. It's okay. As long as it's you. I'm not scared, no matter what's done to me."

Rin pulled her hand away from Haruyuki's back and slipped the pastel-green Neurolinker off her neck. Without a moment's delay, her other hand was putting on the metallic-gray Neurolinker—originally her older brother's—she had been holding all that time.

No sooner had the arm lock gently taken hold of Rin's slender neck than her empty right hand flashed. One end of the slim XSB cable she'd likely pulled out of her bag went into her own Neurolinker. The other went into Haruyuki's.

She didn't give him the time to say anything. The crimson wired connection warning floated up in his view, and the moment it disappeared, Rin murmured a brief command, her lips so close they were practically touching his.

"Burst Link."

All the chaos and confusion, and the bittersweet throbbing he couldn't put a name to, were swept away in the sharp *skreeee* of his thoughts accelerating.

5

HERE COMES A NEW CHALLENGER!!

The flaming text sprang to life in front of his eyes and then disappeared, bringing virtual darkness, and Haruyuki had a strong hunch about what stage would appear before him. Eventually, the soles of his metallic avatar's feet touched the hard earth. He waited until the sensation of descending had stopped before gently picking himself up.

He had, of course, not moved from the expansive underground parking area on B2 of his own condo building. But the real world's multicolored rows of neatly arranged EVs were crushed, burned, rusted, decaying. Even the yellow compact car that had been Fuko's baby, enshrined to his left, was a miserable sight, the hood peeled away, small flames flickering in the exposed engine compartment.

The duel had only just started, so it wasn't as if someone had destroyed them. Looking down, he saw that the concrete at his feet was also covered in hairline cracks, and around him, the thick pillars and walls were crumbling, exposing the rebar. If he went outside, the building itself would probably also be half-destroyed, and he wouldn't be able to get back inside. This image of "destruction completed" was the true nature of the Century End stage Haruyuki had sensed was coming.

And then...

Across from him in the gloom, some twenty meters away, he heard a throaty mechanical roar. This was immediately followed by the irregular rumble characteristic of a V-twin engine idling. A round headlight flicked on, and a warm, yellowish light illuminated his avatar.

Reflexively looking down at his own limbs, Haruyuki found there the smooth, slender armor of Silver Crow and let out a small sigh of relief. The Enhanced Armament Disaster wasn't the type that was constantly equipped, so it wouldn't appear unless he used a voice command to call it. Or it shouldn't, anyway...

"Ngh!" But in the next instant, Haruyuki was made painfully aware of the naïveté of his own outlook.

Silver Crow was not entirely as he had been. Normally, the ten fingers on his hands were so slender as to be ill-suited to fistfighting, but they were now talons with tips tapering like knives. He had three talons on each of his feet as well, and these dug deep into the concrete. When he hurriedly touched his head with one hand, he felt the original round form of his helmet, but protrusions like the vestiges of a visor stuck up from his temples.

So the Armor had indeed already stepped out from the realm of simple Enhanced Armament and was trying to fuse with his duel avatar itself. If Haruyuki's emotions or actions provided any trigger, it would explode and, in the blink of an eye, he would transform into a rampaging destroyer.

The instant he realized this and his body began trembling, he heard *it* growl, quietly but ferociously, somewhere deep in his back. Was it beginning to wake up from its brief sleep, sensing battle and slaughter?

Hey, Beast, he addressed the monster earnestly. *Just sit still and be good for this one fight at least!*

Once he had finished confirming to some degree who and what

he was at that moment, Haruyuki started talking to the headlight in front of him. "Um, Ash?"

The silhouette of the rider that popped up beyond the intense beam of light stayed silent, seeming to simply stare at Haruyuki. The burning remains of cars around them occasionally lit the skull-patterned helmet shield with an orange light.

I can't believe...it's actually a girl under that skull. And I can't believe...she told me that she likes me.

In the fourteen years or so that Haruyuki had been alive, this was the second time a member of the opposite sex had seriously confessed feelings for him. The first had, of course, been his Legion Master and swordmaster, his parent, Kuroyukihime. As she'd moved to protect him from an out-of-control car charging toward them, she had said it: "Haruyuki. I like you."

At the time—no, still, even now, he couldn't completely banish the question of why someone like Kuroyukihime would pick someone like him. Of course, he was so happy when she said that, he practically floated off up to heaven, and he naturally also really liked her. But in his heart, he could see that his own feelings were something akin to worship or respect and admiration. But because he had been in so-called self-restraint mode—right now he was still a short, pudgy, cowardly crybaby, but if he someday became a person worthy of her, then he would definitely tell her—Haruyuki himself had actually never told Kuroyukihime how he felt.

And then a few minutes earlier, in the cramped, closed space of the car, for the second time in his life, a girl had told Haruyuki she liked him. Rin Kusakabe had said, in her real voice, allowing no suspicion of any electronic fraud, and without the slightest reserve, "I like you."

Not only did he not have any idea how to react, he wasn't even clear on how he should take that. He just knew that transforming from his real body into his avatar through the sudden direct duel had succeeded in cooling his head, albeit slightly.

Inside Ash Roller was a girl named Rin. And this Rin had sincerely confessed her crush on him.

He would set these two points aside for the time being. At that moment, what he needed to be thinking about, first and foremost, were Rin's last words. She said she would erase the Armor of Catastrophe with her body. But as far as Haruyuki knew, Ash Roller didn't have any kind of purification-type ability. So did that mean that, just as the sentence that followed—"I'll take. All of your anger and hatred."—indicated, she was planning to suppress the destroyer Chrome Disaster by giving her own self to the Armor as an offering? Maybe she was hoping to take responsibility in this form for creating the trigger for Disaster's return.

"Ash—I mean, Rin." Because they were in a direct duel field where there was no Gallery, Haruyuki dared to utter his opponent's real name. "I'm really happy you want to help me. But you don't have to feel responsible for the Armor of Catastrophe. This armor—this Beast—has been inside me for a long time, for a few months now. I just got carried away by my emotions and summoned it." He glanced down at the sinister tapering talons of his right hand and went to continue speaking, but he was cut off by the heavy yet calm roar of the engine.

Vrrrr! The internal combustion engine shuddered, and the output it generated slowly rotated the fat rear tire. From the darkness ahead of him, the massive American motorcycle revealed itself. The slender rider, a knight on an iron horse, leisurely placed both hands on the handlebars, the skull face hanging so deeply Haruyuki couldn't see the expression on it.

"Rin…" Haruyuki tried to call out to her once more.

In that instant, the black leather gloves clutched the handlebars tightly. While the right hand twisted the throttle, the left dropped the clutch. The engine roared, an explosive howl, and the rear tire spun furiously, sending up plumes of white smoke.

"R-Rin?" Dumbfounded, Haruyuki called her name for the third time. But he didn't have the time to say anything more. From the startlingly close distance of ten meters, the massive American motorcycle charged forward, front wheel lifting slightly.

To his left, Fuko's car. On his right, an enormous SUV. With nowhere to run, Haruyuki stood rooted to the spot. And *wham!* Mercilessly, the bike knocked him down—more precisely, sent him flying.

Not knowing which way was even up anymore and still without the mental reserves to remember to take up a passive posture, he hit the ground on his back several meters to the rear. *Crash!* Sparks shooting up as he bounced, Haruyuki saw the gray tire closing in on him once more.

Wham! Crash!

Wham! Crash!

The combination of the sound of collision and the sound of his fall echoed another two times in the vast underground parking area. The third time, instead of landing on his butt, Haruyuki sprawled out on his back, arms and legs splayed, head spinning from the physical impact and the mental shock.

When the silhouette appeared looming above him in the sky, he cried out, "Wh-whoa!"

But then the enormous, descending rubber ring—the front wheel of the motorcycle—slammed into his stomach. Pressed down by the machine's overwhelming weight, he couldn't actually move, although he could flail his arms and legs frantically. Thanks to the three direct hits and the current crushing, Haruyuki's health gauge had already decreased nearly 40 percent.

She says she's always liked me and then she treats me like this?! Or does she take after Master and this is some kind of violent expression of love?! These thoughts raced through Haruyuki's mind a little late in the game, while a meter and a half or so above him...

The skull-faced rider straddled the seat of the American bike, arms crossed, and spoke in a hoarse voice that both did and did not sound like the real-world Rin Kusakabe.

"You scrawny little craaaow...You dare lay a hand on my baby siiiiiiis!"

"Wh-whaaaaaaaaa—?!" Haruyuki shouted.

As if he could sit there and not shout it.

The real-world person moving the duel avatar that leaned over with the machine, flames of fury burning brightly in the eye sockets of the skull face, was supposed to be the sister, not the brother. Hadn't Rin said that? That her brother, the young ICGP rider Rinta Kusakabe, had been in a coma in a hospital bed ever since a crash two years earlier?

In which case, naturally, it was impossible for him to dive into the Accelerated World as a Burst Linker. And to start with, it was definitely the sister, Rin Kusakabe, who had directed and accelerated with him after falling on top of him in the backseat. Of course, he hadn't actually confirmed through whatever means that she was really the junior high school girl he saw before him—and it wasn't as though Rin herself had declared that she was a girl—but still, in this situation, it was just too absurd that Ash Roller would be denouncing him for "laying a hand on his baby sis!"

"Uh, uh, y-y-you're Rin…right?" Haruyuki asked with a groan, enduring the weight of the front wheel as it made the Armor on his chest squeal and creak.

To which the century-end rider's response was, "'You're Riiiiin'? Damn, man. Who said you could go calling my baby sis by her first name?! Way too soon for second names—nah, third names! Daaaaaamn!"

The opposite of "first name" is "last name."

This was normally where he'd toss off a retort like that, but this was definitely not the time for that. The anger he saw in the rider far surpassed the domain of role-play. Somehow, the personality inside Ash Roller was clearly not the sister, Rin, but the brother, Rinta. So Haruyuki figured he should assume that all the fights in the Accelerated World, the cursing, and at times, the talking had all been with the older brother.

So then that meant…this was a so-called split personality? When the girl Rin Kusakabe dove into the Accelerated World, she switched over to a second personality produced from memories—recollections connected with her brother?

While these thoughts developed in his mind at super-high speed, his health gauge was squeaking down to the halfway mark from the large load damage and finally turned yellow. Instantly, Haruyuki heard, in the center of his back, *it* howling once more with displeasure. *Uh-oh.* If this kept up, the Beast he had managed to put to sleep for a while after rampaging against Iron Pound and Green Grandé in the Unlimited Neutral Field would wake up. Before the duel, Rin had stated her intention to appease the Armor of Catastrophe by putting her own self forward, but he couldn't actually let her do that. First, he needed to escape this crushed state and get into a situation where he could at least *talk* with Ash.

"Uh, uh, uuuuuuuh, Ash— No, big brother!!" Haruyuki called out almost in a trance, as he struggled to try to lift the massive tire with both hands. "Th-th-th-th-that, Rin—I mean, your sister! Um, uhhh…"

If the personality of the girl existed inside the century-end rider above his head, then maybe he could call her out and get her to take over somehow. The moment this plan cut through the jumbled circuits of his mind, a strange conversion process was executed, and:

"P-p-p-p-p-please let me marry your sister!!" The cry jetted from Haruyuki's mouth.

Ash Roller's eyes flashed red. No, they burned. "What. Did. You. Say?"

"Ah! N-no, um, it's, what I'm trying to say—"

"Shuuuut iiiiit! Shaddaaaaaaaap!!" At the same time as Ash's words rang out, sounding like a battle cry, he uncrossed his arms and clamped his hands down on the handlebars. He revved the V-twin engine and the fierce sound of the exhaust echoed in the parking garage.

"You! Made! The rage radiator of my mighty self overheat right into the red!!"

From the mouth area of the skull helmet, white steam jetted up with a sizzling sound. Or at least that's what it felt like to Haruyuki.

Flames stretched out from the dual exhaust, and the front wheel pinning Haruyuki down reared up high. If he took another direct hit from it, his health gauge would drop into the danger zone. Not letting this chance slip by, Haruyuki shook both arms and legs, but the backside of his avatar had been embedded ten centimeters into the concrete floor, and he couldn't pull free.

"Ah! Ah! Wait! Stop! Just a moment!!" The last bit in English. Although there was no reason his panicked cry would reach the older brother in the throes of rage at this stage, no matter the language.

The fat tire descending with a roar was on the verge of smashing Haruyuki's helmet to pieces when it suddenly changed trajectories and crashed into the hood of the German luxury car parked immediately to the right. The rusting panel was crushed flat, and a brilliant pillar of flames rose up from inside. It quickly went out, but the flickering embers reflected in the chrome plating of the car reflected Ash's body, as he snarled in a slightly subdued tone, "You know I'm all two-mountain here. I wanna do this with ya."

After thinking a second, Haruyuki nodded to himself as he got it. *Oh, two mountains—"yama-yama."* A direct translation into English of "very into it."

"Damned crow. I s'rsly owe you now for back there in the Unlimited Neutral Field. So I'mma let you off here. But but! You come near my sis, and next time, I'll make roast crow—naw, chop you up and make a stew outta you! Comprenez-vous?!"

"I—I—I—I—I understand! Yes, sir!" Reflexively reaching for politeness, Haruyuki pulled himself out of the him-shaped indent in the floor before finally taking a breath. He stared hard at the skull mask of Ash Roller, who was returning the bike wheel to the ground.

After a moment of indecision, Haruyuki felt like he had to ask, at the very least. Thus, still sitting on the floor, he took a deep breath and opened his mouth.

"So then…Um, Ash. Just…who are you, anyway?"

Haruyuki and Ash Roller lowered themselves side by side onto the hood of a desperate-looking, huge American-made sedan enshrined a little ways off. The timer in the top of his field of view was already down six hundred seconds—ten minutes. The fifteen minutes until the unlocking of the emergency lock he had set after flying out of the house in the real world was very nearly up. If he was going to put some distance between him and his Legion members, and settle things with the Armor of Catastrophe on his own, he needed to run out of the underground parking lot right then and there, and head off to the condo grounds.

But Haruyuki had no intention of leaving the duel field until the mysteries contained in this Burst Linker Ash Roller were revealed. He couldn't say this wasn't partly out of simple curiosity, but that wasn't the whole story. After his "greatest rival," the one he had dueled and won and lost against countless times in these eight months since he had stepped into the ring of the Accelerated World, was revealed on this other side in the real, he felt he had an obligation to try to understand the situation as best he could.

Fortunately, the Beast was still lightly dozing, leaving Haruyuki's body to himself. As long as he didn't fight any more than he already had, it wouldn't wake during this duel. As he set himself down on the left side of the wide hood, swinging his legs a little, Haruyuki very patiently waited for Ash to speak.

Finally.

"So like, this is just Master Raker's guess, 'kay?" The slightly abrupt nature of the words shook the gloom of the Century End stage. "Like, maybe the memories us Burst Linkers have of fighting and talking like this in the Accelerated World, like, none of 'em are stored in our actual brains."

"H-huh?! If our memories aren't saved in our brains, then where exactly do they...?!" Baffled, Haruyuki shouted out this much before clamping his mouth shut. He opened it again and ever-so-timidly gave voice to his thoughts. "Is it...in the Neurolinker...maybe?"

"Yup. 'Course, not the lock, stock, barrel, everything. Just, like, a part like the key, something you need to replay the whole pile of memories, that's not in your brain but in your Neurolinker. Or that's what Master's thinking, anyway."

Haruyuki took a moment to digest what Ash was saying, and then immediately shook his head back and forth. "B-but that doesn't make sense. I mean, then we wouldn't remember anything about the Accelerated World when we took our Neuro-linkers off."

"Take our Neurolinkers off? But, Crow, where does it come off?"

"Y-your neck, of course."

"Ding, ding! Your neck. Not your head, not your brain. Those little machines, they're *wirelessly connected* to our brains." Ash Roller stopped and tapped on the crown of his own head, the top of his helmet, with leather-gloved fingers. "Totally true, it won't start or signal or anything unless you got it strapped to your neck, right? But, like, that's 'cos it measures distance from your brain or your spine and locks up. You know something? I didn't know until Master came and told me. But before the Neurolinkers went on sale, this big experimental machine, Soul—something or other...But that thing could connect to a brain ten meters away."

"T-t-ten meters?!" Stunned once more, Haruyuki flapped his mouth beneath his silver mask.

If that were true—and if that capacity existed in the current Neurolinkers, there was no need to equip the machine neatly at the medulla oblongata. Couldn't you just put it on your arm or your chest or even just in a pocket or bag, somewhere easy to carry around, take it on and off?

I mean, for someone sweaty like me, it's so hot in the summer, I hate it. I keep putting all those inner pads in the mesh, but they just get soaked, and when I was in elementary, they used to call me "Ari-duh the Sweat Cloth" and tease me so hard...

"N-no, not just that." Kicking the sad memories out of his brain, Haruyuki earnestly set his thoughts back on track. "Umm. So, so, then that means— Is this what you're saying, Ash? Even when we take our Neurolinkers off our necks, they're secretly communicating with our brains, and so we can replay our memories of the Accelerated World? Is that it?"

"That's Master's theory, at least. But, like...There's no other real way to explain why I'm here like this as me right now, y' know."

Haruyuki swallowed hard and timidly confirmed in a hoarse voice. "So then...you really aren't Ri—I mean, Rin Kusakabe's older brother, the former ICGP rider, Rinta Kusakabe...are you?"

The answer took at least a full ten seconds to come back to him.

"Dunno." Ash Roller stared down at the leather gloves on his hands, studded with dull silver rivets, finally opening and closing them, backs turned up, as if testing out how they felt. "Like they say, 'I got no clue.'"

This was a slightly unexpected reply. Because hadn't he definitely referred to Rin as his little sister before? Haruyuki's doubtful eyes upon him, the rider connected his words in faltering groups.

"At least...I got no memory of being a charmed, cursed GP rider in the real world. Actually, I have zero memories of anything before I became a Burst Linker. My very first memory is... watching this duel avatar fight awkwardly."

"Huh? W-watching? From the outside?"

"Yup. In that first duel, the one making this thing move was definitely my baby sis, that kid Rin. And then I watched her from close up. Not the Gallery, man. Whaddayacallit, like a guardian spirit? I was right up close, all see-through, kinda floaty."

Unconsciously, Haruyuki froze with a start. As he glanced at Ash Roller's skull face, the sort of thing that would make a kid cry if they saw it, a hoarse voice slipped out of him. "A—a ghost?"

"N-no way, man! I'm no legless ghost! I got two long and hella cool legs, don't I! I mean, if I didn't have no legs, I couldn't brake or shift or nothing!!" The heels of the black riding boots kicked at the front bumper of the American car that doubled as their bench, and the rusted license plate peeled off and fell to the floor before shattering into polygonal pieces and disappearing. "A-anyway. In the first duel, I was just floating there, thinking, what the hell's this kid Rin fumbling around like that for? That was the very first thought of me sitting here talking with you now. I watched her control the bike, just awkward as hell, and, y'know, I could hardly stand it. I came up and got on behind her, like, I was gonna tell her, this is how you ride a bike, man. But then before I knew it..."

"You became one?" Haruyuki asked timidly, and Ash shook his helmet slowly.

"I...Honestly, I don't actually get what exactly I am, man. All I know's the one who made this duel avatar is my 'little sis' Rin Kusakabe. So that prob'ly means I'm Rin's 'big bro,' yeah? But like, what the hell is his deal, y' know? Is Rinta Kusakabe, sleeping in a hospital somewhere all this time, connected to her Neurolinker super-long-distance, talking to you like this? Or am I, like, a virtual personality the kid Rin made up to fight in this world? I think about it all the damned time, and I get nowhere..." A small sigh.

Swinging tough boots back and forth like a little kid, the mysterious rider continued his monologue. "If the virtual personality thing's right, then, like, that means this person I am doesn't really exist. But, like, Crow. I think that way's seriously better, y'know?"

"Huh? Th-that's—I mean, if that's—then, at some point..." *The Ash Roller of this moment might disappear.*

Haruyuki swallowed the words in his mouth, but Ash seemed to have heard them loud and clear.

"That works," he said, almost whispering as he nodded slightly. "I mean, look, if I am the real Rinta Kusakabe...then, like, that means that even though my dream of being a champion rider burned up and vanished in an accident, I can't give up on those tires—the ashes, they gotta roll, so I'm, like, using my baby sis Rin's mind—nah, man, her soul, right? Like, age-wise, I totally ain't qualified to be a Burst Linker, but here I am taking my sis over, wheeling around all super caz on my bike in the Accelerated World, yeah? And that's craptown, man. Like, she...she should have her own road to race down, y'know."

Ash started to bring a tightly clenched fist down forcefully onto his own knees. But Haruyuki reflexively caught his wrist with his right hand.

"No. That's not it, Ash." He shook his silver helmet from side to side several times. "It's not like...we're fighting here in the Accelerated World to make up for things we lost or dreams we gave up on in the real world. We're doing it to face our own scars and weaknesses, and accept them so we can move forward again. That's what we're here for. Regardless of whether or not you're the real Rinta Kusakabe, you exist right here, right now! You exist, and you've had hundreds of duels with me and other Burst Linkers! That alone...Those memories at least can't be fantasies or illusions!"

Although he was the one talking, Haruyuki wasn't too sure of the point he was trying to make.

Maybe this Burst Linker Ash Roller was a sort of miracle produced by the combination of Rin Kusakabe, a girl who adored her comatose older brother, and the Neurolinker that the older brother Rinta had used. In which case, because of the inherent instability of the miracle, he might at some point stop being the him he was now.

But...be that as it may, that didn't change the fact that his opponent in his first fight, his first loss, his first win as Silver Crow, was Ash Roller. That at least was absolute.

Not knowing how to further put into words the things filling his heart, Haruyuki simply held tightly on to Ash's wrist.

The motorcycle rider didn't pull his arm back or push him away, but just silently stared at the hand of Silver Crow holding his own wrist. The hand that no longer had the slender, weak fingers of the past, but evil talons instead.

"I...Before, in the Unlimited Neutral Field, I was ready for total point loss." Abruptly, a quiet voice. "The attack power of Olive Grab and those other five guys was overwhelming. I mean, even if I'd been up against Olive alone, I prob'ly wouldn't have had a chance. I was trying to at least let Utan get away somehow, but I couldn't do that, either. And I was thinking, *Are we both gonna disappear from the Accelerated World here?*"

"But, like, it's one thing for me to disappear, when I don't even know, like, whether I existed to begin with. But when I thought about U finally waking up, and even Rin, who's somewhere in this avatar disappearing, I just hated it, y'know. But, like, then you came along. Even though you had to know that if you summoned the Armor of Catastrophe, who knew what'd happen to you...Still, you called that armor and rescued me and U with that power. That time, man...It was like, however it happened, me getting to be a Burst Linker, getting to fight in this world, I was lucky, yeah..."

The century-end rider had never once before dropped his wild and easy attitude before, and seeing him faltering however slightly here, Haruyuki felt a sharp pang in his heart again.

Ash swiped his right hand across the nose area of his skull mask, seemingly embarrassed, and his tone was back to normal as he continued, "That kid U, he said the same thing before we left through the portal. Said to say thanks to Silver Crow. And... 'Sorry, ya get me?' Looks like he finally gets it, too. That, like, strength isn't something someone can give you, yeah?"

"That's true. Strength only comes from the process...losing over and over, forced to crawl, but never giving up and always looking up at the sky...the proof of strength," Haruyuki murmured, as if sucked in.

Then Ash Roller twisted around the hand held captive by Silver Crow to catch hold of Crow's wrist. Unwilling to have his own hand stared at now that it was transformed into those talons,

Haruyuki reflexively tried to shake it off. But the black leather glove held fast, not budging an inch. Ash Roller stared at Haruyuki with serious eyes from behind the skull shield.

"Right. Master taught me that, too. But, like, Crow, I could say the same thing to you right now, man."

"Huh? Me, right now?"

"Yeah. You're thinking you can't cut the Armor of Catastrophe from your duel avatar anymore, man. Just charging in to finish things off by finishing yourself off with it. Yeah?"

Ash's words were so on the mark that all Haruyuki could do was nod slightly. Even while they were here like this, his spine tingled with the premonition that the Beast would wake up from its light sleep and try to run wild. If he awoke as the Disaster, Haruyuki might furiously attack Ash Roller. The only reason he was able to hold it in check and keep that from happening was because this was not the Unlimited Neutral Field, the Beast's true hunting ground. And because there was no desire to fight in Haruyuki's heart.

However, this precarious equilibrium could break down at any moment. If, hypothetically, Ash Roller launched just one serious punch filled with real enmity, Haruyuki—no, the *Beast*—would likely react. And each time he became the Disaster, the fusion grew deeper. He didn't know where the point of no return was, but he had seen the example of the former Disaster, Cherry Rook; he knew it wouldn't be too long before the Armor started to interfere mentally with Haruyuki Arita in the real world.

Which was exactly why Haruyuki had locked the door of his house and run off by himself. If the real Ash Roller, Rin Kusakabe, hadn't caught him in the middle of the shopping mall, he would be flying into the Unlimited Neutral Field from some dive café somewhere right about now.

Perhaps picked up on Haruyuki's thoughts, Ash hung his head for a moment. But he soon lifted his face again. "Crow," he uttered in a quiet, but firm voice. "It's not like I don't get you thinking like that. But, like...It's more like this? Like, turning into Chrome Disaster is one part of the process, man. I mean, the Armor lives in you, sure, but I can't help thinking that it's only part of the process, right? 'Cos you can break this curse going on forever in the Accelerated World. So, like, that's why you were chosen. You could think of it like that."

The instant he heard these words, deep in his ears, someone's voice came to fleeting life from off in the distance.

It's all right. I know you can do it, you of all people. You're the one I've been waiting for all this time...

But Haruyuki closed his eyes beneath his silver mask and tried to wipe the voice from his memory. It was a baseless hunch, but he felt like the girl who had once spoken those words to Haruyuki didn't appear when the Beast was excited. Which meant that unless the Armor of Catastrophe could be returned to its seed state, he wouldn't see her again. And that was probably already impossible.

I betrayed her expectations, too.

Chewing on this bitter awareness, Haruyuki murmured, "It's too bad, but...I don't think I'm the one who can break the curse of the Catastrophe. I...When I saw you and Utan being attacked by Olive Grab and them, I felt this intense rage at your attackers, more than any desire to go help you. And, filled with that rage, I summoned the Armor. I moved on without waiting for you guys to regenerate because I probably would've attacked you if I had stayed there. Being able to talk with you normally like this is probably a one-in-a-million miracle."

Even after Haruyuki closed his mouth, Ash Roller showed no reaction for a while. After nearly ten seconds, he released Silver Crow's wrist and brought the leather gloves of both hands together between his knees.

"Just like how my sis—how Rin doesn't have any clear memories of the Accelerated World, I only have this hazy idea of what the real her's doing or thinking in the real world." The words spilled out from the mouth of the downcast helmet.

Haruyuki couldn't even begin to guess at what logic allowed

the two minds of Rin and Rinta to coexist, so he stayed silent and opened his ears to that voice.

"So, like, I don't actually know what Rin was thinking—what she wanted, challenging you to a direct duel. And she prob'ly didn't expect this, either. I mean, she shouts the acceleration command, and the instant she lands in the duel field, control of the avatar shifts to this personality—to me. So basically, there's only one thing I can do right now." Ash Roller cut himself off here and turned his entire body toward Haruyuki, on the hood of the car.

With his right hand, he slowly raised the skull-patterned helmet shield. The "bare face" of the duel avatar that appeared from within had narrowish, pale-green eyes and a design somehow reminiscent of a delicate boy. With that face before him again, Haruyuki could indeed see a faint resemblance to the real-world Rin Kusakabe.

Haruyuki's eyes shouldn't have been visible from that side, but Ash stared into them with his own unmasked eyes, and then lowered his head deeply. "C'mon, you damned Crow," he said quietly. "Silver Crow. Don't go vanishing from the Accelerated World. You're...hope. For Master Raker, who entrusted you with her dream of flying in the sky, and the members of Nega Nebulus, restored and growing stronger bit by bit, of course...but also for the hundreds of Burst Linkers who've dueled you up to now. Win or lose, they looked up at you flying forever like a bird in the sky of the stage."

"Hope," Haruyuki repeated in a voice that was not quite a voice.

"Yeah, hope." Ash nodded, head still lowered. "Still, I mean, it's not like we're putting all this...whatever, expectations, on you—like, you'll prob'ly get to level nine, you'll beat a king or whatever. Your wings are a unique power in the Accelerated World, but, like, no one thinks it's some cheat, or a fake-out or whatever bending the rules of 'same level, same potential.' You...I dunno..."

His hoarse voice paused for a moment, before quickly continuing again. "We're the same, you know. We started at level one, not knowing left from right, gradually getting stronger, sometimes on the verge of total point loss, sometimes getting crushed... And then when we're totally kicked down and we sit down on the ground, we look up at the sky and there you are. Barely avoiding snipers or missiles or whatever, hands thrust out in front of you, you're up there flying as hard as you can. And, like, in the evening, the light of the moon reflects on that shiny silver body, and it's all...glittering brightly up there...Heh-heh, what am I even talking about?"

Ash Roller clenched his right hand and rubbed his own face roughly. Head obstinately still hanging, he continued to speak, albeit falteringly. "Anyway...When I see you up there flying, I feel like yeah, I can still fight a little. And it's not just me, man. In the Hermes' Cord race that time, all those hundreds of people in the Gallery who saw you Disasterfy, the reason they all decided not to say nothing, it's 'cos everyone believes in you. They believe that you...you won't be beaten by something like the Armor of Catastrophe, you'll break free of the curse and all that, and then you'll get back up in the sky, all happy like you do. So...so, like..."

Here, the biker finally lifted his face. The pale-green eyes were a little wet with drops of hazy light, and he could see that those eyes were very much like those of Rin Kusakabe staring at Haruyuki about to cry in the real world.

"So don't give up, Crow. You can't be thinking about disappearing in some corner of the Unlimited Neutral Field with the Armor. You got Miss Lotus, Master Raker, that big blue one, the noisy green one...You got so many friends counting on you, man. You disappear like that, what'll your Legion buddies think? I mean, the ton of Burst Linkers who been staring up at you flying all this time, what'll they think, you know?!" Ash Roller half shouted and hung his head again deeply.

But...

But if I keep going like this and completely become Chrome

Disaster and start slaughtering other Burst Linkers at random…it won't be just me; even my precious friends could end up with bounties on their heads, Haruyuki murmured in his heart, unable to produce a voice.

At the meeting of the Seven Kings the previous week, Nega Nebulus deputy Sky Raker had responded thusly to the threatening manner of the whip-bearing Aster Vine, acting deputy for the Purple Legion, Aurora Oval: Dissatisfaction with the six major Legions and the stagnation they brought to the Accelerated World was growing among Burst Linkers belonging to small and midsize Legions. If the major Legions were to set out to crush the traitor Black Lotus and her Legion through any means, the dissatisfaction smoldering in the Accelerated World would catch fire.

The senior members of the major Legions were most likely aware of this risk. Thus, until that time, they hadn't been able to take the plunge and put bounties on the heads of Haruyuki, Takumu, and the others simply for the reason that they were Black Lotus's subordinates.

But it was a different story if the sixth Chrome Disaster came out of the Black Legion. The kings could give some reason like Lotus was trying to use the Armor to expand her own military power, and thereby put a bounty on the heads of all the Legion members. If they wanted to try and avoid that, Kuroyukihime, Takumu, and the others would have to subjugate Haruyuki with their own hands. Just like the Red King, Niko, giving Cherry Rook, the fifth Disaster, the Judgment Blow while she cried…

It was precisely because Haruyuki loved his friends that he didn't want to thrust such a choice upon them.

"I mean, I—I don't want to disappear from the Accelerated World with everything still half-finished—the Legion's objective, my own leveling up, everything," he muttered, squelching the conflict and the even greater resignation filling his heart. "But once I lose control of the Armor, once I'm not me anymore, it'll be too late. Probably, the Burst Linkers who became Chrome

Disaster before this, they all thought at first that they could control this power. That they'd get used to the Beast raging and they could use the incredible power for justice, for their friends. But... in the end, they were all taken over by the Armor. They attacked a ton of Burst Linkers at random. They ended up not being able to even tell their friends apart, until finally, they were put down like dangerous animals by the kings and vanished from this world."

He paused for a short breath and stared at his hands, transformed into sharp talons. "And...disappearing like that, only the host Burst Linker leaves the Accelerated World. The Armor itself is transferred to the storage of one of the subjugators or it parasitizes them with a seedlike part, and lives on. And then...this cycle of Catastrophe that's been going on so many years is still not broken. Someone else will turn into the next Chrome Disaster and spread the same pain and suffering. The only way I can put an end to it here is if I, someplace in the Unlimited Neutral Field far, far away, where no one ever goes, go into total point loss up against an Enemy, and secretly disa—"

Skreek! The earsplitting sound of metal tearing interrupted Haruyuki.

It was the sound of Ash Roller punching through the hood of the car that served as their bench with his clenched fist.

"Ah! Ash—"

"Then...I'm coming, too."

The strangled words stopped the movement of Haruyuki's mouth.

"Your wings get bad mileage. You won't get too far with 'em. Mighty me here'll let you up on the butt of my bike. To Hokkaido, Kyushu, wherever you wanna go. But, like, going all that way, it's gonna be a real pain to get back to Tokyo. You gonna take the poison, go all the way to paradise, right? Maybe I'll hang out with you and your Enemy? Heh-heh! You and me, like it or not, we're stuck with each other. Gotta see your ugly mug from the very beginning to the bitter end. Not too bad, I guess."

At the same time as Ash Roller stopped with his feigned cheer, hot liquid spilled over from Haruyuki's eyes. Uncontrollably shedding virtual tears beneath the mirrored silver helmet, he shook his head over and over. The voice he earnestly pushed out of his throat warbled thinly, like that of a small child.

"That's…Ash, you don't need to…come with me and disappear, too…I mean—"

"What you're saying is exactly that, you know!!" the biker shouted, his own voice also damp, and grabbed on to the Armor around Haruyuki's neck with the hand he pulled out from the hood of the car. "So you disappear with the Armor of Catastrophe and peace returns to the Accelerated World?! There's no effin' way they all live happily ever after!! You seriously think about how much your parent, your pals, Master, and the kid Rin, too—how much they'd cry and suffer and blame themselves?!"

"So then…" Even if it was a Normal Duel Field, it was dangerous for Haruyuki to get too worked up. And although he knew that, he couldn't stop himself from shouting out the fierce, almost maddening emotions sweeping over him. "Then what am I supposed to do! I keep going like this and fuse with the Armor, I stop recognizing my parent, my friends, I go on a rampage in the darkness, spreading catastrophe, and in the end, I get put down! Are you saying *that's* how it's supposed to end?! If that's what's going to happen, then right here, right now, while I can still be me…"

It's better if I disappear.

Before he could spit these words out, Haruyuki had a shock like a bolt of lightning and swallowed his breath.

It's the same thing. What I'm saying is exactly what Takumu was saying yesterday.

Like Haruyuki, he had been parasitized by a dark power—in Takumu's case, the ISS kit—and with that awesome power, he had massacred the members of the PK group Supernova Remnant. And then, fearing what he would turn into, he had planned to end things by his own hand.

And Haruyuki had told Takumu: "Don't lose—fight. For me, for Chiyu, for everyone in the Legion, fight the ISS kit."

If he gave up on everything here and disappeared alone in the wilderness of the Unlimited Neutral Field, everything he said then would become a lie. And even if he did get rid of the Armor of Catastrophe, the menace of the ISS kits currently blanketing the Accelerated World would remain. Haruyuki had acquired a certain amount of information about where the main body of the kits was thought to be—Tokyo Midtown Tower—and the Legend-class Enemy Archangel Metatron guarding it. He had to at least tell everyone in the Legion this.

But…if I see them all again, I…I know I won't be able to keep running. What should I do? I…What should I do…

"Fight it. Don't give up; hang on until the last thread." The voice echoed abruptly in his ear. Ash Roller's voice, his hand still on Haruyuki's chest armor. "Grit your teeth and fight it 'til the end, just like when you fought me the second time. Crow, you can do that. You're that kinda guy; that's why Rin fell for you… I'll kill you if you touch my sis, but I'll kill you even more if you make her cry."

Haruyuki slowly let out the breath he'd been holding. And smiled, just a little. "That's kinda impossible, you know."

"Shut up. That's what being a big bro's about, y'know!" Ash shouted, seeming embarrassed somehow, and lightly shoved Haruyuki away.

They looked up at the timer in the top of their field of view at the same time; before they knew it, more than 1,700 seconds had passed. In about a minute or so, the duel would be over.

Since Haruyuki's health gauge alone had decreased, Ash Roller moved his hand to request a draw, but Haruyuki pushed it back down.

"I earned a lot of points back there in the Unlimited Neutral Field. This is my treat."

"…You can treat all you want, but I'm still not letting you touch Rin."

"I—I won't touch her!"

After a bit more of this back-and-forth, Haruyuki suddenly remembered something and straightened up. "Oh, right. Ash?"

"...Whut?"

"Um, before, you said your name meant 'spinning tires burned and turned to ash,' but I...I think it's a little different."

Shifting his gaze, he looked over at the large American motorcycle a little ways off. The front and rear tires were indeed not the black of synthetic rubber but a gray somehow reminiscent of metal or ceramic. But there was no sense of the brittleness of embers.

"For me, your name means 'rolling up the earth, swallowed in flames, and turned to ash to create a new path.'"

For a while, Ash Roller said nothing in reply. Finally, he snorted briefly and filled Haruyuki's ears with the same old abusive language. "Dang, that's like some kinda slash-and-burn farm style, man. Totally not the style of supercooooool mighty me! Whatever, I can take it. I ever meet you in the real, I'll toss you a hundred yen for the idea."

"Th-thanks."

That "in the real," however, was probably not the younger sister, Rin Kusakabe, but rather this older brother they weren't sure actually existed or not.

And then the flaming letters TIME UP!! blazed up over that not-very-promising thought.

The duel ended after a full thirty minutes—1.8 seconds in the real world—and the first thing Haruyuki felt upon returning to the real world was a mysterious peace in his heart.

To speak of what he had actually done during the duel, he had only been hit three times by Ash Roller's motorcycle, and then they had simply sat on the hood of an American car and spoken intently. They had talked about some pretty important things, but they hadn't actually come to anything like a conclusion. Haruyuki still basically had no idea what he should do now.

And yet the frustration and remorse—and despair—that had been sweeping through his heart before the duel had calmed, if only for the moment. Eyes still closed, Haruyuki stayed submerged in the gentle warmth filling his body.

A few seconds later, he finally realized that this sensation was not a psychological illusion or false electronic information, and his body froze with a start.

The high-quality elasticity pushing up on his back was the leather of the rear seat of Fuko's beloved car. He was lying on his back there. And on top of him was something soft that smelled good. A sensation a hundred times more alluring than that of the material of the Italian car's interior leather upholstery, an exquisite ratio of elasticity and plasticity.

Very timidly opening his eyes a crack, Haruyuki looked at the ivory knit fabric glued to his own stomach. More precisely, a summer sweater with the badge of a school he didn't know. Even more precisely, the upper torso of a girl the same age as he was, wrapped in that sweater.

"Ngh." A small noise like a hiccup slipping out of him, Haruyuki nervously shifted his eyes upward. A thin, checkered ribbon tie. Slender pale neck and metallic-gray Neurolinker around it. Tapered jaw like a young boy's, thinnish lips, a subdued but solid bridge of the nose. And then two eyes, irises tinged with a light gray.

The girl with her entire body on Haruyuki's—or rather, the girl who pushed him back, XSB directing cable still clutched in her right hand—murmured from extremely close range, eyes as wet as possible as always, "I-I'm. Sorry. My brother. Said so many rude..."

"Uh, uuuummmmm." Darting his eyes around in the great confusion brought about in him by the physical situation and the linguistic information, Haruyuki tried at any rate to cope by producing some kind of voice. "Um, uumm, first, so, you...Do you remember the duel just now?"

He was pretty sure she had said before that she ended up in

a trance of sorts during duels and didn't really remember the details. In other words, the personality that dove into the Accelerated World switched to her "brother," and so no vivid memories remained inside her. Or at least that was what Haruyuki had supposed was happening.

But the girl—the true identity of the Burst Linker Ash Roller, Rin Kusakabe—nodded her head sharply. "Right now. I can still. Remember it. While I have this—my brother's Neurolinker. Equipped."

"O-oh, you…can…"

Perhaps sensing the many questions stuffed into Haruyuki's brief reply, Rin blinked her wet eyes and added by way of explanation in a faint voice, "I. Don't know, either. If the brother that appears in the Accelerated World is my. Real brother. Rinta Kusakabe sleeping in a hospital in Shibuya Ward. Or. If he's a fictional personality I created. But Master. Said to me. There's definitely meaning in the things that happen in the Accelerated World. She says that if I keep fighting together with my brother. As Ash Roller, someday for sure. I'll find a very important answer."

"…You will…"

Rin hadn't actually clearly stated whether the Master she spoke of was the Fuko Kurasaki Haruyuki knew. But listening to her now, Haruyuki became sure of it. Fuko was a Burst Linker who, according to Kuroyukihime, was a "pure positive Incarnate user"—that was to say, a Burst Linker who believed more strongly than anyone in the power of hope and bonds and love. There was nothing more fitting for Fuko to say than this very line.

In other words, the customer who had coolly laid these truths out at the table for Rin when she was working part-time in the hospital cafeteria last summer had indeed been Fuko Kurasaki. Her house was actually near the border between Suginami and Shibuya Wards, and it wouldn't have been strange for her to go to a hospital in Shibuya for maintenance on her cybernetic legs.

Convinced they were talking about the same person, Haruyuki nodded and Rin stared into his eyes. A veil of tears once more covered the drops of gray in her own, and breaking the limits of surface tension, the droplets spilled out and onto his cheeks.

"...Why."

"Huh?" Frozen in place, Haruyuki was unable to understand the meaning of her murmured word.

"Why," Rin asked again, face contorted. "Didn't you attack. Me? Even though I challenged you. I thought. I was okay with you hunting me. With disappearing. Even though. I thought I could do something reckless and. Subdue the Armor of Catastrophe possessing. You."

At these unexpected words, Haruyuki swallowed his breath for a second.

Right. Rin had actually said that immediately before she challenged him to the direct duel. That she would make the Armor disappear, that she would take all his rage and hatred. And it could have really turned out like that, if the duel had played out differently. There had been the possibility that regardless of whether or not the Armor disappeared, Haruyuki would have rampaged and taken Rin on with all the attack power he had.

However, when cool big bro Ash Roller hit hard immediately after the duel started with his you-dare-lay-a-hand-on-my-babysis bit, he had completely taken charge of the duel, and there had basically been no chance for the Beast to wake up. It wasn't like he had planned to yell about that, but now that Haruyuki thought about it, that attitude was really the heart of the countless Ash/Crow battles up to that point.

"I can't hunt you." Haruyuki shook his head gently, an unconscious smile on his face.

"What..."

"I mean, like, Ash is an important...friend." He chose his words carefully.

"...Friend," Rin repeated, turning her half-sobbing face toward him.

Haruyuki picked out the slightest note of dissatisfaction and hurriedly followed up. "Y-yeah. Very important. So, like, even if...I end up controlled by the Armor and totally turn into Chrome Disaster..." He pushed out the words that contradicted his early thoughts as his throat threatened to close over on him. "Don't let Ash do anything reckless. I...I like that guy."

Instantly.

Twice the tears, somehow a different color now, welled up in Rin's eyes. Her small face moved as though trying to catch up with the several drops that spilled over, and smacked into Haruyuki's left cheek. Words riding hot breath poured into his ear.

"I...I'm so happy. That you met. The real me. I was afraid you'd think I was creepy. And I was in a different Legion. So I could only. Fight you in the general duels. And in the Territories...But. That you would...say that to me now..."

She pressed herself more closely against him, and the sensation, alongside its warmth and sweet smell, almost sent Haruyuki's thoughts out of his head.

Even in this situation, the last threads of his reason remarked that the next time they met, Ash was definitely going to kill him, but regardless, his right hand escaped his conscious control and lifted itself up, moving in to touch Rin's slender back—

"Please say what you said before one more time." The murmured voice in his ear stopped his hand cold.

Hurriedly scrolling back through his memory, he replayed the scene in a hoarse voice. "Um. Ash is an important friend?"

"After that."

"So I would totally never hurt you or anything?"

"After that."

"And he's someone I—"

Knock, knock. The hard sound rang out abruptly, quietly.

Eyes half out of focus, Haruyuki turned his gaze absently above his head. He first saw the door panel to the left behind him, and then the rear window came into view above that. Although he was pretty sure the transitional privacy glass had been in maximum shield mode a few minutes earlier, at some point, it had become completely transparent.

And on the other side, smiling quietly, was a woman with long, black hair. She turned the finger that had tapped on the glass and at the same time as she operated the holowindow, the doors unlocked with a light sound. The back hatch was immediately pulled open from the outside, and the woman leaning her top half into the vehicle smiled once more, directly above Haruyuki as he lay back on the seat.

"I'm so glad to see you again, Corvus ♡," she said.

Instantly, Rin, lying on top of Haruyuki facedown, shuddered.

Similarly frozen in place as he pulled a tight smile onto his face, Haruyuki managed to squeeze out a reply to the girl—the deputy of Nega Nebulus, Strong Arm Sky Raker herself, aka Fuko Kurasaki.

"Oh. Y-yeah. Me...too..."

It's okay, it's still okay; this is still not the level of crisis you have to run away from! Because the very person who had ordered Rin Kusakabe currently and admirably holding Haruyuki down was Fuko, and it wasn't impossible for her to decide to interpret this situation as a logical extension of her own order, and in the end if they could talk about it, she would totally understand—he was completely sure of it. For sure.

Haruyuki let his thoughts run off earnestly, forgetting that he himself had tried to literally run away from everyone in the Legion.

However, immediately after that, Chiyuri popped up from Fuko's left and visually confirmed Haruyuki's current status.

Imagining a red overlay flaring up from her feet, Haruyuki shifted his gaze to the door on the opposite side, ready to open it and escape. And there, on the other side of that window, he discovered his Legion Master standing with her arms crossed, and he froze utterly and completely.

Chak! Kuroyukihime opened the door on the right side and bent forward, her special attack "Kuroyukihime's Ultra-Cold Smile" ripping across her face for the first time in a long time.

"Perhaps we're interrupting, Haruyuki?" she said.

Being a young man praised for having reaction abilities of the highest level among Burst Linkers, the response Haruyuki managed to calculate and deliver with all the force of his neural circuitry was the following.

"...I-it's not what you think."

6

The place was once more the living room of the Arita home on the twenty-third floor of the condo. The time was 7:40 PM.

Since Operation Castle Escape had started at exactly seven o'clock that day, June 20, 2047, this meant not even an hour had passed in the real world. But for Haruyuki subjectively, it felt as though he had accumulated several days' worth of events that he still hadn't processed.

The escape from the Castle and Suzaku's fierce attack.

The search for and discovery of Ash Roller. Summoning the Armor, the slaughter.

The encounter with the two members of Great Wall. And yet another battle...

When he had absently retraced his steps to that point, as he sat plopped down in one corner of the sofa set, a mug of café au lait was set down before him, accompanied by a "Here you go."

"...Th-thanks..." He thanked Chiyuri in a small voice and picked up the steaming mug to bring it to his lips.

"Ah! Hawwwwt?!" The instant he sipped at it, the overboiled, scorchingly hot liquid burned his tongue, and Haruyuki cried out in pain.

But Chiyuri, sitting on the sofa opposite him, touched her own café au lait to her lips with a feigned ignorance. "Oh my, I beg your pardon," she said crisply.

Somehow, the cups distributed to everyone else were a suitable temperature, and Haruyuki's alone had been given plenty of heat in the microwave. But only Takumu clucked his tongue and shook his head with a wry grin at this targeted maliciousness; Kuroyukihime, Fuko, and Utai Shinomiya simply turned silently toward their own cups.

This was not because Haruyuki had locked them all in the house and run off alone, or even because he had summoned the Armor of Catastrophe. It was because of the presence of the seventh person, clutching the hem of his T-shirt tightly with her right hand while she sat to his left, on the verge of tears as always. From the time Fuko had pulled her off him in the underground parking lot until she was brought up to the twenty-third floor in the elevator and sat down on the sofa, she had not let go of Haruyuki's shirt.

If, hypothetically, this had been the Red King, Yuniko Kozuki aka Niko, Kuroyukihime would have instantly shouted, *Quit fooling around and let go!* and might actually have even attacked physically. However, when her opponent was a weak-looking girl who constantly sniffled, tears in her eyes, even the Black King apparently hesitated to take action.

Only the sound of Haruyuki blowing on his cup broke the urgent silence.

Finally, Chiyuri set her own cup down. "Leeeeet's see," she said in a voice that was half groan, rubbing her temples with the index fingers of both hands. "I don't understand the situation yet. Actually, I just can't accept it."

Lifting her face, she stared hard at the girl to Haruyuki's left—the girl sitting directly across from her. "Are you really Ash Roller? *The* Ash Roller? The hya-ha-ha-haa-mighty-me-mega-luckyyyyy Ash Roller? The Ash with the missiles on his motorcycle?"

Chiyuri was slightly overemphasizing one aspect in her description, but still, the girl—Ash Roller's real-world self, Rin Kusakabe—nodded clearly. Rin had already switched out her brother's old metallic-gray Neurolinker for her own pastel-green one. If he were to believe what she said before, she already could no longer remember the details of the duel with Haruyuki earlier. But even still, she was apparently fully aware of what kind of Burst Linker she—or her brother—existed as in the Accelerated World. Tears dampening both eyes, she apologized in a thin voice.

"Um, I'm sorry. On the other side. I'm always saying so many. Rude things."

"Y-you don't have to apologize. I talk pretty bluntly in the duels, too."

Unconsciously, Haruyuki and Takumu both bobbed their heads up and down, and once she had frozen the awkward pair with her eye laser, Chiyuri continued. "But—I'm not sure how to put this. I'm just a little surprised because I've never seen anyone so different between here and over there before. I mean, I can't believe you can be a girl in the real and have a male-type avatar."

The instant he heard these words, Haruyuki this time made momentary eye contact with Fuko, who was seated on the love seat to his right.

Since he hadn't explained to Chiyuri and the others Rin's special circumstances, the only people there who knew all about the girl and her brother and the two Neurolinkers were Haruyuki and Rin's parent, Fuko. He took the look in her eyes to mean they would watch for the time to explain it all, and so abruptly opened his mouth.

"Th-that's just 'cos there's over a thousand Burst Linkers. It's not so weird to find someone who seems like an exception sometimes."

Chiyuri turned her hard stare on the girl once more, and then looked away abruptly. "I guess so. Like someone who's all nervous and shy in the real world like this, but then gets all carried away in the Accelerated World and charges on from one thing to the next!"

"Unh!" He reflexively ducked his head at the unexpected attack. As he sipped at his coffee, finally cooled enough to drink, his brain worked at top speed. His plan to escape alone and resolve this himself was ruined, and given that he had been caught again like this, he wouldn't be able to shelve the matter forever. He should at least bring it up himself and apologize. In which case, maybe this was that time.

Haruyuki set his mug down on the glass table in the center of the sofa set and sat up straighter as he took a deep breath. He looked again in turn at the members of his Legion—Kuroyukihime sitting on the far left, Chiyuri and Takumu across from him, Fuko on the right end, and Utai tucked in to his immediate right because of space concerns—and then yanked his head down.

"Um, about what I did there, I'm really sorry. I don't expect an apology to get you to forgive me after all this, but—"

"Do you actually understand why we—why *I* am angry, Haruyuki?" The clear voice that rang out belonged to Kuroyukihime, who had been silent this whole time. Her fingers intertwined as they rested on her knees, and the swordmaster and Legion head stared at Haruyuki with jet-black eyes.

"It's not because you summoned the Armor of Catastrophe and released the sealed Chrome Disaster. Everyone sitting here already understands that you had to do that to save your friends. But you...you shook off the words and hands we reached out to you and tried to punish yourself alone. If...if you had managed to carry out that plan and disappeared to the edge of the Unlimited Neutral Field along with the Armor..."

Her voice trembled the slightest bit, and Haruyuki felt something squeeze his heart. He unconsciously clutched at the fabric of his T-shirt above his chest.

Kuroyukihime blinked once, slowly, before turning slightly

more reflective eyes on him. "Did you really think that we would have been able to continue fighting without you? You, who never once thought to leave us, not Chiyuri held prisoner by Dusk Taker, not Takumu infected with the ISS kit, not Fuko about to give up on her dream of the sky, not Utai sealed away on Suzaku's altar—and not even me, hiding in the depths of the local net for two years! Did you really think that we would just cut you loose and forget you?!"

Her voice gradually increased in volume to become a sharp sword piercing Haruyuki's heart. But that stabbing was not a cold pain; instead, a sweet, sad, and warm throbbing spread out to fill his chest.

Biting his lip, head hanging, Haruyuki pushed back the self that tried to cling to that gentle rebuke. "I'm sorry," he apologized once more in a shaky voice, and quickly continued. "But…but the Four Elements of the old Nega Nebulus and you, Kuroyukihime— Two years ago, you tried to throw yourselves away to protect your friends in the Legion, didn't you? You tried to let the other Legion members get away by putting yourself alone into a state of unlimited EK on the altars of the Four Gods, didn't you? I— Before, I thought the time for that had come for me, too. I thought everyone in the Legion would end up with a bounty on their heads…and I wanted to avoid that at any cost, at least."

"What are you talking about, Haru?! Only yesterday, you told me that rather than sitting and brooding alone, I should believe in my friends and reach out a hand!" Takumu half shouted.

Chiyuri, next to Takumu, gently held him back with a hand. His childhood friend's eyes were completely different from the earlier superpowered fire beam, this time gently urging Haruyuki to continue.

"Sorry, Taku," Haruyuki earnestly muttered. "I actually remembered that earlier when I was direct-dueling with Ash—I mean, Kusakabe." He turned his face back to Kuroyukihime. "And at the end of the duel, Ash said to me that if I was gonna go disappear in the Unlimited Neutral Field somewhere, he'd come with me. And then I realized it: When you lose all your points in the Accelerated World and are pushed to a forced uninstall, it's only you who has all your memories related to Brain Burst erased. So, like, um..."

He struggled with how to express this precious thing that he had realized, but here his language processing engine reached its limit, and Haruyuki simply moved his mouth and his right hand.

"In other words, the death of a Burst Linker doesn't belong to the person themselves." From his right, a quiet, calm voice finished his thought—Fuko. "That's what you mean, yes? Because the Linker forgets they were ever part of Brain Burst, along with who they met in the Accelerated World, what they experienced there, what they were aiming for...Because of that, what really dies...is the him or her inside the people around them, close to them. Only the comrades, friends, and lovers of the person who disappears continue to carry on knowledge of this 'death' in their hearts, in their unlimited accelerated time."

"...Yes." Haruyuki nodded deeply, slowly, and started speaking his words himself again. "That's just it. Which is why...I had the thought that it's actually impossible to begin with, the idea that you alone disappear—it's actually not possible in the Accelerated World. Even if I snuck off somewhere and disappeared after losing all my points to an Enemy...at that time, really, the me that lives inside the people around me I care about would disappear, and that would make a scar, or a hole that size..."

Kuroyukihime kept harsh eyes on him, and he met them first out of the corner of his eye, gradually coming to look directly at her as he spoke his heart in full.

"Which is why I don't think that me alone disappearing will fundamentally resolve anything. Because I know now that it might hurt you all about as much as if I became the Disaster and you had to come hunt me. But...but..."

He clenched his hands into fists as they sat on his knees.

"Making the Armor of Catastrophe disappear again before the meeting of the Seven Kings on Sunday now that I woke it up is probably—no, ninety-nine percent impossible. After fighting with it in the Unlimited Neutral Field, I'm sure of it. The Armor's already completely one with Silver Crow. And not just that. I— At this stage, I might already be getting mental interference from the Armor. I mean—I…"

He was aware that his friends had all opened their eyes a little wider. And he announced to them what he felt himself immediately before he was forced to burst out, when he had been about to set out on a wandering journey together with the Armor of Catastrophe—or rather, the Beast that lived in the Armor.

"I…had the thought that I didn't want to erase it with some outside method. If that had to happen, then…at least I wanted to disappear with it. That's what I thought." Eyes completely downcast once again, Haruyuki bit his lip hard.

UI> Arita. By "it," do you mean the Armor of Catastrophe as an object? Or is it something or someone else? Utai Shinomiya asked him gently, in the chat window, as she sat pressed up against him immediately to his right in the narrow space.

"…That's…" After hesitating awhile, Haruyuki resolved himself and explained.

About the two consciousnesses that lived inside the Armor of Catastrophe. The mysterious girl with the canary-yellow armor inside the original Destiny. And the savage instinct to fight that lived within the Enhanced Armament Disaster, that a twisted fate had given rise to—the "Beast."

"Chiyu also met the girl, and so I think it's pretty clear that she's not a dream I had or some kind of delusion."

"Yeah." Sitting across from him, Chiyuri nodded sharply. "Although I think the world I went to with Haru and Taku, the Brain Burst central server itself, might have been a dream. But the girl we met there was definitely not. I mean, she told us so much stuff that me and Haru didn't know."

"Hmm. A Burst Linker's consciousness lodged in an object. Or perhaps it functions as a pseudo-intelligence. Considering the power of the Armor to interfere with the mind, it's not impossible," Kuroyukihime murmured, a thoughtful look on her face. The dangerous edge in her eyes had faded somewhat as she turned her gaze on Haruyuki again. "Haruyuki. Which was it that you felt you didn't want to disappear? The unknown female-type duel avatar who helped and guided you? Or the Beast that spurs you to fight?"

"...Both— No, maybe...maybe the Beast," Haruyuki muttered, dropping his eyes. "The girl wants the Armor to be completely eliminated, to cut short the cycle of catastrophe that's been repeating in the Accelerated World. So if I disappeared with it, I don't think she'd be sad. And...the Beast wants to erase all Burst Linkers other than itself. Of course, I think that's basically nuts. But if we take what we were talking about before, about a Burst Linker's death, and apply it to what the creature wants...each time it hunts someone and dispatches them from the Accelerated World, it ends up squirreling that death away in its own memory. If it ended up the last Burst Linker in the Accelerated World like it wants...it would be carrying the deaths, the extinctions of a thousand Burst Linkers, on its shoulders. So, like, the Burst Linkers that disappear would live on inside its memory alone. So then, what on earth does it... why would it...?"

Drops of water fell onto his clenched fists. He finally realized that they were falling from his own eyes, and he hurriedly moved to rub his face with his right arm.

Two seconds faster than him, Kuroyukihime leaned forward; slightly ahead of her, Chiyuri was about to offer the nearby box of tissues, but an instant faster than even that, Utai was pulling a handkerchief out of her pocket. But the one who moved even more quickly than these three was the seventh person, sniffling to Haruyuki's left—Rin Kusakabe. She soaked up the tears collecting on Haruyuki's cheeks with the sleeve of her ivory summer sweater.

"It's lonely," the girl in the same grade remarked, in a fairly weak voice. "By yourself. No one. Should disappear. All alone."

"...Oh, yeah. That's, um." Haruyuki naturally froze, but Kuroyukihime, Chiyuri, and Utai all also stiffened up with their own individual expressions on their faces.

What got things moving was a word from the gentle Fuko. "Rin?"

With just that, Rin Kusakabe jerked her body back up to its original position, but as if making some sort of statement, she clutched at the hem of Haruyuki's T-shirt in the same way again.

Still with a complicated look on her face, Kuroyukihime leaned back into the sofa and cleared her throat lightly. "Haruyuki. These feelings of yours...I don't believe that they come from mental interference from the Armor of Catastrophe as you say. Because that is so like you, so like what the Haruyuki Arita I know would say."

Chiyuri, Utai, Takumu, and Fuko all nodded together.

"And thus, I don't believe the possibility of purifying the Armor is completely out of the question. Haruyuki. Just once is enough. Will you give me—will you give *us* a chance?"

Purify.

The word meant that they would burn the Beast together with the Armor of Catastrophe, with the special abilities of the shrine maiden of the conflagration Ardor Maiden—Utai Shinomiya. At this point, the power of Utai's Incarnate, which had melted and buried the protector knight of the Castle's inner sanctuary in a massive pool of magma, went without saying. With her of all people, it might have been possible to selectively burn away—no, to *exorcise*—the Armor, even if it had completely fused with Silver Crow. They had indeed taken great pains to get Ardor Maiden back from Suzaku's altar to carry out that purification to begin with.

But. The Haruyuki of that moment could not be sure that this was really the only correct solution. He couldn't remember the details now, but in the distant past—at the dawn of the Accelerated World—there had been a very sad, cruel incident involving that golden-yellow girl, a metal color that looked a lot like Haruyuki, and the layered avatar calling himself the vice president of the Acceleration Research Society, Black Vise. The metal color, stained with an excessively deep despair, had caused the Arc Destiny and the longsword Star Caster to fuse and given birth to the Armor of Catastrophe, the Disaster.

The Beast, the pseudo-intelligence that lived in the Armor, reacted violently to the memory of this incident and had once even caused a negative Incarnate overflow within Haruyuki in the real world. That was proof that this incident was the source of the Catastrophe, enacted over and over in the Accelerated World. What exactly had happened in the past? Was it really all right to just eliminate the Armor and the Beast without knowing—no, without properly *remembering*, that?

Of course, if he went back into that unknown past—in other words, into the memory of the Beast itself—he would experience even more intense mental interference than he had already. Surpassing even the stage of "fusion" and reaching into "control"— Haruyuki's personality might disappear entirely. The fact that he was struggling like this might itself have been proof that this interference was already progressing.

As Haruyuki hung his head and bit his lip, a small hand reached out from his side and wrapped itself around his right hand. At the same time, text typed out one-handedly was displayed in his view in a cherry-pink font.

UI> Arita. The true purification ability I have is not a destructive fourth-quadrant Incarnate like I used in the Castle.

"Huh? So then...?"

UI> There is absolutely no physical attack power. It

CANNOT BREAK A DUEL AVATAR, NOR AN ENHANCED ARMA-
MENT, NOR AN ENEMY, NOT EVEN A SINGLE TERRAIN OBJECT.
WHAT MY FLAMES BURN IS...THE SO-CALLED "CONNECTION." IT
SELECTIVELY PURGES ONLY THE INFORMATION ROUTE CONNECT-
ING THE PARASITIC BODY AND THE HOST. THUS, THE TARGETED
PARASITIC OBJECT IS SIMPLY CUT AWAY, Utai Shinomiya replied,
a calm smile slipping onto her face.

"It's cut away...without disappearing...," he parroted, and then
shook his head slightly with a "But..."

"But...in that case, even if it works, the Armor of Catastrophe itself will remain in the form of a sealed card again. Right?
If someone takes that card, or we sell it in the shop, or even toss
it into the bottom of the ocean, I know it will call out to its next
host again. Kuroyukihime, the card items, they're..."

When Haruyuki turned his gaze on her, Kuroyukihime
guessed at the implied question and nodded. "Mmm. Impossible
to destroy, without exception. The most certain method of dis-
posing of a card currently known is to feed it to a Legend-class
Enemy with an affinity for item loot...but I can't say that that is
actually foolproof."

A heavy silence filled the living room, illuminated only by the
indirect orange lighting.

Breaking this silence was a faint alarm announcing that it was
eight PM. There was still time before Haruyuki's mother came
home, but it was about time for everyone to be getting home,
especially Utai, who was still in elementary school. Regardless of
how great the problem facing the Legion, the fact remained that
in the real world, they were all students and thus constrained by
various rules.

They did have the option of diving into the Unlimited Neutral
Field to continue talking there or to try Ardor Maiden's purification. But there was one little snag. Because Haruyuki had burst
out with a forced disconnection safety—in other words, his cable
had been yanked out—if he dove into the Unlimited Neutral

Field, he would appear alone on the roof of Mori Tower in Roppongi Hills, far away from this condo. And even that would have
been fine if he could have immediately exited normally through
a portal, but if the mental interference from the Armor began
soon after he dove, Haruyuki himself didn't know what would
happen after that.

"We'll continue tomorrow...yes?" Fuko, the Legion deputy,
said quietly, perhaps thinking the same thing. "We have to first
safely reset Corvus's position information."

Haruyuki had previously explained that he had disconnected
in Roppongi Hills, right before he fled from his friends and this
very room. Yet he still had a mountain of information to share
with them, even though he wasn't able to completely process
his memories inside his own head. He needed to reexamine the
exchange he had with the pair on the roof of Mori Tower—the
Green King, Green Grandé, and the third seat of the Green
Legion's executive group, the Six Armors, a Linker known as
Iron Pound. His memories themselves also needed time to clear.

His Legion Master, Kuroyukihime, looked around the room.
"We in Nega Nebulus made significant progress today," she
announced in a clear voice, "because we managed to bring back
Utai—Ardor Maiden, one of the former Four Elements, from
the altar of a God, a place believed to be impossible to escape.
Although after that, there was a slightly unexpected incident..."
Here, she glanced over at Rin Kusakabe—who continued to
clutch Haruyuki's T-shirt—but then merely cleared her throat
before continuing, "It is an unquestionable fact that Silver Crow's
hard work contributed greatly to the success of this operation.
Haruyuki, that's why it's our turn now to work hard for your
sake. I can understand your indecision and fear. But please. Give
us just one chance."

She repeated her earlier words, turning earnest eyes on him, and
beside her, a small figure pushed forward: Utai Shinomiya, clad in
a white dress-style uniform. She bowed her head neatly, which set

her ponytail swinging, and tapped decisively at the air with both hands.

UI> ARITA. WE NEED YOU. THE FACT THAT I WAS ABLE TO RETURN TO NEGA NEBULUS—THAT I COULD ESCAPE FROM THE STATE OF UNLIMITED EK THAT STRETCHED ON FOR TWO AND A HALF YEARS—IS ALL BECAUSE OF YOU. AND THE REASON I AM HERE RIGHT NOW IS TO CUT THE TIE THAT BINDS YOU TO THE CATASTROPHE. PLEASE. I WANT YOU TO GIVE ME THE CHANCE TO FULFILL THE ROLE I AM TO TAKE.

Finished typing, she squeezed her small hands together at her chest. Fuko, Chiyuri, and Takumu all nodded deeply. Finally, Rin Kusakabe, sitting to his left, tugged lightly on the shirt she still held.

Haruyuki shook slightly, with a momentary yet fierce conflict.

Trying Ardor Maiden's purification meant, in other words, diving into the Unlimited Neutral Field again at the same time as his beloved Legion comrades. In the worst-case scenario, his thoughts would suddenly be under the Armor's control, and it was possible he might attack them without a word. Naturally, however strong Chrome Disaster might have been, Haruyuki didn't think he could simultaneously fight all five members of Nega Nebulus with the Black King at the lead and win. But Kuroyukihime and the others would be forced to choose whether or not to neutralize—no, to push him to—a forced uninstall with the Judgment Blow.

And that was something he didn't want. No matter the cost.

Haruyuki lifted his eyes and looked at Utai and Kuroyukihime in turn before nodding slightly. "I…understand. And I'll ask you guys, too. Please use your power to end the cycle of catastrophe I can't escape. Shinomiya, Kuroyukihime…everyone."

"Haru, are you really okay by yourself tonight? Maybe you should stay over at my place or at Taku's?"

Chiyuri repeated this worry at least five times, and Haruyuki sang his part in the duet, assuring her each time that he would be fine, he *was* fine, while he saw everyone to the door he was still fine, he was fine.

Fuko yanked Rin Kusakabe by the collar of her shirt, forcing her to release Haruyuki's clothes. Rin shoved her feet into her loafers before turning around again. "Um," she said. "The sushi you gave me. Was. Really good."

"Oh! Th-then you should tell Chiyu—Chiyuri Kurashima. Her mom made it," Haruyuki replied.

So Rin turned around once more and bowed her head at Chiyuri, who was already out in the shared hallway. "Thank. You. Very much."

"…It was really nothing. Although I guess I'm not the one to say that…"

Chiyuri returned the bow at a subtle angle, and an even sharper doubt rose up on her face, as it did with Takumu, who stood next to her. Except for the brief self-introduction immediately after they had dragged Haruyuki and Rin to the Arita home from the underground parking area, they had hardly spoken to her, so they were probably still having trouble accepting the theory that Rin = Ash Roller. Haruyuki could relate.

Nonetheless, there was definitely an indescribable air of master and apprentice to Rin and Fuko, as Rin pulled her head in meekly and Fuko clutched the collar of the girl's cardigan. Since Rin would also be part of the operation to purify the Armor of Catastrophe—which they had elected to start the following evening at seven, once more in the Arita home—all of them would get another chance to poke at her and ask her all kinds of invasive questions. This, of course, came with a rather large *if*—if the operation actually succeeded.

Master and apprentice stepped out into the hallway, and once Utai followed them, Kuroyukihime slowly slipped on her shoes. She took a step forward before whirling around to look at Haruyuki. Her lips trembled as though she wanted to say something, parted slightly, and then quickly closed again. After a pause,

Haru's beloved swordmaster let a faint smile rise up onto her lips. "Sorry for always, always making use of your house as Legion headquarters. I hope you don't mind that we're doing it again tomorrow."

"No, not at all. It's totally fine. But isn't it actually tough for you and Master going home?"

"Ha-ha! I'll get a ride from Fuko again today, so I'm fine. Everyone should have an adult friend."

The look on Fuko's face changed slightly behind her, and the others laughed briefly. They then took two steps back, facing backward, and stepped out into the hall.

"So we'll see you tomorrow, Haruyuki."

"Right. See you tomorrow."

The gently closing door hid the faces of Kuroyukihime and his friends, and separated the inside of the house from the outside. The sound of the automatic lock scraped the air. He waited until their footsteps had receded and disappeared before trudging back into the living room.

Chiyuri had taken the large plate with the *chirashi* sushi and *maki* rolls on it, so Haru just had to wash the coffee mugs and return them to the cupboard with the dryer function. He wiped the dining table and the glass table, set the chairs straight, and turned on the AI vacuum cleaner.

Back in his own room, Haruyuki opened his homework app and focused on tackling the math and English problems. Once he had taken care of both, he looked up at the clock and saw that it was just past nine. His mother still wasn't home. On days when she hadn't come back by now, she usually ended up home closer to midnight. Haruyuki accessed the home server and opened the family message board. After thinking for a minute, he typed out a short note…

I'M GOING TO STAY AT TAKUMU'S HOUSE SINCE WE HAVE A GROUP PRESENTATION TO WORK ON. I'LL BE BACK EARLY TOMORROW MORNING.

Naturally, this was a lie. And it was a lie to both his mother and his friends. In fact, it was perhaps a lie that betrayed all the members of his Legion. But he was sure that in the event that his mother did call Takumu to check up on him, he would very neatly corroborate Haruyuki's story.

He hit the ENTER key of his holokeyboard with a stiff finger, cleared his virtual desktop, and stood up. He changed out of his house clothes into baggy camo pants and a printed T-shirt. He put on a cap, slid into some sneakers in the entryway, and opened the door.

The shared hallway seemed even darker and quieter than it had been a mere hour ago. It was only to be expected, but in the space illuminated by LED tubes, there was not a trace of his friends passing through earlier on their way home. Still, Haruyuki took a deep breath and tried to fill his lungs with the air they had all breathed before stepping out of the entryway. Behind him, the lock on the door of the now-deserted Arita house shut tight, along with a small electronic sound of raising the security level.

The reason Haruyuki was going out by himself at this hour was slightly different from when he had locked his friends in and run off. Then, he had intended to slip into the Unlimited Neutral Field from a nearby dive café and lose all his points to an Enemy at the ends of the earth.

However, Rin Kusakabe, Fuko's "child," had blocked his flight with her body in the shopping mall on the first floor, and Haru-yuki had rethought things after talking with Ash Roller, who said he was Rin's brother, in the duel field. He could disappear all on his own, but that didn't fundamentally resolve the problem. And he couldn't do that anyway, not when Takumu had been in exactly the same situation the night before but had still heard Haruyuki out and held his ground.

Just like Takumu, I have to believe in my friends—in the bonds of the Legion, Haruyuki decided somewhere deep in his heart. So the solo excursion he was about to embark on (at a time of night not particularly appropriate for a junior high school boy) was not intended to result in his death in the Unlimited Neutral Field. He wouldn't have had to go to the trouble of leaving his house for that; he could simply shout the "unlimited burst" command from the comfort of his own bedroom.

Haruyuki's objective was outside Suginami—in fact, outside the twenty-three wards of Tokyo: the city of Musashino, spreading out to the west. Of course, it was fully equipped with the social camera net, and thus was a part of the Accelerated World, but it was deserted. Almost no Burst Linkers lived or went there. And he was heading out to his wilderness because he wanted to check if he was still himself even when he dove into the Unlimited Neutral Field.

The worst thing he could imagine happening in the purification mission the next day was him going on a rampage immediately after they dove and attacking his Legion comrades. Even if he assumed Kuroyukihime and the others would be prepared for that, they might decide they could control Chrome Disaster, but Haruyuki couldn't take such an optimistic view of the situation. The sixth's battle ability—being able to use all of the abilities of preceding Disasters—was his own power, but even he couldn't see its depths. Especially the Flash Blink ability left in the Armor by the first Disaster. That was dangerous. This technique rendered physical constraints completely ineffective and turned the user into particles for teleportation. If Haruyuki, one with the Beast, was able to freely control it, it was possible that Nega Nebulus, which lacked anyone with the indirect abilities of yellow-type avatars, wouldn't be able to handle him completely.

Idly considering the possibilities, Haruyuki got on the elevator at the twenty-third floor. The car slipped smoothly downward as he continued along this train of thought.

He could not turn into a crazed Beast and assault his friends in the next day's purification operation. The only way to avoid this tragedy was to dare call up the Beast in the Unlimited

Neutral Field, talk with it or fight it, and gain the right to a certain amount of control. And if he was going to do that, he had to get out of Suginami. If, hypothetically, his plan failed and he was completely taken over by the Beast, Haruyuki—no, the sixth Disaster—would first try to assault the Burst Linkers who made their homes in Suginami. For the same reason, he wanted to avoid Nerima, Nakano, Shinjuku, and Shibuya to the east. But in Musashino to the west, no matter how he might rampage, there were no targets to begin with. If he tried to hunt anyone, he would need to return to the real world through a portal and then take a train or something. During that time, his head might cool, even if only a little.

For these reasons, Haruyuki had decided on this solo trip.

He passed through the shopping mall, where most of the shops other than the supermarket were closed given that it was past nine, and went out into the front garden laid with red bricks. This space, filled with flower beds and benches, was basically taken over by couples at night. At ten o'clock, the main gate was closed, and no one other than residents of the connected condo could pass through it, but he could see the silhouettes of young people sticking around until the last minute, sitting together on benches here and there.

For Haruyuki, this sort of thing was not interesting at all, so when he left the condo in the evening, he tried to use the residents-only gate on the north side. But the south main gate was closer to Koenji Station. Thus, he pulled the brim of his cap down over his eyes, tucked his shoulders in, and tried to pass through the garden at a brisk pace.

"Have a seat."

The voice came from the bench immediately beside him. Startled, he came to an abrupt halt and froze, eyes still fixed forward.

The tone was masculine, but the voice was clearly female. He couldn't mistake that voice, with its silky smoothness, the clarity of melted snow, the sharpness of a whetted knife.

Haruyuki creakingly turned his head seventy degrees to the right, a movement like a gear-driven doll.

Seated on the bench, the swordmaster he had parted from only an hour earlier was looking at him, smiling calmly. Obsidian eyes, black like deep space, announced that they had seen right through him.

7

I never thought the day would come when I—me!—would be sitting with a girl on these benches. And past nine at night! Of course, we probably totally don't look like boyfriend and girlfriend. At best, older sister and younger brother. At worst, the girl lost a dare...

As these thoughts raced through his mind, five slender fingers reached out from beside him to squeeze his left hand sitting on his knees. At the same time, a voice.

"This way we don't look like we're brother and sister. Shall we direct to make extra certain?"

It was almost as if she was reading 80 percent of his thoughts. "N-n-n-n-n-no," Haruyuki squeaked. "Th-th-th-th-th-this is fine." It was likely a wise decision not to add that there remained the possibility that she appeared to be there on a dare.

What was fairly scary was that Haruyuki's current situation could be completely laid bare if Chiyuri were peeking straight down into the garden using night-vision binoculars from the Kurashima house on the twenty-first floor of B wing, which was soaring up above his head. But maybe he was seriously over-thinking this. But he couldn't underestimate her animal-like instincts. He couldn't completely deny the possibility of her suddenly wanting some of the tofu banana au lait (with tapioca) that was only sold at a vending machine in this plaza and coming down to buy some…

"We're not doing anything you'd feel particularly guilty about if Chiyuri or Takumu happened to see, are we? Or is it all right for you to have spontaneous sleepovers with them, but I don't have the right to sit alongside you on a bench?"

"N-n-n-n-n-n-n-n-no. Th-th-th-th-th-th-th-th-th-th-that's not it at all."

If he allowed any additional information to leak out of his brain in this exchange, things would get extremely not good. So Haruyuki cut off his evasive thoughts and finally turned his eyes toward the girl sitting next to him—the Legion Master of Nega Nebulus, Haruyuki's parent, the Black King, Black Lotus aka Kuroyukihime.

To begin with, he timidly gave voice to the biggest question. "Um. I thought you were going to get a ride home from Raker? So then why are you…?"

"Mmm. Well, a simple reason. Fuko's child—Rin Kusakabe, was it? She said her house is in the exact opposite direction as mine, in Egota in Nakano Ward. Uiui lives quite near Fuko, so that's fine, but for her to take me home as well was simply too inefficient. I declined the offer and said I would take a taxi. Incidentally, I didn't go so far as to say what time I would get that taxi, so I haven't lied to Fuko and the others."

"O-oh, right. Wait. Where is your house again?" Haruyuki asked nonchalantly.

Kuroyukihime's eyebrows twitched, followed by a mischievous smile spreading across her face. "Now see here, you. Didn't you look at my student diary?"

He felt like he had heard this line somewhere before, and after a moment of confusion, he hurriedly shook his head from side to side. "I—I—I didn't look inside! And anyway, that was a long time ago!"

"Ha-ha-ha! Eight months ago, hmm? I remember it well." Kuroyukihime laughed for a while, shoulders shaking, and then finally got a look on her face as though she had just remembered something.

"By the way, Haruyuki." Her voice was quiet, and the hand she laid on Haruyuki's squeezed tightly. "I assume you're going out by yourself at this time of night to dive into the Unlimited Neutral Field in a deserted area outside the twenty-three wards. My hypothesis is perfectly correct, yes?"

She cut to the heart of the matter so suddenly that Haruyuki unconsciously bobbed his head up and down.

"Oh! B-but it wasn't to go and lose all my points by myself or anything," he added hurriedly, but Kuroyukihime nodded, as if to say she had even seen through to that point as well, and swiftly piled on another question.

"So then you left some kind of excuse for your mother for going out in the middle of the night?"

"Y-yeah. I said we had group homework and I was staying at Taku's."

He thought for an instant she might reproach him for the crime of perjury, but to his surprise, Kuroyukihime nodded coolly again.

"Mmm. Good. Then we should go." The words were no sooner out of her mouth than she was standing up, still holding Haruyuki's hand.

Dragged along, he half stood, and she started walking jauntily. Toward the condo entrance—no, the main gate to the southeast.

"Huh? Um, what exactly…?" This was the path he had originally been on, but Haruyuki couldn't quite grasp Kuroyukihime's intentions and flapped his mouth in confusion.

But the black-clad vanguard said nothing in response as she cut through the front garden dotted with couples. Without even pausing, she stepped through the gate, off the condo grounds, and onto the sidewalk of the ring road known as Kannana Street.

Apparently, she had at some point made a request from her virtual desktop, and with impeccable timing, a single EV stopped in the lane before them, turn signal winking. It was a taxi, blue lines on the white vehicle, an old-style lamp on the roof. The rear door opened automatically, and without a word, Kuroyukihime pushed Haruyuki in before slipping in after him herself. She offered a simple "thank you" to the middle-aged male driver, who responded with an "of course" as he pulled out smoothly into traffic.

In this day and age, it was normal to send the destination alongside the taxi request, which was sent via Neurolinker to cars driving in the area, so Haruyuki had no idea where they were heading. Half-dumbfounded, half-excited, he peeked out through the windshield and watched as the taxi, which had started out north on Kannana, soon turned left onto Waseda and headed straight west.

So then she's planning to go to Musashino with me? But that's no good. In the fleeting moment Haruyuki had this thought, the car turned left again, not having gone even a kilometer. They went down the residential street, slipped past the elevated Chuo Line, and went further south. In a few minutes, they came out onto Oume Kaido, and this time turned right, and then another left soon after that.

Roughly speaking, from Haruyuki's condo, they had sort of approached the direction of Umesato Junior High and then moved away from it again...or at least, that's what he thought. But their destination remained a mystery. The scene outside the window turned into a residential area again, and the greenery gradually increased. A minute or two later, the taxi stopped, hazard lights flashing.

Payment was also taken care of by Kuroyukihime with her Neurolinker, so it was invisible to Haruyuki. The driver called out a hearty "Thank you!" at the same time as the door opened. Kuroyukihime thanked him back as she got out, and Haruyuki could do nothing but follow her.

On the other side of the quietly departing EV was a sight that seemed impossible in the whole country of Japan, much less in the middle of Suginami Ward.

Stylish white-walled town houses stood neatly and evenly

spaced on excessively large plots, and the street was lined with plentiful lawns and trees. It was almost like the set of an American-made family drama, but the houses had a shared design and were by no standard large.

"Uh, um, where…exactly…?"

"Mmm. Right. You've only just started eighth grade. This comes up in Social Studies in the second term, I believe. This is a URB called Asagaya Jutaku, a condo-type housing complex with a nearly hundred-year history. It was redeveloped at the beginning of this century, but this division alone was basically left as it was."

"Uh, uh-huh." Now that she mentioned it, he did indeed get the sense of architectural cohesion in the look of the residential area, highlighted in the orange of the streetlamps. "So then, it's like a cultural heritage site?"

"Mmm," Kuroyukihime replied to the vague question. "Well, I suppose you could say that." She took Haruyuki's hand once more before starting to walk down the curving street.

Kuroyukihime, what are you trying to tell me by showing me this place? Something the me now needs—no, something important that I have to come to on my own?!

Digesting the place in his mind, Haruyuki walked alongside Kuroyukihime. The humid June air was merely depressing in the inorganic metropolitan areas, but in this place, it seemed almost refreshing, rich with the exhalation of the plants. They advanced a mere two meters or so along the two-lane road, black and wet, perhaps from a short rainfall not too long ago, and then Kuroyukihime stepped into a lane that broke off to the right.

The pavement—which made luxurious use of natural stone tiles—was just barely wide enough for them to walk side by side, and he wondered if it wasn't a public road, but rather a private path attached to a building. But Kuroyukihime did not waver in her stride. However, if they were invading private property, the residents might call the police on them. If Kuroyukihime risked even that to try to tell him something, then…

Haruyuki racked his brain so hard that smoke threatened to come out of his ears, as Kuroyukihime came to a stop in front of one of the town houses. She then raised her right hand without the slightest hesitation and pushed open the black cast-iron gate.

"Huh? What?"

They couldn't just go opening the gates to someone else's house. He didn't even have the time to finish the thought before he was given an even bigger shock, and his eyes and mouth opened as far as they would go.

Not so much as blinking, Kuroyukihime passed through the open gate and reached out toward the doorknob of the house standing neatly beyond it.

"Uh! Um! That's!" Still standing in front of the gate, Haruyuki was startled into speaking. "Wh-what are you doing, Kuroyukihime?! Y-y-you're gonna get yelled at!"

"Mm? Why? And who would yell?"

"Who? Obviously, the person who lives—"

"No need to worry about that." Kuroyukihime shrugged lightly. "This is *my* house."

"...Huh?" His jaw, already on the floor, dropped right through it as Haruyuki reeled.

"When you come in, close the gate," a cool voice instructed. "It locks automatically."

"...Okay." Any other reaction was beyond him.

A bungalow with a loft, one bedroom, a living room, a dining room, and private garden. This was the dwelling of the beautiful girl in black and her many mysteries.

After Haruyuki took off his shoes and stepped into the house in a trance, Kuroyukihime led him to a spacious living/dining area of about twenty square meters.

"I'm going to go change. Make yourself comfortable." Leaving with these words, she disappeared through a door in a wall on the west side.

Haruyuki staggered into movement once more and came to a stop in the middle of the living room, before attempting to at least gather some visual information despite the fact that his brain was at a standstill.

Given that it was a one-story house, the design was compact, but the floors and pillars were lavishly made from natural wood, and the south-facing windows were large, so there was a sense of openness. Unexpectedly, the room wasn't decked in black. The wallpaper and the ceiling were a light gray, the area rug and curtains covered in brown stripes. Furniture was on the sparse side, with a small table and a beanbag chair, plus a ladder-type rack placed up against the western wall. In the adjacent kitchen on the other side of a counter, he could basically only see a small fridge, a multipurpose microwave, and a slim cabinet. He didn't get the impression that any cooking took place in there.

The thing that drew the eye in this extremely restrained interior design was a large tank in the southeastern corner. Haruyuki moved as if drawn in by it, and peered into the aquarium lit by orange LEDs.

There were maybe twenty small tropical fish. He felt like that was too few for the size of the nearly meter-long tank; what occupied the water world instead were a great number of water plants. There were all kinds—one like a shaggy carpet, one with thin, elliptical leaves trailing, one that looked like a micro bamboo grove—but the plant that stood out had several thin, long stalks soaring from the center of the base up to the water's surface.

Since the top of the tank was closed with a lid that had devices to maintain water quality and temperature, Haruyuki crouched down and peeked up at the water surface from below, feeling like a fish gazing up at the outside world from inside the water. The dozens of distinctive round leaves floated on the water at the ends of stalks, some even seemingly stretching their heads up into the air.

He had seen the shape of these dark green leaves somewhere before. *But, I mean, I've never been interested in water plants or anything.* He cocked his head to one side and then suddenly remembered.

In the fourteen or so years of his life, there had been just one time. He had spent several days gathering information online, and then struggled for over an hour once he was actually at the shop, where he bought a marine plant that cost all the allowance he had saved up. The plant with the long stalks and round leaves he had chosen, put into a vase, and taken to a certain hospital was a tropical water lily.

"The water lily you gave me, I looked it up. It's a Lindsey Woods," a voice suddenly murmured in his ear.

Haruyuki jumped and whirled around.

Kuroyukihime had changed from her Umesato uniform into a sleeveless housedress that hung straight down, and was bending down to peer into the tank. It might have been housewear, but the dress was all black, so it had the air of a party dress somehow. Here, finally, Haruyuki's brain was jerked out of its idling, almost-stalled state and regained about 80 percent of its output, forced into an acceptance of the situation.

At this time of night, when it's coming up on ten o'clock, I am at Kuroyukihime's house for the first time, and it's just the two of us, and on top of that, I left a message at home saying I wouldn't be back today. So, like, what?! What is even happening?!

The thought flashed through his mind, but since he felt it was extremely dangerous to consider what might lie ahead, Haruyuki earnestly jumped on the information before him.

"I-it is? I—I—I—I picked it just for the color," he replied, turning back around and peering into the tank once more.

Kuroyukihime laughed. "I didn't know the name of even one ornamental lily at the time, either. I only learned about them after you gave me those flowers."

After she sustained serious injuries last fall, Haruyuki had brought a bouquet of tropical water lilies when he went to visit her on the day she was moved from the ICU to a general ward room. Of course, the selection had been connected with Kuroyukihime's duel avatar, Black Lotus, but four or five leaves other than the lily flowers had been added to the bouquet the shop clerk make for him. Because he remembered the round shape of the slender stalks, even without seeing the flower, he could guess that those were water lilies growing in the tank before him.

"S-so then, are these lilies the same as those flowers?"

Kuroyukihime shook her head, a playful—or perhaps innocent—smile slipped across her face, almost like a young child boasting. "They are indeed the same genus, but that's not all. The plants I'm cultivating here are the very flowers you gave me eight months ago. Well, more accurately, the 'children' of those flowers."

"What?!" Haruyuki was stunned, and he stared hard at Kuroyukihime's profile, illuminated by the tank lights. "B-but the ones I bought were cut flowers! I thought they wouldn't grow roots even if you put them in soil."

"Mmm. That's exactly right. But I learned after doing some research that some lilies, including the Lindsey Woods you gave me, are called 'propagule species.' They grow new leaves and roots from a propagule you can cultivate from the base of a leaf; in other words, a bud."

"Huh? F-from the leaves?"

"Exactly. After I learned this, I took a good look at the five leaves that were in that bouquet, and there was just one that had developed a bud. I got it to sprout in a pot of water, and then after I got out of the hospital, I moved it to this tank. It was actually quite some work to get them to grow to this size these last eight months. Unfortunately, it will apparently take another month or so to get them to bloom."

Surprise at the vitality of plants and a deep emotion at the trouble Kuroyukihime had gone to, her *connection* to the life of the flower he had bought, filled his heart, and Haruyuki focused his gaze on the stalks swaying in the water. Like this, they passed a few seconds, or perhaps a few minutes, in a strangely peaceful silence.

Eventually, however, Kuroyukihime leaned forward and gently touched Haruyuki's back. "Come and see them again when the flowers bloom," she said. "Now, shall we sit already?"

The beanbag chair on the rug laid out by the living room window was fairly large, and Kuroyukihime sank down into one side of it. When Haruyuki remained frozen in place, she pulled on his arm and mercilessly made him sit next to her.

The fine powder beads changed shape to smoothly hold his weight. Inevitably, his body turned toward the center of the cushion, and he slid down the tiniest bit toward Kuroyukihime, to his right. Their arms touched, and Haruyuki's consciousness once again threatened to fly off beyond the stratosphere. But Kuroyukihime lifted her right hand in a relaxed gesture and quickly flicked at her virtual desktop.

The lighting in the living room dimmed until it was just barely on, and the curtains automatically opened about a meter, while the transparency of the variable privacy glass increased. On the other side of the window, the broad-leaved trees and the lawn of the garden rose up in the restrained illumination of the street lamps, and then off in the far distance, the lights of the redeveloped high-rise housing complex glittered, almost cutting into the night sky.

It was like he was peeking into metropolitan Tokyo of the current 2047 from some long-past century. Haruyuki realized all over again that Kuroyukihime probably—no, *definitely* lived all by herself in this small town house in one corner of Asagaya Jutaku. "How long have you lived here?" he asked slowly, unconsciously.

Her reply came after a delay of five seconds or so. "I moved out of the house I originally lived in and started living here right before I started at Umesato. To put it more accurately...that would have been six months after I took the head of the first Red King with this hand."

Haruyuki swallowed his breath and thought about the meaning of her words. Actually, it was obvious without thinking about it: Kuroyukihime was telling him that she had not left home for the reason of attending junior high school in the real world, but rather because of the murder of the Red King, an incident in the Accelerated World.

But what exactly was that supposed to mean? Haruyuki understood that she had forced Red Rider into total point loss through the level-nine sudden-death rule because she was resisting the mutual nonaggression treaty the Seven Kings were attempting to conclude among themselves at the time. In other words, both cause and effect started and finished in the Accelerated World alone, so how did that connect with why she had to leave home?

"I've actually...never told anyone that before. Not even Fuko and Utai and the others..." Abruptly, Kuroyukihime leaned her head on Haruyuki's shoulder. "Red Rider wasn't the only king I hunted. I also tried to subjugate another king with these hands. And not through an ordinary duel. A physical threat in the real world. In other words, through a real attack, with violence."

"What?!" He inhaled sharply again. Kuroyukihime wouldn't even allow the use of the acceleration command during a test, and yet she had attempted the loathsome real attack—i.e., a PK. The fact that that had even been possible meant—

"K-Kuroyukihime, do you know the real of another...king?"

After a long silence, she murmured briefly, simply, "I'm sorry."

She then turned to the left and touched Haruyuki's right side with not just her head, but her entire body. Once more, his consciousness threatened to fly off at the softness and warmth communicated to his five senses, but he just barely held on again. Because this gesture of hers reminded him somehow of a young child clinging to someone and seeking protection.

"Someday...when the time comes that I can talk about it, I'll definitely tell you." Her voice was at a volume that he could almost hear, almost not hear.

Haruyuki nodded slightly. "Okay."

That was all he could manage, but Kuroyukihime clutched the hem of his T-shirt and murmured, "Thank you."

Several minutes of peaceful silence passed. Since there was nothing by way of clocks around the room, he could only check the time by looking at the corner of his virtual desktop. However, from Haruyuki's perspective, the small digital numbers were displayed on top of Kuroyukihime's chest. And apparently, these creatures known as girls had a super sense for detecting the rude gazes of boys.

Haruyuki had suffered Chiyuri's harsh verbal attacks more than a few times—"What are you staring at, Haru, you perv?!" He would have liked to have argued that it wasn't intentional eye movement, but rather a command issued by the most primal regions of his brain, but in the current situation at least, something precious would have been ruined if Kuroyukihime were to misunderstand him in any way. Thus, Haruyuki had no choice but to tackle the high-level technique of sliding his entire virtual desktop to the left, while looking down to the righ—

"That reminds me. I still haven't gotten an explanation of what you were doing."

At the sudden voice, his gaze froze with a start. "What I'm doing? N-nothing. I mean, tr-tr-trying to look at the clock."

"You can look at your clock all you want. That's not what I mean." Kuroyukihime lifted her face, pursed her lips together somewhat poutingly, and continued. "I'm talking about what exactly you were doing in Fuko's car with that Rin Kusakabe."

The attack came from such an unexpected angle with such unexpected force that Haruyuki froze again. Now that he was thinking about it, Kuroyukihime had clearly witnessed Haruyuki and Rin glued together in the backseat of the EV, directing with each other.

"Uh, um, that, well, it, Rin— I just was talking with Kusakabe in the duel field, and there was absolutely nada else to it."

"Hmmmm. Still, I feel the look on her face was incredibly emotional. Is that really all?"

Under the hard stare of her slitted eyes, Haruyuki was forced to remember, whether he liked it or not. In fact, it was hard to definitively say that was all. Rin had come straight out and bluntly told him she liked him. And there was no other way to interpret the simplicity and strength of the way she said it.

"Uh, um, uh. Oh! Really, nothing happened with *Ash*! I was trying to run off to the ends of the Unlimited Neutral Field, and he said he'd give me a ride, but that was about it, uh-huh."

That was true. Between the Burst Linker Ash Roller and Haruyuki, there was nothing other than the friendship that had grown out of their rivalry. Because the one moving that century-end rider in the Accelerated World was not Rin Kusakabe, but either her actual older brother Rinta Kusakabe or a simulation of his personality.

At this explanation, which was just barely not a lie, Kuroyukihime pursed her lips suspiciously once more. She, Chiyuri, Takumu, and Utai didn't yet know about Rin Kusakabe's special circumstances. They thought the extremely teary-eyed, weak girl had a personality flip and was doing some ha-ha-ha-*vroooom* role-playing in the Accelerated World. But Haruyuki couldn't be the one to tell anyone the truth. It should be Rin herself, or at least her parent, Fuko Kurasaki, telling that story.

Fortunately, Kuroyukihime's expression softened abruptly after a few seconds, and she pinched Haruyuki's round cheek. "Well, I suppose I should say that adding one to our numbers makes no great difference in the battle situation at this point."

"Wh-what?" She put some force into her fingertips, and Haruyuki hurried to shake his head back and forth. "Nho, hit's hine, hit's hine."

"Honestly." Again with the faintest hint of a smile slipping out, Kuroyukihime released his cheek and smoothly turned herself on the beanbag chair to stare up at the ceiling as she continued. "Even still, I was honestly surprised. To think that inside your very first duel opponent, that biker, is a girl younger than I am. Until this very day, I never doubted that he was that sort of boy in the real as well."

"Yeah, me, either."

"Well, I can accept it somewhat with Fuko being the contact point. She told us a little of the story when we were walking down to the parking area. Apparently, they met at a family hospital. It seems they just clicked at first sight. The same as when I found you."

"Uh, uh-huh. I wonder just how they clicked…"

"Mmm. Then shall I quote everything Fuko said? 'If the strength of a certain button being pushed inside me was a hundred points with Corvus, it was two hundred with Uiui, but it was a thousand with Rin. The instant I saw her, I knew I had to train her.'"

"She. Said that?" Haruyuki replied, in a hoarse voice. If she would shove him off the top of the old Tokyo Tower when he had a hundred of whatever points, then what kind of training exactly would she inflict on Rin with a thousand? Simply imagining it was frightening.

However, Kuroyukihime then added something unthinkable with a wry smile. "Incidentally, according to Fuko, I was a hundred thousand points at the time we met. I suppose I should be glad that I am not her child but her friend instead."

"Sh-she. Said that?"

Kuroyukihime and Fuko had been friends since they were both low level, so he guessed that they had probably been in elementary or junior high school when they met. He could even imagine, from looking at the current Kuroyukihime, what kind of child she had been.

"I—I wish I could have met you ages ago, too. We could've done so much together as members of the old Nega Nebulus," Haruyuki muttered to himself, and Kuroyukihime popped her head up.

Centimeters away from his face, she peered into his eyes. "What are you talking about? At that time, there would have been no points of contact between you and me in the real, so the possibility's stronger that far from Legion members, we would have first encountered each other as enemies."

"Oh! R-right. I guess so." Haruyuki began to hang his head despondently, but slender fingers held his cheeks back.

"Well, in that case, I likely would have done whatever it took to recruit you into the same army. If it really had been like that—in other words, if I had invited you to transfer when you belonged to the Legion of a different king, what would you have done?"

The question sounded like a joke, but at the same time, there was something serious hiding deep within it, causing Haruyuki to falter momentarily. However, he soon returned Kuroyukihime's gaze from a slight diagonal. "I think I would have moved to the Black King's Legion, no matter how hard I had to work," he replied. "I'm not just saying that, either. I guess Taku—Cyan Pile—got into some seriously real trouble when he was transferring from the Blue Legion, Leonids, to Nega Nebulus last fall. I keep asking him, but he won't actually tell me the details. I'm sure I'd do that, too, though. I mean, even if you weren't my parent or my Legion Master, Kuroyukihime—Black King, Black Lotus, you're my..."

He was speaking in earnest, but here he came upon the limits of his linguistic powers. If he had been typing with the text editor in his Neurolinker, the predictive engine would have displayed a list of appropriate words for him, but right now, he had to find them himself. After opening and closing his mouth several times, Haruyuki finally declared, "You're my hope."

It was how he truly felt, completely and honestly. Kuroyukihime let her gaze wander for a bit as if she was thinking, and then a smile that was half-happy, half-complicated rose up on her face.

"Hope, hmm? Welcome words. But that is the very thing I would say to you. Actually, I believe I've said it to you any number of times since we met. Haruyuki, I've told you you're the fastest Burst Linker in the Accelerated World and that someday you'll surpass even the kings and reach the source of that world. Yes. And I believe I also said this."

Here, the tiniest bit of color bled into the snow-white features of the black-clad beauty as she turned her body for the third time and wound both arms around Haruyuki's neck, pulling their bodies together.

Her cool touch, sweet, refreshing scent, and supple elasticity sent an overload signal racing through his sensory system. And then she struck the final blow.

"Haruyuki...I like you."

He was seriously on the verge of passing out at the shock, so great he could even believe some of the circuits in his brain actually burned out, but at the last minute, he managed to avoid a system outage.

"I like Silver Crow of the Accelerated World and Haruyuki Arita of the real world the same amount," Kuroyukihime continued, her words flowing into his right ear with a light sigh. "With these feelings as a guidepost, I was able to stand up once again as a Burst Linker and come this far. That itself is indeed...a true miracle, going far beyond the Incarnate System or anything like it. It seems I could do anything if it was for you, and I now believe I can go anywhere if you are holding my hand."

"...Kuro. Yukihime." It was all Haruyuki could do to murmur her name in reply. He wasn't worth anyone telling him they liked him—he was now finally able to brush aside this extremely negative self-definition, but even so, it wasn't as though that instantly made him capable of calmly accepting such a declaration.

And—although thinking about another girl in this situation was an absolutely unforgivable sin—two and a half hours earlier on that very day, when he had been glued to Ash Roller's real-world self Rin Kusakabe, that girl had also told him in the most straightforward way that she liked him. The experience of having two girls confess their feelings of affection to him one after another on the same day was nearly impossible for Haruyuki's brain to even process, much less accept.

His mind on the verge of complete burnout, he wondered exactly to what extent the law of cause and effect would have to be twisted to allow for this to happen. And then, abruptly, he understood.

It was all because Haruyuki had tried to disappear, of course, in front of his Legion comrades. In full view of his war buddies. From the Accelerated World itself. To extend a hand and hold him back, his most frequently fought rival, Rin Kusakabe, and the person he had spent the most time with, the swordmaster Kuroyukihime, were turning feelings, priceless like gems, into words and letting Haruyuki hear them.

I am a fortunate person. Is there any other Burst Linker—no, junior high kid—as fortunate as me? he whispered in a corner of his heart. The thought was, for Haruyuki, as revelatory as being reborn into this world.

All this time, he had hated himself. He had loathed himself. He had been glad of the smiles and feelings his friends— Kuroyukihime, his Legion comrades, Niko, Pard, Ash Roller— turned toward him, but he had come along thinking he didn't have the right to really respond without changing how he looked and how he was inside.

But, in that moment, for the first time, Haruyuki thought, *Maybe I'm okay the way I am.* He still didn't have enough mental energy to say so definitively, but someday...someday, the time would come when he could honestly be positive about himself...

"Kuroyukihime...I— Me, too," he murmured hoarsely, and moved to gently place his hand on her slender shoulder. But he couldn't do it. And his mouth, too, stopped before it could get any other words out.

Because *someday* might never come for Haruyuki. If they couldn't purify Silver Crow—no, Haruyuki himself, more than half-fused with the Armor of Catastrophe, he would no longer be a Burst Linker whether he went and lost all his points alone at the end of the world or he was done in by assassins of the Six Kings. And at that time, he would probably lose a large part of his memories and feelings related to Kuroyukihime, including even the sad ache filling his heart at that moment.

But even if my memories are erased, the truth can't be erased.

The fact that Kuroyukihime said she likes me. The fact that I was able to think of myself as fortunate. So even after everything is all over, these facts will encourage me and guide me. Like a gem in the palm of my hand, even if I don't know why I have it.

At this thought, two of the tears he had been trying so desperately to hold back spilled out of his eyes. They fell from the corners of his eyes onto the cheek of Kuroyukihime, pressing her head against his chest.

And then the slender arms wrapped around his neck doubled the strength of their grip. At the same time, a voice that was almost soundless said, "Haruyuki. You belong to me. I will not give up. I cannot tolerate losing you. Absolutely not."

She announced it as if carving each word into both of their hearts and slowly lifted her face. On those pale cheeks, a trail separate from the tears Haruyuki had shed glittered silver, slipping out from her own eyes. The two of them were so close, they were on the verge of touching, and her lips trembled.

"Even with Utai-class purification—with the most powerful purifying ability in the Accelerated World—it's a big gamble as to whether or not the Armor can be cut free now that it's fused with you. I crossed swords with that berserker more than once, and even I couldn't see the bottom of the darkness it contained."

Haruyuki held his breath and let the words pour into him. Kuroyukihime stared into his eyes and continued in a voice that had regained a little of its tension.

"But there is possibly one way to increase the chances of success for the purification. In a certain situation, the activation of the negative will of the former Disasters always decreased. And that was...immediately after a fierce battle with a powerful enemy. And not simply a fight to the death where hatred slams up against hatred, but a fight that could be called a true duel, an exchange of high-level techniques and Incarnate on both sides. Do you remember? When you and I and the little red girl challenged the fifth Disaster, immediately after that close-range battle we fought body and soul? He was unable to dodge Rain's main armament and was seriously injured. Normally, the Disaster would have repelled that attack with just his aura."

Now that she mentioned it, he did have the feeling that the fifth, aka Cherry Rook, seemed different at the turning point of the ferocious sword fight with the Black King. And without a reason like that, he wouldn't have tried to run away from Haruyuki, when he had only just made it to level four and didn't even know how to use Incarnate.

There was no need to even go back to the fifth. The current status of Haruyuki, the sixth, indeed supported this hypothesis. He took a deep breath before nodding twice, then three times, and opening his mouth. "Kuroyukihime, maybe that's the reason that I can be here like this as my regular self."

"Oh?"

"Um, before, I didn't really tell you all the details at the house, but I said I got into a fight with members of another Legion at Roppongi Hills in the Unlimited Neutral Field, right?" He closed his mouth for a minute and swallowed hard before announcing the rest. "My opponent was, um, a senior member of Great Wall. I guess they're called the Six Armors? Um, this level seven named Iron Pound—"

"What? 'Fists' Pound from GW?!"

"Oh! Y-you know him?" he asked.

"Do I know him?!" Kuroyukihime moved her arms while his head was still turned and yanked on his ears with both hands. "He's an old enemy of 'Strong Arm' Raker. One of the legends of the Accelerated World is how Pound knuckled under and got a flying tool just to shoot Fuko out of the air."

"Oh, that rocket punch was for that..."

It made sense. He nodded and quickly thought back: He had been told ages ago about the relationship between Sky Raker and the Prominence deputy Blood Leopard, fierce enemies on the surface and friends below it, but apparently, Raker had also dangled the Leonids' deputies Cobalt Blade and Manganese

Blade from the top of the government building in Shinjuku. And on top of that, she had also clashed loudly with the Aurora Oval deputy Aster Vine. Just how many old enemies did she actually have...?

A chill ran up his spine, and Haruyuki brought his straying thoughts back on track. When he met Kuroyukihime's eyes, a faint, wry smile crossed her face.

"So once again you happen to meet something incredible. I see," she murmured. "You fought Fists, then, did you?"

"Oh! Um, it wasn't just Pound..."

"What? Other members of the Six Armors were there, too? It couldn't have been someone higher up than Fists?"

"I guess you could call him higher-up." With Kuroyukihime still clutching his ears gently, Haruyuki ever-so-nervously gave voice to the name. "Th-the Green King, Green Grandé, was also there. And I don't know, things just happened..."

Kuroyukihime yanked hard to stretch out Haruyuki's earlobes. "Whoa," she commanded, in a fairly strained voice. "You can't mean...? D-did you fight? That shield man as well?"

"Sort of. Really, we just smashed sword and shield together once."

The swordmaster let out a long, thin breath as she released Haruyuki's auricles, which bounced back like rubber. Winding her arms around his neck once more, she stroked the back of his head. "I had intended to not be surprised at your recklessness at this late stage, but...So if you brought your sword down on it, then you got hit with the extra effect of that great shield Strife, yes? Incredible you made it out all right."

"E-extra effect? What kind of power is that?"

"The shield takes in any attack and counters with double the power. In other words, the only way to break the defensive barrier of that shield is to get rid of it in a single super, superpowerful blow, or to create gaps through endless, successive attacks and aim for the main body of the avatar. Although I have no memory of seeing either of these succeed."

"C-counter? Maybe. It did. Probably." That moment where he fought sword against shield, Incarnate against Incarnate, with the Green King as his opponent felt like the long-distant past, but even so, a chill ran through him. "But that force probably all went into the air around us. We sent half of Mori Tower flying."

"Mm-hmm. So that was that explosion, then? We saw it from the southern bridge of the Castle."

Haruyuki thought for a minute and then shook his head in tiny increments. "No. I think that was probably something else. After the battles with Pound and the Green King, another big thing happened...but I'll tell you about that after. I want to go back a bit. Before, you said that if the Armor of Catastrophe fights an intense battle with a strong enemy, its activity drops for a while, right? That's exactly where I am right now, I think. The Beast that lives in the Armor's asleep. It's drowsy because it fought both members of GW so ferociously and squeezed out the last drop of Incarnate. Which is why I could talk with R—Ash normally and why I can be here like this with you now. But at some point—no, definitely tomorrow—it's going to wake up. And then it'll try to get me to go hunting for fights. Whether or not I can resist that and stay myself...to be honest, I...have my doubts..."

For Haruyuki, being able to conclude such a long speech without stammering—and while he was holding and being held by the person he adored most in the world—was a fairly difficult task. But he was unaware of this as he finished speaking, and Kuroyukihime, who had simply listened quietly, smiled faintly, for some reason.

"Mmm. That's a wonderful theoretical analysis. I believe that's true myself. In which case, in order to succeed in the purification tomorrow, there is just one action we should take now."

"Huh? A-a-a-a-a-action...Wh-wh-wh-what do you mean?" Haruyuki stammered and spat with a force strong enough to cancel out his earlier long speech.

Kuroyukihime smiled again before manipulating her virtual desktop with quick movements.

Next to them, something gradually rose up with a whine from the natural wood flooring where there had previously been nothing. The cylindrical device, about fifteen centimeters in diameter and fifty centimeters high, was probably an integrated terminal connected to the house's home server. Normally, this device was used to control household appliances without a Neurolinker, but Kuroyukihime apparently used it in a different way. She pulled a wind-up XSB cable from the middle of the small tower and inserted the end into her Neurolinker.

"Haruyuki, you burst out because of the forced disconnection on the roof of Roppongi Hills, yes?"

At the abrupt and unexpected question, all he could do was nod dumbly.

"Mmm. Then five—no, three seconds. After I accelerate and three seconds pass, pull the cable out."

"Huh? Um. What exactly—?"

"I'll explain later. Understand? I'm counting on you. Unlimited Burst." The command was uttered nonchalantly, and then Kuroyukihime's body slumped down, lifeless.

Haru didn't know what was what anymore, but at any rate, all he could do was follow her instruction. The instant the digital digits in the lower right of his field of view increased by three, he yanked the plug from the piano-black Neurolinker.

Kuroyukihime's eyes flew open before him. "I'm back, Haruyuki," she said with a serious face.

"Um, Kuroyukihime, I have no idea what is even—"

"What do you mean? Isn't it obvious? I moved from Suginami to Roppongi Hills in the Unlimited Neutral Field."

"H-huh?!" Unconsciously, he cried out wildly. The command he'd heard earlier was indeed definitely the one to dive into the Unlimited Neutral Field. But even if it was a world where the mind was accelerated by a thousand, three seconds of real time was still a mere fifty minutes on that side. In a world where taxis and the like didn't exist, you'd have to run from Asagaya to Roppongi, and really kill yourself running as hard as you—

No, no. That's not what he should have been thinking about. The real question was why Kuroyukihime did it. And the answer was self-evident, wasn't it? To rendezvous with Haruyuki on the other side.

"Y-you can't, Kuroyukihime! Once I dive into the Unlimited Neutral Field, the Beast could wake up at any—"

"That's why," she asserted, deadly serious. "That's why we're going." She pulled a second cable out from the integrated terminal. As she brought it to Haruyuki's neck, their faces also grew closer. When he could feel her sweet breath, a voice clearer than neurospeak came at him.

"Haruyuki. While you and I are parent and child, we are also master and student. In which case, at some point, *the time* definitely comes. And that time is now. You needn't this development or the results. All you have to do is stand in front of me, just as you are now."

"Kuroyukihime." As he said her name in a voice that was not quite a voice, Haruyuki earnestly tried to move his frozen head from side to side.

What she was saying was perfectly clear.

Fight. They would fight. If the Beast living in the Armor of Catastrophe used up some kind of energy through intense fighting, then the Black King herself would be his duel opponent and guide the Beast into a certain slumber until the purification mission the next evening. However…however…

"I— Around the time I became a Burst Linker, I made a decision. That I would never fight you, no matter what happened. That if it came to that, then I would uninstall Brain Burst of my own will," Haruyuki argued fiercely, sounding like a child on the verge of tears.

Kuroyukihime smiled gently, wryly, and patted his head admonishingly. "Although it is indeed a fight, it's different from a conflict fueled by hatred. It's a duel. The sole and greatest reason Brain Burst exists. Or…" Puffing out her cheeks slightly, she added, "...are you saying you can duel Ash Roller—I mean, Rin Kusakabe—but you can't duel me?"

"N-no, it's not like tha—"

"Listen. There is indeed something in the Accelerated World that has to be communicated not in words, but with fists and swords and bullets. And now that I'm thinking about it, didn't you yourself seek out a duel with me the night before the Hermes' Cord race? You told me many, many precious things then, not in words, but with both fists. Now, it's my turn to tell you what I have to say. As your parent."

"...Kuro...yukihime..." All kinds of feelings welled up in his heart, and all Haruyuki could do was groan.

Kuroyukihime nodded with a kind smile before gently inserting into Haruyuki's Neurolinker the plug of the second XSB cable she pulled out of the integrated terminal. "Now, me, too," she urged.

Haruyuki finally realized he was still clutching the first XSB cable. Even though his heart was in chaos, his fingers moved on autopilot, and the plug clumsily approached Kuroyukihime's Neurolinker.

She accepted the connection with eyelids closed, and the wired connection warning had no sooner disappeared than she was murmuring in a low voice, smile still on her lips, "We go on the count of five. If we both make it back safely..." Her lips kept moving, but he couldn't catch the words they made.

After a pause, a louder voice began to neatly carve out the time. "Now then, starting the countdown. Five, four, three, two, one."

If he shouted the command now, he might not be able to come back as himself again. Full of resolve and indecision in equal measure, Haruyuki braced himself and quietly said with Kuroyukihime:

"Unlimited Burst."

8

Forty-five years had already passed since the completion of construction on Roppongi Hills Mori Tower, but it remained an enormous building poking its head far above the rest of the buildings in the Akasaka neighborhood. The roof was six thousand square meters, much larger than the sports grounds at Umesato Junior High. With a height of two hundred thirty-eight meters, it fell short of Tokyo Midtown Tower soaring up to the northeast by ten meters, but the floor area was one and a half times that other giant.

Thus, the superb view that leapt into existence the second he opened his eyes stole his soul for a moment or two. Perhaps best called an enormous sky garden, walls and pillars reminiscent of Greek ruins were scattered around, made of a white, porcelain-like limestone. Small flowers he didn't know the name of sprang up in the cracks and crumbling bases of the stone, and clouds drifted leisurely through the sky, shining madder red. Off near the horizon in the western distance was the sun, a large gold coin.

A Twilight stage, a "natural" stage with earth attributes. Its features were: terrain objects that were easily shattered; though apparently entirely comprised of stone, many things were flammable; and surprisingly dark in areas of cover. Nothing particularly spectacular.

However, for Haruyuki, this place had personal significance.

Last fall, a time he would never forget, he had been given the key to another world by a black spangle butterfly who descended suddenly before him, and the first place they had visited was this land of eternal dusk. That butterfly had reached a hand out to Haruyuki, who was obstinately hanging his head, and asked, "Do these virtual two meters feel that far to you?"

Yesterday, eight months after that day, when they direct-dueled in the nurse's room at Umesato Junior High, Kuroyukihime had shown Haruyuki a modest, but true, miracle. She had denied the attributes of her own duel avatar through the Incarnate System—the phenomenon of overwriting—and changed the sword of her right hand into five slender fingers. The newly born "hand" shattered in a mere seventeen seconds, but that Incarnate in and of itself was nothing but a loud declaration: That Kuroyukihime herself would also close the two meters from that day in the past.

This thought drifting through his mind, Haruyuki started to shift his gaze to seek out Kuroyukihime. However, immediately before that, he realized he had forgotten the thing he should be checking first and foremost.

He hurriedly raised his hands and stared at his spread fingers. Silver Crow's ten fingers—normally so slender that it was hard to believe he was a hand-to-hand combat type—had doubly thick armor and tapered into claws at the ends. They were basically in the same condition as when he direct-dueled with Rin Kusakabe before. He next checked the form and color of his body and found that these, too, were about the same as three hours earlier, a mix of 80 percent Crow and 20 percent Disaster. Finally, he closed his eyes and focused on the center of his spine deep within his consciousness, but it seemed that the Beast that lay there was still dozing. He couldn't perceive its piercing pain, or its low howl.

"Just stay asleep like that a little longer," Haruyuki murmured, as he lifted his face and once again surveyed his surroundings.

The roof of Mori Tower was large, but due to the terrain effects of the Twilight stage, countless pillars and stone walls covered it in a labyrinthine configuration, and Haru couldn't see all the way to the other side. Clearing his ears, he couldn't hear anything besides the howl of the desolate wind blowing.

"Kuroyukihime?" Haruyuki called out to the person he was waiting for in a slightly tense voice. But he couldn't see a single active object, much less obsidian armor. But now that he thought about it, Kuroyukihime had said simply that she'd moved from Suginami to the roof here in Roppongi Hills; it would have been impossible for her to precisely grasp the position where he would appear. She had to be somewhere in the maze searching for him just like he was her.

With this thought, Haruyuki started walking along the narrow path between the chalky stone walls. Unlike the main tower building, the decorative walls and pillars were likely not very strong, so he might have been able to smash through them in a straight line, but he seriously hesitated to do so. The rare Twilight stage was, for him, a place to memorialize, a sacred space.

The path hit a wall soon enough and branched off to both sides. He turned right on a hunch. Taking care not to step on the small flowers blooming on the left and right of the cobblestone path, he headed toward what he thought was the center of the roof. He turned right several more times, and then left, and then he slipped through a crumbling arch to find a plaza about twenty meters in diameter, slightly lower than the surrounding area.

The center of the roof of the real Mori Tower was also a heliport, a meter lower than the wooden deck around it. So this was probably the center. Of course, there was no *H* mark for the heliport; instead, a dozen or so pillars stood in a ring. In the center of these there was a remarkably thick, tall pillar; water flowed smoothly from the top of it, and at its base was a shallow pond.

He stepped down into the plaza as if pulled in and walked over to the central pillar. He brought his hand up to the wet limestone surface, and just as he was about to touch it—

"Crow." He heard a low, calm voice call his name from the other side of the pillar.

"Oh! K-Kuroyukihime!" *Is this where you were?* he was about to say, moving around the pillar, but the voice continued and held him back.

"Stop. Don't move, just listen."

"Huh...? O-okay."

The diameter of the pillar standing in the center of the plaza was, generously speaking, eighty centimeters at best. She might have been small, but with her design emphasizing the edged areas of her limbs, Black Lotus would have had to strain to hide completely behind this pillar. Unintentionally imagining how she looked, all scrunched up, Haruyuki stopped in place.

"Silver Crow. I've been thinking for a long time about how I can help you now that you're parasitized by the Armor of Catastrophe." Kuroyukihime's voice came from the other side of the stone pillar once more, with just the slightest bit of a flat echo, as though she were deliberately suppressing any intonation. Haru held his breath and waited for her to continue. "I examined several ideas, but this did seem to be the best method. Crow. Unfortunately, you have become too great a danger now. For the Legion, for the Accelerated World, and for me."

"...K-Kuro...yukihime...?" An inexpressible confusion. The words she uttered did in fact express reality, but that way of speaking, somehow businesslike—no, even cold...

"Thus, this is my decision. Disappear from this world."

The completely emotionless voice slammed into his ears from the other side of the pillar.

At basically the same time, something pierced the thick limestone before him and reached out in a straight line. A sharp, black blade. A sword— No, the Black King's hand.

Dumbfounded, Haruyuki stared at the ebony tip aimed precisely at the center of his own chest, the most critical point for a duel avatar. His thoughts stopped, and he had no sensation in his limbs. But perhaps his body reacted on its own; he leaned his torso to the left a mere five centimeters.

Whuk.

With a very modest impact, the black blade plunged deeper and deeper into the right side of Silver Crow's chest, until it came out through his back.

An instant of a chilly, cool sensation. And then—an incandescent, fierce pain.

"Unh...Ah!" A hoarse cry slipped out of him, and he focused every bit of his strength in his legs to jump straight backward. The sword slid out of his chest, giving rise to a new round of pain, and the bright-red light of the damage effect in the air shimmered like fresh blood. He staggered, bathed in that light, and plunged his left knee into the ground.

Although he had evaded a direct hit to his heart, he had taken serious damage to his torso, and his health gauge abruptly dropped over 20 percent. Naturally, his special-attack gauge was also charged by an amount corresponding to the damage, but there was one other obvious change inside him.

....*GRAAAR.*

A low howl. The first drop of the molten iron, the red-hot rage that was about to spill out of him. The Beast was waking up. Haruyuki hadn't managed to dodge—albeit by only a few centimeters—the black blade's surprise attack by chance or his own reflexive action. The Beast had moved his duel avatar.

"Kuro...yukihime...why...!" Haruyuki squeezed a voice out, pressing his right hand to the wound on his chest—or holding back the rage of the Beast trying to gush out from it. "Why... would you...?!"

It was true that they had dropped into the Unlimited Neutral Field to fight. However, this—the surprise attack, not letting him see her—had simply fanned the Beast's rage and called it to complete wakefulness.

Wait. Did Kuroyukihime ever have any intention of dueling?

Was her plan all along to bring him into the Accelerated World, beat him down, and solve this problem in one fell swoop with the Judgment Blow?

*GRAAAAR...*ENEMY...IF THIS IS AN ENEMY...THEN ONLY... SLAUGHTER...EVEN IF...THAT IS YOUR PARENT, a creaking voice echoed forlornly in the depths of Haru's mind. He could no longer stop the Beast's awakening.

But down on one knee, body curled up into itself, Haruyuki started speaking desperately to the pseudo-intelligence living within him. *Wait, Beast! You're wrong. You're totally wrong!*

Exactly. It *was* wrong. He couldn't believe that the voice calling to him from the other side of the pillar and the blade that pierced his chest belonged to anyone other than Black Lotus, but...even still, it was wrong. She wouldn't say that. She wouldn't *do* that. So then, someone was faking the Black King's voice and techniques. That was the only conclusion—no, the truth.

Haruyuki slowly stood up and glanced down at his body as his armor darkened with the awakening of the Beast. "Come out from behind that pillar ple— I mean, come out! Who are you?!" he shouted resolutely.

Momentarily, the wind stopped as if afraid, and even the flowers at his feet hid their faces.

Finally, a smooth voice. "It's sad, Crow. You hear my voice with those ears, feel my technique with that body, and still, you can still ask a question like that."

The chalky pillars in the center of the roof of Mori Tower shone golden in the Twilight stage, illuminated by the setting sun from the right, with the left side sinking into shadow to create a strong contrast. From that shadow, a silhouette stepped out smoothly, silently.

A face mask that tapered into a V from both sides. Armor skirt patterned after the petals of a water lily around the incredibly slender waist. Arms and legs in the form of long swords. And the Armor of the entire body a real black, more concentrated than the shadow.

"...That..." Haruyuki felt a pitch-black despair drop into his heart. And like a drop of ink in a glass of water, the darkness seeped into the interior of his avatar.

The volume of the Beast's howl increased in step with this stain. *Kree, kree.* With a dry metal creaking, his hands and feet grew larger into claws. The protrusions on either side of his forehead shot out abruptly, and his visor began to shift into something resembling the maw of a wild animal.

But unaware of the changes coming over him, Haruyuki simply continued to stare at the jet-black duel avatar standing in the shadow of the pillar.

That form. And no avatar besides the Black King had that coloring. So then, those words before, were they Black Lotus's true feelings—Kuroyukihime's? Those cold words, announcing she would cut away Silver Crow—no, *Haruyuki Arita*—as a dangerous element and eliminate him from the Accelerated World...?

Skreenk! His limbs transformed into thick, blackish-silver armor with sharp edges. The top and bottom halves of the visor enclosing his round helmet had already finished generating; all that was left was for him to bring the fang-shaped serrations together and bite down hard.

THAT IS THE ENEMY. OUR ENEMY. CALL THE SWORD. BOIL WITH FLAMES! the Beast commanded Haruyuki, with an increasingly clear voice.

But still, Haruyuki gritted his teeth beneath his visor and shook his head slightly. "No. I can't accept that. I don't believe it. That's not Kuroyukihime," he groaned, half talking to himself. The voice, the form, and even the color might have been those of the Black King, but that was not Black Lotus—Kuroyukihime. His instincts, his soul, were screaming it.

The pronounced shadow of the large pillar, characteristic of the Twilight stage, swallowed up all details and painted over everything, obstructed his vision—no, all five of his senses. The avatar that looked like the Black King did not move, instead keeping her body sunk in the darkness, as if she was trying to flee the light. He felt something artificial in it.

Wasn't there any way to make her move away from the shadow, even if only for a moment? Smash the pillar— No. If he carried out any physical attack now, the Disasterfication would be completed instantly. *Don't destroy it; illuminate it. With a new, powerful light.*

Beast. Let me just check. Don't get in the way of me activating my Incarnate, he murmured, and the pseudo-intelligence howled with dissatisfaction.

GRAAAAR...IF THAT WILL ALLOW YOU TO CONFIRM THIS IS THE ENEMY, THEN DO AS YOU WISH.

...Yeah...I'll confirm it. Exactly what that is, there.

Haruyuki slowly turned the five fingers of his right hand, transformed into sinister claws, toward the Black King of the darkness—it was a movement like he was bracing to withstand an intense destructive impact. But in contrast, his heart was calm like the surface of a lake. He probably only had one chance, one moment. He had to focus on the image, activate, and release in less time than ever before.

Light. The image of light. He mustered up every ounce of concentration from every corner of his body to focus on the mental image that was the source of his Laser Sword, the Incarnate technique he had shot off any number of times in the past and condensed in the depths of his right hand. This image, honed so small and sharp that it didn't even generate an overlay—he had to release it all at once!

"Light!!" he shouted out unconsciously. At the same time, a pure white light jetted out from the right hand of the more-than-half-Disasterfied Silver Crow, until it illuminated the world.

That was when Haruyuki saw it.

The form was indeed exactly that of the Black King. But it was a form that took shape only when seen from a very limited angle. In other words, it had no *depth*. The swords of the four limbs, the Armor patterned after flower petals, it was all just cut from panels thinner than paper—a shadow picture. The avatar perfectly resembled Black Lotus in the darkness, but this was its true form, exposed in the momentary flash of light.

"You— Who are you?!" Haruyuki cried, thrusting the talons of his right hand out.

The shadow avatar, sinking back into the darkness created by the pillar, didn't move, as if it had been burned in place by the strobe light. In the gloom, it really was an almost perfect copy of Black Lotus, but now that he had seen its true form, he realized it was different from the Black King in one important way. Normally, the tips of the Black King's toes floated a couple centimeters above the ground, since she usually moved by hovering. But the points of the shadow avatar's feet were digging into the ground slightly. A minute, but decisive, difference.

Even bathed in Haruyuki's unflinching gaze, whoever it was who was pretending to be the king maintained their silence for a few more seconds, but finally, perhaps deciding that any further deception was impossible, they leisurely spread out the swords of both arms—or rather, the thin, weak panels patterned after them. At the same time, a voice:

"I've underestimated you. The fact that you still use the Incarnate of the first quadrant although the Armor has penetrated you so deeply means you've grown, hmm?"

The tone was again basically a perfect reproduction of Kuroyukihime's in the Accelerated World. But the choice of words and the intonation made Haruyuki's memory ache uncomfortably. He had the feeling that he had met someone who talked like this somewhere, sometime before. It was— Right, in the Unlimited Neutral Field...in a stage colored in the same thick shadows...

"You...you..." Almost at the same time as Haruyuki moaned quietly, the dangerous thoughts of the Beast sounded in the depths of his head.

You. Are. You are...That. That time...

Even faced with the hostile gaze containing the animosity of two beings, the shadow avatar stood calmly in place—or rather, was pasted there. Bringing down the extended arms in a slightly mechanical motion, he launched into another monologue.

"Coming into contact with you Black Legionnaires here was entirely unexpected. But, well, this sort of opportunity doesn't come along too often, does it? Metatron on the Midtown Tower was raging after three days of quiet, so I was on standby just in case, when I was surprised by unexpected guests."

The tone, aloof and somehow reminiscent of a teacher giving a lecture, stung at Haru's memory sharply once more, but a physical unease great enough to override this moved Haruyuki's mouth. "You were on standby?"

Metatron—"Archangel Metatron"—was the Legend-class Enemy guarding Tokyo Midtown Tower, which soared up five hundred meters to the northeast. Haruyuki had indeed seen the terrifying, invisible monster use a dreadnought laser attack to create a massive crater in the urban center of Roppongi in reaction to the rocket punch launched by Iron Pound. Most likely, the shadow avatar before him had hidden himself here on the roof of Mori Tower, a position that allowed easy monitoring of the other skyscraper, in order to search out whoever had caused the monster to attack.

But in reality, that was impossible.

Haruyuki had seen Metatron attack about three hours ago in real-world time. So, in the Unlimited Neutral Field, it had already been three thousand hours since then. *One hundred twenty-five days* had actually passed. No one could possibly wait for a hazy *something* for that massive amount of time without even sleeping.

The instant his thoughts got to this point, Haruyuki belatedly remembered he had been shocked once before in the same way.

The final battle in the Unlimited Neutral Field with Dusk Taker, a powerful enemy who had stolen Silver Crow's silver wings. Despite the fact that Haruyuki and Takumu had taken the greatest measures to keep Dusk Taker from breaking his promise and setting up an ambush, people were already lying in wait on the Umesato Junior High grounds, where the fight was to take place.

Dusk Taker had triumphantly told the tale to an astonished Haruyuki and friends. About how *he* was the only one in the Accelerated World who could stay on standby for incredibly long times. Because he was the only one who could stop the acceleration of his thoughts during a burst link due to the brain implant chip in his head, the lone "deceleration" user...

"You...you're..." Whirling to face the two-dimensional avatar, thin like a paper cutout, Haruyuki called out in a creaking voice:

"...Vice president of the Acceleration Research Society...Black Vise!!"

The instant he heard the name, the shadow avatar held his right hand up in front of his chest, bent at the waist, and bowed courteously.

His entire body then neatly rotated ninety degrees on the pivot of the toes of his right foot, which dug lightly into the ground. Because his every part was made of extremely thin panels, at this angle, he looked to Haruyuki's eyes like nothing more than a single line. But Haruyuki didn't get the chance to look too closely; the thin pieces separated once more into ten or so panels on each side and lined up neatly with a few centimeters between them. What was produced was a "layered" avatar, like a detailed radiation fin cut out into the shape of a person. This was nothing other than the true form of Black Vise, the avatar who had once made Haruyuki and his friends suffer so terribly with his unusual powers.

Vise was still courteously bent forward, right arm at his chest, but unlike when he was the fake Lotus, his left arm was missing from its socket. Still, he wasn't injured...This strange avatar had the ability to freely detach the panels that made up his body and manipulate them over long distances. If he'd activated that ability now, then his target was likely...

"You...her, the Black King, what did you...?"

The fact that the real Kuroyukihime still hadn't shown up on

the roof of the tower like she was supposed to no doubt meant that Black Vise had gotten to her first. Haruyuki started toward Vise to press the question, when—

Suddenly, a fierce, red-hot pain pierced the center of his spine.

"Graaaaaaaar!!"

Haruyuki didn't know whether the tremendous roar of rage sounded in his mind alone, or if it actually jetted out from his mouth. But the next time, definitely in his head, he heard the crazed howling of the Beast.

You…Kill! Kill! Killkillkillkill!

Haruyuki staggered at the incredible explosion of negative thought, as though something had slammed into him physically. At the same time, scenes flashed across his view in quick succession.

A large mortar-shaped hole dug out of the ground. A female-type avatar with golden-yellow armor standing at the bottom, restrained by a jet-black cross.

From the deep hole next to the cross, the figure of a strange snake slithered into view. With a mouth lined with countless fangs, it ate the girl, chewing up her armor with a loud *crunch*.

On the edge of the basin, a couple dozen Burst Linkers silently watched over the tragedy. In one corner, three shadows stood a distance from the rest of the group. A small avatar with four eyes that glittered eerily. An avatar cloaked completely in white light, such that her actual form wasn't visible. And a matte-black layered avatar, several thin plates put together in the shape of a person…

This figure burned into the Beast's memory was overlaid perfectly on the Black Vise before his eyes.

Haruyuki felt a large amount of information flowing into his mind like red-hot molten metal. Or maybe it existed within him right from the start. The "dream" he had had two days earlier, during the short nap he took after breaking into the Castle with Utai Shinomiya…Forgotten until now, that long, sad dream—or rather, all the memories of the first Disaster Chrome Falcon—suddenly came back to life.

It's him.

He was the one who had set a trap for the golden-yellow girl, Saffron Blossom, the avatar who had held the ideal of zero total point loss. He had had the hell snake Jormungand kill her over and over and over. The very person who had brought about the incident that twisted the sixth star of the Seven Arcs, the Destiny, and the high-level Enhanced Armament Star Caster and turned them into the Armor of Catastrophe, the Disaster, was actually the Black Vise standing before him now.

"You...*you*..."

Now the Beast's rage was Haruyuki's. As if guided by an overwhelming urge to kill and destroy, the light armor covering his body abruptly transformed into something blackish silver and heavy, as a long tail slithered out from his back.

"*You...killed* Fron...!!" As he cried out, his facial visor came down with a sharp metallic *clank*. His view was dyed a pale gray, and only the figure of his enemy was set in sharp relief.

Even after Silver Crow had completed his transformation into Chrome Disaster, the layered avatar continued to stand calmly where he was. "Hmm. Very interesting," he said to himself quietly, tilting just the thin panels of his head. "You know me—or, rather, you remember me from the past?"

The voice was not the one that had sounded so much like Kuroyukihime only moments earlier, but rather the low, relaxed voice of the boy once more. It was extremely quiet, but Haruyuki's enhanced hearing clearly picked up the words uttered.

"How COULD I...forget...I HAVE continued to exist IN THIS world IN ORDER TO kill YOU." The halting words were no sooner spat out than they turned into pure red flames and scorched the air.

Essentially, the reason the Armor of Catastrophe existed was to obliterate all Burst Linkers. The source of that dreadful urge was, of course, the death of Saffron Blossom. Blossom had had the ideal of building a mutual burst-point-sharing system and removing the fear of total point loss from the Accelerated World. For it, she was betrayed by thirty or more Burst Linkers, who set a trap for her. So then, he would give them the elimination they desired that resulted from total point loss. This resolve of the first, Chrome Falcon, had become lodged in the Enhanced Armament and spurred those who wore the Armor after him to endless slaughter.

However, in the end, the core of this massive, swollen compulsion was a hatred toward the three people who had orchestrated Blossom's tragedy. None of the three had shown themselves center stage in the more than seven years of real-world time since that incident, and now Black Vise, the "restrainer," happened to run into Chrome Disaster in an awakened state.

The highly pressurized desire for vengeance caught fire, and the tremendous, murderous urge that subsequently exploded in him easily blew away what little control Haruyuki's sense of reason held over the avatar. An aura of even more concentrated darkness rising up from his dark silver armor, Haruyuki—no, the sixth Disaster—took a heavy step forward.

"I WILL NOT STOP slicing you UP UNTIL YOUR body is TRANS-FORMED INTO a pile of scraps," Haruyuki said, words riding on incandescent breath, and raised his right hand high.

The beautiful madder-red sky of the Twilight stage suddenly clouded over. Dark cumulonimbus clouds appeared from nowhere and gathered together in a spiral, swathed in pale lightning. A remarkably fierce bolt of lightning appeared from the center—the sword once called Star Caster, about to be summoned to Haruyuki's raised palm.

Black Vise moved.

The panels making up his right arm quickly slid in from the outside as they sank into the shadows at his feet. With almost no delay, two thin sheets gradually rose up from Haruyuki's own shadow to slam up against his avatar on both sides and tried to catch him. He had been hit with this before. It was Vise's restraint attack, Static Pressure.

Haruyuki paused the summoning of his sword. "Flash Blink!" he called out quickly.

When he had been pinned between these panels two months earlier, the only way he had been able to escape was to crawl and yank himself free, losing all the Armor on his torso in the process. However, for the Haruyuki of the present, there was a way to evade it without injury: the ability left in the Armor by the first, aka Chrome Falcon—pseudo-teleportation. Long, long ago, Falcon himself had fled the super pressure of the thin panels with this technique.

Haruyuki's body turned into countless minuscule particles and started to move forward at super-high speed.

Almost as if anticipating that reaction, Black Vise murmured, "Hexahedral Compression."

Haruyuki's field of view was closed off by darkness. Though it wasn't that the light had been lost. No, a new panel had appeared before him to block his way.

His avatar, a mass of particles charging forward, slammed into the wall and bounced backward, rematerializing. As he staggered, his back hit a panel that appeared behind him. Flash Blink was basically almighty as a close-range movement ability, but it was still not true teleportation. His particulate body couldn't move to a place unconnected to his starting point. There needed to be a hole or gap it could pass through.

"Grar!" A cry of rage. Completely surrounded by matte-black walls on all sides, Haruyuki had nowhere to go. So then: up. He decided instantly and moved to jump. But perhaps this action had been anticipated as well; with a *bang*, the gaps directly above and below him were closed off with black lids.

All light was extinguished, and Haruyuki understood that he was completely locked inside a rectangular box. And that wasn't all. The panels on all six sides were closing in on him with a slow but certain movement. A fearsome pressure pushed against his head, shoulders, chest, back, and the soles of his feet, and his armor creaked fiercely, sparks flying.

"Gr...raaaaaar!" Howling, Haruyuki tried with all his might to push back against the panels. Unlike the total speed-type Silver

Crow, Chrome Disaster was all-powerful, with a balance of speed and strength. Haruyuki was currently incomparably stronger than his former self. And yet the six panels didn't even flex, almost as though they were the borders of the very world itself.

Then: He heard that voice, reminiscent of a young teacher somehow.

"Crow—no, Disaster. Just like it seems to be for you, this is also the second time I've seen this technique of yours. Before you slipped out on me, you see? So I made a few adjustments."

The voice seemed like it was coming from all six directions. In fact, it likely was. It was the six panels themselves that were speaking.

"*Graar...Graaaaah!*" At Vise's composed words, Haruyuki—or the Beast mentally fused with Haruyuki—emitted another roar. He pressed the claws of his hands against the jet-black walls and tried to rip through them. But even these claws, which had torn through the Armor of any and every duel avatar, only scattered futile sparks. If he had at least had his longsword at hand, he might have been able to pierce the walls, but this enclosed space apparently prevented the summoning of Enhanced Armament; no matter how he called for it, there was no response.

Howling like a wild animal, Haruyuki beat furiously on the walls with both hands and kicked with both feet. As if sympathetic to the out-of-control destroyer, the voice echoed gently once more.

"It's a little sooner than planned, but I'll be collecting and analyzing this armor. Unfortunately, Crow, I'll have to have you exit the Accelerated World, but what you really want likely isn't to wander the Unlimited Neutral Field in this state, either. Well, depending on the intentions of the president, there might be another road, but..."

Thmm.

The rectangle enclosing Haruyuki sank straight down. A deeply unpleasant sensation enveloped him, like both feet stepping into a lukewarm mucus. This was the "shadow." Black Vise was sinking into the shadow with Haruyuki trapped in the box, in order to carry him somewhere.

A numbing cold spread out from his shadow-immersed feet and stole the strength from his body. Fused with the Beast, Haruyuki tried even now to rage, but the movement of his limbs gradually lost force. The level of the shadow increased in the blink of an eye, rising up to his thighs, his hips, his stomach.

Then, suddenly, a crimson line cut from left to right across the center of Haruyuki's field of view.

The extremely thin line of light kept going around the right side, turned ninety degrees behind him, and then bent once more to join up with its starting point. When the red thread all around him disappeared, he could see the tiniest bit of the outside world through a thin gap.

Abruptly, there came a crashing sound, like thick glass shattering, and the jet-black hexahedron holding Haruyuki crumbled. Swallowed up to the chest by the shadow, he was shot out and tumbled heavily across the white paving stones of the Twilight stage.

Wide-open eyes caught his captor Black Vise standing straight, right arm missing as well as his left.

And about ten meters away from him, standing quietly near the western entrance to the circular plaza, was another black duel avatar.

Four flowing swords. Hip armor patterned after a water lily's flower. A face mask reminiscent of a bird of prey on the verge of taking flight. The silhouette strongly resembled the shadow produced earlier by Black Vise. But he lacked the ability to perfectly re-create several features of this figure, standing in the golden light of the evening sun.

First, the semitransparent armor that caught the afterglow within itself and glittered beautifully, like black crystal. And the eye lenses shining a bluish purple, filled with fierce resolve.

Finally, ten or twenty minutes behind Haruyuki's dive, the

real Black King, head of the Legion Nega Nebulus, the traitor Black Lotus, advanced about three meters in an easy hovering motion. When he looked closely, the embers of a faint red aura twined around the sword of her right arm. There was no doubt a long-distance attack had been launched from that sword to sever Vise's Hexahedral Compression and free Haruyuki.

However, the Black King stopped without so much as a glance at the fallen Haruyuki, instead favoring the inky layered avatar with a bloody gaze. Black Vise didn't flinch, although just a look from the Black King was enough to send a newbie into zero fill. He smoothly moved armless shoulders up and down.

"I am indeed always surprised by you, hmm, Black King." He spoke leisurely, voice uncolored by nervousness or anything near it. "Since you broke through so easily before, this time, I took the initiative of completely restraining and rendering the swords of your hands and feet ineffective, but…how on earth did you slip out? Though it seems that it didn't come without injury."

Just as he said, the sword of Black Lotus's left arm was cruelly shattered about twenty centimeters from the tip. But more than enough remained of the blade itself. If all four of her sword limbs had indeed been held fast by some restraint created by Vise, then she had, by some means, first destroyed her own left arm and then, with that newly freed arm, cut her right arm and her legs from their bondage.

"I'm under no obligation to disclose my secrets to you." The Black King's response was curt. "After all, you were the one who preached the disadvantages of being too eloquent when we happened to meet before."

Her cool, sharp tongue brought a light, wry smile onto the face of the layered avatar. "Ha-ha! That's a point for you. Perhaps I am indeed a little too talkative today, hmm? But just when I had waited in vain for over two hours, prepared for it to end as a fool's errand, an unexpected and wonderful present happened to come along. It was inevitable that I should get a little excited."

"Hmm. From time to time, unexpected presents explode when you open them, you know. From the look of it, you've taken more damage than we have, and although I'm sure you've planned all sorts of petty tricks for my partner, I believe the situation remains two against one."

Exactly.

Even while he was listening to the exchange between Kuroyuki-hime and Black Vise, the majority of Beast-fused Haruyuki's mind was occupied with a cool calculation of how to completely destroy the loathsome layered avatar for good.

Given that he was able to set up simultaneous, large-scale restraint attacks for both Black Lotus and Chrome Disaster, Black Vise was indeed a formidable foe, but both restraints had been destroyed, and Vise had lost both of his arms. In other words, this likely meant he could no longer use larger-scale techniques, including Hexahedral Compression.

However, as he had declared before, his greatest ability was fleeing.

Just as he had said, Vise did have what was essentially the ultimate escape technique; he folded his own body up into a single panel, sank into a shadow somewhere in the stage, and moved that way. Countless pillars and walls were crammed together on the roof of the Twilight stage Mori Tower; it would be an easy feat to move through the shadows they cast to the edge of the roof. Once he reached the shadow created by the wall of the massive building, he could run off anywhere. For instance, the shadow cast by all two hundred thirty-eight meters of Mori Tower, as it stood illuminated by the westerly sun, swallowed up over a kilometer of the urban center of Roppongi by itself.

Thus, to make sure he brought down his sworn enemy and peeled one panel after another from his body until he brutally slaughtered him, Haruyuki couldn't simply charge in recklessly. First, he had to remove the avatar's avenue of escape.

"*Grar...*" With a low howl, Haruyuki slowly picked himself up and crouched down low, checking his gauges with a glance. Thanks to the first surprise attack to the chest and the pressure damage from being inside the box, his health gauge had decreased by just over 30 percent. But his special-attack gauge was nearly zero, crushed after he activated Flash Blink. He wouldn't be able to use his wings or any other abilities for a while. In which case, rather than first aiming for Vise's body, he should target the large pillars in the center of the plaza. *Destroy those and take away the shadows Vise is in constant contact with.*

Haruyuki himself couldn't have been aware of this, but being able to run through these sorts of calculations even while completely fused with the Beast was an ability the previous Chrome Disasters had not had. Once they were clad in the Armor of Catastrophe, all they could do was rampage, propelled onward by the instinct to fight. As a result, their mental strength was gradually worn away, and in the end, each was as hungry as a large animal caught in a trap.

However, even while spurred on by an inexhaustible rage toward Black Vise, Saffron Blossom's murderer, the sixth Chrome Disaster, aka Haruyuki, maintained the ability to analyze and judge, arguably Silver Crow's greatest power. Was this because not much time had passed since he'd become the Disaster? Or because he was more deeply synced with the Armor than anyone else had been?

The answer came unexpectedly quickly—a mere minute or so later.

Surprisingly, the first to move was Black Vise. He leisurely stepped out from the shadow of the plaza's central pillar, which he had stubbornly stayed so close to, and exposed himself to the light of the sun.

Under the red light of the sunset, he had an obviously different quality from the Black King, similarly ruled by the name *black*. Unlike Lotus's semitransparent armor, shining like an obsidian crystal, the thin panels that made up Vise's avatar were a matte black, which basically absorbed light.

On the tips of the toes—even these looked like simple pieces of black paper in a row—Black Vise turned toward the crouching Haruyuki. "Two against one. I see," he stated calmly. "You believe in this boy that deeply, even now when he's changed into the Catastrophe entirely. The bond of parent and child, hmm? To be honest, I'm jealous. Right from the start, I've never had any connections."

Abruptly, the outermost of the panels that made up Vise's right leg broke away. No sooner had it turned into a square in midair than it began to spin at high speed. In an instant, it looked like nothing more than an extremely thin, blurry gray disc.

"I *am* jealous. So shall I at least take that bond with me?"

At the same time as he spoke, the disc began to shine red like blood. Overlay. Some kind of long-distance Incarnate attack was coming.

Haruyuki braced himself, but he was somewhat confused after reading the row of information displayed in his view. Because, all it said was: PREDICTED ATTACK: INCARNATE ATTACK; RANGE/POWER ENHANCEMENT: SEVERING TYPE; THREAT LEVEL: 5. The predicted trajectory shown in red was also a simple straight line. If he were to believe the analytic powers of the Armor, the technique was such that it could be dealt with by moving a single step or simply repelling it with his arm.

However, this attack was not actually carried out.

"I will not allow it!!" the Black King shouted sharply, and charged toward Black Vise. The sword of her right hand was wrapped in a vivid blue overlay.

"Death by Piercing!!" She called out the ominous name of the special attack at the same time as she activated it, boosted with the power of Incarnate.

The tip of the sword shot forward, containing enough power to shake the entire massive tower, threatening to pull it to pieces—and the inky layered avatar did not move to dodge or defend against it.

Instead, the instant before the attack hit its target, his body changed form once more. In the blink of an eye, every part of him came together into a single thin panel, including the piece spinning at top speed. His body, now an extremely thin line, rotated dozens of times before drawing out a human shape into the air again.

A flimsy shadow portrait appeared before Haruyuki once more, again with no depth. But it was not the fake Black Lotus he had tried to deceive Haruyuki with before.

The edges were short hair turned up at the bottom. Armor at the shoulders and waist reminiscent of flower petals. Slender arms and legs, a cute baton gripped in the left hand.

The shadow portrait, which should have been a solid black, in that instant alone, reflected the eternally fading light of the Twilight stage, and glittered a dazzling golden yellow. At the same time, Haruyuki heard a name spill out of his own mouth.

"...Fron."

On top of this trembling voice came the hard sound of impact. The sound of the thrusting technique the Black King had released deeply piercing the chest of the golden-yellow girl-shaped avatar.

As the girl slowly reeled back, she reached a hand out toward Haruyuki. Deep, deep in his ears, he felt like he could hear a hazy voice, like a faint breeze.

...Fal...

Crack!! A dreadful spark popped inside Haruyuki's head. His entire field of view was dyed red, and the sky, the ground, and each and every terrain object disappeared. In the bloodred world, only the two entangled silhouettes stood out in sharp relief.

The girl with the sharp sword plunged deep into her chest dropped lifelessly to her knees and fell on her side before disappearing completely, as if sucked into the ground. The other figure was briefly fixed in position, at the end of her technique, but eventually, she, too, turned her face away from him, as if repelled. But he could no longer recognize this other, dark avatar.

Sparks burned his consciousness a snowy white. In that moment, the reason of Haruyuki, of Silver Crow—what little remained in the form of the power of judgment—disappeared completely. All that was left was a lone Beast, seeking vengeance and slaughter.

"*Graaaaaaaaaaaaar!!*" He roared with enough force to shake the heavens, and black clouds appeared, whirling in the sky once more. From their center, a bolt of obsidian lightning poured down into his right hand, extended high into the air. Instantly, it gained form and became a sinister longsword.

"*Graaaar!!*" Howling once more, the Beast kicked hard off the ground and headed toward the black avatar standing frozen a few meters away. That avatar was the attacker who had killed the girl he loved more than anyone else—his enemy.

Charging, he brandished the sword high above his head. The slashing attack carved out a trajectory of black sparks, filled with an incredible power. But as long as its target had a certain level of expertise and read the timing, it would have been an easy thing to avoid it.

But his enemy didn't dodge. Instead, she crossed her sword-shaped arms—although the tip of the left had been shattered—and a vivid green light grew there.

The longsword clad in dark thunderbolts and the green cross drawn by the two swords came into contact. The incredible energy of their clash compressed into a single minuscule point and glittered like a new star.

Kwaaan! The power was immediately released and radiated outward into the surrounding air. Swallowed up by this energy wave, the countless limestone objects lining the roof of the tower crumbled silently and disappeared. Although the building itself was not taken apart like it had been when he'd hit the Green King, the impact was still powerful enough to turn the entire roof into a vacant lot instantaneously.

Even after the shock wave died down, the two fighters stood with swords locked. Each time the intersection between them creaked, dazzling sparks illuminated their faces.

Bluish-purple eyes narrowed in what looked like anguish beneath black mirrored goggles, his enemy appeared to be desperately shouting something as she held back the longsword of the Beast. But words did not reach the Beast, transformed now into a mass of senseless fighting instinct.

"Graar!!" Howling briefly, the Beast beat at the slender body of his enemy with a tightly clenched fist. Although his opponent tried to deftly respond by going around to the right, he vibrated just the right side of the wings, abruptly rotating his entire body to change the trajectory of the punch. This was an application of the technique Aerial Combo, which the Burst Linker who was now a vessel for the Beast had once trained intently to master, but even that memory no longer remained within the creature.

Wrapped in dark aura, the fist caught the enemy's right side and drilled into it mercilessly, breaking and cracking her armor.

As though she had been blindsided by an enormous hammer, the enemy flew sideways more than ten meters, bounced off the wall of the empty roof, and fell. Before his opponent could stand again, the Beast used his wings to fly fiercely toward her. He had no sooner straddled the body lying on its back than he cried out once more.

"Grr...aaaaaaar!!"

He thrust the sword in his right hand into the ground, across the enemy's uninjured sword-arm as a means to check her movement. Then he removed his hand from the hilt, tightened it into a fist, raised it—until he smashed it into the mask of his enemy.

The single blow sent cracks like spiderwebs racing across the black mirrored goggles. He clenched his left hand as well and slammed it into her chest. The tiny fragments that went flying glittered red, reflecting the sun.

Right, left, right. Howling endlessly, the Beast alternated fists to beat at his enemy.

This could no longer be called a duel, or even a fight. It was an explosion of the ultimate ugliness of resentment and hatred built up over many, many long years.

In the back of the Beast's mind as he lashed out wildly with both fists, someone's voice sounded weakly, kindly.

It's…better this way.

I will take. Everything. That pains you.

Because I am your parent, your teacher, your senior…

And because I love you more than anyone.

The once-beautiful black crystal armor was smashed beyond recognition, countless fragments dancing in the air. In between these fragments, several drops of a different hue, a silver light, hung perpendicularly.

The source of the light was the sinister visor covering the Beast's face. From the gap between the top and bottom biting together like the maw of a carnivorous animal, droplets of silver fell one after another, pouring soundlessly onto the shredded and destroyed black armor. Almost like rain.

Like tears.

9

At the bottom of a hole so deep not a ray of light reached him, Haruyuki cowered, clutching his knees to his chest. Above his head, from somewhere very high up, the sharp, heavy sound of an impact rained down periodically. He didn't know what the sound was. But Haruyuki dimly felt it.

Something that must not happen was happening outside this hole—this jail. And when that sound stopped, everything would be in a form that could never be repaired.

Several times, he tried climbing up the walls of the hole. However, there weren't even handholds on the black perpendicular surfaces, much less a ladder. On top of that, he couldn't make a single scratch on them when he dug his nails in. And, of course, flying out was absolutely impossible.

Because right now, Haruyuki was not his duel avatar Silver Crow. He was his plump and rotund real self. There were no tools in the pocket of his uniform, and there was no way that he could climb up a perpendicular wall with this body that could only do two pull-ups.

So he held his knees with helpless arms, pushed his face down as hard as he could, and just kept listening to the low, heavy sound counting down to the end of everything, all while large tears spilled from between his tightly closed eyelids.

I've always been like this.

The time my indoor shoes were hidden for the first time, in second semester of third grade. The time when I was in fifth grade and was forced to imitate a pig in the classroom. Even after I started junior high, each time I had my pathetic allowance ripped off or I got punched for no reason at all, I ran away to some secret hiding spot, held my knees, and cried.

So even if everything ends, I'll just go back to those times. I'll just wake up from a fun dream and go back to reality. Murmuring this in his heart, Haruyuki tried to shut out the sound pouring down from above.

But the hands he brought up to plug his ears stopped halfway for some reason. He lifted his head the tiniest amount, cracked his eyelids open, and stared at the two appendages in front of him.

Short, round fingers. Pasty palms from being kept hidden in pockets for so long. Hands that had so intently refused to reach out toward anyone, to clench for a fight…

Do these two virtual meters feel that far to you?

Abruptly, he felt like someone's voice echoed faintly from far off. And then his own voice in reply:

They do.

"…But…" As he crouched at the bottom of the dark hole, Haruyuki spoke aloud his response to this exchange that reached him from some long-distant memory. "If I reach out, I get a little closer. If I take one step, I get even closer. Someone…very important taught me that."

He placed his hands on his thighs and staggered to his feet. He looked up above his head, but he couldn't see any exit. Just perpendicular walls reaching up forever.

Wiping away the tears spilling out of his eyes with the back of his hand, Haruyuki turned around and faced the black wall rising up before him—the infinite cliff he had tried to climb countless times before, until he inevitably gave up.

But suddenly, he remembered: The memory was hazy, but he felt like he had done something like this before. He had been beaten down to the depths of despair, but he had climbed up a tall wall from there and found a new path.

Unconsciously, Haruyuki clenched his right hand tightly. He stared alternately at the cool wall, shining black, and the softness of his real-world fist. Gritting his teeth, he steeled himself and raised his arm.

It was an awkward punch, lacking speed and power, but even so, the instant his fist hit the wall, a burning pain shot through his right hand and into the core of his brain.

"*Unaaah!*" Haruyuki cried out.

Just barely staying on his feet, he cradled his throbbing hand to his chest. The skin was scraped away where the bones jutted up, and blood was oozing out. Naturally, there wasn't even a single crack in the wall, much less any kind of indentation.

Shoring up his faltering resolve, he clenched his left hand. "*Unnh!*" He pushed it forward with a pathetic yell.

Bam! The sharp impact and then the fierce pain again. The tears he had calmed welled up again suddenly. He pressed his fist—blood oozing up on this one, too—to his mouth and frantically worked to hold back sobs.

He wanted to sit down. He wanted to lean back against the wall, hold his knees, and plug his ears and cover his eyes until everything was over.

However, somewhere in his brain, Haruyuki understood that if he did that, it wouldn't just end with him returning to his original place in the world. The many friends he had gained in a new world would be sad, along with the childhood friends who had stood by him forever—and he would cruelly hurt *her*, the person more important to him than anyone; he would lose her, and block forever the road she should be walking down.

"*Unh…aah!*" He hit the wall again with his injured right fist. A little blood flew onto the black wall, and a dizzying pain pierced the core of his brain.

"Aaah...Aaaaaah!" Now the left. His flesh was crushed; his bones creaked. Tears and snot mixed together as they ran down his face, before falling in large drops on his chest.

The wall was so hard, beyond stone or steel, it didn't seem like the sort of thing a mere flesh-and-blood fist could do anything to. But Haruyuki kept shouting, half in pain and with a crumpled face, beating at the wall with his clenched fists. Right, left, right. From far above, the sound of a gong beating out destruction continued to rain down on him. He matched that pace and punched the wall. *Punch.*

Soon enough, both hands were covered in blood and slowly swelling up. He had passed the stage of feeling pain as pain, and now a burning sensation that was hard to endure raced along his nerves, like they were being scorched directly with fire. If he slackened his focus for even a second, he might collapse and not be able to get back up again. So Haruyuki gritted his teeth so tightly they threatened to crack, and as high-pitched shrieks made their way through the gap, he punched the wall over and over.

Again and again. Right, left, right, left, right again—

"It's no use."

A small voice came from behind him.

Haruyuki dropped his battered fists for a moment and looked back over his shoulder.

A much younger boy was standing at the bottom of the hole. His face was unfamiliar. He had on a T-shirt and knee-length shorts, and his longish hair hung over his forehead. From the fact that the boy was much shorter than Haruyuki, and his youthful face as well, it was probable that he was in second or third grade at best.

The boy turned a nihilistic, somehow pitying gaze on Haruyuki. "It's no use," he said again. "You can't break that wall."

Panting wildly, Haruyuki returned faintly, "That's...You don't know. Unless you try."

His hands were indeed on the verge of shattering, but they still moved; they could still clench. And he had his feet as well, he had his shoulders, he had his head, even. He had no intention of stopping until his body was completely destroyed and he could no longer stand up.

He looked back at the boy, his eyes brimming with tears at the thought, and then started to turn back toward the wall.

But before he could, the boy, shaking his head in tiny increments, said, "It's impossible. I mean, this 'despair,' it's not yours, it's mine. This is the hole in my heart."

"What…"

"You're the first one who's ever come down this far. But even from way, way shallower parts, there's never been anyone who could get out of the hole. Not the person before you, or the person before that, or the person before that…This hole will disappear when the Accelerated World itself disappears. Until those guys who betrayed Fron and made her suffer have all disappeared, every last one of them, my despair won't end."

The instant he heard this, Haruyuki understood.

The young boy before his eyes was the first. The Burst Linker who had twisted the Arc Destiny, and the longsword Star Caster with the Incarnate of his overly massive rage and despair, and changed them into the Armor of Catastrophe, the Disaster, at the dawn of the Accelerated World.

Chrome Falcon.

"Have you…been here all this time?" Haruyuki asked hoarsely. But of course he had. Because the one who produced the pseudo-intelligence that lived in the Armor, that "Beast," was this boy. It wasn't strange at all that hidden in the depths of the core of the Beast was Falcon's heart.

However, if that were the case, then how ironic. Somewhere inside the data that made up the Armor of Catastrophe, the heart of the Saffron Blossom Falcon loved also survived. But Blossom, that golden-yellow girl, could not appear when the Enhanced

Armament was activated as Disaster. And similarly, Falcon could not appear while Destiny was summoned. Sweethearts infinitely close and yet never to meet...

No.

No, that wasn't it. Whatever form was summoned, Destiny and Disaster were one and the same. Haruyuki had seen it in the Brain Burst central server. If both of their hearts remained inside the zeta star of the Big Dipper that had glittered dazzlingly bright in the center of that trembling galaxy, then they had to have already met by chance.

Forgetting the pain in his hands momentarily, Haruyuki thought hard about the fundamental difference between the Armor of Catastrophe, aka the Disaster, and the Arc, the Destiny.

It was the fact that the Armor swallowed up the longsword Star Caster when in the Disaster state, while the two were separated when in the Destiny state. Only when the sword was separate, in other words, when it was calculated independently, could Saffron Blossom appear.

It wasn't the Armor Blossom lived in. It was the sword. The small companion star shining faintly beside the zeta Kaiyou. She herself might not have realized it, but Blossom's thoughts existed inside that sword.

The memory of the long, sad dream, brought back to life by the complete fusion with the Beast. At the final curtain of that tragedy, Saffron Blossom was devoured and killed endlessly by the Hell snake Jormungand, and then Jormungand dropped the item Star Caster. Almost like a present from the dead.

"Is...that it?" Haruyuki murmured, in a voice that was not a voice.

If his guess was right, then there existed only one way to break the curse called Catastrophe and sever the cycle of tragedy that had played out unbroken in the Accelerated World. Maybe. But to try it, he had to escape from this dark hole somehow. Before everything ended.

"I...can't give up," Haruyuki said, staring hard at the young boy—at Chrome Falcon—standing there, head hanging. "I mean, I still exist here."

Turning around, he raised his battered right hand. None of his fingers worked to his satisfaction anymore, but he endured the pain and started with his little finger to bend them all into a fist.

"*Unh*...Aaaaah..." Raising his voice, he brandished that fist with everything he had.

"Aaaaah!!" And slammed it straight into the wall with a desperate cry.

Crack! A hard sound rang out, and a crimson light raced around the core of his mind.

"*Ungah*...Aaaaaah!!"

Next, his left fist. The straight punch, with the angular momentum and weight of his body riding on it, charged forward, and fresh blood scattered on the wall.

"It's impossible..." A quiet murmur spilled out from behind him. "No one can break out of this despair. No one can sever the shackles of Catastrophe. Not until there's only one left at the end of the world."

"...Do you...seriously...want that?" Haruyuki asked, brandishing his right fist. "Being the last one...means that you would bear all that sadness all by yourself. It means that you alone would carry the memories of the Burst Linkers who disappeared. Is that loneliness...really what you want?!"

Crack!! He beat at the wall with all his might. Blood dripped from the hand he pulled back.

"What I want? No, that's not it," the voice replied quietly, coolly, sounding even sad somehow. "They're the ones who want to destroy everything with fighting. The ones who betrayed and killed Fron. I'm just trying to give them what they want."

"Then...then I'm asking you!" Haruyuki shouted, as he slammed his right fist into the wall, blood flying off and hitting his face. "What about what *Saffron Blossom* wants?! What about her wish to make it so that no one ever had to disappear from the Accelerated World?! Aren't you betraying Blossom's hope right now?!"

For a while, he got no answer. Then finally, an even quieter voice shook the thick darkness.

"Fron's not here anymore."

One more time.

"Fron's gone. And a world without Fron doesn't need hope. Those guys who killed her have no right to wish for hope."

"You're wrong…You're wrong!!" Haruyuki screamed, alternately swinging his bloody fists. "Even if Blossom's gone, her hope lives on. It's here right beside you!!"

"…You're lying."

"I'm not lying!! If you reach out your hand…If you just reach out your hand a little to the other side of this wall…"

"You're lying!" Here, finally, the boy that was the residual thoughts of Chrome Falcon erupted in a shout. "The only thing that exists in this world is despair! No one can escape this pit of despair! Not you…and not even me!!"

"Do you think…you're the only one…who knows despair?!" Haruyuki howled, blood and tears flying. "If this wall is your despair…then I am going to smash it!! Me, Pigita, Barfuyuki, Pizzamaru, Piggy—Haruyuki Arita…!!"

Convinced that his fist would shatter completely with the next blow, Haruyuki nevertheless pulled his right hand as far back as he could. Adding the force of a charge to it, the force of slamming it with his entire body—"I will smash it!!"

Claaaang!! A crash roared through the dark pit, sounding like a fierce collision with Silver Crow's metal armor.

A moment of silence.

Krk!

A crack—extremely faint, but definitely there.

And then Haruyuki saw it. A fine white line radiating outward bit by bit from the point of contact between the wall and his right fist.

The world shuddered. The crack stretched out, picking up speed as it did, and reached the floor from the curving wall.

"…You…," a voice muttered from behind him.

Haruyuki slowly turned and looked at the boy standing there, stock-still. Unconscious words flowed from his lips, which oozed blood because of the number of times he had bitten them.

"I'm the same as you," Haruyuki said. "...I'm sure, deep down, everyone in this world is like you..."

Hearing this, the boy, Chrome Falcon, finally lifted his hanging head, albeit only the tiniest amount. Haruyuki couldn't read his expression, but the instant his clear eyes caught Haruyuki's...

The world of darkness became countless shining shards of glass, and shattered.

"Graaaaar!!" With an ominous roar, the right fist wrapped in dark metal armor was about to set out on its downward course yet again.

Reflexively, Haruyuki slid that trajectory to the right, and below the fist, cracks radiated outward in the limestone paving stones, until the expanding shock wave made the entire tower shake slightly.

Immediately to the left of that arm was the face mask of the Black King, Black Lotus, so thoroughly destroyed it seemed impossible for it to get any more so.

The V-shaped side horns were both broken in half, and cruel cracks ran throughout the slickly shining mirrored goggles. The damage extended to her entire torso, to the point where it was hard to find an uninjured part of her.

It was clear that the fists of the Disasterfied Silver Crow had inflicted this damage—Haruyuki's own hands. As he opened both eyes wide in shock, his avatar's left arm trembled and came back up on its own, ready to launch the next blow.

Still straddling the Black King, Haruyuki mustered up his willpower and stopped his fist. Instantly, inside his head, a roar full of the Beast's rage echoed wildly.

WHY DO YOU FIGHT ME?! THIS IS THE ENEMY!! AN ENEMY TO BE DESTROYED!!

Haruyuki's entire body shook once more, but did not move any further. At the very least, the right to operate this duel avatar was currently his.

No!! Haruyuki called back desperately in his mind, left fist still raised high. *This person is not the enemy!! She's…more important to me…than anyone…!!*

But he forced himself to cut the thought off there. He had no idea how long he would maintain priority with the avatar. Before he fell into a berserker state again, there was something he had to do.

The ominous form of the longsword was plunged into the earth, crossing the right arm of battered and nearly unconscious Kuroyukihime. But this sword had not always had this form. In the long-distant past, Saffron Blossom had been devoured by the Hell snake Jormungand, and the silver sword appeared from inside that Enemy, like she was trying to communicate her dying wish. A dying wish that had been twisted by Chrome Falcon's rage and grief and incorporated as one part of the Catastrophe.

If, as Haruyuki had guessed, the soul of Blossom still remained inside this sword, and assuming that what produced the Catastrophe was Blossom and Falcon's eternal separation, then he had to make them meet again. And he could think of only one way to make that happen.

But an enormous obstacle still remained.

It was obvious why the Beast ran wild and attacked Black Lotus. In the instant before the Black King attacked, Black Vise changed his own shape into a shadow portrait of Saffron Blossom and pried open the origin of the Beast, its greatest pain.

According to Haruyuki's memories up until the moment his mind was sent flying to the bottom of that darkness, after the Black King's special attack pierced her chest, the fake Saffron had pretended to crumble and fall to the ground, dying, and then sunk into the shadows at their feet.

And then immediately after that, every single terrain object, the walls and pillars that had stood on the roof of Mori Tower, had been completely blown away in the aftershock of the clash between Black Lotus and Chrome Disaster. Which meant that the shadows those objects made had also been eliminated. The power to move from shadow to shadow was no longer useful.

In other words—Black Vise was still hiding in a shadow carved out in the ground before his eyes.

Right now, he likely hadn't realized that Haruyuki had escaped from his berserker state. But there was no doubt that if he sensed the slightest abnormality, he would come up out of the shadow and strike up his next demonic plan. If he wanted to pummel the layered avatar with a counterattack before that, Haruyuki wouldn't be permitted a single misstep in the action he took now.

The ones who had pushed Saffron Blossom and Chrome Falcon into that cruel trap and created the opportunity for the Armor of Catastrophe to appear were precisely Black Vise and the Acceleration Research Society. Could he sever the cycle of tragedy looping over the seven years of real-world time since then—or would he be caught by the Society and turned into their trump card?

Here was that watershed. The moment of victory or defeat.

"Graaaaar!!" A sinister howl surging out of him, Haruyuki used his left hand to pull the blackish-silver longsword out of the ground nearby and up into the air.

Without a moment's delay, he stretched out his right arm and tightly grabbed hold of the slender neck of Black Lotus, still lying motionless on the ground.

I'm sorry, Kuroyukihime! I'll apologize later, so, so much!!

Sword secured in his left hand and the Black King in his right, Haruyuki threw his whole body back and howled again.

"Gra...aaaaaah!"

His long tail twisted, and he spread out the metal wings on his back. He kicked fiercely at the paving stones and took to the air. On a spiraling trajectory, he aimed for the golden sun spanning the western sky. What was important was distance and angle. Keeping an eye on Mori Tower in one corner of his field of view, he flew thirty meters or so before settling into a hover.

Perhaps roused by the sudden change in gravity, bluish-purple eye lenses flickered faintly beyond Black Lotus's cracked goggles.

Haruyuki stared down at the Black King, eyes desperate

beneath the visor that was modeled after the maw of a carnivorous animal. A voice on the verge of disappearing touched Haru's hearing.

...Haruyuki...?

Kuroyukihime! Kuroyukihime!!

Earnestly fighting his tug-of-war with the raging Beast as it tried to wrest back control of the avatar, Haruyuki returned the thought with everything he had. *After I hurt you like this, you probably won't believe a word I have to say. But right now, just for this moment! Please trust me!!*

And then he felt like the Black King smiled faintly...*What. Are you talking about...? I've always trusted you. Up to now...and from now on, too...Forever...*

These words spilled into Haruyuki's mind and glittered like multicolored gems, and a passion so powerful it threatened to drive him mad filled his heart. He wanted to throw away the sword in his left hand and hug Kuroyukihime to him. But doing that would be the end of everything. He still had a job to do. To undo the curse of the Armor and end the chain of sadness, he had to make those two meet one more time.

"*Graaa...aaaaaah!!*" Haruyuki made a remarkably fierce roar ring out through the eternal twilight, and twisted the longsword he clutched in his left hand to face him, brandishing it high.

To anyone looking up and watching from below, the action would have looked like nothing more than the sword in his left hand going to pierce the avatar he held fast in his right. And because his back was completely turned to the tower, the point of the sword would have been hidden by the large extended wings of the avatar, and thus be invisible.

He held his breath, concentrated every ounce of willpower he could muster—the positive Incarnate that could be called a prayer or wish—in his left hand and brought the sword down.

The sharp tip passed to the side of the Black King's body, merely brushing up against it, and lightly pierced the center of the Armor of Catastrophe—toward Haruyuki's own heart.

*   *   *

Do you betray us?! Even you?! You betray and try to destroy us?!

A dreadful howl of rage from the Beast rang out inside his head. However, this cry almost seemed to contain the slightest echo of sadness.

No! I'm not going to destroy you or anything! This sword can't hurt you!!

Haruyuki intently turned his thoughts toward the Beast. But right away, an overwhelming torrent of hatred threatened to swallow them up.

Lies! All who exist are deceivers, cheaters, traitors!! I trust no one!!

The voice sounded somehow like a sob, and several threads of a jet-black aura spilled out of the hole dug out of his chest armor. These tangled up around the blade of the longsword and tried to push it back from the chest.

Desperately fighting the reaction, Haruyuki shouted, *I'm not telling you to trust me!! But there's one person in this world who loves you and cares for you!! Her...Trust her!!*

A pure white light gushed from Haruyuki's sword-hand. The aura, glittering dazzlingly, began to wrap around the sinister form of the greatsword, moving from the hilt to the tip. The parts the light touched changed design, evaporating, and the figure of a new sword appeared from inside. A flowing silver longsword with several stars caught inside the semitransparent blade. The Enhanced Armament Star Caster.

"Unh...aaaaaaah!!" Together with a fierce cry in his own voice, Haruyuki stabbed his own chest with the longsword that had regained its original form, up to the hilt.

The blow generated no numerical damage. He didn't feel pain or even the impact. Instead, Haruyuki took in a single image with all five senses: an infinite darkness filling a thick, superhard shell.

A small fissure ran along the metal shell covering his world. Through the crack, a brilliant white light reminiscent of the spring sun came pouring in. The fissure grew bigger before his eyes, and the light steadily grew stronger. From beyond this dazzling shine, almost too bright to look at directly, someone was flying into the world of darkness, both arms outstretched.

Wrapped in golden-yellow armor with a flower-petal motif. Glittering drops of light spilling out of sky-blue eye lenses. The girl who had lived in the longsword Star Caster and had continued to pray earnestly for so, so long—Saffron Blossom.

Gently descending, Blossom stood tall and faced the center of the world of darkness.

An enormous something existed there, its body covered in jet-black flames, a something with eyes the color of blood and long fangs. The Beast.

Not frightened in the least, the golden-yellow girl walked over to it, reaching out with her right hand. "I'm sorry. I left you alone for so long. You must have been sad…It was so hard, wasn't it?"

A low groan spilled from the massive maw of the Beast. It tucked its head in and shook it quickly, back and forth, as though it couldn't believe the girl was standing there before it. It tried to step back, tail hanging.

But Blossom approached with a resolute step and didn't hesitate before taking the enormous head into her outstretched hands. She stroked the conflagration of fur. "We'll always be together from now on. Always, always together…"

Pop! The black flames covering the Beast burst. A massive energy wave spread out within the shell and was finally absorbed it. And then, standing there—

Not a duel avatar, but a real-bodied little girl. Her hair was cut boyishly short. She wore a large-ish hooded sweater and culottes. And in both arms, she held a small black cat.

The girl smiled gently and, still holding the kitten, took a few steps forward. A little ways off stood the boy—Chrome Falcon. His lips trembled, and he timidly raised his right hand.

The little girl started running toward him. The two grew closer with each passing breath until the tips of their outstretched fingers touched, clasped, and held each other tightly.

Fal!!

Fron!!

Their voices became a gentle wave and echoed throughout the metal shell.

And then the thick shell enclosing the darkness turned into a myriad of flower petals and broke apart abruptly.

As if melting into the dancing snowy white lights, all the suffering, hatred, and sadness that had filled the Armor sublimated away. Riding on the twinkling, fleeting sound of a bell, it all flowed, drifted, and receded.

On the verge of returning from the world of the image to the madder red of the duel field, Haruyuki felt like he could hear that voice.

FAREWELL, MY FINAL COMRADE. YOU...ARE STRONG. STRONGER THAN ME. I DESTROY AND AM DESTROYED AGAIN BY ALL THOSE PEOPLE. I PRAY YOUR LIGHT REMAINS IN THE WORLD AND YOU CUT OUT THE ROOT OF THE EVIL...

At the same time as the voice faded, Haruyuki was restored to the Accelerated World—the sky of the Twilight stage. In his right arm, the body of the injured Black Lotus. His left hand held nothing at all.

And the metal armor of his body reflected the light of the setting sun, shining a pure, mirrored silver.

10

"Kuroyukihime." Haruyuki gave voice to this one word, filling it with every drop of the flood of emotions within him.

He couldn't help but feel such guilt that he wanted to rip his own body apart for falling into the berserker state and injuring so severely the swordmaster he had sworn to protect, Black Lotus—Kuroyukihime.

However, Kuroyukihime had dared to stop Haruyuki's fists with her own body after he'd lost himself and gone wild. Given that the king had enough actual power to inflict serious damage on even a Super-class Enemy like the God Suzaku, she should have been able to at least counter the blows, even if her opponent was the rampaging Chrome Disaster. But instead, she had taken every bit of the beating he had mercilessly brought down on her. She had believed that Haruyuki would regain himself again…

In Silver Crow's arms as he hovered in the air, hearing the trembling voice calling her name, Kuroyukihime blinked bluish-purple eye lenses irregularly beneath her battered, mirror-finish goggles. Her endlessly kind and gentle response flowed out on the faint wind of the stage.

"…Welcome back, Silver Crow. You did…well…" The half-broken sword of her left hand gently stroked the surface of the round helmet.

"Kuro…yuki…" Once more, he squeezed a faltering voice out and desperately suppressed the sobs rising up in him.

He wanted to bury his face in her chest and wail like a little kid. But this was not yet the time for that. There was still one more thing he had to do. He had a promise to keep with his erstwhile partner, the pseudo-intelligence of the Beast. It would probably take a long time to fulfill his vow to cut the root of evil from the world, but he would fire the first shot into this battlefield. To show the pride of the Black Legion and his own as a Burst Linker.

Kuroyukihime seemed to pick up on his intent through their armor touching. She nodded once, very slightly. "We have one chance, one moment. We're both close-range types, so we'll have to carry out the attack with long-range Incarnate. But we don't have the luxury of slowly mustering up the image…You focus on targeting, I'll provide the power."

Despite the fact that she was so thoroughly injured that, viewed from any angle, it seemed any further fighting was impossible, Kuroyukihime's words were filled with a firm resolve to fight. Haruyuki returned her nod and cleared his mind.

"We go from a count of three. Two, one, zero!"

In time with the instruction, he whirled his body around abruptly.

Below him, an enormous chalky spire rose up in the center of his field of view, bathed in the evening sun—Mori Tower. The roof had been swept clear of objects in the earlier clash between Black Lotus and Chrome Disaster, and transformed into a perfectly white plain.

In the center of this bled a single small, black dot. It was the shadow produced by Haruyuki and Kuroyukihime midflight with the sun behind them. However, for this moment alone, it was not simply a lighting effect of the virtual world: It was also the hiding place of his sworn enemy, the Burst Linker for whom, no matter how great the hatred in Haruyuki's heart became, it would never be enough.

Yes. In that instant, within that tiny shadow hid the layered avatar who called himself the vice president of the Acceleration Research Society, the restrainer, Black Vise. One branch of the root of all evil the Beast had told Haruyuki to cut out.

"Crow! Your hand!!" Kuroyukihime shouted sharply, lifting her right sword high.

The tip of her sword-arm shone with a hazy golden overlay and separated with a *snap* to produce five slender fingers. Instinctively, Haruyuki reached out with his left hand and tangled his fingers tightly around them. From their clasped hands, the brilliant light of two auras—one crimson red, one silver—jetted out.

At that point, no doubt guessing something was amiss, a single, thin black panel slid out from the blurred shadow on the roof thirty meters below. Black Vise. The panel slid along as if glued to the floor, heading for the inner edge of the roof—more precisely, the enormous shadow that fell on the eastern wall of the building. If the roof had remained covered with its original pillars and walls, this layered avatar, with the unusual ability to move from shadow to shadow, would have been able to leisurely escape the battlefield without exposing himself.

But every single object capable of producing a shadow had already been destroyed. And the tower was the tallest building in the area. The only shadow etched onto that roof was that of Haruyuki and Kuroyukihime. And this was no coincidence— Haruyuki flew at these coordinates after precisely calculating the angle and distance that would produce this condition.

For these reasons, Black Vise could not, as he had done so many times before, sink into the shadows and escape—he could not, in his own words, show off his "greatest ability," fleeing.

This was their one moment, their one chance.

Haruyuki concentrated the image of light in his left hand as fast as he could, pushing up against the limits of the speed he had managed up to that point. The crimson overlay produced in Kuroyukihime's right hand carved a spiral in the silver one he generated, fusing with it.

"Laser Lance!!"

"Vorpal Strike!!"

The two different technique names rang out, one over the other in perfect unison.

From between their clasped hands, the two auras extended, carving out a trajectory like the double helix of DNA to produce a single, enormous lance.

Movement synchronized, the pair threw the lance toward the tower below. The silver-and-crimson javelin plunged ahead, ripples spreading out around it in the virtual atmosphere, and quickly closed in on the thin black panel quickening its slide away. The two parallel tips touched the center of the panel.

And then Haruyuki saw it.

The jet-black sheet scattering into countless fragments and radiating outward.

The lance did not stop there; it touched the white roof and easily dug into it, as if pushing through the surface of a body of water.

Leaving behind only a high-pitched *skrnnn* of resonance, it disappeared into the two hundred thirty-eight meters of the massive building.

A few seconds later, from far lower on the building, a vibration wave like the earth trembling came racing upward. The decorative windows of the building's outer walls shuddered violently, along with the pillars and bas reliefs straight out of temples of Ancient Greece, some of them even cleaving from their homes. And the damage didn't stop there: Deep cracks raced, one after another, along the entire outside wall, a torrent of flaming energy erupting from inside…

In the next instant, Roppongi Hills Mori Tower, a landmark and without a doubt one of the largest structures in the Accelerated World, began to collapse, reduced to an infinite amount of falling rubble.

The phenomenon itself was incredible, but for Haruyuki, the complete destruction of the enormous building was just one more thing to fill his special-attack gauge. More important was the burst point addition system message that scrolled in small letters along the left side of his field of view. This meant, then, that the earlier combined Incarnate attack had pushed the health gauge of his sworn enemy Black Vise down to zero—he was dead.

Of course, death in the Accelerated World was, for the majority of Burst Linkers, an everyday occurrence. Their points simply decreased a certain number as a penalty, and they came back to life perfectly fine in the next duel in the Normal Duel Field, or an hour later in the Unlimited Neutral Field. However, there was an exception to this rule.

"Kuroyukihime!" Hands still intertwined, Haruyuki turned toward her and shouted, "How about it?!"

The question omitted the subject, but the Black King still shook her head slightly. "No. From the number of points added, he seems to be level eight."

"...He is, huh..." Haruyuki said, letting out the breath he'd been holding.

If the restrainer Black Vise had reached the same level nine as Kuroyukihime, the sudden-death rule would have applied to him now, and he would have lost all his points in one swoop and been forever banished from the Accelerated World. Given Vise's history—basically one of the oldest residents of this world—and his unfathomable powers, Haruyuki had anticipated that it might at least be a possibility, but unfortunately, that schemer had apparently stopped at level eight.

Which meant that the layered avatar, instantly dying when pierced by the Incarnate lance, remained in the field as a small death marker and would regenerate in an hour. If they challenged him again there without letting him run off and defeated him over and over again, at some point, they would press him to total loss...but...

"It'll be quite the chore to find his marker in that mountain of rubble."

At the sound of Kuroyukihime's voice, Haruyuki looked down

at the enormous pile of destruction that had been Mori Tower. He couldn't begin to guess how many tens or hundreds of thousands of wreckage objects were stacked up in that pyramid; it was indeed a fact that it would be difficult to turn each of them over to find the death marker.

"And there are a lot of shadows on the ground, too. I feel like next time would probably just end with him running off at top speed."

"Mmm. That's exactly it…Well, at any rate, we did defeat him once, he who is so proud of his fleet-footedness. That should serve nicely as a declaration of war," Kuroyukihime responded before gently untangling her hand from Haruyuki's. The five slender fingers made an ephemeral *crack*ing sound before shattering.

"Ah!" Haruyuki cried out.

The Black King turned a gentle smile on him. "Just over two minutes. A new record."

"…Kuroyukihime." He reached out his right hand once more and wrapped it around the half-broken jet-black sword. Even though he had so much he wanted to say, so much he *had* to say, the words were obstructed by the enormous vortex of emotion welling up in his chest.

Everything was over—even though in actuality, it wasn't. Although the curse that produced the Armor of Catastrophe, the Disaster, had been broken and the Armor had disappeared superficially, it still existed in some form or another system-wise somewhere in the data that made up Silver Crow. Until it was separated from him as an item through purification, the current mission was not over. And he still couldn't see the big picture strategy of the Acceleration Research Society, who he assumed were the source of the ISS kits.

Pushing back once more the impulse to clutch the battered and bruised Kuroyukihime to his chest with all his might, Haruyuki slid his hovering body a little to the northeast. His eyes caught the majestic Midtown Tower, soaring higher even than Mori had been, about five hundred meters ahead.

"Can you see it, Kuroyukihime? The transparent Enemy lurking at the top of Midtown there."

A few seconds later, Kuroyukihime assented quietly. "Mmhmm."

At first glance in the fiery light of the setting sun, it appeared that there was nothing around the tip of the massive tower. But squinting hard, he noticed the presence of an enormous *something* bending the rays of sunlight slightly.

"Iron Pound from GW said it was the Legend-class Enemy Archangel Metatron. He said someone tamed it and moved it from the bottom of the Dungeon up over there."

"So Metatron has left the Cathedral? Then that means...that that tower is basically unapproachable outside the Hell stage, which has an extremely low appearance rate."

"That's exactly it. The huge explosion you guys saw in the south during the last dive was when Metatron there reacted to Pound's rocket punch and shot off an incredibly powerful laser."

"I see...The scope of that explosion makes sense now. And this means that Midtown Tower is itself..." Kuroyukihime trailed off.

"Yes," Haruyuki said. "That's the location of the ISS kit main body—the headquarters of the Acceleration Research Society."

With sharp eyes turned toward the massive spire in the distance, Kuroyukihime maintained the silence for a few seconds, then relaxed slightly and murmured, "I dearly want to go and raid it right now, but...Fuko and the others would be angry if we went ahead without them. Let's leave this Castle attack for later enjoyment."

At this extremely bold line, Haruyuki couldn't stop his mouth from softening beneath his helmet. Perhaps sensing this, Kuroyukihime smiled slightly before continuing in a different tone, "Now then, it's about time for us to be getting home. The nearest portal is..."

"Oh! Oh, no. It would have been inside the tower. If the building was totally blown away, then..."

"Ha-ha-ha!" Kuroyukihime laughed at Haruyuki's panicking. "It's fine. No matter what sort of attack they come under, the leave-point portals cannot be destroyed. Their coordinates are completely fixed, so even if the tower was destroyed, it should still be floating in the place where it normally is."

He sent his gaze racing around. The blue circular form was indeed floating in space several dozen meters diagonally below them. There was no mistake that the shimmering he saw there, so like the surface of still water, was a one-way door to the real world.

Haruyuki gently cradled Kuroyukihime's injured body in his arms and spread the silver wings on his back—now restored to their former sheen—to start a gentle glide through the air. Before his eyes, the portal hanging in empty space grew larger, welcoming them with a gently pulsating light.

On the verge of plunging into the surface of the blue water, he flipped himself around and took in the eternal evening of the Twilight stage spreading out around them. Beyond the neighborhoods of Roppongi and Shirokane and past Shinagawa, he could see Tokyo Bay, reflecting the orange light of the setting sun and glittering brightly. For some reason, the sight called up a bittersweetness in Haruyuki so strong that he wanted to cry.

The instant they slipped through the ring of blue light and returned to the real world from the Unlimited Neutral Field, something elastic was pressed tiiiiightly up against his face, completely closing off his view. Unable to immediately recall where he had dived from and in what position, Haruyuki frantically flapped his hands.

And then from his fingertips came an incredibly soft sensation like silk thread—although, of course, he had never actually touched real silk—and he unconsciously caressed it. The delightfully smooth texture was something so...*right*. It was really similar to the feel of Kuroyukihime's long hair when she had directed with him in an audacious posture on top of him in bed in the nurse's room at Umesato after he was carried there when he collapsed during the basketball game. Or maybe it was exactly the same thing?

"You really did so well, Haruyuki," a voice murmured abruptly in his ear.

In an instant, Haruyuki finally remembered where he was. The living room of a stylish town house in one corner of the URB Asagaya residences in southern Suginami Ward, on top of a large beanbag chair by the window. And the person holding his head with all her might was none other than the master of this house, Haruyuki's parent, head of the Legion Nega Nebulus/vice president of the Umesato Junior High School student council, the Black King, Black Lotus, aka Kuroyukihime.

Kuroyukihime invited me to her house for the first time...We sat together on an enormous beanbag and directed...We used the "unlimited burst" command and dove into the Unlimited Neutral Field together...and then...

When his brain finally caught up, a fierce shudder ran through him. His voice spilled out as he moved his lips slightly, unawares. "K-kuro...yukihime...I—I hurt you...so, so much—"

"That's enough!" A sharp voice cut off Haruyuki's river of self-reproach. Gently pulling away from his head, which she held cradled to her chest, Kuroyukihime looked into his eyes from extremely close-up. "There is not a single thing you need to apologize for," she said, her tone easing. "You fought wonderfully and accomplished what needed to be done. That's all. If anyone here is to be reproached, it's me for failing to consider even the possibility of an ambush."

"Th-that's— I mean, I, I should have been watching out. I knew the place we'd appear after diving was really close to their headquarters."

"Even if you had very seriously warned me, it's doubtful whether or not I would have been able to respond to the surprise attack by that annoying panel avatar. In that sense…I suppose we could say that we both put up a good fight. After all, we're here like this now, talking, the same people we were before the dive."

Her endlessly smooth and silky voice gently soothed Haruyuki's exhausted senses. As the sensation of the hand gently stroking his scalp sank in, his mind threatened to wander far off, but right before it did, he remembered something and opened his eyes once more.

"Oh, that reminds me, Kuroyukihime. You said something right before we dove, didn't you?"

"Mmm. Did I, then?"

"Umm. Something about if we both come back safe or something?" He turned a puzzled gaze on her.

For some reason, the porcelain of Kuroyukihime's skin was dyed a cherry pink. She jerked her head back, but perhaps the movement was too sudden, and she lost her balance on the beanbag chair.

Haruyuki stretched out a hand, but to no avail. Her bottom hit the floor with a wonderful *thump*. Two seconds later, the black-clad beauty stood up with a look on her face like nothing had happened and cleared her throat deliberately before continuing.

"Ahem. D-did I say something like that? Let's see. That was, then, if we both returned safely, I would whip up some of my excellent cooking in celebration."

Although he felt that both her tone and facial expression had a fleeting awkwardness to them, the majority of Haruyuki's thoughts were carried away by the word *cooking*. The last time he'd eaten was the enormous plate of sushi around six thirty, shared among the six Legion members—well, seven if he counted Rin Kusakabe. He hadn't moved much physically, but so many things had happened that weighed heavy on his mental capabilities. Just roughly listing them, he had…

* * *

June 20, 2047. Seven PM: Haru dove with Utai Shinomiya/Ardor Maiden into the Castle inner sanctuary in the Unlimited Neutral Field. He gained the assistance of the mysterious young samurai avatar Trilead Tetroxide aka Lead, and defeated the guardian Enemy while escaping from the Castle.

Immediately following that event: Haru made contact with the Super-class Enemy, the God Suzaku, on the large bridge outside the southern gates of the Castle. After bringing Maiden to safety, he used the Incarnate flying technique Light Speed to fly vertically upward outside the atmosphere while rescuing Kuroyukihime and Fuko, who were acting as bait. When Suzaku lost the divine protection of flames, it was crushed by Kuroyukihime's superdreadnought Incarnate attack, Starburst Stream.

Continuing from there: The escape into the Unlimited Neutral Field from the southern bridge was completed. They carried out the mission to rescue Ardor Maiden, but Haruyuki set out alone to find Ash Roller, who was supposed to join them.

After that: Haru discovered Ash Roller under attack by a group of six ISS kit users on Meiji Street in the Shibuya Ward. He lost his composure and summoned the Armor of Catastrophe from its seed state. With his power as the sixth Chrome Disaster, he instantly slaughtered the kit users and then fled the scene.

Thereupon: He met the Green King Green Grandé and his escort Iron Pound on the roof of Mori Tower in the Roppongi area. Haruyuki crushed Pound after a fierce battle and exchanged a single blow with the Green King before bursting out through the emergency disconnection safety activated in the real world.

Seven twenty PM: Haruyuki fled, after locking his friends from his Legion within his home. But in the shopping mall on the first floor, he was captured by Fuko's child, Ash Roller/Rin Kusakabe. They moved to a car in the underground parking area and, after talking, entered a direct duel.

Seven forty PM: He was recaptured by Fuko, Chiyuri, and Kuroyukihime. He promised not to run off by himself, and at eight PM, they dispersed. He then quietly did his homework in his room.

Nine PM: He exited the house once more, leaving a note to his mother that he would be on a sleepover that night. However, he was recaptured by Kuroyukihime in the garden in front of the condo building. He was put into a taxi and taken to Kuroyuki-hime's home in Minami Asagaya. After talking for a long time, the two of them dove back into the Unlimited Neutral Field.

Ten fifteen PM: The battle with the vice president of the Acceleration Research Society, Black Vise, on the rooftop skydeck of Roppongi Hills Mori Tower. Although an evil trick plunged him into an unprecedented state of wildness, he happened to meet Chrome Falcon, the first Chrome Disaster, in the deepest depths of the imagination circuit. He suddenly understood the secret of the two Enhanced Armaments that made up the Armor of Catastrophe and finally succeeded at removing the curse.

All of these too-numerous incidents had happened one after the other in just over a mere three hours. But by his own reckoning, the *mental* energy Haruyuki had burned was up to 2,500 kilocalories, and thus, it was inevitable that the incredible appeal of *Kuroyukihime's cooking* would steal away with his thoughts.

He tumbled out of the beanbag chair with a *thud* himself and trotted after Kuroyukihime as she headed toward the kitchen.

The kitchen space off the living room was fairly large for a one-person dwelling, but the sink and the induction cooktop sparkled; the sense that it wasn't used much was not that different from the Arita house. On top of that, he couldn't spot anything in the nature of a pot. But he interpreted this as something along the lines of *a masterful housewife is also good at cleaning up*.

"Uh, um, I'll help," he called to Kuroyukihime, as she turned toward the refrigerator. "I'm not actually so good at cooking, but I can peel potatoes or something at least."

"Oh-ho, impressive! Teach me the trick to it next time. When I peel them, they strangely lose mass."

"O-okay. Anytime. Wait. Huh?" Haruyuki blinked quickly, surprised at the admission. He'd assumed she was an excellent chef.

She yanked open the door of the fairly large refrigerator-freezer. The inside was stuffed not with vegetables or meat or fish or fruit, but countless white square packages piled up neatly.

"Haruyuki, jwestchiitaspagerfren, which do you prefer?"

This question posed to him with a serious face, he thought a moment. *Jwestchi* was "Japanese, Western, Chinese," so then if *ita* was "Italian," the rest were "Spanish, German, and French"... right? In that case, a single artless question came to mind.

"Uh, um, how is Western different from *itaspagerfren*?"

"Mmm. It's obvious, isn't it? 'Western' is a Western-style meal. And I'll just say this. Western is traditional Japanese cooking, you know. I like beef stew and macaroni gratin."

"R-right...Th-then I'd like 'Western' beef stew."

"Understood. In that case, perhaps I'll have the gratin." With practiced ease, Kuroyukihime pulled two packages from the tall white towers, put them into the high-powered microwave next to the fridge, and pushed a button. "Dinner will be ready in five minutes. Go wait at the table."

He felt it was a bit hazy as to whether or not this could actually be called cooking, but at the very least, the finger of Kuroyukihime herself had pushed the HEAT button. As he tried to convince himself, Haruyuki slid back into the living room.

The steaming beef stew was transferred from the package to a ceramic plate, and regardless of its origin, it was incredibly delicious. While the flavor was a fair bit blander than the mass-produced frozen dishes, it had a solid savor to it, and there were plenty of root vegetables. Considering the fact that the packaging was extremely simple, it was probably the private label product of some famed restaurant. A salad was also included, so there didn't seem to be any problems at all on the nutritional front, but as he intently moved his spoon, Haruyuki couldn't help picking out the lone commonality with the frozen pizza that was his own daily fare. And that was, in other words...

"Let's trade, Haruyuki. C'mon, aaah!"

Together with these sudden words, a fork was thrust in the direction of his mouth, so Haruyuki reflexively opened it. The large-ish bite of macaroni covered with plenty of velvety béchamel sauce had a firm al dente texture despite the fact that it was a frozen meal, and he chewed it in delight.

Turning a gentle smile on this ecstatic Haruyuki, Kuroyukihime dropped her gaze to the table. "So then, in exchange, that enormous carrot there..."

"Oh! Sure..."

"The super-enormous piece of beef next to it."

"Oh! Sure— Hey, wait! You can't! I've been taking good care of this little one until now."

"You accepted a trade without asking the conditions. That was your error. Now, 'aaah'!" she continued, and closed her eyes as she opened her mouth wide, leaving him no choice but to weepingly offer up the little meat baby he had kept aside to enjoy last.

Enveloped in sadness, but still just a little excited somehow, Haruyuki brought the meat to the other side of the table with his spoon, and after she had disposed of it mercilessly with a chomp and some chewing, Kuroyukihime raised her eyelids and laughed cheerfully.

"Food really does taste better when you eat it with someone else, hmm?"

This hit exactly on the thought struggling in the back of his brain earlier. No matter how good a cook she was or wasn't, Kuroyukihime was sitting at this table by herself every night.

Eating alone was sad. Before the question of flavor or nutrition… just sad. Haruyuki knew that only too well.

"Um, Kuroyukihime?" Forgetting the pain of having his chunk of beef stolen, Haruyuki opened his mouth, heart full of emotion welling up.

"Hmm? You can ask me to give it back, but it's too late, you know?"

"N-no, it's not about the meat. It's, um…" He clutched the spoon tightly in his hand like a protective charm, and stared intently into the jet-black eyes eighty centimeters ahead of him. "Um, I know we can't right away, but…I was thinking it'd be kinda nice if someday…we could eat dinner together like this every day."

There had to be a way—even if *every day* was more a figure of speech than literal truth—some means of increasing the number of suppers where Kuroyukihime wasn't alone, by having her stop by his house on the way home from school or somehow getting past the mandatory departure time at school and staying with her in the student council office or something.

This was Haruyuki's intention in saying this, but…

Kuroyukihime's reaction was rather unexpected. She dropped the fork in her left hand onto the plate of gratin and dipped her fingertips in the fiery hot sauce when she went to pick it up. Crying out "Ah!" she reached out for her glass of ice water and even knocked that over as well.

Fortunately, it was basically empty, and Haruyuki hurried to catch the glass as it fell. Standing it upright again, he looked with puzzlement across the table.

Kuroyukihime had frozen solid, right hand clutched to her chest in her left. There was an excessively strong red element to her coloring, but he couldn't manage to read the look on her face. She seemed surprised, but also like she was ruled by a different emotion entirely.

After a few seconds, she finally relaxed her shoulders a little. "Again? Again, really?" she said briefly.

"Huh? A-again? What is—? Did we talk about dinner before?"

"No…This trick is a first, but…this is the second time you've done something to trouble my circulatory system." She followed up this fairly incomprehensible statement by letting out a long sigh. Catching the eyes of a dumbfounded Haruyuki again, the gentlest of all faint smiles—one he had seen somewhere before—spread across her lips.

"Understood," she said. "I promise: We can eat together as many times as you like."

Standing up, she moved around the table to stand next to Haruyuki and stretched her right hand out in front of her, her pinky finger extended from her loose fist. "Here, pinky promise."

Just as he was told, Haruyuki timidly raised his hand and wrapped his own plump finger around it. Shaking their hands slowly up and down, Kuroyukihime smiled faintly once more.

"It's a promise. Someday, we will eat supper together. Every day."

11

The next day, Friday, June 21, seven PM.

Gathered together in the Arita living room were, as on the previous day, the six current members of Nega Nebulus. Unfortunately—or not, as the case may have been—Ash Roller, aka Rin Kusakabe, was not there. Since she had broken her curfew of eight PM the previous day, she had apparently been categorically prohibited by her father from stopping anywhere on the way home.

"You know, I did wonder why she almost never dueled at night, given her character," Chiyuri remarked, as if it all made sense to her.

Fuko chuckled. "Well, when it comes to vehicles, she's actually pretty terrible with even a manual bicycle, much less an electric scooter. Just like there are duel avatars in the Accelerated World who are a Perfect Match, albeit very few, Rin is one of those you could call a 'perfect mismatch.'"

"Ah-ha-ha! True! And he's not on the level of a mismatch, but Haru's toeing that line, too, huh?!"

The point of Chiyuri's spear suddenly turned toward him, Haruyuki dropped the somen noodles from between his chopsticks.

Given that they couldn't very well have asked Chiyuri's mother to make another big meal for them for the nth day in a row, the menu that day was prepared by the group. That said, the two boys had just boiled the noodles, while the squad of girls had prepared the toppings and dipping sauce. The dinner table took twenty minutes of actual work to put together, but somen noodles crisply chilled in water were exceptional to eat on a hot, humid day at the end of June. Even more so when surrounded by good friends.

After slurping up the noodles he'd rescued from the excessively large glass bowl, together with some chopped ginger, Haruyuki launched his counterargument. "Th-there's stuff in common between me and Silver Crow, you know. Um...we're not easy to hit, bad fuel economy, we hate getting zapped with static electricity..."

UI> THOSE ARE ALL WEAKNESSES, Utai Shinomiya typed politely, after neatly returning her chopsticks to her chopstick rest, and everyone burst out laughing.

Fifteen minutes later, when they had finished cleaning up after dinner and moved to the sofa set, he could see a bit of nervousness in his friends' faces.

Seated at one end, Kuroyukihime let her eyes run over them all before saying in a calm voice, "Just as was explained earlier, thanks to Haruyuki's efforts last night, the negative residual will that could be said to have been the energy allowing for the existence of the Armor of Catastrophe was released. Currently, that armor has no will of its own and has returned to being normal Enhanced Armament...or it should have."

At a glance from Kuroyukihime, Haruyuki nodded firmly. He had given Takumu and the other three an overview of the events that transpired after they had dispersed the previous day in an email, one carefully composed over lunch break that day. Still, he had been forced to leave out the part about being invited to Kuroyukihime's house.

"Nevertheless, the Armor still remains deep inside Haruyuki's avatar in the system as a parasitic object. Unless we completely remove this using Utai's power of purification, those thick-headed kings will not recognize the Armor's elimination. Utai?"

They shifted their eyes, and the youngest present tapped at her holokeyboard with resolution.

UI> LEAVE IT TO ME. THAT IS PRECISELY WHY I AM HERE NOW. HOWEVER, IF THE TARGET IS AN ARC-CLASS, SUPER-HIGH-LEVEL ENHANCED ARMAMENT, AN EQUIVALENTLY LONG TIME HAS TO BE ANTICIPATED FOR THE PURIFICATION. MOST LIKELY, IT WILL TAKE AT LEAST AN HOUR.

"Mmm. So then, the other four of us are there to protect Haruyuki and Utai from Enemies or other Burst Linkers, although these are not very likely. Naturally, we will select an area away from the patrolling courses of large Enemies, but as you well know, they are drawn by the 'scent' of the Incarnate…"

When Kuroyukihime closed her mouth, Takumu spoke with a reliable grin. "If that happens, then we'll earn back the points all of us spent heading into the Unlimited Neutral Field, Master."

"Ho-ho, that's exactly right. If it comes to that, we can simply lure the Enemies into Shinjuku and have them get cozy with an Enemy hunting party in the vicinity of Leonids," the actually scary Master Raker said brightly, and everyone forced stiff smiles onto their faces, at which point the meeting ended.

Just like they had the previous day, they connected their Neurolinkers directly, going through the Arita home server as a safety measure.

This was actually the fourth time that Haruyuki was visiting the Unlimited Neutral Field that week. However, when he cried out the "unlimited burst" command with the others, there was no longer any unease or fear in his heart, just the warmth of the feeling of believing in his companions.

Ardor Maiden, shrine maiden of purification, one of the Four Elements of the first Nega Nebulus. Haruyuki was already more than well aware of the tremendous power Utai Shinomiya possessed. He was convinced that the flames of the maiden—with which she had defeated the ISS kit–using Olive Grab unscathed, burned a similarly equipped Bush Utan right out of the Field, and then caught and melted in a pool of magma even the massive knight Enemy that had been guarding the inner sanctuary of the Castle—contained an attack power of the greatest order in the Accelerated World. However, the true nature of Utai's power was not destruction. Haruyuki was about to learn that firsthand.

The location selected as the stage for purification was Koenji—not the area, but the large temple near Haruyuki's own condo that gave the area its name. The temple grounds. Everyone thought a Shinto shrine would have been more appropriate given that Ardor Maiden was a shrine maiden, but she herself said that she had absolutely no issue with a Buddhist temple, and there were no shrines nearby to begin with, so that settled the matter.

Still, bathed in the moon's cool, clear light in the Moonlight stage, a powerful sense of the sacred drifted up and around the temple grounds. Not a single element rejected the presence of the shrine maiden in her white robe and crimson *hakama* pants. Utai stood Haruyuki in the center of a large space, moved about three meters away, and then turned to face him before stretching her right hand out in front of her.

Small flames rose up in the slender fingers, flames that quickly turned into a snowy white hand fan. The fan was opened with a quietly satisfying *snap*, and the shrine maiden began to wave it leisurely from left to right.

Red flames shot up in front of Haruyuki to the right, then the left, then behind him to the right and left. While Kuroyuki-hime, Fuko, Chiyuri, and Takumu stood a ways off and watched with bated breath, Utai brought the fan back in front of her and stepped onto the earth with the tip of her *tabi*-socked foot.

"'Fleeting cherry blossoms…The sins of the fleeting cherry blossoms scatter and take root'…"

The instant the "song" she chanted shook the cool atmosphere of the Unlimited Neutral Field, a roaring conflagration broke out inside the four fires encircling Haruyuki. His field of view itself was dyed crimson, and the air carried with it a physical pressure pushing against the body of Silver Crow from over a meter away.

However, Haruyuki didn't feel the slightest bit of fear; he simply gave himself over to the power. He felt no heat or pain, and his health gauge in the top left of his vision did not flinch from its full state. He felt the overwhelming power of this fire was indeed burning something away—no, "cleansing" it. To borrow Kuroyukihime's words, the flames were likely burning the object parasite status in the system, but with all five of his senses bathed in the raging fire, the words *connection* and *attachment* floated up in the back of Haruyuki's mind.

Right. It was the Armor itself that had initially parasitized Silver Crow's back. After that, the Beast, that pseudo-intelligence that lived in the Armor, would occasionally speak to Haruyuki, deepening the level of fusion until, finally, he awoke completely as the sixth Chrome Disaster. But it would have been a lie to say that in the process, an "attachment" hadn't been born in Haruyuki's own heart, to power—to a desire for the overwhelming destructive power that the Armor held. Put another way, if that feeling of attachment hadn't existed, the Armor wouldn't have fused with him to such a deep level.

In the middle of the powerful, cool blaze produced by Utai Shinomiya's Incarnate, Haruyuki felt the faint egotism remaining inside him being gently burned away. He closed his eyes, and as he leisurely spread his limbs, he whispered deep in his heart to his former comrade in arms:

Hey, Beast.

I didn't hate you, you know. Working together with you and fighting…It was pretty fun.

If we meet again someday in some other form, let's duel for sure then. One-on-one or in a tag-team match—either's fine. A real duel.

He got no reply. But Haruyuki felt like, somewhere far, far away, he heard the fierce, beautiful Beast wrapped in those flames of darkness howling at the moon.

*   *   *

Ardor Maiden continued to dance beautifully for an hour and thirty minutes. The feared interruptions from Enemies or Burst Linkers did not come. When the movements of the shrine maiden gradually grew slower and finally stopped altogether, the pillars of flame also turned into countless sparks and scattered, melting into the night wind and disappearing.

Feet alighting on the earth, Haruyuki realized that two small objects had materialized in his hands. Square cards glittering silver, transparently, in the light of the moon.

Carved on one of them was the text STAR CASTER; on the other, the name THE DESTINY glittered brightly. The sword and the Armor. These were nothing other than the initial forms of the binary stars that had appeared at the dawn of the Accelerated World and transformed the destinies of so many Burst Linkers. The fact that both had returned to a sealed card state meant that the Disaster no longer existed anywhere in this world.

Clutching both cards tightly, Haruyuki took a few steps forward and bowed deeply toward Utai Shinomiya, who did indeed appear to be mentally exhausted.

"Thank you, Mei. It's over. All of it…"

"This is not something I alone accomplished. It is because you were able to say a proper good-bye to the Armor, C." A small hand gently stroked Haruyuki's helmet as she spoke.

When he lifted his face, beyond Utai he came to see Kuroyuki-hime, Fuko, Chiyuri, and Takumu—all with the same grins on their faces.

Ardor Maiden took a few steps back, and Sky Raker moved to support her. In her place, Black Lotus silently hovered forward and nodded forcefully.

"Crow, you did well. Now there will be nothing to criticize you for at the meeting of the Seven Kings this coming Sunday. Most likely, at the meeting, the policy on dealing with the ISS kits and the Acceleration Research Society will be the main topic, but you can stand up tall and declare you are free. And as for what to do with those two Enhanced Armaments, I'll entrust them to you. Think about it carefully and make your decision."

While he was pleased with the unconditional trust implied in his Legion Master's words, Haruyuki shook his head slightly. "No, um. Actually, I've already decided."

"Oh?" The Black King cocked her head to one side, and Haru took his eyes off her to look around at his friends.

"Everyone, especially you, Mei...I know you're all tired, but... could you help me out just a little more?"

First, Haruyuki touched his own health gauge to bring up the Instruct menu and then deposited both cards temporarily into his nearly empty storage. Then he randomly smashed terrain objects outside the temple to fully charge his special-attack gauge. Holding Utai in his right arm and Chiyuri in his left, he floated up into the air a little, so that Takumu could dangle from his legs. Kuroyukihime climbed onto Fuko's back, equipped with the booster-type Enhanced Armament Gale Thruster.

In this formation, the six headed due south, following Kannana Street. They left the Setagaya area, shifted east on Meguro Street, and headed toward Shibaura-futo alongside Tokyo Bay, avoiding the city center.

Coming down in a spot from which he could see the Shibaura parking area off the Daiba Route of the Shuto Expressway to the north, Haruyuki waited for Fuko and Kuroyukihime to catch up with a long jump using the booster, and intently compared the surrounding terrain with his hazy memory.

In the Moonlight stage, the storehouses of the wharf were transformed into buildings in the style of splendid sanctuaries. The wide road for trucks that stretched between them running east-west met an intersection—

"It's here." He turned toward the other five, who had no idea what that was exactly, and said, "Um, there should be an item on the ground somewhere in that intersection."

"An item? Not a card, an object?"

He assented to Takumu's question with a nod.

"But, like, things dropped on the ground of the Unlimited Neutral Field, don't they get swept away and disappear in the Change every time?" Chiyuri asked, and Haruyuki brought his head up and down once, only to then move it from side to side.

"Yeah, usually, that's how it works. But I feel like I heard that for supervaluable things, even when the Change happens, they don't disappear, not after days...even years. That's right, isn't it, Kuroyukihime?" He turned his gaze on Kuroyukihime, likely the most senior Burst Linker in that spot, and she nodded slightly.

"Mmm. That is exactly right. But items with infinite endurance are relatively limited. Legion Master quest achievement proof... proof of passing through the four great dungeons..."

"And the key to your own house, right?" Fuko noted casually.

Haruyuki nodded firmly. "That's it!" he shouted. "What I want you to look for is a key."

The ground of the Moonlight stage was thinly covered with a crisp, dry, superfine white sand. Because of this, it could hardly be said to be the perfect place to look for something, but it was still better than the Corroded Forest stage, with its poisonous bogs all over the place, or the Purgatory stage, swarming with repulsive insects. Haruyuki considered the various options as he turned his energies to digging in the white sand spread out over the large intersection.

In truth, it wasn't as though he had any proof that a key was buried in there. But on the other hand, he also had a certain confidence that he was in that place now because something—or someone—had led him there. The dream he'd had inside the Castle, that long, long dream...If the final chapter of that sad tale was indeed historical fact, then they would definitely find the key there. When he was really little, he had picked up a tiny obsidian arrowhead in the mountains of Okutama when he was climbing there with his parents. Just like that stone implement, the key had to have been quietly waiting here this whole time, waiting for when someone would come along and find it.

As the fingers of his right hand stroked the sand for the however-many-hundredth time, *tunk*—they touched something.

His hand froze, and then he began to carefully grope around below the sand. He grabbed on to something and pulled it up: a small silver key, completely unblemished even now after an eternity had passed. He guessed it must have been nearly *seven thousand years*.

"...I found it...," he murmured, and stood up. Noticing him, his friends stopped their own searches and came over to him. He held up the small object, which shone in the light of the moon, so that everyone could see it. "I found it," he said again. "This is what I was looking for."

"Crow...what is that key for?" Chiyuri asked.

"I'll take you there now," he replied. "Of course, it's not my house, but...I think the owners would forgive me."

After he carefully put the small key away into his item storage, Haruyuki started out toward their next destination. But there was no need to fly a long distance this time. Across the Rainbow Bridge from Shibaurafuto into Odaiba, due south, they descended on the northern side of a place that was called Akatsuki Futo Park in the real world.

Along the narrow road, there was a small house with slightly different coloring than the other terrain objects. If Haruyuki hadn't picked up the key earlier, he wouldn't have been able to even find the house, much less touch it. Because this was a so-called player home, which granted access only to the Burst

Linker who had purchased the extraordinarily expensive key from one of the shops dotting the Unlimited Neutral Field.

The house, standing there with walls of white rock bathed in the hazy moonlight, somehow resembled Kuroyukihime's home, which he had visited the previous evening. Haruyuki took a few steps into the modest front yard and looked back over his shoulder.

"This is Chrome Falcon and Saffron Blossom's house," he announced.

All five of his companions opened their eyes wide. Although he had only really given them all a rough overview of the story tied up in the Armor of Catastrophe, they all seemed to understand right away. The reason why Haruyuki had worked so hard to find the key, why he had come to this place.

"So then, the intersection before at Shibaurafuto," Utai murmured, and Haruyuki moved his head up and down in assent.

"Yes. It's where Blossom lost all her points and disappeared from this world...and it's also where Falcon was finally subjugated after that, when he became the first Chrome Disaster. So I figured whichever one of them had the key, it would definitely still be there."

"I see. Indeed, there is no more suitable place than this to put those two Enhanced Armaments to rest," Kuroyukihime said, turning her eyes on Haruyuki, and nodded deeply as if to say, *This is good.*

After Haruyuki nodded back, he opened his storage and turned the three items in question into objects. With the two card items in his left hand and the small key in his right, he slowly walked toward the house. He didn't even have to put the key into the doorknob; at his approach alone, the cute door opened without a sound.

"Pardon my intrusion," he said, and slipped through the doorway.

The inside of the house had been carefully customized

with a variety of furnishings and small items, and even in the bluish-white light of the moon, it looked very cozy. But he did feel a thick sadness hanging in the long, still air. That was only natural. The two who had once lived in this house no longer existed anywhere in this world.

Glancing back, he saw that Kuroyukihime and the others had apparently decided to wait in the entryway and were silently watching over him. In that case, he couldn't make them wait too long. He had already made Utai in particular, who must have been tired after the long purification, keep him company for nearly two hours.

Haruyuki turned his gaze back toward the inside of the house. "Blossom," he said. "Thanks to the help you gave me, I was able to return to the people I love again…Falcon, I'm going to keep thinking about what it is you wanted, what you were trying to destroy…Thank you."

It was all he could do to put the many thoughts filling his heart into these brief words, what with his impoverished language abilities. Even so, he felt sure that he had managed to communicate what needed to be said to both of them, and he took a step forward. On top of the table where the two who had loved each other had eaten, talked, and gazed at the other, he placed the two card items. Next to these, he set the silver key.

"Good-bye."

He took a step back and turned around, heading toward the door, where his friends were waiting. Just as he was about to leave the room, he felt like he heard someone calling out to stop him. Turning around again, Haruyuki saw…

A slender, somewhat dark-silver avatar that looked a lot like Silver Crow standing to one side of the table. Beside him, sitting on the white chair, was a golden-yellow girl-type avatar. And on the girl's lap, curled up in a circle, eyes closed happily, was a small black cat.

The three figures were half-transparent in the moonlight and flickered hazily. But Haruyuki was sure that they were no simple illusion. The boy and the girl, and the kitten their love had produced, had finally returned to the place they were meant to.

Good-bye. Someday, we'll meet again.

Holding back tears that threatened to spill over, Haruyuki once more murmured a farewell in his heart. And then he took a large step back, to return to where his friends were waiting for him outside the door.

12

Once again—the following day, Saturday, June 22, 2:30 PM.

Haruyuki was walking by himself in the yard at Umesato Junior High. Since it was Saturday, his classes had, of course, ended in the morning. Apparently, for a while, starting at the end of the previous century, there had been a dreamlike era when the majority of elementary and junior high schools had had a five-day system—in other words, they had Saturday and Sunday off—but the number of schools reopening voluntarily for Saturday classes skyrocketed in the 2010s, and now, in 2047, the Ministry of Education acted as though there had never been a five-day system right from the start.

But then, if Haruyuki had hypothetically had Saturday off, he couldn't have simply spent the whole day lying around the house anyway, since the Brain Burst Territories were held at five PM every Saturday. This event to fight for control over areas in team battles of a minimum of three against three could be said to be the very reason for the existence of Legions.

The Black Legion, Nega Nebulus, had managed to protect the entire Area within Suginami Ward with five people until then, but starting that day, they would be six. Naturally, this was because one of the former Elements, Ardor Maiden—Utai Shinomiya—had come back to the Legion. Not only did this mean they could split up into teams of three and simultaneously defend two territories, they also added to their ranks the long-awaited red long-distance type. Thus far, they had been mercilessly routed in battles that had someone with ridiculous defenses in the vanguard of the attacking team and someone else slamming them with massive firepower from behind that wall. But starting that day, that strategy would no longer work so well for his enemies. He would love to have Utai on the same team as him and, just once, be action-movie cool in their formation: "Mei, I'm gonna go smash that weapon in the back—cover me!"

At some point, Haru realized he had stopped dead in the middle of the yard and was grinning to himself, and he hurriedly began walking again. His destination was, of course, the wooden animal hutch in the northwestern corner of the Umesato grounds, which the majority of students didn't even know existed.

Ever since the lone three members of Nega Nebulus had started fighting in the Territories the previous autumn, Saturday afternoons were, for Haruyuki, a time of boredom. They were released from the classroom at 12:50 PM, after the long homeroom in fourth period. Once he ate lunch in the deserted cafeteria after that, it was barely one thirty, and it felt like an eternity until the Territories started at five.

Kuroyukihime was busy with student council work and Takumu and Chiyuri both had practice, so he couldn't get any of them to hang out with him and kill time. Since they could take part in the battles from anywhere in the Suginami Area, there was no issue with him just going home, but then he couldn't share the joy of victory (or the sadness of defeat) with the other three diving from the school, which was just too depressing. Thus, up to that point, he had done things like flip through the pages of picture books in the library or challenge himself to get new high scores in various games on the local net, but that lonely existence had also abruptly ended this week.

Haruyuki had finally been assigned a job to devote his time

to on Saturdays: president of the Umesato Junior High Animal Care Club.

Arriving in front of the animal hutch, he peered in through the wire screen to begin his agenda with a greeting. It might have been a hutch, but it was relatively large inside, where two tree perches stood. On the highest branch of the one on the left sat the figure of a bird. He held on with one foot, eyes closed sleepily. It was a bird of prey about twenty centimeters in length, a gray pattern on its white plumage, sharp beak buried in the down of his chest—a northern white-faced owl, Hoo.

Since it had still only been five days since they'd met, Haruyuki didn't really feel that the owl was ready to open up to him, but even so, perhaps sensing his presence, Hoo raised just his right eyelid and stared at Haru with a beautiful, copper-colored eye.

"Hey, Hoo. Pretty hot today, huh?" As he spoke to the bird, he manipulated his virtual desktop and connected with the body weight and temperature sensors embedded in Hoo's perch. Both were within the normal range, and his weight, which dropped a little immediately after he moved here, seemed to have basically returned to normal.

At Haruyuki's greeting, the white-faced owl flapped a wing in restless annoyance before once more going into nap mode. Haruyuki smiled wryly and went to wirelessly open the door's electronic lock so he could first wash and replace the paper laid out in the hutch.

From behind, he heard the quiet sound of footsteps on the mossy ground. He turned, thinking that Hoo's original owner, Matsunogi Academy fourth-grade student Utai Shinomiya, was already here. But there, Haruyuki saw someone not only completely unexpected but completely unfamiliar.

The white, short-sleeved shirt and gray skirt with the hint of green in it was the uniform of Umesato. The ribbon around her neck was blue—eighth grade. The loosely curled long hair, the thinly plucked eyebrows, and the eyeliner just barely light enough so it wouldn't be called out by the teachers all indicated that she belonged to a school caste that Haruyuki had basically zero connection with. The Neurolinker peeking out of her collar was also the "deco" type, a glossy pink studded with rhinestones.

Approximately 0.2 seconds after looking at the beautiful but somehow coercive face, Haruyuki dropped his gaze toward the ground. "Uh, um, did you…lose something?" he mumbled. "If I find it, I'll make sure to note it in the lost and found in the local net, so…" He said this, assuming that there would be no other reason for a student like this to ever come out to this part of the school grounds. But a few seconds later, he got another surprise.

"What, you forgot? You're supposed to be the president, y'know."

"Huh?" Reflexively, he jerked his head up and looked at the girl's face again, for 0.5 seconds this time. And then he did actually feel like he had met her somewhere before. They were in the same grade at the same school, so he had probably passed her or something in the hallway, but it wasn't that— Wait. *President?* Did she mean of the Animal Care Club?

"Oh! R-right, you're, uh…Class B…I-Iza—" He dug intently into the deepest layers of his memory for the name.

"Iiiiizeeeekiiii!" a scary voice corrected him. "Reina Izeki!"

No longer able to look at the girl's face, Haruyuki bobbed his head up and down. He had completely forgotten she existed, but this Izeki was essentially Haruyuki's colleague—a member of the same club. She was one of the three people newly elected at the beginning of this week, to accommodate the animal (Hoo) from Matsunogi Academy, which was part of the same corporation as Umesato. Haruyuki had announced his candidacy and ended up president, so forgetting the name and face of a member was absolutely unforgivable.

He panicked slightly at the dangerous mistake, at the super blunder, but fortunately, rather than reproaching the president any further, Izeki simply moved briskly over to the hutch. She peered in through the mesh. "Oh, wow!" she said, the swords gone from her voice. "It's, like, really an owl. Damn! It's, like, super fluffy, right?"

Her tone, at any rate, expressed simple surprise, and she was even taking care to lower her voice out of consideration for the clearly sleeping Hoo, so Haruyuki was slowly released from his state of fear.

"Y-yeah. An owl. It's a northern white-faced owl," he noted timidly.

Izeki glanced back at him, her curls swinging. "Is a white-faced owl different from a regular owl?"

"Oh! Um. A white-faced owl's a type of owl. More precisely, Strigiformes order, Strigidae family, Otus genus."

"Whoa. What's its name?"

"Hoo."

"...That is some seriously simple naming there. Who named it?"

"A-apparently, they voted on it." Although it was just him somehow answering questions when asked, he was at any rate managing to carry on a conversation.

Izeki nodded with a "huh" and turned her eyes back toward the hutch. She put a hand to her mouth and called out quietly, "Hoo, Hooooo."

There's no way that extremely unsociable Professor White-face there is going to respond to someone he's only just met in the middle of the day like this, Haruyuki thought. But the instant Hoo heard Izeki's voice, he snapped open not one, but both eyes. He turned his head around and seemed to identify the person standing beyond the mesh, but what surprised Haruyuki was that he spread both wings and flew off his perch.

"Whoa! Wow!" Izeki cried out at the sight of Hoo flying majestically inside the hutch. "It's flying! It's flying! Crap! It's super gorgeous!"

...I show up and I get one eye open. What's with the big show here? Haruyuki unconsciously grumbled in his heart, but Hoo flew around a full five times in feigned ignorance before

returning to the perch and sleep mode, holding on with one foot, ear coverts tucked back. Izeki watched with even greater enthusiasm.

Turning toward her face in profile, Haruyuki hesitantly asked, "So, um, Izeki…why all of a sudden today?"

Instantly, she was glaring at him out of the corner of her eye, and he froze up once more. "Well, I *am* a member of this club, too. Not a crime for me to show up?"

"Th-that's true…but on the first day, you didn't—you didn't seem so happy to be in the club…I kinda thought, but—"

"That's 'cos I was seriously crazy tired then, and you said it was okay, so I just went home! But then I saw the activity log actually being uploaded, and I dunno, I kinda regretted going home, like, I figured making you clean that shed all by yourself, totes impossible! That a crime?!"

Unable to tell whether he was being blamed for something or apologized to, Haruyuki shook his head from side to side. "N-no, that's not a crime."

"That's why I thought I should hurry and say sorry, but then you didn't give us any jobs at all! You just do the club stuff by yourself every day, so I had to come to you, you know! *That* a crime?!"

"N-no, that's not a crime at all." Shaking his head from side to side once more, Haruyuki worked hard to process and synthesize the convoluted story, and reached a conclusion. Looking up at Izeki, he nervously sought confirmation. "Umm. S-so then, uh, Izeki, you came to do the club work, to take care of Hoo?"

"That's what I been saying this whole time!"

Really? He stopped himself from cocking his head to one side and let out the breath he'd been holding in a long sigh.

If that was the case, then even if it was someone from a class he had absolutely no connection with in everyday life, and a girl on top of that, he was honestly glad to have her. The hutch was big, and cleaning it was pretty hard. Plus, when he was by himself, he had to be really careful about opening and closing the door. He sucked the June air, with its scent of green, into his empty lungs. "Okay, then," he said boldly. "Umm, a whole bunch of leaves have piled up in front of the hutch again. How about we clear them away first? We can just sorta push them together with a broom."

"Okay!"

Fortunately, this time, rather than grumbling about how tired she was or how annoying this was, Izeki accepted the bamboo broom Haruyuki held out to her. He felt secretly relieved at the sight of her awkwardly sweeping away the damp leaves, and then he also started working.

Hoo appeared to no longer be paying attention to the pair of humans working in front of the wire mesh; he simply continued to doze on the perch. The white-faced owl was totally at home in his new residence five days after moving in, and Haruyuki spoke to him in his mind as he worked.

Hoo, I have to thank you. This is the first time I've ever taken care of a living creature, but I actually feel like you're teaching me all kinds of things instead. The meaning of living, of flying. I can't put it into words properly, but I think it's because I got to meet you that I could fly faster and higher than the God Suzaku.

I'm still totally hopeless in the real world and in the Accelerated World…and even still, it's only bit by bit, but lately, I've started feeling like I'm moving forward…

Digesting these thoughts, he actually moved to take a step forward.

Instantly.

Something was yanking on the back of his shirt.

"Ngh?!" Startled, Haruyuki looked back, and found yet another wholly unexpected personage.

She was also in a school uniform, but the ivory summer cardigan and the plaid skirt were not that of Umesato Junior High. Short, fluffy, unruly hair, bright-green Neurolinker. The fingertips of her right hand were holding tightly to Haruyuki's shirt, and for some reason, both eyes were damp. Her appearance here was unexpected, but she was not unknown to him.

"R-R-R-Rin Kusakabe," he said, right cheek stiffening. "Wh-wh-what are you…?"

And then, for some reason, suddenly tears. Blithely dodging both the vocalized and unvocalized questions, the Great Wall member, level-five Burst Linker Ash Roller—and the girl Rin Kusakabe in the real world—opened her mouth slightly. "Who… are you?"

Naturally, the question to establish identity was not directed at Haruyuki. Rin's gaze was turned toward Izeki, the Animal Care Club member standing a little ways off, bamboo broom still in hand, gaping. When Haruyuki froze, unable to comprehend the current situation, she strode over somewhat haughtily.

"I could ask you the same thing," she remarked, in a voice that was just the slightest bit thorny. "That uniform's Shibuya Sasajo, yeah? What's a little princess doing in a place like this?…Wait. Huh? What? Is that it?"

Haruyuki had basically no idea what *it* was, but he did feel something improper somehow in the eyes Izeki was shooting back and forth between him and Rin.

To at least put the situation on hold, he waved his hand. "I-I-I-Izeki, h-h-h-hold on a minute!"

And then he moved over to the wall of the second school building, dragging Rin still clutching his shirt. "Uh, um, uh, Kusakabe—" he said, with a quiet urgency.

"My brother's Kusakabe, too, so you can just call me Rin."

"R-R-R-R-R-Rin, um, okay…What are you doing here?! We have the Territories later— Oh! A-a-a-are you maybe going to go in from here? I mean, are you—?"

You're not actually going to transfer Legions today? Leave Great Wall for Nega Nebulus? So then starting today that mighty-me-mega-lucky century-end rider's my comrade?

Rin moved her head at a slight angle. "I'll be. Fighting," she said. "But…I'm on the. Attacking side again. Today. Transferring Legions. That's for. My brother to decide."

"Oh! Th-that's…" He nodded, tasting something like relief,

something like regret, and then was stunned once more. "A-a-a-attacking side?! B-b-b-but the Territories are a minimum of three people. Where are the other two?"

"They're on standby. On the border between Shibuya. And Suginami. It's U and..."

U was the familiar *Ya feel me?!* Bush Utan. Although he had been swallowed up by the magical power of the ISS kit, after he was betrayed and hunted by his friends, he had apparently been able to return to his old self. Even if the kit hypothetically remained within the avatar, it was possible to have him purified by Ardor Maiden after the Territories were over that day or something.

"...the other is Iron Pound."

"Huh, okay. Even if he is on the enemy side, I'm glad Utan's back to his old— Wait, whaaaaat?!" Haruyuki involuntarily shrieked at the third name Rin uttered so casually. If he had heard right, Rin's attacking team included the fearsome boxer avatar, number three of GW's Six Armors, also known as "Iron Fist."

"Heeeeey, Prez! How long you gonna jabber over there? Job's not even close to done here!"

Izeki had apparently overcome her numbness, and at the sound of her voice, Haruyuki was forced to once again put the situation on hold. Before the Territories, he had to first take care of his club work right now. It was unclear how Izeki was interpreting Rin's presence, but if Haru neglected to explain it, he had the feeling that by next week, an extremely suspicious rumor would be flying around the second floor of the main school building.

Returning to the hutch with Rin still hanging from his shirt, Haruyuki blathered on with an explanation he forcefully twisted out in an even shriller voice. "Uh, um, Izeki, this is Kusakabe, but she's, uh...You know there's a special Matsunogi Academy member of the club, right? So she's a friend of her friend, and she came to help out today."

It wasn't a complete lie. Fuko Kurasaki, who was a "friend" of the special member Utai Shinomiya, was the "master" of Rin

Kusakabe. That she had come to help was something Haruyuki made up on the spot, but it was possible to make that true after the fact. He would just have to get Rin to actually help with the cleaning now.

"Hmmmm." Izeki made a long, noncommittal sound, perhaps accepting this, perhaps not, and she flicked her eyes back and forth between Rin and Haruyuki. "You got it going on, huh, Prez? Maybe, like, I'm in the way?"

"I-I-I'm not doing anything! And y-y-you're not in the way at all; you're super helpful, super!"

Possibly acknowledging his shrieked reply, Izeki nodded her head, sending her curls swinging. "'Kay," she said. "Anyway, I'll keep cleaning or whatever. What're we gonna do after collecting all the leaves? Burn 'em?"

"I-if we burn them, the patrol cars'll be here super fast, super!"

"That was a joke." Grinning, his colleague returned to the hutch, and Haruyuki followed her with a heavy breath.

Rin finally released his shirt, and he handed her the broom he had in his right hand before setting himself to fetch the dustpan and a garbage bag from the small cupboard beside the hutch.

Suddenly, a bolt of lightning snapped through the space between his eyebrows.

Murderous intent…?! Before he leapt back, a voice announcing a new danger rang out through the yard.

"Ah! Haru, what exactly is going on here?!"

His entire body froze with a start, and Haruyuki seriously considered whether he should turn toward the east, the direction the voice had come from, or run away to the southwest, toward the central courtyard. If Izeki hadn't been there, he might well have chosen the latter, but the president couldn't very well abandon his members in the middle of work and flee.

Left with no other choice, his body creaking like the wheels of a gear, Haruyuki turned and saw Chiyuri in her tracksuit, holding up a shopping bag full of what were likely refreshments.

To her left stood Utai Shinomiya, red backpack slung over her shoulders, carrying a second bag with a meal for Hoo in her hand. Farther back, smiling brightly, but still clad in an aura that forced Haru to conjecture certain things, was Fuko Kurasaki. And then, walking to Chiyuri's right, dressed in her jet-black custom uniform, her beauty almost intimidating, the look drifting across her face reminiscent of an unsheathed blade, the vice president of the Umesato Junior High student council, Kuroyukihime.

The similarly tracksuited Takumu coming in and out of view behind the four girls was some comfort, but the grin on his face said, *Don't give up, Haru.* Haruyuki shook his head furiously back and forth and desperately tried to make his face say, *Help me, Taku.*

"So, like, it's a whole party. They all helpers, too?"

Glancing back, he saw Izeki, broom in one hand, looking at Haruyuki with a truly exasperated expression.

"Prez, what exactly are you?"

"I-I'm nobody!" he replied, in a small voice.

Finally abandoning the hope of fleeing, Haruyuki straightened his back and turned to face Kuroyukihime and the others, as he repeated once more in his head:

Right. By myself, I'm absolutely nobody. Nothing but a regular, nothing-special-about-him, timid, socially phobic, game-obsessed junior high school boy.

But just when I'm with my precious friends, I can definitely be someone. I can try a little harder than when I'm by myself; I can stand a little straighter. And I can believe in myself, just a tiny bit.

Inside the animal hutch, perhaps sensing that Utai had arrived, Hoo flapped both wings forcefully. Haruyuki took a step forward as though that flapping were pushing at his back and waved his right hand in a wide arc at the five people approaching.

END

AFTERWORD

Reki Kawahara here. Thank you so much for reading *Accel World 9: The Seven-Thousand-Year Prayer*.

This is the volume on the Armor of Catastrophe, Chrome Disaster, which first appeared in Volume 2, and was taken up as a main part of the story in Volume 6. But in Volume 9 here, we finally get to see the end, for now at least. I really do appreciate all of you putting up with the "to be continued" at the end of Volumes 6, 7, and 8, and sticking with me right up until "the end."

But since there are still so many plotlines left stacked up in here (or rather, so many were added in this volume…), it doesn't look like we'll reach the conclusion of the story itself anytime soon. What will Haruyuki aim for in the end? What is hiding in Kuroyukihime's past? Why does the Accelerated World exist? Although it's not entirely certain that I'll really be able to write everything out to that extent, I'd like to keep going the way I have been, one volume at a time, having fun with it myself. At any rate, I want to make Volume 10 something cheerful and fun that is complete in one volume! Yes!!

And I wasn't sure whether or not to touch on this, but maybe just a little…Those of you who have read Volume 8 of my other series *Sword Art Online* were no doubt wondering "Who is that?!" when you saw the new girl character standing in the way in the spread with the preview of *Accel* Volume 9 at the end of the book. Who exactly that was is made clear in part four of this volume, but I had no intention of announcing, "So-and-so is a girl!" through her appearance there. (At any rate, I'll avoid spoilers.)

I'm sure I'll have a chance to write about her in more detail in the future, so until then, I'd be pleased if you could be in anguish over it...It would help, anyway. (lol)

Since I only have a few lines left, I'll make one announcement here. I believe it's probably also noted on the obi band of Volume 9, but *Accel World* is being turned into a television anime show. Sunrise is doing the production. *The* Sunrise. I'm right in the middle of the *Gundam* generation, and the structure of the duel avatars has been influenced in a variety of ways by the Sunrise robots, so I couldn't be happier at just getting to see Crow and Lotus moving on-screen. I do sincerely hope you will all take in the anime version of *Accel*!

To my illustrator, HIMA, who put heart and soul into the design for said new character; my editor, Miki, who gave me more corrections than basically ever before on the scene with that character (lol); and, to repeat myself, all you readers who stayed with me right until the end of the Armor arc, thank you so much!

Reki Kawahara
August 11, 2011

THE CHART-TOPPING SERIES THAT SPAWNED THE EXPLOSIVELY POPULAR ANIME ADAPTATIONS!

SWORD ART ONLINE, VOL. 1-9
LIGHT NOVEL SERIES
SWORD ART ONLINE © Reki Kawahara
KADOKAWA CORPORATION ASCII MEDIA WORKS

SWORD ART ONLINE, PROGRESSIVE 1-4
LIGHT NOVEL SERIES
SWORD ART ONLINE: PROGRESSIVE © Reki Kawahara
KADOKAWA CORPORATION ASCII MEDIA WORKS

SWORD ART ONLINE, PROGRESSIVE 1-4
MANGA SERIES
Sword Art Online: Progressive
© REKI KAWAHARA / KISEKI HIMURA
KADOKAWA CORPORATION ASCII MEDIA WORKS

SWORD ART ONLINE, VOL. 1-4
MANGA SERIES
SWORD ART ONLINE: Aincrad
© Reki Kawahara / Tamako Nakamura /
KADOKAWA CORPORATION ASCII MEDIA WORKS

SWORD ART ONLINE, GIRLS' OPS, VOL. 1-3
MANGA SERIES
Sword Art Online: Girls' Ops © REKI KAWAHARA /
NEKO NEKOBYOU
KADOKAWA CORPORATION ASCII MEDIA WORKS

VISIT YENPRESS.COM
TO CHECK OUT ALL THESE TITLES AND MORE!

www.YenPress.com

Dive into the latest light novels from
New York Times bestselling author REKI KAWAHARA,
creator of the fan favorite *SWORD ART ONLINE* and
ACCEL WORLD series!

©REKI KAWAHARA ILLUSTRATION:Shimeji

©REKI KAWAHARA ILLUSTRATION:abec

SWORD ART ONLINE Light Novels

©REKI KAWAHARA ILLUSTRATION:abec

And be sure your shelves are primed with Kawahara's extensive backlist selection!

SWORD ART ONLINE Manga

©REKI KAWAHARA/
TAMAKO NAKAMURA

©REKI KAWAHARA/TSUBASA HADUKI

©REKI KAWAHARA/
NEKO NEKOBYOU

©REKI KAWAHARA/KISEKI HIMURA

ACCEL WORLD Manga

©REKI KAWAHARA/HIROYUKI AIGAMO

ACCEL WORLD Light Novels

©REKI KAWAHARA ILLUSTRATION:HIMA

www.YenPress.com

HAVE YOU BEEN TURNED ON TO LIGHT NOVELS YET?

IN STORES NOW!

SWORD ART ONLINE, VOL. 1–9
SWORD ART ONLINE, PROGRESSIVE 1–4

The chart-topping light novel series that spawned the explosively popular anime and manga adaptations!

MANGA ADAPTATION AVAILABLE NOW!

SWORD ART ONLINE © Reki Kawahara ILLUSTRATION: abec
KADOKAWA CORPORATION ASCII MEDIA WORKS

ACCEL WORLD, VOL. 1–9

Prepare to accelerate with an action-packed cyber-thriller from the bestselling author of *Sword Art Online*.

MANGA ADAPTATION AVAILABLE NOW!

ACCEL WORLD © Reki Kawahara ILLUSTRATION: HIMA
KADOKAWA CORPORATION ASCII MEDIA WORKS

SPICE AND WOLF, VOL. 1–17

A disgruntled goddess joins a traveling merchant in this light novel series that inspired the *New York Times* bestselling manga.

MANGA ADAPTATION AVAILABLE NOW!

SPICE AND WOLF © Isuna Hasekura ILLUSTRATION: Jyuu Ayakura
KADOKAWA CORPORATION ASCII MEDIA WORKS

IS IT WRONG TO TRY TO PICK UP GIRLS IN A DUNGEON?, VOL. 1–7

A would-be hero turns damsel in distress in this hilarious send-up of sword-and-sorcery tropes.

MANGA ADAPTATION AVAILABLE NOW!

Is It Wrong to Try to Pick Up Girls in a Dungeon? © Fujino Omori / SB Creative Corp.

ANOTHER

The spine-chilling horror novel that took Japan by storm is now available in print for the first time in English—in a gorgeous hardcover edition.

MANGA ADAPTATION AVAILABLE NOW!

Another © Yukito Ayatsuji 2009/ KADOKAWA CORPORATION, Tokyo

A CERTAIN MAGICAL INDEX, VOL. 1–10

Science and magic collide as Japan's most popular light novel franchise makes its English-language debut.

MANGA ADAPTATION AVAILABLE NOW!

A CERTAIN MAGICAL INDEX © Kazuma Kamachi
ILLUSTRATION: Kiyotaka Haimura
KADOKAWA CORPORATION ASCII MEDIA WORKS

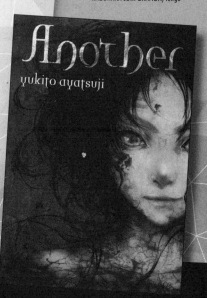

VISIT YENPRESS.COM TO CHECK OUT ALL THE TITLES IN OUR NEW LIGHT NOVEL INITIATIVE AND...

GET YOUR YEN ON!

www.YenPress.com

ACCEL WORLD, Volume 9
REKI KAWAHARA

Translation by Jocelyne Allen
Cover art by HIMA

This book is a work of fiction. Names, characters, places, and incidents
are the product of the author's imagination or are used fictitiously.
Any resemblance to actual events, locales, or persons, living or dead, is
coincidental.

ACCEL WORLD
© REKI KAWAHARA 2011
All rights reserved.
Edited by ASCII MEDIA WORKS
First published in 2011 by KADOKAWA CORPORATION, Tokyo.
English translation rights arranged with KADOKAWA CORPORA-
TION, Tokyo, through Tuttle-Mori Agency, Inc., Tokyo.

English translation © 2017 by Yen Press, LLC

Yen Press, LLC supports the right to free expression and the value of
copyright. The purpose of copyright is to encourage writers and artists to
produce the creative works that enrich our culture.

The scanning, uploading, and distribution of this book without permission
is a theft of the author's intellectual property. If you would like permission to use material from the book (other than for review purposes), please
contact the publisher. Thank you for your support of the author's rights.

Yen On
1290 Avenue of the Americas
New York, NY 10104

Visit us at yenpress.com
facebook.com/yenpress
twitter.com/yenpress
yenpress.tumblr.com
instagram.com/yenpress

First Yen On Edition: March 2017

Yen On is an imprint of Yen Press, LLC.
The Yen On name and logo are trademarks of Yen Press, LLC.

The publisher is not responsible for websites (or their content) that are
not owned by the publisher.

Library of Congress Cataloging-in-Publication Data
Names: Kawahara, Reki, author. | HIMA (Comic book artist) illustrator. |
    Beepee, designer. | Allen, Jocelyne, 1974– translator.
Title: Seven-thousand-year prayer / Reki Kawahara ; illustrations, HIMA ;
    design, bee-pee ; translation by Jocelyne Allen.
Description: First Yen On edition. | New York, NY : Yen On, 2017. |
    Series: Accel world ; 9
Identifiers: LCCN 2016035666 | ISBN 9780316502702 (pbk.)
Subjects: | CYAC: Science fiction.
Classification: LCC PZ7.K1755 Se 2017 | DDC [Fic]—dc23
LC record available at https://lccn.loc.gov/2016035666

ISBN: 978-0-316-50270-2

10 9 8 7 6 5 4 3 2 1

LSC-C

Printed in the United States of America